Crossways:
The Wayman Chronicles

By Michael J. Allen

Three Ravens Publishing
Chickamauga, GA USA

For my mentor Larry Dixon, who in the spirit of Gene Wilder and Danny Kaye inspired me to embrace my inner weird. This Big Madness in a Little Novel is all thanks to you.

For B, B & E, J & J, & L.

CROSSWAYS: THE WAYMAN CHRONICLES By Michael J Allen

Published by Three Ravens Publishing
threeravenspublishing@gmail.com
P O Box 851, Chickamauga, Ga 30707
https://www.threeravenspublishing.com
Copyright © 2022 by Three Ravens Publishing

Publishers Note: This is a work of fiction. Names, characters, places, and incidents are a product of the author's imagination. Locales and public names are sometimes used for atmospheric purposes. Any resemblance to actual people, living or dead, or to businesses, companies, events, institutions, or locales is completely coincidental.

Credits:
Crossways: The Wayman Chronicles was written by Michael J Allen
Cover art by: Jacqueline Sweet

Paperback ISBN: 978-1-951768-61-4
Hardback ISBN: 978-1-951768-57-7
Ebook ISBN: 978-1-951768-58-4

Table of Contents

1: Chased

A sallow, rotund figure fled as fast as he could, desperate to find the last stolen microdots. Phantasms pursued him through dim hallways, deepening his desperation to finish and escape before the ghosts devoured his soul.

He turned right down another identical hall.

Why hadn't he been forewarned? How were the entities controlled? Intelligence had provided him with a few super-soldier stimulants that somehow held off the ghosts' deadly touch.

He turned left. He ran down another hall.

He'd consumed the drugs already escaping several close calls. Without more, every moment his mission dragged on worsened his chance to escape.

He turned right and ran a short hall before taking another right. A long hall stretched out before him, disappearing into shadow.

A ghost slipped around the corner hot on his tail, hunting him in its eerie silence. He raced forward, still managing his top speed despite what felt like hours of running.

A corridor appeared on his right. He darted into it and glanced around another right-hand corner, intent to follow its path. Another ghost slipped into view.

He bolted the other way, darting right just ahead of the ghost he'd thought to escape. Another rightward corridor appeared, but he couldn't chance another ghost cornering him against the first two.

Crossways

He ran all out down a familiar corridor. Ahead lay several short, sharp turns he'd used before to slip his pursuers.

He made it to the end, turning right twice. Two quick lefts brought him back to where he'd been forced to use his first stimulant. A third ghost glided around the corner ahead. He spun on his heels, but his pursuers were too close.

No hope.

No escape.

He reversed once more, hoping this new ghost might flinch against all expectations.

It didn't.

He collided with it. A draining cold washed over him. Loud, boisterous laughter boomed over the sounds of his dissolving body.

Sam Bridger

"You ain't never going to beat my high score, Mack, not if you keep letting Pinky kiss you."

Mack released the red joystick and scowled at the blond, bearded man. "I work for a living, Bridger, rather than spending my time playing Pac Man or dodging the dispatcher."

"If you'd been married to that ugly, old shrew, you'd dodge her too."

"That why your loads include stops in the seediest neighborhoods and on the worst worlds?" Mack asked.

"Any world without Beatrice is a vacation paradise. You've got to remember Sam Bridger's rules about ex-wives."

Mack snorted.

"Rule one, they only hate you because they still want you. Rule two, it's nev--"

A sharp female voice cut him off. "Samuel Oswald Bridger, what the hell are you still doing here?"

Sam spun to find Beatrice in the doorway. He brightened for the barest instant before he recognized her expression.

The late-twenties woman glared at him over folded arms. Her big, brown hair almost brushed the door's frame. Despite Sam's words, his ex was still striking and attractive.

Like the small rotund figure, Sam spun on his heels and darted out the opposite door, pausing only to snatch a beat-up Detroit Tigers ball cap.

He took a hard right out the door, ran the hall and then spun hard-left sliding on yellowing linoleum. He regained his footing in time to stop dead before a force rivaling ghosts and ex-wives - his boss.

Percival Wiggins's red and blue paisley necktie bisected a pressed white shirt. Despite the formal attire, he wore a silver Member's Only windbreaker rather than a sports jacket. Thin greasy hair lay atop the boss's head in a hopeless comb over while the ridiculous rectangular collar strip dangled loose down the jacket's front.

Behind Wiggins, a young, bespectacled corporate clone beamed enthusiastically at Sam.

"Glad I caught you, Sam." Wiggins's whiny voice rivaled his fashion choices for World's Most Annoying. "Kenneth here is our newest driver. I'd like you to--"

Sam recognized the onramp to trouble without highway signs and headed Wiggins off fast. "With all the respect you're due, I'm not taking some baby wayman with me to Audoria— too dangerous. I'm also not taking him under my wing. Sam Bridger doesn't explain the nuts and bolts of these eleven universes to nobody."

"I'm afraid I'm going to have to make it an or--"

Beatrice's voice echoed off the walls, her winter boots stomping ever closer. "Samuel Bridger, you lazy, good-for-nothing buffoon, come back here right this moment. I'm not through with you yet."

Sam called back over his shoulder. "If you still wanted me, you shouldn't have divorced me. I'm not that kind of guy."

"Sam!"

"Bridger," Wiggins snapped.

"Kenneth." Sam winked at the newbie and bolted around Wiggin at a dead run. He called back once more. "Sorry, brother, can't talk now. Maybe later."

Sam wove through the warehouse, dodging broken down forklifts, cargo crates and demands he repay long overdue loans. He careened into the exit door's push bar and out the door. The icy steps robbed him of his footing, forcing him to grab the frigid rails with his bare hands.

And I left my jacket in the break room too, damn it.

Two dock workers huddled over an industrial heater, their hands cupped around their cigarettes to keep the stiff wind from blowing them out.

"My rig ready?" Sam asked.

The nearest man nodded.

"You should really consider giving up smoking, brother. Standing around in this weather'll kill you."

Sam slowed enough once on the ground for his work boots to maintain traction, but only just. He slid around the front of his newly painted Kenworth K-100 cab-over truck, grabbed the glossy red door to stop his momentum and climbed inside. He started his rig, shoved it into gear and pulled away from Crossways Transportation's headquarters.

The moment he was safely underway, Sam checked the itinerary holographically projected overtop of the glowing, aluminum disc called a passport. The device mounted atop his dashboard enabled interdimensional travel as well as altered his rig's shape and characteristics into something appropriate for their environment. His passport switched out the floating itinerary for a multicolor series of lines and waypoints, offering alternate routes to Sam's delivery point in the Audoria universe.

The first route suggested he drive his load to the closest waygate, crossing over into Audoria and then making his way across that other world to his destination. Terrain impediments, wars and worse often made cross country navigation across some of the ten worlds - universes really - impossible.

The second outlined crossing the United States to a waygate outside Bend, Oregon. He'd enter Audoria a few miles short of his drop-off point skipping Audorian travel across its hostile and almost endless Intner Plain.

Beatrice's voice came over a small high-tech radio tucked under the CB. "Truck twenty-three, HQ Dispatch, come in."

"Toledo and a quick exit it is," Sam said.

"Twenty-three, come in."

Sam whistled to himself, negotiating traffic onto the busy winter highway.

"Twenty-three, if you don't answer me, I'm going to order your passport to drive your truck back to base."

Sam glanced at an aluminum Frisbee mounted on his dashboard. A pool of blue neon light dominated its center, radiating similar lines of spider-webbed circuitry. "You wouldn't do that to me, would you, baby?"

Chirps and whistles emanated from its surface. Sam knew several drivers who thought they'd worked out their passport's language, but he preferred to search the notes for an emotional equivalent—in this case, a lecture.

"Traitor." Sam pushed a button on the communicator. "Twenty-three, Bridger here."

"About damned time, Sam. When we call, we need you to--"

"You want to save the lecture for when we're not on the communicator? You know how much those dwarves from Ryalox charge for cross-world roaming."

"I've uploaded a pickup to your itinerary."

"You didn't need to call. I'd have seen it."

Contempt filled her voice. "Sure you would, like you promised me an anniversary I'd never forget but instead skipped waygates so you could drive to the Cayman Islands for an impromptu fishing trip."

Considering how many times she's brought that up, I delivered on my promise.

"Twenty-three acknowledges itinerary update, Bridger out." Sam sighed. "A mere twelve hours late and won't ever let me forget it."

"You left me waiting at a restaurant, disappeared without a word," Beatrice's voice cracked. "I thought you'd died or something."

Sam's gaze shifted to the communicator.

Her voice hardened into an icy knife "Instead, you showed up the next morning with lame excuses and a Pac-Man machine."

"Look, Beatrice, I--"

"HQ Dispatch out."

Sam drove down the highway, wishing he hadn't taken her call - not that she'd left him any choice. As bad as the company was doing, Sam had been hoping she'd transfer to an undermanned facility or even quit before Crossways Transportation could lay her off.

Either she sticks around to harass me or is too blasted stubborn to give up on the company, he thought.

He glanced out his window.

A small, grinning boy held up a red and blue robot from the backseat of a VW Vanagon. He held up a single finger, bidding Sam to wait while he fiddled with the toy below Sam's sightline. The kid presented the transformed red toy truck so that Sam could see how his toy matched Sam's truck.

Sam threw the kid a thumbs-up and honked his horn twice.

The kid beamed.

The trip to the half-finished weigh station on I-75 south of Toledo, Ohio took about an hour. The construction wouldn't ever be finished, though commuters and local bureaucrats might wonder why.

They all probably figure someone diverted the tax money to something else. Sam snorted. Tax dollars didn't pay for this station. Not human tax dollars, anyway.

The empty station remained free of ice and snow despite heavy accumulation on either side of the highway. Three of the passport's six spindle legs unwrapped from the dashboard and flexed over a central disk of blue light. A globe of energy grew between the metal tips. A shimmering globe replaced earth's image with an icon that signified Audoria - the same icon that decorated banners over The Audorian peoples' seating section at the HQ enclave for the United Planes Organization.

Sam didn't bother slowing despite rapidly approaching the barricade. Whether he could see the entrance or not didn't matter. Neither did his speed. Ten miles per hour or a hundred, every trip between dimensions propelled his rig to the same breakneck speed.

Darkness swallowed his rig. Multicolored lights streaked past his window. The rig banked left, dove, rolled right, climbed and spiraled down once more.

Sam chuckled. Space Mountain on steroids.

Careful not to touch anything else, Sam grabbed the handles edging his bucket seat and planted his feet in the chair's stirrups.

A nonstop, electronic chittering spewed from his passport.

The truck changed.

The whole rig wriggled and writhed despite being metal, or metalish. Regardless of repeated warnings throughout his training, Sam had been unable to resist touching the change field enveloping his rig that first year as a wayman. It'd been a damn good thing he'd emerged near a UPO doc able to change his arm back into something less slimy and more Sammy.

His roof vanished.

The dashboard and doors melted into a sweeping curve half his height.

A shaft grew out of his truck's nose, then budded into four high-tech rocking horses. Pivoting thrusters formed instead of rails or legs. They burst to life, dragging his rig forward. The truck's surfaces changed to a deep bronze.

Sam glanced backward.

Another shaft connected his rig-become-chariot to a long sled with a leading edge identical to his pilot compartment. They both rode a cushion of magnetic energy that offered a smooth ride over rough terrain—even though it played hell on digital watches. His passport carefully sized the cargo trailer for a snug fit so that the now bronze crates crammed the sled.

They slid out of the waygate into Audoria.

Sam surveyed his rig and chuckled. *This design always makes me feel like we should be towing waterskiing, bikini-clad babes.*

Audoria resembled a bastard child of Ancient Greece and Buck Rogers. Though the world's terrain felt reminiscent of Clash of the Titans–though no one in Audioria resembled Burgess Meredith. Its primary peoples – the Tauron – even resembled the ancient Minotaur. They wore light, simple clothes, rugged despite a silky, futuristic appearance.

"Some early Greek probably glimpsed a Tauron while they were tinkering around on Mars." Sam chuckled. "After all, those dwarf cyborgs caused our whole anti-hitchhiker movement."

His passport chirped in the same tone Beatrice used whenever she'd accused him of spouting outlandish nonsense.

Same tone she uses when she calls me a stubborn idiot too.

The always grumpy computer resembled an astromech far more than a TRS-80, originating as it had in another UPO universe. The divorce intensified her disagreeable nature in a shift Sam attributed to solidarity between chicks.

Sam shrugged. "I mean, really, you can't blame those dwarves, can you, baby doll? Who wants to waste their vacation studying customs or learning the native language? They weren't really crazy axe murderers. Those axes are just their version of blankies."

Disgruntled beeps and whistles escaped Sam's passport.

A family chariot hovered by him. A small boy who hadn't yet grown into his horns waved, then tapped twice on the air in front of him. Sam tapped the button above his controls and sounded his chariot-transport's trumpet. The boy grinned and waved again.

Sam pulled off the main thoroughfare, grabbed a couple gyros for lunch, and continued toward his drop point. He'd once mistaken Audoria's orangish sky for a forest fire. Wildfires weren't possible, not after the Taurons engineered a thick under bark liquid layer on all their trees.

Sam had crossed Theta province far enough to down two drinks and water a few plants before something unusual—at least more unusual than animal headed people—brought him up short at the entrance to the Intner plain. Smoke poured from the engine compartment of a chariot crushing roadside vegetation and some rancher's fence.

Do minotaur raise cattle? Would eating steak count as cannibalism?

A little old Tauron doddered around the broken down vehicle, reminding him of a Holstein from his grandfather's dairy - give or take her horns. A check of his digital watch found it making oddly artistic geometric patterns, but Mickey's hands on his pocket watch informed him he was running late.

Guess I'll be later then. Just can't leave some little old lady broken down on the side of the road.

He pulled the rig to the side and slid off the back of the chariot.

"Broken down, ma'am?"

She gestured at the smoke coming from under the control board. "Was it the aroma of burnt insulation or my cursing that gave you that impression?"

Sam shrugged. "Just thought to offer a hand, but guess I'll head on my way."

She scrutinized him. "Sorry, wayman, been a day. It's hot, and I'm late." She wiped her brow and patted an enormous handbag. "Got a present to deliver to my grandson's wedding."

"I'm no expert, but I can look under the panel for you."

"Very nice of you, son."

Sam returned to his rig and donned the communicator's headset. "Base, twenty-three, get Bob for me."

He snagged a toolbox out of a recessed compartment and climbed into her chariot. He crawled under her control panel and waited, tools at hand.

A soft, soprano voice filled his ears. "Hey, Sam, what's wrong? Your passport's not reporting any issues."

Sam lowered his voice. "This isn't about my rig."

Even her flat tone sounded like music. "What are you doing?"

"Little old lady broken down in the heat. Needs to get to her grandson's wedding."

"You know how much these comm calls cost. I have to log it, and the reasons for it," Bob said.

"Come on, darling, have a heart."

Bob's voice softened. "Okay. Get the translink from your tool box and plug it into the computer module."

"The computer module looks like what again?"

"Sam." Bob's tone could have withered spring crops.

"I just can't remember what it looks like," Sam hastily added, "on this model."

"See the cable end on the translink?" she asked.

"Yeah."

"Find the little box, size of a deck of cards - I know you know what those look like. It'll have a port that fits the cable."

"Got it."

"Hold on. Coming up now." Bob whistled. "Not good. Most of her control systems are fried."

"What's the cause?"

"I'll download the system and look through its sensor logs," Bob said. "If I figure it out, you can let her know on your way back by."

"Okay, thanks, Bob. I owe you one."

"You owe me dinner."

"You got it. We can get some dogs at a Tiger's game."

"Baseball season isn't for another five months."

"Didn't want to cramp your schedule, babe."

"Right, because I have such a busy life," Bob said. "Dinner, New Year's Eve."

"Well, I suppose, if I'm not working, but you know that's less of a dinner and more of a--"

"You heard me. Base out."

Sam unplugged the translink and stood, wiping hands on his black jeans. "Looks like it's not going anywhere."

Rather than being where he expected her, she scowled at the rig's controls from his seat.

"Ma'am?"

Her expression softened. She lifted big cow eyes up to Sam's face. A single tear ran down her cheek. "I really wanted to see my only grandson's wedding."

Sam fidgeted. He took a deep breath, eased it out, and gestured for her to move to the copilot seat. "Not supposed to take hitchers, but who's going to know?"

She smiled sweetly. "Thank you, son."

Sam climbed into the rig.

"Was that your sweetheart?"

"Bob? Nah, we're just friends."

"And she lets you address her like you're lovers?"

Sam blinked at her. "What? No, just being friendly is all."

Grandma shook her head. "You might think so, son, but I'd be careful. You're liable to offend someone...or give them the wrong idea."

Sam started to object but arguing with little old cows seemed like a bad idea. He started up his rig, and they sped down the road.

2: Telltale

Sam Bridger

Grandma pointed down a narrow canyon set between what passed for Audorian high rises. Ten-story buildings in signature Audorian styles lined both sides of the road, their wide balconies blocking out most of the sky. Laundry lines hung out in the sun marred their high-tech architectural lines.

A pack of Anubians crossing the street forced Sam to slow. Human bodies with legs and heads of Doberman pinchers, Bob had once told Sam there was a word for their kind, Therio-something-or-other. They froze midway across and wrenched weapons out of shopping bags from The Trench.

Sam brought the hover chariot to a hard stop.

The lead Anubian's bark-like speech took Sam a moment to comprehend. "Give up the weapon, wayman. "The Canis Liberation Army will not lie down and beg before Tauron oppressors."

Sam licked his lips. "Well, now—"

Movement on balconies above them stole Sam's attention.

On his right, a flock of Horusians fluttered onto a balcony, their hawkish heads eyeing him like a field mouse. They turned energy rifles on him and the Anubians.

"The weapon, wayman, and you fly free," she said. At least, Sam assumed it was a she by the very feminine screech. "The Horusish Independence Front won't cower in their nests under threat."

On the opposite set of balconies, a third group with heads and wings of a vulture rather than a hawk mirrored the Horusians. "The weapon, wayman! This isn't your fight." A male planted a talon on a balcony rail. "The Nekhbetian Freedom Talon won't hesitate to crack your eggs if you oppose us."

Sam shook his head and glanced at his side mirrors. Behind him a gaggle of crocodile-headed cheerio-buggers crawled out of a sewer entrance and trained what appeared to be rocket launchers toward his rig.

"Wayman," one of the crocs Sam thought were called Sobekan said, "we will have the weapon."

"That's it?" Sam craned around to face them. "No faction name? No manifesto?"

"No," a smaller Sobekan replied. "We just want the weapon."

Sam rubbed the back of his neck. He reached over his shoulder and whipped a sawed-off shotgun from behind his seat. He put it to his passenger's head just as she drew an energy pistol from her bag.

"There's only one thing I want to know, Grandma," Sam said. "Why does this sort of thing keep happening to me?"

She blinked angry cow eyes at him.

Bob's voice leapt from the communicator. "Sam, I had a look at those logs. Her chariot was damaged by energy weapon fire."

Sam took a deep breath and bent to press the communicator button with exaggerated slowness. "Thanks for the update, Bob."

"You'll steer clear, right?" Bob asked.

"First chance I get. Bridger out."

"Sam?" Anything else she might have said was drowned out as the four varied factions opened fire.

"Ah hells," Sam cursed. "Button up, baby, button up fast."

The passport's glow intensified, and the rig shuddered. An armored shell grew over Sam's head and the cargo so fast it practically materialized.

Weapon blasts rocked the rig.

"Bob's going to skin me alive," Sam glared at Grandma. "But you're going to tell her this wasn't my fault."

A swirling, lightning vortex appeared just beyond the newly-grown windshield. All weapon fire halted. The vortex disappeared as quickly as it had formed, leaving a man standing with one foot on either of two of the hover horses - a gleaming knife handle protruding from one polished black boot.

He raised his chin, metallic-looking burgundy vestment and pants shining in the sunlight. His voice echoed off the buildings. "Citizens of Chronosphere string fourteen this action violates the Tycho Conventions set down in the 34th eon." He pointed a single, golden gloved hand, stretching out his arm to display the black symbols along his silver sleeves. "You're instructed to lay down your arms, cease all hostile activity, and return to your place, plane or time of origin."

"What's your name, brother?"

"You can call me Alden, Sam."

"Well, Alden, they're about to hand you your shiny ass."

Alden smiled. "Not this time."

The factions opened fire.

Alden extended his ringed hand. A spherical force field sprang up around the rig. He unsheathed his knife. Instead of a knife however, a single-edged sword slid free, its blade etched with glowing circuit paths.

"Knife to a gunfight?" Sam asked.

Alden flourished his wrist. The sword transformed into a long barreled energy blaster. He whipped it toward the Anubians. The shield blinked off and back again. Alden fired twice between, adding burnt dog hair to the breeze. He pivoted and fired up at the Horusians with similar results.

Two rockets impacted the rig, shaking them despite the suddenly wavering shield.

Alden glared at Grandma. "Stay there."

The spherical shield shrank to a simple disk of protective energy. Alden moved, leaving after-echoes of himself. He darted across spaces, sometimes seeming to teleport in and out of warped, swirling whirlpools of light. Fists, feet and blaster fire lashed out at the Anubians.

Alden vanished a moment ahead of weapon blasts. He reappeared on one balcony, fighting the Horusians.

Sam blinked. He rubbed his eyes.

One Alden fought on each balcony. Both appeared and reappeared, streaked across spaces in a cascade of after echoes.

A cry brought Sam's attention to those behind him.

A third and fourth Alden wrestled two of the Sobekan crocodile-men.

Sam craned his neck to be sure the mirror hadn't cracked and given him a false image. Two Alden fought Sobekans with blinding speed, appearing and vanishing at will.

A Nekhbetian and a Horusian cried out at the same time.

Sam whipped around.

Three Alden fought a Nekhbetian and two more fought the Horusians.

"Does that seem strange to you, Grandma?"

A sixth Alden planted a foot atop the lead Anubian.

A seventh appeared once more on the horses before Sam. "Neat trick, brother."

Alden gasped for breath. "Thanks."

Every Alden vanished, taking their assailants with him. He reappeared on the rig's hood and glared down at Grandma. "Essie Bell, lower your weapon."

"I'll shoot him," Grandma said.

"Pull the trigger, and I'll take your weapon before you can finish," Alden said.

"Hold on there, boss. Not sure I like that idea."

Grandma pulled the trigger.

Another Alden appeared in the back seat, snatching her weapon and vanishing as the mechanism triggered.

Alden's glare hardened "Do you have any idea the kind of headaches that causes?"

Sam set his shotgun in his lap and held both hands up in surrender. "Man, I didn't do anything. I was just trying to be a good samar--"

"Samaritan," Alden finished. He rubbed the bridge of his nose. "Yeah, you said that last time, too."

"Like some kind of déjà vu?" Sam asked.

Alden nodded behind his hand. "Occupational hazard."

"What are you going to do with her?" Sam gestured.

Grandma and her bag no longer occupied the other seat. Sam blinked. "She's getting away."

"No, I've already taken her into custody."

"With you still here?"

"Yes and no. Now, Sam, I'd really appreciate it if you'd listen to me this time and be a bit more cautious from now on."

"Even though we've never met."

"Correct."

Sam smiled. "You got it."

"You promise to stay safe?"

"Yeah, I know the deal. Drive fifty-five, stay alive."

Alden smirked. "And don't exceed eighty-eight miles per hour."

Sam stared at him.

"Too soon? Right, next summer. Forget I said it," Alden waved his bare hand, gold ring gleaming in front of Sam's face. "You won't remember seeing me. You decided to take a shortcut to her grandson's wedding, driving through a bad neighborhood and into an impromptu gang war. Shortly after entering, they all ran off. You delivered Essie to the wedding."

"Did I get any cake?"

"The last thing you remember is Essie sending you off with a piece of cake."

"Except I don't remember any cake."

Alden repeated all of his instructions, watching Sam expectantly.

Sam grinned. "Mind trick not working?"

Alden grimaced, slapped the ring against his thigh and waved his hand once more.

"Sorry to break it to you, brother, but those things only work on the weak minded, and if there's one thing Sam Bridger ain't its weak mi--"

Sam blinked.

His rig idled in a side street for no particular reason. He had a vague recollection of a gang war spontaneously occurring, inconsiderately damaging his rig and then vanishing just as quick. He remembered cake that tasted like the smell of fresh mowed grass.

"Why do I have a sudden overwhelming urge to play things safe?" Sam snorted. "I make tea and scones in the face of danger. American, not the *foreign* kind."

He chuckled. Helen from records would be so proud.

Sam checked the time and cursed. He shoved the rig into gear and glanced over at the passport. "Give me directions to our drop off, baby, and don't spare the short cuts—the safe ones."

The device let out a disgruntled set of chirps and projected a holographic set of directions.

"You're a doll."

They entered the delivery destination via a high-speed drift with seconds to spare. Sam double-checked for any pending local pickups while others unloaded his rig.

Nothing? What about that add on? He frowned. Whoa, never been to a dead universe before.

He glanced out the window at the late afternoon sunshine. A gelato stand caught his eye. "Work us up a route, will you, baby doll? I'll be right back."

Sam leapt out, ignoring the passport's irritated noises. He strode across the street to a small plaza. Taurons and a small family of Anubians - only parents and six pups – lounged over coffee and snacks as if on holiday. He sidled up to the stand just as a beefy Tauron woman walked away with two cones of brown gelato.

Sam pointed after her. "I'll take one of those, brother."

A Tauron adolescent with a paper soda jerk cap snorted in acknowledgement. Within seconds, the boy had a waffle cone filled with brown gelato.

Sam whistled softly. Kid's got that skill down, pretty handy with the scoop too.

The young Tauron handed Sam the frozen treat and passed the barcode of Sam's wayman badge across the payment scanner.

"Thanks."

Sam strolled from the kiosk, bringing the gelato to his mouth. A warm, buttery flavor like brown gravy flowed from the icy treat across his tongue. He glanced at it, shrugged and took another taste.

A small Tauron girl with a string of bells tied around her horns skipped up to him.

Sam smiled down at her.

"Where do you come from?" she asked.

"A long time ago Sam Bridger had a mommy and daddy."

She scrunched up her nose. "That's not what I meant."

"What do you mean, darling?"

"I live here. Where do you live?"

Sam liked Audoria, though he didn't get many trips into the fractious universe. Taurons and their fellow there-and-back-againite minorities knew about waymen though they didn't know about the crossways. In a world filled with animal headed humanoids lacking in primates, it was hard being a human-headed humanoid, particularly one so handsome and memorable.

Sam turned toward the horizon and made an expansive gesture with his gravy gelato. "Sam Bridger comes from a land far, far away."

"How far away?"

"Far, far away."

"How far is that?"

Sam frowned and looked around for her parents. "Far, far, far away?"

She turned and skipped back to several other children. "He doesn't know where he comes from either."

"Cute kid." Sam chuckled and turned toward his rig. A brain-frying, glowing-magma orange muumuu polka-dotted pink and violet brought him up short. He stared, blinking away spots independent of the dress. A dozen impressive teats strained against the supernova of fabric, struggling for notice amidst Sam's overloaded vision.

A high-pitched voice bit through the noise. "What're you looking at?"

Sam tore his gaze up to meet deep blue eyes beneath luxurious lashes and a bristle of blonde locks. Slender, pearl-pierced ears framed a haughty expression. The Porcina female pursed her matching orange lipstick above a similarly bristled chin. He gestured at her. "Wow, baby doll, just wow."

She glanced down her front and then slammed a twin-fingered hand across Sam's face. "Swine."

Sam cradled his cheek, watching her march away, snout skyward.

"I meant the dress, baby, but yeah, with bacon like that, who'd ever want the roast beef?" He chuckled under his breath and returned to his truck. "You ready to go, babe?"

Sam licked his gelato and examined the holographic map. He scowled, shaking his head. "Just tell me where to turn."

The passport berated him with a disgruntled set of noises and turned on the rig's left blinker.

Sam followed the blinkers to a nearby waygate he'd never used before. He drove into the rollercoaster ride through to Earth. His rig emerged inside a large empty warehouse. He drove out through open doors onto a sunny beach road.

The left blinker directed him away from the waterfront. Sam's attention lingered on the boardwalk, bikini-clad women, and inviting surf.

The left blinker clicked louder.

"We've done a lot of work today. Time for a break."

Sam pulled the rig into a few parking places. He fed all of the meters and strolled along the boardwalk with his half eaten gelato.

Florida license plates dominated the cars. Mostly English chatter floated up and down the beachfront. New waymen often got hung up on time mismatches between universes.

Just means it's always time for a beer.

A little boy sat on a bench outside a souvenir shop, his tongue racing to catch melting trails along his large strawberry ice cream cone.

A sunburnt woman in a t-shirt-covered, hot pink bathing suit held up a keychain. A New Englander accent so thick it was almost an alien language escaped her. "What do you think about this, Pauly? Think Joey'll like it?"

Pauly shrugged and tried to recover lost footing with the ice cream exodus. One large lick sent the ball of strawberry goodness tumbling to the boardwalk. He raised tear-brimmed eyes toward his mother, but the woman had vanished further into the shop.

Sam glanced down at his own cone. He shrugged and walked up to the boy. "Here, you can have what's left of mine."

A grin stopped the tears as he took Sam's gelato.

Sam strolled away with a smile.

Something cold slammed into the back of Sam's head. He put his hand to the spot and brought back melted brown gelato. He turned toward Pauly to find an angry, disgusted look on the boy's face.

Passing tourists stopped for the show.

"You don't like gravy?" Sam glanced at the watching tourists. "Who doesn't like gravy?"

Pauly ran into the shop. "Mama!"

Sam strolled back to his rig, wiping away more gelato and occasionally licking his fingers.

3: Ruins

Sam Bridger

Sam drove from Daytona's boardwalk, thoughts straying to his bootlegger cousin. The US Government had covered up the whole nightmare with Morgan and her children.

Nice lady despite the whole slaughter and eat IRS agents thing...one seriously hot mama too.

The massive death toll had eliminated pretty much all of the witnesses, but the authorities still tried to hang the whole noose around Sam's neck. Crossways Transportation and the UPO intervened, waggling a finger at Sam before sending him off to his next delivery.

Sam considered swinging by Cousin Ler's place. A load of moonshine sold in some other universe's black market would help dig him out of the lingering divorce debts.

Instead, he drove through the beachfront tourist town to a closed-down drive-in theater. Sam pulled his rig past a half-rotted flea market sign, startling an alligator sunning itself next to a speaker post.

He glanced around for the subtle signs marking a waygate.

A faded scene of vintage life covered a fence beneath the large screen. A boy dragging his probable sister dead center in the mural pointed upward at the screen.

"That's it, right?"

His passport watched him without a chirp.

Sam put the rig into gear. "Hope we don't end up in someone's pool again."

He sped through the drive-in, up and down the low rises. His passport chittered at him.

"We'll chitchat later, doll. I'm busy."

Moments from slamming into the fence line, Sam raised his arms over his face and let out his best horror-movie scream. His high-pitched wail dissolved into choking belly laughter.

The loud crash of a rig smashing through old wood cut off his mirth. He slammed the brakes. His truck skidded to a halt a single pace away from a small boy playing in a sand pit.

"You could've warned me." Sam shifted his glare from the passport, smiling and waving at the boy.

The boy waved back.

Sam honked the truck's horn, expanding the boy's grin. He backed out of the boy's yard, keying his communicator. "Twenty-Three to base."

Beatrice answered. "Base here, what do you want, Sam?"

"Got a six-twenty here that I need resolved."

"Where's your brain?"

A woman in a housecoat stepped out onto the back porch. The boy ran up to her, bouncing and pointing.

Sam slunk down in his seat, offering the woman an embarrassed wave. "Look, base, I've never had a pickup on Vuria. So I've never used this gate before. I thought I marked the entrance, and since my passport didn't tell me different, I drove through. You going to taking care of this or not?"

"Fine, we'll clean up your mess, again. Give me the address and gate number."

He did.

He rolled down his window and handed the woman a business card. "My office will come out to take care of this. If you don't hear anything by tonight, call this number."

"You drove through a drive-in screen and *my fence*."

"Awful sorry about that, darling. Wasn't my fault."

"Not your fault?" She asked. "How'd you not see a three-story wooden wall directly in front of you?"

"I thought I'd phase right through it," Sam shrugged.

She sized Sam up for a straitjacket.

"Blame my passport, sweetheart."

"I'm not your sweetheart!"

"How many times have I got to tell you women don't like being objectified, Sam?" Beatrice asked.

"Ignore my ex, babe. You don't have any objection, right?"

"I'm calling the cops."

"For calling you sweetheart?" Sam asked. "You like 'baby' better, princess?"

"You crashed through my fence and nearly killed my son!"

Sam shared a disgusted look with the boy. "Overreacting is like a mom superpower, am I right, buddy?"

The boy giggled.

"If you want to make a federal case of it, make your call."

"Sam!" Beatrice snapped.

"What?"

"You do know if the local authorities get involved, cleaning up after your mistake becomes harder and more expensive," Beatrice said.

Sam pointed at the communicator. "The old ball and chain's right, darling. It'd only mean brain damage for you and some innocent smokey when the corporation erases everyone's memory."

"Damn it, Sam, shut up and get out of there."

Sam smiled. "You heard the lady. I've got to go now."

"You can't leave," the homeowner said.

"Got a pickup, ma'am, can't be late." He pointed his fingers at the boy like a gun, pantomimed firing as he clicked his tongue and winked. "Catch you later, buddy."

Sam pulled the rig away, hunting for the gate.

She chased him across the drive-in, fluffy yellow slippers slapping as she ran. When he paused to look around, the panting woman raced over to the drive-in's exit and extended her arms wide to block his escape.

UPO markings caught Sam's eye. He threw the truck into gear and drove between the speaker posts toward the concession stand.

The woman screamed something. Sam's rig slid into the waygate a foot from crashing into the building, the crossway's horizon cut off her words.

Sam stood next to his futurized semi-truck, wishing the breathing mask covering his face didn't pinch so badly. Scarlet treads replaced his rig's tires, clashing with a pastel, tie-dye rendition of the Aurora Borealis painting the truck's exterior.

A hard wind struck him. Blown debris and bone fragments threatened to knock him over. He took shelter behind one of the ruined, lava lamp-shaped buildings. A magenta sky roiled beneath a violent storm thrashing the ground horizon to horizon.

The detritus of war littered the clearing before him. In the center, crate-stacked skids arranged in a triangle awaited him. Sam crossed to them.

A sudden squeak made him jump.

He whirled around, wishing he'd brought his shotgun from the rig. Looking down at the offending boot, revealed a blue rubber doll. An over-large perfectly round head capped the body of a tadpole. Big eyes and outstretched arms begged him for comfort.

I don't like it here either, and I just arrived.

Sam dusted the toy off and continued evaluating his pickup. An uneasiness drew his eyes back to the horizon. Sam had just relaxed when a flash of movement back near his rig caught his attention. Sam squinted through the dust and wind, watching until his eyes watered.

Nothing moved.

Sam rubbed the back of his neck. "Don't like this neighborhood, but a job's a job."

A tablet on the nearest cargo stack itemized the shipment.

Invoice looks authentic. Identity code matches Beatrice's message. He shrugged. *Guess we're good to go.*

Sam raised his voice against the wind. "Lower the trailer, will you, darling?"

His passport lowered the cargo ramp.

He strode up into the enclosed trailer and approached the grav-lift mounted just inside. He unclipped the straps and thumbed the lift's power button. The invaluable tool hummed only a moment before sparking and belching smoke.

Sam cursed, searching the lift for a set of discrete marks. *Yup, this is my unit...unless someone counterfeited...nah.*

Sam locked the lift back into place and dug a back brace out of his sleeper. Strapping the support in place over his flannel shirt, Sam trudged back to the waiting cargo.

His neck hair tingled.

He checked the horizon.

Sam old buddy, you're jumping at shadows. He reversed course once more only to stop short. Cargo wasn't arranged like that before, was it?

He recounted crates. Finding their number unchanged, he assessed the rising wind. It didn't seem strong enough, at least not yet. Sam shrugged, hefted a crate, and started loading.

Thunder exploded overhead. Buildings trembled around the clearing. "Damn, need to finish up and high tail it."

The crate in his hands blinked up at him.

Sam screamed a battle cry normally only heard when a Girl Scout cookie stand is encroached upon by Boy Scouts. He hurled the box away, raced to his rig and reclaimed his shotgun. Sam approached the crate cautiously, circling weapon at the ready to blast the first eyes that winked at him.

None appeared.

Lightning reflected off a couple bolts? He shoved the shotgun into his belt. Get a grip, man.

He resumed loading. No bolt-eyed boogeymen jumped him.

Pity. He smirked. Could've asked for help loading.

A full-body stretch popped his back. He climbed inside to find his passport projecting a map above its surface. Sam rubbed his neck. "Whatever, babe, just tell me where to turn."

They drove across the ruined countryside stretching out like a post-apocalyptic version of a Doctor Seuss illustration. Sam didn't know much about Vuria. The world might be composed of a singular, limited environment like Quiss or Dorsun. On the other hand, the universe might somewhere contain pristine, unravaged countrysides or even other planets for him to explore.

Guess I could ask Bob. He reached for the communicator but hesitated. She'd be pissed if I used the comm... or worse, rope me into another...date.

He watched the landscape slide by. Tall buildings built of spheres and interconnecting curves broke up the landscape without managing to hide dead foliage and dying trees. Doorways pockmarked each sphere, ignoring distance to the ground.

Sam caught occasional movement in the upper windows. *Scared people or shifting curtains?*

His earlier unease grew mile by mile. Waymen told stories about Vuria. Even so, no one he'd asked remembered what the world had looked like before.

A clicking blinker dragged his eyes from the broken Seussian world. He checked for cross traffic despite empty roads. As he did so, a small figure half a block away peered around a dirty, rounded wall.

He stopped his rig.

She – *really too young to be sure* - resembled the forlorn doll in his passenger seat.

Sam grabbed the doll and got out. He pushed through the wind with slow, measured steps. His too-tight facemask muffled Sam's voice. "Hello there. My name's Sam."

She darted behind the building.

Sam spoke in soothing tones, presenting the doll. "No need to be scared. I found this doll. Would you like her?"

The Vurian child didn't peek.

Sam eased the doll down onto what might've been a manhole cover. Patting his pockets, he found a half-eaten Big Hunk candy bar. "She's lonely, hungry too. Hope she likes candy."

He propped the candy in the doll's arms before returning to his truck. One of his backward glances caught her peeking, but she didn't break cover.

A scar from the Audoria gangland war marred the cab's nose. He glared at his passport. "You can completely transform the whole rig and wipe out my paint jobs, but you can't fix a dent?"

It emitted a single beep.

Sam climbed up into his cab and watched.

The girl's pale, grime-blunted blue skin emerged little by little. She bobbed up and down, the swish of her tadpole tail propelling her from the ground. Out in the open, the poor child looked painfully gaunt.

Sam cursed. *Nothing else I can give her.*

She rose, eyes bigger than the doll's locked on Sam's rig. She swam the last few yards in a rush, scooped up the candy, and shoved it into her mouth - wrapper and all.

"Please tell me what you can do with the change field can make her some food."

The passport let out a forlorn tone.

The child glanced toward Sam one more time before snatching up the doll and speeding back toward cover. Once safe, she peeked out one more time and offered Sam a wave.

Sam beamed back and honked the horn.

She bolted.

He slapped his forehead. *Stupid. Stupid. Stupid.*

Sam pulled back onto the road. She appeared in his side mirror, cuddling the doll as she waved once more.

Sam arched his eyebrows at the small, remote warehouse. As his company or the broken grav-lift in his trailer could attest, UPO members seldom popped for the deluxe package when it came to shipping cargo through Eleventh World. The ramshackle warehouse in a derelict Versailles industrial park didn't herald a change of philosophy.

Sam knocked on the door.

No one answered.

The manifest read: 1049 Route de L'Envers, Versailles.

He double checked the warehouse wall. Metal numbers one, zero, four and nine hung from nails in an odd curve.

"That's the frogs for you." Sam adopted a French accent, "Always the artistes."

The door proved unlocked.

Go in or face Beatrice. He shrugged. Won't be my first French trespassing charge.

He tightened his grip on the shotgun and stepped into the dark warehouse. The light switch worked. Fluorescents blinded him, sending three fist-sized cockroaches and a rat-brontosaurus crossbreed racing for cover.

"Hello?"

No one answered.

"Bon Jorse?"

Silence.

Sam cursed. "Got to call it in after all."

Something seized his arm. Sam whipped around, wrenching himself from the grip of an ancient black man. Sam stared.

"Where the hell did you get Superman's grip, Gramps? You look two minutes past due for cremation."

"Quai?"

"Delivery?"

"Monsieur?"

"You speak Americano? Maybe learned it during the revolutionary war?"

He grinned, nodded and gestured toward the loading bay.

Sam chuckled. "Right."

He left the old man behind with the cargo, heading for a nearby French Motel Six equivalent. He could've just slept in his rig.

I hate the idea of sleeping in a truck run by a computer with mood swings. I could end up in some backward universe or even off a cliff if she succumbs to one of those once-a-month-serial-killer-female things.

The next morning, Sam sought out a good breakfast. Instead, he ended up with warm, flaky croissants and some anorexic omelets filled with fruit of all things. He checked both for saliva.

I don't know what that waiter's problem was. A man ordering toast in France expects syrup and powdered sugar.

Four bowls of phenomenal coffee soothed his irritation.

Thankfully his truck still waited where he'd left it.

An itinerary update waited too.

Sam started with the local pickup. He relocated luxuries and other resources through six countries on four continents. He enjoyed a hearty lunch in Cuba before dropping off one last cargo in Audoria and knocking off for the night in a Tauron wayman hostel.

4: Ultimatum

Taleh

Taleh paced up and down the narrow central aisle of her RV. Her high, leather heels didn't so much as whisper against the thin carpet worn shiny by feet her true form didn't have.

Tall, buxom and brunette, Taleh'd stolen the illusion she wore from a popular but forgotten television show. The disguise often drew a bit too much attention, but the spare amount of time she spent on Earth's streets limited her reasons to construct another.

Hopefully she doesn't suffer for what I'm about to do.

A knock and a giggle halted her mid-pace. "Mistress, everything is ready."

She exited from the RV onto an asphalt parking lot to a small man in a tweed suit. He performed an archaic bow, gesturing toward a tent erected at the end of a rest area service road. His customary queer grin - almost a grimace - clung to his face. "This way."

She studied him, still unable to determine his origin universe. *No matter where, he's a godsend—despite that unsettling giggle.*

He and his brethren found her, swearing service to her and her mission. She needed them so desperately, she didn't pry into the how, why or even their origins.

"Thank you, Mite."

He bowed once more with a soft titter, leading the way.

Crossways

Cables snaked out of the tent to the nearest of two posts. She stepped over them through tan canvas flaps. Inside, a collapsible framework dotted with cameras filled two alcoves. A thick backboard of communications electronics connected everything to the signal relays through the wires outside.

"There is no way for them to trace us?" Taleh asked.

His head shake seemed lopsided. "They will trace, but we're bouncing our connection through crossways in eight of the eleven universes. They'll not locate us in time."

"Unless they have an agent nearby."

"We do what we must."

She hunted through the controls, trying to remember all the extra steps Mite's predecessor had taught her. Anticipating her as usual, Mite flipped on encryption and scrambler devices.

She thanked him with a nod and turned on the drone screen. The humming display floated into the framework's center, centering itself in preparation to move whichever direction her attention shifted. "Everything ready?"

Mite nodded. "All awaits this historic event, Mistress."

She closed her eyes, took one last breath, and initialized connection with the UPO Council Chamber located in the little pocket universe which had been the testbed for Eleventh World. "Begin communication."

Taleh's immense, three-dimensional head and shoulders appeared above a massive forum's empty center. Walkways split ten sections of organized disorganization, each beneath the flag of its origin universe. She glanced down, the floating screen moving with her attention to display her desired view.

The council wasn't in session.

Had they been, the speaker would've noticed me before I got my bearings...and my courage.

Small groups of UPO officials conversed throughout the room. They didn't notice her until her voice boomed through the chamber. "U. P. O."

Representatives jerked and spun around. She gestured to someone off camera and restarted at a more reasonable volume. "U. P. O. I require your attention."

A man with sun-browned skin, swept loose robes to one side as he strode toward the screen. "I'd say you have it."

"Corlan's correct." A Tauron with massive horns snorted. "What's the meaning of this?"

A slight elf in silvery gowns folded her hands behind her back. "Ambassador Onklus's question notwithstanding, audiences must be scheduled with the executive assistant for the adjunct to the associate of audience scheduling."

Taleh grimaced at the very bureaucracy responsible for her desperation. "This won't wait, Ambassador Felisian." Taleh's hand halted the elf's objections. "I have within my control a bomb. Accede to my request or...or I'll destroy Eleventh World."

The Tauron Onklus threw back his horned head and laughed.

A stout dwarf sporting a dozen blue-steel braids joined him. Expelled air rippled his matching handlebar mustache. "Ridiculous. You'd never get it onto Eleventh World. Procedures and safeguards aplenty prevent--"

"My world-ender is already on Eleventh World."

A crystalline owl perched on an old woman's robed shoulder hooted softly. The magus gave her symbiote a single nod. "A good question. What do you hope to achieve by destroying Earth?"

"Perhaps she dislikes her fellow vermin," Corlan sneered.

Felisian lowered her voice. "Let her speak."

Taleh swept an accusing finger across the assembly, hesitating a moment longer as her gaze fell upon the Vurian assembly. "If you do not provide me what I request, I'll destroy your crossroads, stopping your waymen from delivering your comforts, luxuries, and even desperately needed resources."

"You can't. My people need those resources," Corlan said.

"I can." Taleh closed her eyes for half a breath. "I can and I will destroy all commerce between the worlds, handicapping your greed and turning poor and wealthy citizens against you for your part in this."

"How exactly are we complicit?" Felisian asked.

"It's your greed, your contentious ineptitude, your inaction that drives me to this course, Ambassador," Taleh said. "If you want to save Eleventh World, your offices received my initial demands moments ago."

"What proof do you offer that you even have a world-ender?" Corlan asked.

"I have no lesser threat to offer you, Ambassador. Defy me and I'll obliterate Eleventh World and all within her."

"You should've prepared more leverage," Felisian said.

"I said lesser, Ambassador, not only. Earth is merely the least valuable universe I can destroy." Taleh's expression hardened. "Which of yours will be next?"

A young Anubian raced into the chamber, thrusting a digital tablet into Onklus's hands. He scanned the contents and snorted once more. "Not exactly an auspicious list for someone holding an entire universe hostage."

"Consider it a test of your cooperation. You'll receive new lists at each new drop off to ensure your honesty."

Felisian glanced around the Tauron's beefy arms. "I see no delivery location."

"The wayman will be notified." A smile flickered over her face before she straightened it. "Almost forgot, my shipments are to *only* be transported by Samuel Oswald Bridger."

The electronics around Taleh shut down, leaving her in silence. "Did they trace us, Mite?"

"No, mistress, they weren't expecting us. Next time perhaps."

She left Mite to see all the equipment disassembled and packed for their return to Mars. Taleh marched across the rest area and into the RV. She collapsed into a chair, cradling her face in shaking hands.

It had to be done. It had to be.

The RV door opened. After a lengthy silence, she lifted her gaze to find Mite's grin bent by worried eyes. "Mistress, a problem, perhaps so, a problem."

She tensed. "They traced us? They know we're here?"

"No, not that, no, not at all."

"What then?"

"The bomb, Mistress?"

"What?!"

Crossways

"The package..." Mite giggled. "...seems to have been lost in shipping."

5: Quiss

Sam Bridger

Sam toweled his hair dry and joined another three waymen around a dining table set by an old, wrinkled bull. Plates held greenish knots of honey-smothered, deep-fried bread beside bucket-sized mugs of coffee.

Sam inclined his head. "Morning, Mister Waret. Morning, boys. Just five of us?"

Two remained silent, slowly chewing mouthfuls of breakfast. A young, dark-haired wayman shifted enough bread into one plump cheek to answer without spraying too much food. "Yeah."

"Thanks, Bats." Sam grinned, dumping the heavy, nutty bread off a neighboring plate onto his own. Gnawing off a chunk, the earthy flavor underpinning the potent honey intensified the longer he chewed it. Chewning down small bites of Tauron knot-bread to swallowing size took forever. Sam's double portion would require chewing long after nightfall, but a single serving sated hunger for at least a day.

"How're you, boys? Arthur? Ross?" Sam asked.

The plain looking Brit cleared his mouth with a dainty sip of coffee, pinky in the air. "I don't suppose you'd do me a favor, would you, Bridger?"

Knot garbled Sam's reply. "Wha'cha need, Arty?"

Arthur's brow arched. "I've got a pickup in Quiss, but Mumsy requires I join her bridge game and meet her latest matchmaking hopeful."

"Where's it going?" Sam asked.

Crossways

"Dorsun."

"Sure, run's worth a few bucks. Transfer it over."

"Personal profit?" Bats asked. "You know better."

Sam shrugged. "Company's broke. Got to repair the old rig somehow."

A southern drawl infused Ross's laughter. "And another paint job, I imagine."

Sam met Ross's brown eyes with a forbidding glare. He managed it for a three count before he cracked up laughing. "That, too. Damn passport keeps changing the paint."

Ross's teeth glowed white between his dark lips. "She tell you why?"

"No idea, I don't speak beep."

Confused expressions watched him. A moment later, they burst out laughing.

Wasn't that funny.

Sam's truck writhed around him. The eyesore color scheme it took on in Vuria dissolved. Truck and trailer merged together into a long submersible painted light daffodil. Wheels extended, became propellers, changed directions and grew sailplanes. A moment later the waygate dumped him into a world of solid water amidst a blizzard of air bubbles.

A modified dashboard accommodated up and down blinkers in conjunction with left and right. Down and right blinked and Sam turned his rig until they both blinked off.

Quiss resembled the deep Amazon jungle of aquariums. Leaves blotched with bioluminescence illuminated the murky blue world of tangled green. Free-floating plants grew fathoms long. Orange vinecrabs hung onto leafy extensions with two claws while snapping at tiny fish with their other two. Species from which whales, rays and sharks might have been designed slid through the living weave, snacking on lesser fish and avoiding greater.

Sam's passport erupted in a cascade of noises just before the collision light flashed an angry red. He shoved the steering wheel forward just in time to avoid a whale the size of several aircraft carriers. As yet unchewed lengths of foliage trailed several blocks long from the corners of its mouth.

Sam jerked the rig up once more, sailing into the massive corridor cleared by the plant nibbler.

Sam belched. "Ugh, smells like mowed grass."

The freshly eaten highway allowed Sam to push his rig up to full speed. His destination, Perudathe, soon came into sight.

A forest of arena-sized habitats, shaped like diver bells, floated together like a massive school of jellyfish. Within each, Quissians lived, worked, shopped and on occasion died. Car-sized submersibles swam between them, as brightly colored as the surrounding aquatic life.

Larger clusters housed factories more advanced than anything on Earth, turning native and imported resources into needed goods. Just beyond one cluster, a colossal mud ball was anchored to them all. He turned toward the cluster, merging into the three dimensional traffic patterns.

The mud ball took on a shine the closer he came to it. Bio luminance, shed by the buildings themselves, augmented by electric lighting glinted off an insulating layer consisting of the industrial equivalent of fish egg jelly.

He aligned the rig beneath a delivery port and raised the truck straight up into it. Flaps of plant flesh extended around and beneath his rig, cradling it and sealing in the only kind of atmosphere Quiss offered - that generated by the huge plant structures and used by their inhabitants.

Sam climbed out of his rig. The ground beneath his feet shifted. *Like walking on a waterbed.*

The ground stiffened the further across the warehouse floor he walked until it became solid floor.

A merman with long blue hair and a matching utility jumpsuit descended a set of stairs to meet him. He made a trio of popping bubble sounds with his lips, then smiled. "Greetings, Wayman."

Sam chuckled. "Good to see you, Laris. How's your mate?"

"She is well, Sam Bridger. She has a sister yet single."

"Thanks, brother, but I've swam that current. I'm not interested in doing it again, if you catch my meaning."

Laris nodded. "We have your barrels prepared."

"They at least resemble wood this time?"

"Yes, Sam Bridger, though they remain polymer."

"Good enough," Sam rubbed his neck. "Don't suppose I could get another half dozen added to this shipment?"

Laris scanned his manifest.

Sam handed over his waymen card. "Charge me the difference, unless you want me to bring back dirt on my next trip."

"Your credits are good. Shall I add it to the manifest?"

"Let's put these on a separate one."

Laris typed the changes into his pad. He handed Sam a slip of transparent plastic which slid out the base. "Preparing disguised barrels will take half an hour. Would you like to wait in the office? We're watching Sharkhunter's newest episode."

"What's that one about again?"

"Sharks, hunting."

Sam chuckled. "I'll hang out near the rig this time."

Laris disappeared back into the office.

Beatrice's voice emerged from the cab. "Truck twenty-three, HQ Dispatch, come in at once."

Sam drew a slow hand across his shaking face.

"Twenty-three, this is a priority seven."

Sam's head shot up. He turned toward the passenger door. Something flashed past his mirror. He whirled around. Tools and assorted boxes lay conspicuously still.

Knots must not be agreeing with me. He belched fresh grass smell, climbed into the copilot seat, and keyed the comm. "Bridger here."

"Sam, you need to return to HQ immediately."

"I'm in the middle of a run, Bea."

"Forget it. Bring your cargo back and someone else will drop it off."

Sam muted HQ and regarded his passport. "How much travel time to our Dorsun drop point?"

A holographic route appeared, complete with estimated start and end times.

Sam rubbed his neck. "I'm a bit off the beaten path here, Bea. It'll take me several hours to get back."

"Do whatever you have to," Beatrice's voice softened. "Don't screw around this time, Sam, this's important. HQ out."

Sam scowled at the communicator. *What's knotted her panties?* Memories from one of their good anniversaries flashed to mind, invoking a grin. Both fled. *Your own damned fault, brother.*

He took a cleansing breath. *Why rush me back to HQ? Surely, someone else could handle...whatever.*

Rush orders, even those costly rather than profitable, happened somewhat regularly. With bigwigs in ten universes as their primary customers, everything was a rush. Pissing matches between honchos over who had priority often left waymen feeling like two-headed pack mules being drawn through the crossways in opposite directions.

He rubbed his neck. Something about her tone though... Maybe I should cancel the side order.

Sam assessed the barrels of nutrient-rich water waiting to be loaded. Their contents offered miraculous benefits to Dorsun's desert tribes. Quiss's water transformed barren areas into lush, bumper-crop fields for a growing season and a half.

Sam didn't have to buy water from Laris. Water anywhere in Quiss would've done the same. Quiss authorities enacted severe punishments on anyone exporting, purposely or not, microorganisms filtered out of their export-approved water.

On Dorsun, these inexpensive barrels fetched a fortune. Earth and rock purchasable for almost nothing on Dorsun likewise offered extreme profits on Quiss. Select leaders of both worlds used the knowledge to make themselves richer, careful not to flood the market and lower their profit.

And I'd get drummed out like Laz if they catch me profiteering. Sam chuckled. Not that the smug bastard had just been smuggling.

Sam wasn't too concerned. Landfills were tidier than HQ's record keeping.

Any route through Dorsun's geonations teamed with tribes desperate for more of the imported water. Crossways Transportation limited smuggling temptation with waygate passport check-in and minimizing consecutive Quiss-Dorsun runs.

Sam rubbed his neck. Priority Seven, someone probably forgot to order ahead for their dinner party. Still...

Laris reappeared.

Better cancel.

A golf-cart sized mechanical crab scrambled into the room with his additional cargo.

"Open it up, Sam Bridger. We'll load it straight in."

Sam pulled a lever. The rear of his submersible parted to admit the cargo. He tapped his foot while they loaded.

I'll just make the Dorsun run a fast one.

"Sam Bridger, you're out of room."

"Hold on a moment." Sam spun toward the passport. "What're you doing to me, doll? Relax and let them shove it in."

It offered him one angry chirp.

"Come on, babe, I need to repair the rig. What if I got you some flowers or something?"

It repeated its chirp.

"You heard Beatrice. We're in a hurry but we've also got to do this job, as a favor to Arthur. Please?"

"Okay, Sam Bridger, you're all loaded."

Sam glanced back to see the cargo area close. He kissed his hand and planted it on the passport. "That's my girl."

Sam ignored the passport's disgruntled noises and waggled his hand in a hang loose gesture. "Keep it swimming, Laris."

Sam mounted up, double checked all the pressure seals and gave Laris a thumbs up. Laris threw a lever which sent sparks playing along the floor's edges. The living petals retracted, dropping Sam's rig back into the water. Sam navigated toward the nearest waygate and opened up the throttle.

Crossways

In and out before whatever's going on at HQ blows up in my face.

50 | Page

6: Dazzling Peril

Sam Bridger

That the waygate nearest Perudathe exited onto Earth on opposite ends of a supermarket parking lot from one to Dorsun always amazed Sam. If their worlds hadn't been physically antagonistic to one another - not just to tourists - they could've been connected directly. Dorsunian knowledge of Quiss, and vice versa, could've built twin paradises.

Of course, such connections would've eliminated any need to create Eleventh World and the glorious accident of Sam Bridger.

Sam chuckled. Wouldn't have mattered. Their politicians wouldn't have allowed uncontrolled prosperity.

He drove out of the Quiss waygate, his still yellow truck once more a mere semi, across the rear parking lot and into the Dorsun crossway.

His rig transformed once more. Ahead of him, a half dozen tan horses - resembling real animals enough to make Sam wonder. Tack and harnesses connected them to a long thin shaft connected directly to Sam's wooden cart. The passport's silvery exterior and neon lights hid beneath a dull wood grain. The cart's wheels reshaped for a wider surface area, their cross-section becoming an almost hourglass shape. The cab's configuration accommodated desert climate at the cost of Sam's air conditioning. A veiled litter replaced his sleeper, and an awning stretched light fabric overhead to protect him from sunburn in the sunny, entirely subterranean universe.

Crossways

Sam's passport projected their route.

In an example of the universe's grudge against Sam, the easy Dorsun gate exited nowhere near his destination—ever.

He didn't have time for an excruciatingly long haul through the maze of Dorsun geonations. "I don't need that, baby doll. Just control the horses. It's a short trip."

The map vanished with a disgusted whistle.

They emerged into a hollowed out sphere of rock ten miles in diameter. Its walls were smooth, free of debris and rubble. He'd long wanted to run the wagon team full out around the sphere's inner surface to see just how much horsepower the team really had.

Sam sighed. "Never enough time to play, huh, darling?"

The passport remained wooden.

Sam dropped the reins to the wagon floor and held them there with his boot. He stood, folded back the canopy and stretched beneath a tiny, blazing star floating in the center of the massive empty geode. "What say you change us into a flier, and we check out the star?"

His passport didn't answer.

Sam gave a few slow, lazy flaps of his arms, doing a bad Sidney Poitier imitation. "They call me Mister Icarus."

With a shrug, he stripped to his briefs, wiping sweat from his eyes. He removed a bundle of clothing from a box beneath his seat and donned a desert aba. Wrapped in the light robe, though still wearing his combat boots, he added a head and face wrap as tradition required of Dorsun men.

Dorsun's primitive matriarchal tribes didn't know about waymen. The similarity between human and Dorsun disguised the waymen and other safeguards protected Sam and his brethren.

He dropped onto the bench, missing the padding of his pilot seat and flicked a hand forward. "On Dasher, On Dancer, On Binky and Mister Ed, on...well, everybody else."

The passport chirped at him.

Sam sighed, reclaiming the reins. "Yes, dear."

He flicked them and the horses picked up speed. The well-traveled road led up the side of the wall. Despite the incline of such a small sphere, gravity never varied. The path descended into a shadowy, narrow tube. The stone straw's diameter stretched just wide enough for two side-by-side wagons without the curvature tangling their cargos.

The tube let Sam out into a sphere fifty times larger. Sand, trees, rocks and other desert terrain stretched out to the available horizon. Above, a logically larger star warmed and lit the new geonation.

Sam trundled down a right fork at his best speed. He passed a small caravan reminiscent of old Bedouin tribes. The woman leading wore sheer veils over studded leather armor and tanned skin. She glared at him.

Guess I'm supposed to clear the road for her highness. Screw that, road's wide enough for us both.

Her hand went to a steel scimitar.

Sam flipped a medallion out of his robe's collar.

She glared but didn't unsheathe her blade.

His road meandered the desert, ascending a rise. To Sam's right, a halo of farmland surrounded a wide clear lake. Bob believed the lakes interconnected geonodes the same way the access tunnels did the geonations. True or not, lakes were heavily guarded even if not as precious as his current load.

Despite being fundamentally horse-drawn, they made good time. He stopped for a meal just inside the geonation's exit.

Rice with the occasional chunk of spicy lizard or goat filled the flat bread.

A shadow fell over him, welcome relief from a late afternoon sun. When it didn't depart, he glanced up.

A statuesque beauty in veils glowered. "I require this table."

Sam gestured. "Have a seat, baby doll."

A blade pressed against his throat before he could lift another bite to his lips. "What did you call me?"

Sam placed fingertips on either flat of the blade and pushed it away. "I'm happy to share the table but keep your cutlery to yourself."

"Remove your unworthy self from my table and my sight before I water the desert with your worthless male blood."

Sam frowned. "You're mite rude. Careful, girl, you're treading deep water here."

"I've killed greater men than you and for far less."

"You might think so." Sam eased his medallion free of his aba. A stylized ten-pointed star surrounded the blue-green sphere. "Water bearer, toots. Draw *my* blood and your tribe dies of thirst."

She stiffened. "How dare you threaten an anointed Sun Cavalier?"

"Look, no hard feelings. Have a seat. I'm almost through."

"I'd rather breed with a diseased lopenar."

Sam winked at her. "You just go do that."

The sword swept toward his throat. Metal rang against metal, the blade stopped by the two barrels of Sam's shotgun. She swept it to one side then back at him only to meet the shotgun once more. Sam leapt to his feet, snatching a combat knife from one boot. He pushed the sword away with the knife and extended the gun.

"This here is my thunder stick, honey."

She eyed it with undisguised disdain.

Sam's expression hardened and his voice took on an airy quality. "Might not seem big to you, but if you want to throw down it'll leave you moaning on the ground with holes big enough to herd goats through. So the question you've got to ask yourself is, do you wanna dance, punk?"

They met each other's glare, fighting a silent war. Sam let out a great guffaw. He beamed at the startled woman. "Sorry, babe, I just couldn't resist. You've got one hell of a stare. Table's yours."

Sam collected his food and strolled away.

"Whatever tribe birthed you, they've disgraced themselves promoting a mere male to the sacred role of water bearer."

Sam turned. "Mere male? I don't know what you problem is, lady, but men—"

"Are worthless, beasts of burden suited only to be used up and once so, put down like the filthy mongrels they are. "

Sam stared at her a moment. Such narrow mindedness baffled him. *And they all treat their men like that.* "You live in one screwed up universe, toots."

He shook his head, leaving the angry, ignorant woman to seethe behind him.

Sam emerged from a stone tunnel into a new geonation's bright sunlight. Glare off a sea of white sand made him blink. Cloth swathed figures exploded from the dunes around him.

Hard eyes and polished wooden crossbows pinned him in place.

An exotic beauty in silver veils sashayed from around a boulder, her movements the savage beat of heart pumping music. Beneath the veils, supple honey-colored leather struggled to constrain muscled curves. Elaborate silver plates armored the soft leather, designed to match the twin swords riding high over her shoulders.

She drew both with terrifying elegance.

Sam reached for the shotgun hidden behind his seat. Sharp pressure against his spine from her accomplice's blade aborted his grab for the modern weapon.

"Just ain't gonna be my day, is it?" Sam asked.

"Silence, male," her eyes flashed a fierce emerald under desert-blonde hair cascading like silk.

Sam inched his left hand toward his medallion. Her sword flashed up, slicing a shallow cut across the back of his hand.

"You got any--"

Her second blade sliced across his face, parting cloth and drawing a red line along his cheekbone. "I know precisely who you are. You will not deliver water to our rivals."

"Babe, I--"

Another line appeared on his opposite cheek. "Further, you will take me to the source."

Sam narrowed his eyes but held his tongue. She sheathed one sword, flicked hair off of her face, raised her nose and addressed him without looking at him. "You may speak."

"Let's forget, for a moment, the penalties involved in attacking a water bearer and come right to the point. What the hell are you talking about?"

She gestured a sword toward the water barrels being unloaded. "In exchange for your worthless male life, you'll take me to where this water originates. A more than a fair exchange."

"There's nothing mere about Sam Bridger, baby."

Her eyes narrowed. "Speak thus to me again and there won't be anything male about you, bearer."

The figure behind Sam punctuated her sentence with the sharp point of his knife, no doubt leaving little crimson beads that would lengthen into commas.

Rather than express his distress over new holes in his favorite shirt, Sam eyeballed the desert beauty. He shrugged and smiled. "Whatever you say, doll."

A hand tightened around Sam's throat and the knife pressed deeper into his back. The assailant pushed Sam forward until he and the woman were eye to eye.

Her voice lowered to an ominous whisper. "I am Princess Niri Hivrus of the second Taite Dynasty. You will address me as Your Royal Highness or Phred will cut out your tongue."

"Whatever you say, your wonderfulness. Pokey coming with?"

"My manservant attends me everywhere," Niri said.

"Bath too?" Sam's brows rose. He glanced over his shoulder. "How'd you luck into that gig?"

Niri's sword tip pressed into the hollow of Sam's throat. "You will take us now."

Sam grinned. "Absolutely. Climb aboard."

Sam attempted to make conversation across the Dorsun deserts. One sword in her lap, she remained silent, perched pointedly at the bench's far end. Phred rode behind, not jabbing Sam on bumps or jostles.

Doubt it's sheathed though. Sam spoke over his shoulder. "Don't mean to be rude, Phred, but what's with the all-white aba? Not exactly subtle assassin attire, even in the desert."

"Phred is my manservant," Niri snapped.

"Nope, not buying, not considering his stealth and weapon choice. Still unsure how he expects to blend into crowds in bright white—tan maybe, or cream."

"Shut up, bearer. You will not speak unless I request it."

Sam shrugged.

An hour later Beatrice's voice broke the silence. "Truck twenty-three, HQ Dispatch, come in, Sam, now."

Niri leapt to her feet, swords in hand and eyes searching for its source.

Phred's dagger slid ahead of Sam's throat.

"Damn it, Sam, answer the comm."

"Who is that?" Niri pointed a blade. "Speak."

The knife across his throat eased its pressure.

"My former wife, Bea."

Fear tinged Phred's boyish voice. "You're haunted by your murdered wife?"

Sam chuckled. "She haunts me alright."

"Answer her, appease her spirit," Niri said.

"Hand's free, will you, babe?" Sam cleared his throat. "Twenty-three, Bridger here."

"Where are you?" Beatrice asked. "You're needed at base."

"Bit busy here, doll."

"Doing what?" Beatrice asked.

"Being abducted by a princess."

"Samual Oswald Bridger, I didn't buy that excuse the first time, I'm not buying it now. Get your ass back here."

Heat entered Sam's voice. "Sam Bridger is a lot of things, *woman,* but he's no liar."

Niri pressed her sword tip to his chest. "You will address your wife's shade with respect."

"I am!"

"Who was that?" Beatrice asked. "So help me Sam, if I find out you're playing around with some harlot when you're--"

"Silence, shade," Phred said. "Princess Niri is no--"

"I don't know what kind of perverted orgy is going on in your rig, and I don't care, Sam," Beatrice said. "Leave her unsatisfied already, tuck it away, and get your ass back here."

Niri fell into her seat, mouth moving without sound.

"Fine. Bridger out."

Fearful awe softened Phred's voice. "Our water comes from the underworld? We defile our food fertilizing it with corpses?"

"What? No, of course not," Sam said.

"Then how can you rejoin your wife's shade?" he asked.

"She's not dead—even if it's a nice thought on occasion."

They entered the last sphere and Sam headed for the dead-end tunnel housing the crossway. A smirk clung to the side of his face opposite Niri.

Oh, they're going to love this.

"What are you doing, bearer?"

He faced her, flicking the reins for more speed.

"That's a dead end," she said.

The dagger tip reappeared in Sam's spine. Clipped precise words filled his ear. "Answer her."

"This is the way," Sam said.

"You're a liar. Phred, kill him if he continues."

The knife pushed deeper. Warmth trickled down Sam's back.

Sam tossed the reins off the wagon and folded his arms. "Sam Bridger is a lot of things, but liar isn't one of them. I mean, there was that one time, and of course, there were the twins, but I really couldn't tell them apart and then--"

"Pick up the reins," Phred said.

Sam flourished his hands. "Open says me."

The swallowing dark of the tunnel became the starlit darkness of a crossway. The rollercoaster ride threw them up, right, left, right and up once more.

Niri shrieked, grabbing Sam's robes for support.

Sam perched his feet in stirrups formed near his feet. He was tempted to let the change field have her too, but her grip threatened to transfer it. "I'd pick up those sexy legs of yours if you want to keep them."

Wood shimmered, writhed, and transformed into metal.

Niri cried out, jerking her legs away from the light.

Phred's shriek drowned out Niri's curses.

Sam didn't look. The sensation of even a mere arm in the change field wasn't a horror soon forgotten. He couldn't imagine the torture wracking the fully enveloped assassin.

"What's happening to him?" Niri asked.

"I might have mentioned it," Sam smiled. "But you told me to shut up."

7: Ignoble Defeat

Princess Niri Hivrus of the second Taite Dynasty

Their horses dissolved, silently digested by the vast blackness. Niri's heart plummeted past her stomach, one headed for her feet and the other her throat.

Her neck blistered. *How dare this male keep such information from me?* She grabbed the water bearer's aba with every intention of spitting him on her ancestral blades.

Phred's screams drew her eyes. The water bearer's sorcery inflicted horrors on Phred beyond her imagination. Her eyes widened as Phred's changes grew more and more drastic. *I won't look away. I won't. A good leader is honor bound to bear witness to the fates she orders her men to endure.*

Despite the torture, Phred stabbed at the water bearer with an arm thin as silk and six times normal length. Phred's dagger of station resembled an unknown orange and white fish. A desert orchid capped with a thistle tuft replaced his other arm. Three individual breasts grew from his shimmering chest, taking turns lighting red, yellow and green. His legs shrank to stumps while his feet grew metallic, webbed and to enormous proportions. An odd hunch slithered into place on his back, part of it ripping out of his robes to end in windmill blades which grew flowers.

The bearer winced. "Unpleasant looking change, nice breasts though. I once got a cyborg arm with three little glowing hearts along in a stripe."

"Change him back!"

"Nothing I can do, baby doll. I didn't cause this."

"But you knew!"

Sam shrugged. "Your fault. I did *exactly* what you told me."

"You betrayed us. I'd kill you--"

Sam smirked. "Not if you want him changed back—unless *you* know how it's done."

She opened her mouth to refute him when the darkness broke. An azure sky painted golds and pinks stretched out without end. Fluffs of cotton floated through the sky, white, orange, violet and grey. To her right, massive structures stood upon a smooth field of building stone.

Two young males - scandalously unveiled and small clothes - stopped frolicking atop strange wooden platters. One waved.

Sam slapped twice on the strange wheel replacing his reins. Some kind of mating call bugled out.

Phred's cries died away, replaced by pained wheezes.

She gasped. We're imprisoned in metal. Where's the wood gone? Who would waste so much precious metal on a carriage?

The water bearer intoned a few musical words under his breath, "...Somewhere under the rainbow..."

Directly in front of her, a metal discus bleeding light made noises approximating smaller birds.

"Hold on to your hat, babe."

Niri regained her composure. She poised her sword to strike. "Stop this wagon at once."

"Too late."

Blackness swallowed them once more. The vehicle dove and darted, tilted and toppled though a darkness lit by shooting lights. Phred's screams renewed. The soft glow she now knew part of the change magic enveloped him once more.

A strange pair of metal tubes pointed at her from Sam's outstretched arm. "Behave, your worshipfulness, I'm a bit tired of you poking me with that pig sticker."

"I should fear this short length of metal?"

"Unless you want that beautiful face splattered across the far window."

"I demand you return my manservant to himself and deliver us from this sorcery."

Sam wiggled the shotgun. "This here thunder stick says I make the rules now. Now, I'm granting you three wishes."

Her eyes widened. The implication of his words bringing understanding at last. "Your wife's not in the underworld, she's a wind spirit. You're djinn."

A corner of his mouth turned upward. "Her gob never stops blowing, but no. Sure could go for a gin though, little ice and a squeeze of lime, delicious."

Phred's silence heralded an unbelievable sight beyond the glass. Water surrounded them. Lush green plants and vibrant creatures - some larger than houses - swam around them.

"Wish one granted," Sam said. "Take you to the water."

I... I can't believe it. So much...

A shudder ran through her. Flashes of near drowning swam in her memory. She'd been touring a lakeside farm with her mother. Niri's throat closed in on itself, the terrifying sensation of sinking through water returning from her nightmares. Her lungs filled with phantom water.

Master yourself. You are a Sun Cavalier, not a little girl.

A dozen horse-sized copies of Phred's fish sped by the clear walls.

"I don't understand," Niri said. "I demand an explanation."

"Say please."

Phred's arm swept into view, slapping his fish against Sam's ear. She glanced at Phred, rage stealing her breath as much as the endless water.

"Say please and tell Slappy back there to be nice or he can stay like that."

Her chest tightened. "You would do that to him?"

Sam rubbed his neck with his free hand. For an instant his eyes glazed, no longer watching her, but the moment ended before she could take advantage of it. "No, but I'm damned tired of getting hit by a clown fish. It's not funny. Neither is your attitude."

"My attitude?" *Why am I repeating this male like an ill-educated servant?* "You abducted us, ensorcelled my manservant, stole us from the normal world, threatened me and brought us to this cursed place!"

"Now look here, honey. You ambushed me. You cut me. You demanded I bring you," Sam gestured out the window. "If you don't like what you got, then be careful what you wish for."

A tirade rushed her lips. She closed her mouth against the escaping words. *Blast the Sun, he's right — obscene as being corrected, let alone lectured, by a mere male.* She'd lost the upper hand. Without sorcery, the most she could do is slay the bearer. That meant putting her nightmarish manservant down. Doing so might be a mercy, but a well-trained male was a resource worth protecting. A smile curled her lips. *Well trained...controlled...easy enough with the right encouragement.*

She lowered her sword and drew in a deep breath to accentuate her bosom. Widening her eyes, she shifted positions to minimize everything except her chest and batted her lashes. "Water bearer--"

"Sam."

She infused her voice with a breathiness. "Sam, please forgive me. Your mighty magic frightened me. Such strength filled me with a sandstorm of confusing emotions. I was overwhelmed and acted badly." She ran a hand along her thigh. "Perhaps, I should be punished."

"It's alright, baby, the weaker sex never could resist Ol' Sam Bridger."

"Oh, yes." Repulsion filled her. *Play the part to leash the mage.* "So *manly*."

"Just sit your pretty self right there." Sam lowered the weapon. "I'll take care of everything."

Niri smiled. You're mine, bearer, heart, soul and genitals.

She glanced back at Phred. Murder lurked in his two large green and four tiny black eyes. *You'll pay, bearer. I'll avenge myself and my manservant for your vile sorceries.*

Any thoughts of vengeance evaporated from her mind as a collection of massive underwater plants swung into view.

"Welcome to Perudathe settlement," Sam said.

Settlement? It's larger than most of our cities.

In all her days, she'd never considered such a thing of alien beauty. The once more altered wagon joined a school of metallic fish. Green-skinned people sat oddly calm within transparent bellies of their devourers. Their smiles gave no indication that digestion discomforted them. A girl child with magenta curls waved.

Niri raised her hand to wave back, but Sam struck the rein-wheel twice, summoning his vehicle's mating call once more. The girl bounced up and down inside the fish digesting her, clapping her hands with glee.

The bearer's wagon slowed to a stop beneath a great gaping maw. Long, fleshy lips reached beneath them, drawing them inside the beast.

Niri grabbed Sam's arm. "Beware, we're being eaten!"

Sam patted her hand. "Just trust old Sam, babe."

She flinched away from his touch, heat exploding in her chest to ignite her eyes.

His jaw tightened.

He noticed, but is he still mine?

Phred hit him in the ear with a fish.

Sam turned around, controls abandoned. "Had just about enough of you, squid boy."

Niri lurched over, seizing the wheel. She overestimated the distance and fell across his lap.

Sam chuckled and pushed her upright. "Bit over the top for an apology, don't you think, your highlightedness?"

Her cheeks heated. How dare he suggest? Control, I need this fool.

The wagon stopped. Instead of blood and entrails, the cavernous beast's insides contained an odd assortment of swallowed objects.

But no water.

"It's some kind of structure," she said.

Sam rolled his eyes and exited the vehicle. Checking Phred she pounced into Sam's empty seat. Despite her efforts, she found no way to flick the wheel like she might reins.

Sam watched her through the glass.

He's laughing at me. This male's laughing at a Princess of the second Taite Dynasty!

A pitiful whine escaped the backseat, bringing her attention to the horrid creature the bearer's dark magic had made of him. Her neck burned. An ache squeezed her chest. "Rest, Phred, you've my word I'll see this fool pays once you're restored."

Her manservant's breasts blinked, but he had no mouth to answer her.

Niri slipped out after the bearer, drawing both swords. The ground moved in unexpected ways. She lost her footing. Her attempt to catch herself drove one sword into the floor. The structure's fleshy lips recoiled, knocking her from her feet. She Niri hit the soft ground beside where the injured lip's retraction opened up a portal into the bottomless depths.

Sam helped her up.

Pent temper flared as too-familiar hands touched her as no male was allowed. Niri struck him with a pummel-anchored hand.

"I've had about enough of you, baby doll." Sam heaved her into the air. "Time you cooled your jets."

His strength surprised her.

Niri scrabbled for any purchase as he discarded her into the gaping hellscape's center. Bottomless water raced toward her with heart-stopping slowness. Icy water swallowed her whole.

Her throat seized up, phantom water burning lung still filled with fresh breath.

The pinkish building monster floated away from her.

Niri flailed, desperate to reverse her doom. The swords in her grip fought the water hampering her efforts to reach the retreating wedge of light. A giant's hand crushed her chest. Black spots invaded her vision.

I must surrender either life or my swords.

Crying tears no one would ever see, Niri released her precious ancestral swords. Her sacrifice bought little. She still sank, still drowned.

Metallic fish swam around her. Swallowed people looked on with concern or her rather than themselves.

Crossways

A sleek, muscular someone shot downward at her through a cloud of bubbles. The mostly naked, mostly green male shot past her. *Why come to my rescue but abandon me?*

Her chest ached for air, the pressure to breathe blinding.

Hands seized her wrists. She followed the corded arms to the bearer's muscular, lightly furred chest. He reversed orientation, pulling her body against his bare chest. One arm wrapped beneath her breasts. Her hand speared out over her shoulder, knifing into his throat.

He released her to clutch his neck. A litany of probable curses bubbled out his normally buffoonish expression. Fury darkened his face as he swam down past her.

Niri tried to keep him in sight, but the bearer moved like a fish. He thrust a hand between her thighs from behind and another over her shoulder in a lengthwise lock that compressed her breasts.

Her elbow caught him in the kidney.

He released her, yanked her around to face his purple glare, and speared three tightly grouped fingers into her gut.

The last of her air escaped in an explosive exhale. Her body sucked in breath as her mind flashed back on happier times.

This fool male is groping me while I die.

Water filled her lungs, building painful pressure up in her chest. The invading spots retreated from her vision. The burning ache for air faded.

The green man shot by them, pausing to grin and shake his head at the water bearer.

Sam regained his original grip around her midsection. His efforts lifted them toward the tiny sliver of light. Even so, it took all of Niri's will to resist lashing out.

When her chest tightened once more, she sipped breaths of water. The foreign sensation satisfied her lunch and eased her terror.

The green male helped the bearer lift her onto the odd floor. Nausea gripped her.

Beyond arm's reach, the bearer vomited water on hands and knees. She gasped, but no breath filled her lungs. The bearer seized and flipped her bodily, sliding arms beneath her breast once more. *Will this bearer's perversions never cease?*

He jerked his arms tighter around her chest, squeezing painfully. His grip slipped, sliding over her wet clothes and cold breasts. Before she reacted, he replaced them at her sternum and squeezed once more.

Water gushed from her lungs, spraying through her lips over and over. The moment her convulsions started, he released her. Niri gasped air, ejected water, and gasped air again. Recovery took minutes slowed to hours.

Sam panted, uncharacteristic menace in his glower.

Niri rose, holding herself in a regal stance and marched over to him. Her hand struck his face loud enough to echo. "That's for my family swords."

"Missy, you'd best keep your--"

She slapped him again. "That's for fondling me."

"Damn it, girl, if you don't stop--"

She slapped him a third time. "That's for throwing me into--"

Face red from more than her handprint, Sam's large flat hands slapped across her face. "I ain't in the habit of slapping girls, but enough is enough."

She stared. He struck me. A male...struck...me.

A horde of fire horses galloped up her neck. She snatched a knife from her boot and shoved it into Sam's stomach. "No one strikes Princess--"

Two strong arms wrapped around her head and neck from behind. Several men rushed to the bearer's side. Others snatched her hands from the impaled knife. They bound her hands. A flop sound brought her eyes to poor Phred, struggling to come to her rescue without any control over his strange form.

"Give me my knife so I can stab him again!"

The man holding her head passed her to others. He bent beside the bearer. "Be at peace, Sam Bridger, a medic comes."

"The bitch stabbed me, Laris!"

"We saw, Sam Bridger."

"Ambushed my rig, stole the water, cut my face and now the God damned bitch stabbed me."

"What shall we do with her?"

Sam coughed blood. "Stole your shipment. Abducted a wayman. Here to steal more. Bitch stabbed me."

"You're quite right, Sam Bridger. Imprison this woman for trial."

Niri gasped. "How dare you? No male may sit in judgment over a Sun Cavalier, high woman or member of a royal line."

Sam held his gut. "You ain't in Kansas anymore, Daisy."

8: The Big Bad Dwarf

Alabaster Roxx

Alabaster Roxx hadn't enjoyed the journey from Ryalox.

He'd waylaid a wayman named Bats. The man prattled endlessly about some ludicrous stick and ball Earth game. Alabaster ignored most of it, one ear cataloging the information while records scrolled across the heads up display of his cybernetic eye.

Despite his mission's urgency and the wayman's protests Alabaster performed a full vehicle inspection.

A task put off is a duty failed.

His audit found three outer blemishes, a broken down grav-lift, and an interior light replaced with the wrong model bulb. His scan measured the cargo weight at twenty kilo over manifest. Filing a three day's pay withholding via his right arm's holographic computer silenced Bats the rest of the trip.

The horrid waymen delivered him to a frozen white world. Red optics tinged the world pink. He wore clothing ill-suited to the winter conditions, but Alabaster ignored the temperature's effects. *A dwarf does not let the weather hamper his duty.*

At a set of entry stairs, three men sucked on burning weeds beside an exterior fire. He measured the distance between them and the nearby fuel storage tanks. Fifteen centimeters separated them from a UPO safety infraction.

I'll check their position later.

Crossways

His heavy metal foot clunked on the steps and into a warehouse floor, lifted and deposited by his replacement leg with only the smallest of limps. His targeting reticule scanned his surroundings, identifying items, judging distances, designating possible threats, and otherwise filling him with disgust.

If the initial warehouse indicated the norm, the Crossway Transportation Company's systematic gross negligence was as complicit in the villain's plot as the wayman Samual Oswald Bridger.

No wonder they were able to sneak a bomb onto the primary world of this dismal, misnamed universe.

The dwarf auditor marched through the building, cataloging violations and sending natives scurrying away toward no doubt dark corners. Two natives hurried into the warehouse and toward him. Alabaster's internal database designated them as Percival Wiggins, facility manager and Beatrice Bridger, primary dispatch operative.

They stopped meters from him, Percival opened his mouth, but Alabaster addressed the dispatcher first.

"Ms. Bridger, UPO operating instructions require the primary dispatch operative to maintain position at her station at all times, excepting a single three centi, excuse me, minute lavatory break during her third and sixth hours, and a fifteen minute meal break between the fourth hour and the end of its first quarter. You have thirty seconds to resume your duties or be reported for dereliction of duty."

"I asked her to come," Percival said. "She speaks Ryalox."

Alabaster scanned the man, noting wardrobe shortcomings but nothing outside regulations. He gestured at the warehouse "You seem unaware of your operating guidelines. Facility managers are required to understand all UPO recognized languages."

"All sixty?" Percival asked.

"Indeed. I've also catalogued forty-four violations since arrival, including equipment broken or outside operational specifications."

Percival bristled. "We're doing the best we can with the funds provided."

"Very well, I'll report your inability to provide satisfactory results within budget and request a replacement."

"I don't need to be replaced. The regulations need to be updated to match the budget cuts."

Alabaster shifted his attention. "Your thirty seconds have expired, Ms. Bridger. Where is your mate? Committing more acts of terror?"

Beatrice shoved a finger bearing a colored nail longer than regulation length into Alabaster's hardened chest plate. "Now listen here, you stunted little jerk."

"Auditor Roxx," Alabaster corrected.

"Fine, stunted little auditor jerk. Sam Bridger isn't my mate, and he's not some kind of terrorist either."

"Where is he?"

"He's not back yet," Percival said.

Alabaster glared. "I ordered him recalled."

"We recalled him," Percival said. "But he was on an extended run. He's returning as we speak."

"Insufficient. Did you at least comply with my orders not to inform him as to why he was recalled?"

"Yes," Beatrice said.

Alabaster scowled. "I wasn't speaking to you. You were dismissed back to your station."

Beatrice folded her arms and offered a smug smile. "I'm not on shift."

"Existence on company property outside a fifteen minute buffer on either side of your assigned shift is a violation of UPO--"

"Shove it up your bearded ass, you half-metal tyrant!"

"Bea," Percival warned.

Alabaster cocked his remaining eyebrow. "Familiarity between management and employees is--"

"We're no more familiar than you are human," Beatrice said.

"Thank the Great Crafter for that." Alabaster gestured his living hand through the proper motions required to display deific gratitude. "Until Mister Bridger arrives, assuming he doesn't run, I shall perform an inspection of this facility. Attend me, Mister Wiggins. Leave the premises, Ms. Bridger."

Sweat beaded Percival's forehead, weighing down his comb over until it drooped enough to display bald skin. "Auditor Roxx, you're empowered to audit our facility, file reports, perform investigations in this crisis and even recommend things to the UPO oversight board. You're not permitted to give orders to myself or my employees."

Alabaster smiled. "Very good, Mister Wiggins. Excellent, in fact. Please conduct me through your facility. Any exceptions or extenuating circumstances you claim will be filed alongside the violations reported."

"He speaks English, Bea," Percival said. "You can go home if you want."

"I'm not letting this little weasel out of my sight until Sam's vindicated."

"I find it odd, Ms. Bridger, that a woman reportedly harboring so much disdain for her former mate would so vehemently defend him. Are you a co-conspirator, perhaps?"

She scowled. "Absolutely not, and let me tell you one more thing: Sam has a lot of faults, a lot. Hell, he can be the world's most inconsiderate boob on occasion, but treason, disloyalty and terrorism aren't in him."

"We shall see, and that was more than one." Alabaster turned to Percival. "Lead on, sir."

Sam Bridger

Bob looked up as Sam helped Phred toward Buford. "Sam? What're you doing here?"

"Got to help slappy here back to his original shape."

"Slappy?" Bob asked.

"Long story." Sam heaved the electrical junction cabinets open, swinging them out of the way of the giant microwave that was Buford. He helped Phred inside, closed the door and donned a blast helmet and lead apron.

"You, um, need any help?"

"Thanks, babe, but I've got this. Don't let me derail what you've got going."

She returned to the engine she'd been rebuilding.

Sam checked his watch only to curse. He'd run by his locker for another one. The company that made them only allowed so many warranty replacements. So he'd bought extras.

"Hey, Sugartits!" Gabriel Manx marched into the garage.

Bob's shoulders tensed. She smiled at the other wayman. "Something I can help you with?"

"My rig's still not running right."

"I fixed your truck myself, corrected the fuel—"

"I know you did the work, toots. You know how I know? It took twice as long and now the horses under the hood are limp as a geriatric in a whore house."

Heat prickled Sam's skin. He checked Buford's progress. Until the device finished, he dare not walk away lest Phred end up cooked.

"Someone recalibrated your engine," Bob said. "I—"

"Screwed it sideways. Look, baby doll. I know they put you in charge down here." Gabriel eyeballed her. "Probably had *good* reason, but how about you do something useful like assign one of the boys to fix it while you get your hair done or something?"

Bob opened her mouth.

"Great, glad you're onboard." Gabriel marched toward the exit, nodding as he passed. "Bridger."

Sam checked Buford once more and then Bob. She stood ramrod straight, head down with her hair curtained around her face. Her shoulders shook and she held the wrench in her hand in a death grip. She made no noise and Sam couldn't see her face, but he'd have sworn she was muttering.

"Bob? Are you all right?"

She didn't look at him. "Fine, Sam."

Not sure I believe her.

He glanced at the timer and decided to chance stepping away. Restoring not to mention not cooking Phred was important, but not as important as his friend.

Sam approached her, easing a hand onto her shoulder. "Bob?"

She jumped.

Bob looked up, her face pale and splotchy—no mean feat considering her skin tone.

"Are you all right?"

"I'll be fine, Sam. Nothing I can't handle." Bob gestured. "Don't let him cook in there."

Something in his gut told Sam that Gabriel had upset her. He just wasn't sure why.

Questioning her skill?

"You know you're the best mechanic in all Eleven, right?"

"Thank you, Sam."

"You sure you're all right?"

She smiled up at him. "I'll be fine. I promise."

He nodded and returned to Buford. He turned back to ask her if he could do anything, but she'd gone.

Maybe I should send her some wrenches, something to cheer her up.

Beatrice

Beatrice sat in the corner of Percival's office. Her boss cradled his head in both hands while the dwarf auditor barraged him with violations.

She hadn't been lying when she said there was nothing between herself and Percival, nor when she told Alabaster she wasn't Sam's mate. Nonetheless, she very much wanted to take one of Bob's larger wrenches to his head, preferably not the section covered by a metal skull plate. Each new violation exited his mouth with enough pompous breath to send ripples in the thick, auburn mustache braids that hung to his collar.

The office door opened, drawing all eyes to the dark-haired woman. Grease marred Bob's face. Her tan forehead wrinkled. "I-I'm sorry, sir. I didn't realize you were in a meeting."

"Did you need something?" Percival asked.

Bob glanced at Beatrice, one brown lock of her almost black hair in the corner of her mouth. "N-no, it'll wait."

Beatrice eyed her rival, trying to keep heat from rising in her chest. Bob's not my rival. I divorced Sam. If she wants to crush on him, it's her heartache.

Confusion tempered Beatrice's envy. Bob's constant self-assurance had fueled Bea's jealousy of the woman before Bob set her sights on Sam. It wasn't that Beatrice was a wilting flower, but as a mechanic, Bob dealt with the company's most chauvinistic bullies.

Woman's got an iron constitution. Bea noticed the chewed hair and the stuttering. Except where Sam's concerned.

Beatrice eyed the Cherokee woman, connecting the dots.

Alabaster wanted Sam.

He'd ordered them to withhold all information from her former husband, especially the auditor's purpose at HQ.

We're all worried about Sam, but this...oh, no. Sam's back.

Alabaster rose. "Miss Zephyr, your biometric readings indicate prevarication."

Bob narrowed her eyes.

"Such an expression, translatable as displayed hostility or inferred threat, warrants entering a formal reprimand in your record."

Bob spat out a litany of Native Indian words. Beatrice couldn't translate the words, but the tone seemed pretty clear. Alabaster looked on with a blank expression indicating he couldn't translate it either.

"We're busy, Bob," Percival said. "See me later."

Bob glowered daggers at Alabaster but departed without further curses.

Alabaster smiled. "I shall be interested to see if her curse takes effect."

"What curse?" Beatrice asked.

"Miss Zephyr words invoked a curse in the People's tongue."

"You understood her?" Percival asked.

"Once I assimilated her language from my stored archives, but the real question is whether such primitive superstitions hold any actual power on Eleventh World."

"Why would that matter?" Percival asked.

"A great deal of magic went into creating your universe. It only follows that same may remain and be accessible to certain persons. As her file links Miss Zephyr's heritage to a medicine man and a spirit walker mother, she may well be able to inflict a rather uncomfortable future on my person."

Good.

"In the meantime, Miss Zephyr's visit, vitriol, and biometrics indicate Mister Bridger has returned."

Alabaster

The yellowing linoleum halls Alabaster marched down desperately needed a paint job. Mister Wiggins and Ms. Bridger trailed him. He wasn't sure whether they represented a threat. Still, between the discomfort the terrorist wayman caused and their potential violence, Alabaster was tempted to trigger his conversion circuit to transform his arm into an energy blaster.

I could take them bare handed. As for the traitor, his execution waits until I've coerced the bomb's location from him. Until the threat is resolved, he lives.

Alabaster shoved open the rearward maintenance bay manned by the Cherokee mechanic unaccountably called Bob despite her real name.

Bob interposed himself. "What're you doing?"

"Apprehending Mister Bridger."

"You can't go in there yet."

The lights flickered. "What nefarious activity are you covering up, Miss Zephyr?"

Percival flinched as the lights dimmed once more. He rubbed his face with one hand, letting out a soft groan.

Bob looked at Beatrice.

Interesting, nonverbal pleading for assistance. The two women could both be Bridger's lovers, each a termination level violation of the coworker fraternization statutes.

Ms. Bridger interposed herself. "Bob's right. It would be unsafe for anyone to enter right now."

Theory substantiated.

Alabaster split the two with a sweep of his arms and marched to a heavy metal door.

"It's your skin," Bob said.

"Literally," Beatrice added.

Alabaster muscled the door to one side, noting its lubrication had not been maintained within operational specs. Sensors alerted Alabaster to higher than normal radiation levels. Samuel Oswald Bridger wore a blast helmet and lead apron over jeans, a flannel shirt, and ball cap. Cabinets Alabaster mistook as wiring junctions hung open, displaying a heavy radiation door reminiscent of the clunky microwave oven in the company break room, a jury-rigged control console, and a horrifying series of safety violations.

The lights dimmed further and finally flickered out. Sparks from the console illuminated Sam Bridger's grin. A single bell-like ding sounded.

Sam passed Alabaster with a nod of his chin, rounding the console to drag open the heavy door.

A short man in torn, bloodstained white robes knelt in the chamber. His long, sweat-soaked, brown hair hung over his face as he checked the number of digits in one hand.

"There you go, Pokey, good as new," Sam said.

"Who is this man?" Alabaster asked.

"Who're you, Cyclops?"

Beatrice sucked in a breath.

"My name is Alabaster Roxx, formerly Major of the One Hundred and Eighth Ryaloxian Dragoons, three time awardee of the Bronze Axe of Valor for actions including the Gogri Butterfly Incursion of Fifteen Two-Eighty."

"Well," Sam's head wagged side to side. "Lah. Di. Dah."

"I'm also the UPO auditor sent to execute a performance review of one Samuel Oswald Bridger."

Sam snorted, the noise turning into full blown laughter. "Kind of a long fall, huh? That explains the short legs."

Alabaster felt his single ear burn. His hands clenched into fists and his targeting reticule marked critical injury points on Sam's body.

"Well, General Paper Pusher, this here is Phred. Phred and his mistress ambushed me in Dorsun, stole my load, abducted me at weapon point, and dragged me back to Quiss. Phred enjoyed the mean end of a change field. He's getting sorted out, so I can return him to his mistress on Quiss."

"What is a Dorsun woman doing on Quiss?" Alabaster roared.

"Pointy things at my throat, I thought I mentioned this in the last thirty seconds. Matter of fact, I'm sure I did since I was standing right here when I did it. Where were you? Playing cartoons in that computer eye?"

Alabaster smiled. It was a smile he'd practiced over the years, employing it against uppity sergeants, smart-mouthed soldiers and the occasional self-righteous junior officer. Anyone who'd known him long, knew it impended the removal of skin from a living subject.

Sam Bridger's smile broadened. He clapped Alabaster's shoulder. "Caught you, huh? No harm done, it's not like we're going to lose her. I had them lock the princess up."

Alabaster rationed the tirade of words perched on his lip and readied to storm a battleground. He released them one at a time slow enough for the humans - living examples of unintended consequences caused by poor planning - to understand. "Do you have any idea how many UPO regulations you've broken by transporting nonindigenous, crossway-ignorant sentients to another universe? How many safety protocols you violated by introducing a Dorsunian into the Quiss environment without proper quarantine? Or even the number of laws involved in abducting and imprisoning royal personages?"

Despite the measured increase of heat in his tone, biometric readings of Sam Bridger didn't vary so much as a fraction until he opened his mouth to speak.

"Hey, *she* abducted *me*." He rubbed his stomach. "Bitch stabbed me, Mister Alabastard."

"Auditor Roxx," Alabaster spat between clenched teeth. "How many?"

Sam shrugged. "Two?"

"Twenty-nine."

Sam's brows shot up. "Really, twenty-nine at once? Is that some sort of record?"

Beatrice's tone begged caution. "Sam."

"If not, it should be."

"Sam," she repeated.

Alabaster shoved Sam backward with a single thick finger. The memories of past combat missions filled him, adrenaline pumped out from his attachments in response to his sudden need to act. His command voice rose from the depths and dusted itself off. "You will accompany me back to Quiss to liberate her from incarceration. Dress out for an infiltration and meet me back here in fifteen minutes, do you understand me?"

"Not really," Sam said.

"Get your gear, soldier. We've got a princess to rescue."

"Bitch stabbed me."

"Suit up, man!"

"Couldn't we just ask for her back?" Sam asked. "I mean surely there are protocols--"

"Move!"

Sam rushed from the room, glancing over his shoulder several times.

Alabaster approached Phred. "You will surrender your weapons."

Phred wound his headwrap over his face. "I answer only to my mistress."

Heat boiled in Alabaster's gut. "I'm in charge here."

"I answer--"

Bob slid between them, irritatingly forestalling Alabaster with an upraised hand. "Phred, right?"

Phred nodded, not taking his glare from the dwarf.

"Phred," Bob placed a hand on his arm. "Please place your weapons on the table there. Once Auditor Roxx has cataloged them, you can all go to your mistress's rescue."

Alabaster's display showed a spike in Phred's vital readings, tracing them to increased airborne pheromones.

Phred looked from her to Alabaster and back. A soft pink crept into his tanned skin. "Yes?"

Bob grease-smudged mechanic's smile increased Phred's heartrate another notch. "I'd really appreciate it, Phred."

Phred turned to the indicated table and unloaded seven knives, two spools of fine wire attached to wooden toggles, a dozen small bolts, a collapsed hand crossbow, and four vials of liquid. He glanced at Bob's watchful expression, adding a blowgun ringed by six tiny darts from his lower back.

Bob leaned in, drew aside cloth covering his face and kissed the man's boyish cheek. "Thank you."

Alabaster tried not to roll his eye. He removed his auditor clothes, revealing camouflage fatigues beneath. Dipping into one pocket, Alabaster produced camouflage paints and drew lines across his face. Checking his HUD chronometer, he indicated Phred. "Come with me, that idiot ought to be ready by now."

"It's only been five minutes," Beatrice objected.

"War waits for no man's leisure."

"You don't know Sam," Beatrice said. "He'll be late for his own funeral."

"If he's late, it'll *be* his funeral," Alabaster said.

Alabaster's march to the complex locker room trailed an audience. "Bridger?"

An odd accent filled the reply. "Just a moment, old chap."

"Hurry it up."

Sam emerged attired in a formal tuxedo and flashed a smile.

Chemical pheromone levels shot up in the humid locker room air. Phred's gaze reached the women before the dwarf's. Both women held themselves at odd angles, pupils widened, and lips moistened.

Sam strode to Bob, a finger stroke lifted her face toward his. Bob's lips parted and her lids narrowed.

Sam's British imitation continued. "Bob, a jewel among pebbles, have you brought me anything from Q-Branch?"

Seemingly unable to speak, Bob shook her head.

"What the hedrin is that getup?" Alabaster asked.

Sam turned aside, kissing Beatrice's cheek. "Hold down the fort, old girl. We'll be back in time for tea."

Alabaster's voice rose despite his iron control. "What are you blathering on about, man? And what in the Great Crafter's name gave you the idea that's infiltration gear?"

Sam straightened his bow tie. "Name's Sam, Sam Bridger."

9: Track That Package

Taleh

Taleh regarded her grinning assistant. "Still nothing?"

"No," Mite said. "Perhaps your wayman found the bomb?"

She sighed. "My agent hasn't reported. I guess they were both discovered."

"This wayman is a crafty one. Perhaps choose another?"

"To what effect? If they found the bomb..."

"Tell them that package was a ruse, a false trail. There is time enough to bring another bomb in."

"Not with them watching."

A giggle escaped Mite's lips. "I've located a former wayman who might serve, or we create another locally. A poorly guarded locale in their Soviet Union contains sufficient nuclear materials to rival the damage of a world-ender."

Taleh scrutinized Mite. One assistant at a time, his people had offered zealous service to her cause. Never seeing two at once, she didn't know whether they were skittish like they told her, or bloodthirsty. All she knew is that each suffered from nervous giggles. "I have another bomb already here. I'm just concerned about our credibility."

Mite bowed. "As you say, mistress, but what shall we do about the original?"

"Ascertain if either agent or bomb were discovered. If not, we find our wayward explosive."

"I shall redouble our search efforts."

"No, Mite. Relocate us someplace we can contact the UPO."

Taleh entered the readied pavilion. Two sets of video equipment were divided into small alcoves. Mite sat in one of the alcoves, speaking with a blue-haired woman on the screen. "I'm sorry, sir, but the wayman's logs indicate your package was delivered on time."

Taleh left him to his discussion and stepped into the other alcove. She took a deep breath and studied the controls around her, trying to remember all the extra steps Mite's predecessor had taught her.

Once engaged. the drone screen floated before her. She found the location scrambler and encryption controls. Taleh engaged both, double checking they were online before taking one last deep breath and initializing connection with the UPO Council Chamber

Taleh studied the room, several adjuncts nudging their distracted ambassadors. Vuria's ambassador watched Taleh with large, piercing eyes.

Onklus, Felisian, and the Dorsun Ambassador Corlan shifted their attention to Taleh in silence. The crystal owl on Ambassador Leahna's shoulder screeched. All eyes turned to her and then up toward Taleh. Tuweine and Ryaloxian ambassadors rushed into the room.

Seven, where are the other three?

"What do you want?" Corlan snapped.

"My first shipment."

Ryaloxian Ambassador Gramoard brushed his blue handlebar mustache. "We've sent an auditor to facilitate your demands."

"Then where are they?" Taleh asked.

Mite replied to the blue-haired woman at the edges of Taleh's hearing. "I appreciate your position, Marge, but the package has not arrived."

"There was some difficulty tracking down your chosen wayman," Felisian said.

"He's on his way to the first pickup now," Onklus said.

"If you can tell me what you purchased and from where," Marge said. "We'll be happy to order a replacement."

Taleh suppressed a cringe. She held up her hand. "A moment please, honored representatives."

She bolted out of view of the UPO transmission, shouldering Mite out of the way. "Marge, right? Marge, my shipment contained family heirlooms. It's vitally important you locate it."

"Could you describe it for me, miss?" Marge asked.

"One moment," Taleh rushed back to the other alcove. "I need to know you are taking my threat seriously. If I don't get my first shipment in the next two days, you will see how serious I am."

"You'll destroy Earth?" the Vurian, Hullis, asked.

"I've come into possession of some nuclear material here on Eleventh World." Taleh used childhood memories to fake a genuine-looking smile. "Allowing me to temper my first response to your refusal to cooperate."

"How benevolent," Onklus said.

Corlan snorted.

"I realize they're important to you," Marge said, "But you don't have to resort to vulgarity. Misplacing heirlooms for a few days isn't exactly the end of the world."

"Two days," Taleh shut off the communicator and raced to the other alcove. "Marge. Sorry, my brother can be very surly on occasion, but we really need those heirlooms."

"I've done all I can," Marge said. "I'll contact our driver and see if we can't learn anything more."

A chill ran up Taleh's spine. She considered telling the woman not to bother to avoid the wrong kind of attention but backing out now would be just as suspicious. "Wonderful."

"Can I have a comm number to contact you when we find it?"

Mite giggled. "Don't call us, we'll call you."

Marge's expression turned scandalized. "I never!"

Mite killed the communication. "Dangerous, Mistress."

Taleh nodded. "Get me a nuclear bomb, Mite."

His leer turned into a hungry smirk, though a shadow palled his features. "My pleasure."

"Everything except the fission material." Taleh scrutinized him, careful to note everything about his reaction.

Mite's brows shot up, showing more wrinkles than graced his forehead the week before. "Mistress?"

Taleh noted spots on his neck and new wrinkles other than his forehead. Mite's death neared.

What will I do without him?

The thought left her feeling selfish. "A casing will serve for now. They know we're interested in nuclear material. Buying it now would show them we were bluffing."

"I assure you, Mistress, I'll acquire it without anyone becoming wise."

"How? Mind control?"

Mite giggled.

"Just get a casing, and double check the first delivery site is secure."

"Even though we haven't given it to them yet?"

"Yes." Taleh rubbed her throbbing head. "Have you found any more issues with the crossway generator?"

"Not yet, mistress, but without our ransom payment, I can perform no further test. Shall I fetch you some tea?"

She nodded into her hands. "Please."

10: Works with Superman

Sam Bridger

Sam let Phred into the cab's rear, then assumed his seat. Across from him, Alabaster climbed into the passenger side.

Sam continued his Connery imitation. "Going to need a bit of extra seating, darling. Be a good girl and accommodate our guests."

The passport filled the cab with irritated chirps and beeps, but a second row of pilot seats grew from the floor.

Alabaster quirked his eyebrow, then leveled a glare at the passport. He cleared his throat, grunted, then vocalized a similar series of noises.

Sam stared at him, open-mouthed.

The passport answered.

Alabaster shot Sam a withering look, turned back to the device and replied. They went back and forth for several moments.

"How did you do that?" Phred asked.

"What?" Sam asked with his normal voice.

"You ensorcelled those women. Is this more of your magic?"

Sam brushed his sleeves. "The right outfit makes the man."

Alabaster snorted. "Mister Bridger, I'm required to inform you that I have chastised your passport for change field operations outside normal safety constraints. It seems however that this oversight is due to poor calibration, owing to its operator not providing proper guidance."

Sam folded his arms. "I don't speak beep. If you've got a problem with her, lecture her."

"Your passport is a he," Alabaster said.

Sam blinked at him. "Excuse me?"

"Your passport's personality matrix is male, something you would know if you'd engaged the neural tap as instructed on page four of the wayman passport operation manual."

Sam stared at him.

"Further, while the serial number of this passport corresponds with inventory and maintenance records, the device uptime does not—indicating tampering."

"Don't look at me," Sam said. "I haven't even thumped her-him-it to improve the reception."

The dwarf gave Sam an assessing look.

Sam faced forward and started the truck. "Give me the signals, bab-uddy."

The passport responded with a set of long-suffering notes and turned on a blinker.

Alabaster muttered something in beep.

The passport replied.

Alabaster harrumphed. "Idiot."

"Could you teach me?" Phred asked.

"Beep?" Sam pulled onto the highway.

"No, this mastery of women," Phred said.

Sam shrugged. "Sure, we'll pick up a couple Bond flicks on our way back to Dorsun."

"You'll do nothing of the sort, Bridger. Your pollution of this man ends now."

"Geez, lighten up, we're only talking about a movie." Sam noticed a pair of boys in the back window of the car ahead of them. They pulled down on open air, wide grins on their faces. Sam honked his truck horn. Both boys offered him double thumbs up, turning back forward in their seats.

Sam flashed a smile at his passengers.

Alabaster glowered. "That constitutes unnecessary wear and tear on company property."

"Is honking the horn against the rules?" Sam asked.

The dwarf folded his arms. "No."

The trip to Quiss followed a simple pattern. They drove for a while. Phred asked a question. Sam started to answer. Alabaster snapped a rejoinder. Interspaced into the byplay, Alabaster lectured Sam about every UPO regulation or protocol violated and offered long corrective dissertations on local state highway laws.

Sam had never been so happy to enter a crossway in his life. "Feet up into the stirrups."

Maybe this'll shut Alabaster up for a few minutes.

The truck slipped into darkness, twisting and turning an erratic course between shooting stars. Phred flinched when the changes started but settled down when it didn't harm him.

Sam's passport transformed his rig into a submersible but didn't repaint it as was its custom.

Phred leaned over Sam's shoulder, gazing out at the water and wildlife swirling around them.

Alabaster vocalized beeps and the windows all tinted solid black. The steering wheel retracted into the dashboard. He nodded to himself, a smug smile on his lips.

"What gives? I can't see to drive. Can't drive either."

"Protocol," Alabaster said. "Ren-2-3 will take us in."

"Bet you shut down peep shows too."

Would dumping the little pain into the drink short him out? Sam's head came up. "Ren-2-3?"

"Passport's designation."

"You mean his name?"

Alabaster shrugged.

"Alabastard."

The submersible halted, and Ren-2-3 chittered.

Sam reached for the door.

Alabaster snatched Sam's hand away. "Are you mad?"

"We're here, right?"

"We're docked to a maintenance port outside the building."

"And why aren't we docking like normal?" Sam asked. "Laris will bring her right out."

"This liberation must be conducted in secret to limit the political ramifications," Alabaster said.

"Did they carve out some of your melon when they gave you the shiny metal hat?" Sam asked. "I might not be the smartest--"

"Below average exceeds your reach," Alabaster grumbled.

"Tell me, how is sneaking in and stealing a prisoner the less politically damaging move here? And why aren't there protocols against it?"

Alabaster glowered. "Going through channels could take months, the Quissians might want reparations that would bankrupt the princess's tribe. They might refuse to surrender her, sparking an inter-universe war..."

"How the hell could they bankrupt her tribe? A hundred truckloads of dirt and sand would make the Quiss think they'd struck black gold and moved to Hollywood. It wouldn't cost her high-and-mighty-bitchiness almost anything."

Alabaster shot a look at Phred and glared at Sam. "We do this my way."

Sam shrugged.

Alabaster climbed back into the sleeper cabin, getting boot prints on Sam's bed. He crossed to the newly formed airlock and checked the other two for a ready sign.

Sam retrieved a small black handgun from the glove compartment, holding it beside his face.

"Not the thunder stick?" Phred asked.

Sam summoned his best Connery. "Walther PPK, favored gun for a British agent."

"You were born in Altoona!" Alabaster shoved open the airlock, one arm transforming into an energy weapon.

Bet it's got no stun setting. Alabastard's too used to lecturing people to sleep.

"Move out!"

Phred trailed behind Sam and Alabaster.

Alabaster hacked a security terminal, locating Princess Niri. He led along a circuitous route. The dwarf slipped from shadow to shadow, kneeling low to peer around corners.

"This reminds me of our infiltration of the Gogri warren," Alabaster whispered. "Their cursed butterfly men retreated to their fortress with our Holy Ale Keg, and we were forced to-
-"

"Butterflies? You fought a war with butterflies?"

"You've got no idea what you're jawing about. They'd have killed you without breaking a sweat. They were naturally armored, and they spit--"

Sam leaned forward; his interest kindled. "Acid? Fire?"

"Dizzydust, I believe you call it LDS."

Sam cradled his face. "You mean LSD."

"Intimately familiar I see."

"Well, I can spell it."

Alabaster harrumphed.

"So, you eventually beat the free-love, trip spitting, flower-power butterflies?"

Before Alabaster answered, a Quissian couple walked around the corner at their rear.

The dwarf dove, rolling to one side. He came up to one knee, leaning left and right. "Shoot them, Bridger. I can't get a shot around Phred."

"But--"

The couple cowered in each other's arms.

"Shoot them, man!"

Sam aimed at the Quissians and pulled his trigger. A thin stream of red-dyed water squirted into their chests.

They stared down, screamed and raced back up the corridor.

Good. Sam grinned. Ridiculous dwarf.

Alabaster charged around the corner but returned empty-handed. He snatched Sam's gun, scanning it with a visible red light. "Water? You brought a water pistol?"

Sam smiled. "Superman is weak against kryptonite."

Alabaster tilted his head to one side, eye wide.

"Kryptonite is from krypton, he's vulnerable to the essence of his birth world."

Alabaster licked his lips. "And the food dye?"

"Seemed unfriendly to kill them with regular old water, the authorities might not know the cause of death. People need closure, after all."

Alabaster dropped Sam's gun, stomping it to powder with his mechanized foot. "They live *in* the water, you idiot. If it were deadly to them, they'd already be dead!"

Sam rubbed the back of his neck. "That'd make freeing the princess easier. Dead men recite no poetry, after all - don't shoot back either."

Alabaster snarled and rushed around the corner. "We've been seen. We have to move."

Sam smirked.

Phred turned to him. "You're not this simple."

Sam cocked his head to one side. "What makes you think so?"

"Your guile turned the tables upon Mistress and me."

Sam winked and followed Alabaster down the hall.

Their clandestine rush through the Quissian halls met no further resistance. Alabaster removed a small disk from his artificial leg and set it along the seam of a locked door. A storm of electricity enveloped the door. He made several hand gestures Sam didn't understand, wrenched open the door and stormed inside.

A short hallway stretched a half dozen meters. A door capped both ends. "I've got the left! Bridger, Phred, take the right! And breach!"

The auditor kicked in the left door, charging into the room like he was in a Schwartzenagger movie.

Leaving Alabaster to storm Laris's storage shed, Sam sauntered over to the other door. He opened the patio access and strolled into a pool party.

Laris's wife Rheeta and her green-haired, single sister Vella relaxed in lounge chairs on the far side of a swimming pool. Laris stood behind a small grill in a 'Kissing fish do it better' apron, a pair of tongs held motionless in shock.

Alabaster's voice came from behind Sam. "Bridger, are you all right?"

"Sure thi—zoinks!"

Princess Niri emerged from beneath the pool's surface, shaking her hair clear of water and smiling. Water glistened along voluptuous tan curves. Phred and Sam stared, mouths agape.

If this were Tuweine, Phred would have to chase down my eyeballs while someone got a forklift for my jaw.

Niri smiled at her manservant. "Good to see you restored. You have my thanks, wayman."

"Can I offer you some grilled crappie, Sam Bridger?" Laris asked.

"Sure." Sam sidled across the patio and seated himself in an empty chair. "Been a crappie kind of day."

Alabaster charged the room, weapon pivoting back and forth to cover all of its occupants. "Princess Niri, I'm here to rescue you."

Sam smirked. "Aren't you a little short for this ride?"

"Bit late, too. I've already rescued myself," Niri said.

"Come with me, we must return you to your people," Alabaster said.

Niri shook her head. "I'm not through with my negotiations."

"There's no time for this!" Alabaster stomped forward and seized her arm. Niri kicked him in the chest, driving him back. Before he closed the distance, she slid a pair of swords from beneath her lounge chair.

"You have to come with me now!"

"I have to do no such thing."

"I'm not taking no for an answer."

"It's the only answer you're getting."

Sam's head bobbed back and forth between them. "Have a seat, Al. Laris'll get you a crappie, beer, maybe some chips."

Alabaster retracted the energy weapon arm and replaced it with a long-handled hammer. He drew a small cylinder from his belt, flicking a wrist to convert it into a short, wide-bladed sword. "You're coming with me whether you like it or not."

The two clashed - sword to sword and sword to hammer. They fought around the pool, overturning furniture and inadvertently slaying a yellow ducky floatation belt.

"Hey, that was a gift," Sam said.

Both fought like experts, maneuvers ranging in speed and skill from impressive to unbelievable. After several seconds of battling across a narrow pool, Alabaster used some kind of technology Sam didn't understand that wrenched away Niri's swords. They dropped into the water out of her reach.

If he'd expected the desert princess to shirk away from water rather than reclaim her swords, the graceful dive which sent Sam's pulse stampeding ended any misapprehension.

Alabaster smiled, stepped closer to the pool, and shot it full of electricity.

Sam sprang to his feet, knocked Alabaster out of the way and dove in after her. He grabbed her stunned, sumptuous frame and kicked off of the bottom as hard as he could. His rise brought him to the pool's lip with enough force to help him deposit her body on the edge.

Laris and Rheeta descended upon her, helping her dislodge the aerated water from her lungs.

Sam pulled himself out of the water, tuxedo dripping on the beige patio tiles. He whirled to charge Alabaster, jaw and fists clenched.

Alabaster's eyes widened.

Sam glanced down. He's afraid of my fists?

The great dwarf warrior fell forward, his artificial body parts hitting the deck with a heavy clank.

Phred lowered a blow gun from his lips. "He had no right to touch my Mistress."

Sam held his hands up. "I was just trying to help, brother."

Phred inclined his head. "And thus have nothing to fear from me...brother."

Sam smiled. "Didn't he take your weapons away?"

Phred shrugged. "He turned his back."

"Remind me not to make that mistake," Sam turned toward Laris. "Crappie?"

Laris rose, leaving Niri to Rheeta's attentions.

"Absolutely." Sam glanced over at Niri. "Crappie, princess?"

She shook her head.

"Kelp salad?" Vella asked.

Sam found a peculiar smile on her face and offered one of his own. "Sure, baby doll. I love greens."

11: Grudging Respect

Sam Bridger

Phred stayed with Niri, while Sam and Laris loaded Alabaster up in the truck's sleeper. They loaded up a double order to replace the stolen water, and Sam headed for Dorsun with the unconscious dwarf.

Sam didn't bother rushing. He exited the entry geode and made it halfway across the second geonation before he pulled off of the road for the night.

Sam set a small camp with a modest fire amidst cacti and palm trees, rough scrub, and a dark, starless night. With the geonation's star doused to a tiny pinprick, desert chill crept into his bones. Far off, the hunting screech of a night flier echoed oddly off of the dunes. A baleful cry answered, whether in supplication or opposition Sam wasn't sure. Locusts darted into his campsite in ones and twos, diving into the flames with a sudden, sharp pop.

He poked the fire with a thin stick. *Wish I had some marshmallows or could sleep in my rig's sleeper.*

"Where the hedrin are we?" Alabaster glared across the small fire.

"Dorsun."

Alabaster's good eye narrowed. "Who told you?"

Sam shrugged. "Arthur transferred the delivery to me before Beatrice called me back to base. Since we were in Quiss, I got the water to finish the delivery."

"Then the princess made good for her theft before you dropped her at home?"

"Nah."

"Then how are you paying for this, Bridger?"

"Used my own credits."

The dwarf scrutinized Sam. He took a seat across the fire. "You'll expense it?"

"Probably not."

"Good...man." The words sounded as if they cost the dwarf something. "Yes, you got caught with your britches down, but it's an honorable soldier who takes responsibility for his mistakes."

Sam opened his mouth to correct the dwarf but stayed silent. Actually, that sounded almost friendly. Best not mention the profit I've made while he slept.

"How did her highness take being forced home?"

Sam rubbed his neck. "I didn't force her."

"She came willingly?"

"She stayed in Quiss."

Alabaster leapt to his feet. "What?"

Sam misquoted one of Alabaster's protocols, then added, "So I couldn't interfere with a royal in negotiations with--"

"That's not what that protocol means."

Sam threw up his hands. "I look like some gold-plated legal robot to you?"

"We have to go back for her."

Sam's brows rose. "I have a delivery to make."

"Bridger, it's important."

Sam stood. "Sam Bridger took on this delivery and Sam Bridger never fails to deliver what he promises."

"We're going back."

"Have a nice walk."

"You know full well I can't use a crossway without a passport."

Sam shrugged. "Figured you had one tucked in all your gizmos somewhere."

Alabaster resumed his seat. "Just as well, I suppose. We have a pickup to make."

Sam sat with a grin. "See, it all worked out. Everything does if you give it enough time."

"No." Ambassador Corlan said.

Sam glanced from Corlan to Alabaster.

Alabaster glanced at Sam. "This waymen is not cleared for the details of my assignment. Perhaps we could have this discussion elsewhere?"

Sam's brows rose.

"No," Corlan repeated.

Alabaster purpled. "We are to pick up a pregrowth geonode for delivery."

"You cannot have a PGN."

"Are you aware, Ambassador, of the repercussions of not making this item available to us?"

"The end of his world."

Alabaster glanced at Sam.

Sam's brows furrowed. What the hell is going on? I thought PGNs were only picked up by armed convoy – on the very rare occasions they're used outside Dorsun at all.

"I won the right to represent my mistress, dwarf," Corlan said. "I fought, bled and nearly died to beat out all the others.

I won my place at the UPO enclave, representing my mistress and through her my world."

"I'm sure it was a valorous achievement. But the UPO needs--"

Corlan shoved a finger into the dwarf's chest. "Dorsun is my concern, not the UPO. You want an item of inestimable wealth to save something that means nothing to us."

"Dorsun agreed to the construction of--"

"And has gotten nothing for all the expense and trouble. Do you have any idea how many PGNs we sacrificed for the waygate network? How many more we give up for repairs? We're better off without access to Eleventh World."

There must be a Dorsun crossway on the fritz. How am I going to trade water and dirt if Dorsun's locked off?

"Ambassador, surely--"

"Don't you get it, dwarf? We're not going to give you the geonode. Let that woman do whatever she wants. If she isn't bluffing, which seem the most likely, ignoring her improves Dorsun's lot and mine as well."

"Yours?" Sam asked. "And what woman?"

Corlan looked down his nose at Sam. "Here, I'm a slave. At the enclave, I have power, live in a community combining the best technologies in ten universes. Telling you no means spending even more time there."

"I'm going to lodge a formal protest," Alabaster said.

"Do that," Corlan said.

"Come along, Bridger. We have another pickup to make."

Sam watched the dwarf storm away. He rubbed his neck. "This isn't about Dorsun's benefit, is it?"

Corlan smiled. "As it happens, my interests coincide with my world's."

"And your mistress agrees with you?"

Corlan's dark skin lightened. "Of course."

"Bridger! We're leaving."

Sam fixed Corlan with a steely gaze. "I've got a pickup order for a pregrowth geonode. Sam Bridger always delivers."

"Run along, wayman. You'll be lucky not to hang when that dwarf's done with you."

We'll just see about that.

Alabaster grumbled the rest of the way across Dorsun. They transitioned to Earth and headed cross country toward Nevada. Alabaster grumbled across the United States too.

"That's the third turn you've almost missed."

"I didn't miss them," Sam said.

"If you paid attention to the holomap instead of honking the horn at children, you wouldn't have to make last minute turns."

"Let's stop for a beer."

"We have a job to do."

"Even with the best short cuts, we've got hours of driving ahead."

"And you'd prefer to do that driving intoxicated?"

Sam gestured at the passport. "Sh-he can drive for us, if need be, but what I really want is some peace and quiet."

"You can barely hear me over that noise you call music."

"But I can *still* hear you. That's the problem."

Alabaster glowered.

"Look, maybe if we stop, you get a brew or four in you, you'll relax a little. I thought dwarves liked beer."

"Despite stereotypes perpetrated by your world's bad writers and worse movies, not all dwarves are wanton drunks."

"So you don't like beer?"

"I didn't say that."

"Then you do like beer."

"I didn't say that, either."

Sam slammed on the brakes, changed lanes, and pulled off an exit ramp to the dismay of his fellow highway drivers. He pulled into a parking lot of a roadside bar and grill called Miley's. "Do you like beer or not?"

"Yes."

"Would you enjoy a beer?"

Alabaster scowled. "A beer might be refreshing."

Sam threw up his arms. "Then why are we arguing?"

Alabaster opened his mouth, but Sam exited the truck without another word. He wove his way through a couple dozen motorcycles and stepped inside.

The inside of Miley's resembled most roadside bars Sam patronized. Given his druthers, he preferred truck stops to bars, but plenty of routes included one but not the other. Most of the small tables were pulled to one side, occupied by hairy, muscular men in leather vests or jackets.

Sam chuckled. Dwarf ought to feel right at home.

Sam sat between a pool table and an Asteroids machine. A worn-out looking woman sidled up to him, one hip jutted out and a pad in her hands. "I'm Steff, what do you want?"

"Anything good?"

"We've got an open-faced roast beef sandwich."

"Mashed potatoes and gravy over all of it?"

She nodded.

"Great, we'll take two and two of the biggest beers you can offer."

"Draft?"

Sam rubbed his neck. He shrugged. "Yeah, if he doesn't like it, I'll drink his."

Steff glanced around "He who, honey?"

"My companion. He'll be inside in a minute."

As if on cue, the door opened, and Alabaster entered. His clothes were something Wiggins might have worn, but not someone who frequented roadside bars. Long sleeves covered his cybernetics, and a single black glove hid his metallic hand. A patch covered most of his red, robotic eye.

Alabaster took a seat across the table as Steff headed for the kitchen. Snickers and several sidelong glances drifted over from the bikers, but the dwarf didn't notice.

"I ordered us some food too. To save time."

Alabaster gave a single nod.

Steff returned with the beer.

Alabaster took one drink and sprayed Sam with it. "You call this beer?"

"Hey! Look, just because you don't like it doesn't mean I want to wear it. We'll order you a different kind."

Alabaster glared up at Steff. "I'd like a rich, hearty brew, not cold human urine."

"Don't blame me for what he ordered," Steff said.

"Do you have any real ale or mead?"

"Like what? How about a brand name?"

Alabaster rattled off a few.

Steff shook her head, looking to Sam for help.

Sam shrugged. "He's from...Germany."

"I'll check the cooler," Steff said.

"It should be served warm," Alabaster snapped.

Steff fled.

Sam leaned closer to Alabaster. "You don't have to bully everyone."

"You offered me beer."

"And you got some, whether you liked it or not."

Steff returned with a few dusty green bottles. "No one around here'll drink this. Guessing that makes it your brand."

"Thank you," Sam said.

The dwarf's tone rose. "Don't thank her until we find out whether she's competent."

"Lighten up on her, Al," Sam offered her an apologetic smile. "Thanks, Steff, how's dinner coming?"

She took the hint and made good her escape.

Alabaster opened a bottle with his gloved hand, not bothering with the opener she'd left on the table. He took a sip.

"Good?" Sam asked.

"What makes you think that?"

"I'm not wearing it?"

"We serve stronger drinks to toddlers. Your people really are the worst accident in the universe."

Chairs on the opposite side of the room scraped the floor. Most of the biker group got to their feet with expressions as disgruntled as Alabaster's.

"You got a problem with Americans, metalhead?"

Alabaster didn't bother looking up. "No more than with the rest of you."

"Bet you got that plate in the war."

Alabaster looked up. "Yes."

"Can I buy you guys a round?" Sam rose, but the nearest biker shoved him back into his chair.

"You like this Nazi?"

"Al's not a Nazi," Sam said. "He's--"

"A white Michael Jackson?" a biker laughed. "What's with the one glove, Adolf?"

"Alabaster," the dwarf glared up at him. "If I told you, you'd have to die."

"Why's that?"

"Your brains are too weak for a mind wipe."

Sam's head fell forward into his hands. He sucked in a huge breath and stood. "Look, fellas, this is all just a misunderstanding. His English isn't real good, he didn't mean--"

"I meant every word, wayman."

Sam glanced around at angry faces. He rubbed his neck and nodded at the group. "I guess there really isn't much hope of getting out of this without a fight, is there?"

Several produced knives, brass knuckles, and short lengths of chain from their persons.

"Sam Bridger's an even-tempered man, but he doesn't shy from a fight."

"Who the hell is Sam Bridger?"

Sam picked up his drink. "Sure I can't offer you a beer?"

Before anyone else could answer, he threw the beer into the nearest faces, followed with a series of punches before the biker nearest him recovered.

Two bikers grabbed Sam and a third slammed a fist into his stomach. Sam kicked his assailant before he could land a second blow. He pulled free from one man, slammed the other into him and snatched up a green bottle.

Bikers swarmed Alabaster. The dwarf disappeared beneath them. A moment later his voice rang out. "Hedrin, yeah!"

Bikers flew in several directions, crashing into tables. One hit the Asteroids machine, producing a series of electronic explosion noises.

Sam ducked a punch and smashed the bottle over his attacker's head. He waved the broken glass at another biker, following it with a sucker punch when the man avoided the glass and charged in.

Alabaster took a chain-covered left hook to the jaw that probably should have put him down. He shook off the blow and returned it with interest by means of a golf swing of his hammer hand.

Sam retreated from a switch blade, coming to an abrupt halt with his back to the pool table. His attacker charged. Sam spun out of the way like a ballerina, snatched up the eight ball and brought it down. "Ole!"

Alabaster kicked a downed biker and slammed his left into a second. "A Tauron teach you that?"

"Bugs Bunny," Sam replied. "Could really do for a well-placed anvil right now."

Two bikers tackled Sam. His eight ball slammed down into one and his elbow the other. Blows pummeled into Sam.

Alabaster dropped another biker. Two gazelle-like bounds brought him to Sam's aid. He wrenched a biker off of the wayman, taking a knife gash across his flesh. He brained the knifeman with his hammer.

Alabaster heaved Sam to his feet. "No one ever found victory in the dirt."

"How about linoleum?"

Alabaster snorted.

A crowd of bikers formed a curved wall of leather-clad vengeance between them and the door.

Sam backed up to the wall, snatching a pool cue from a rack poking him in the back. He brandished it back and forth, taking on a civilized accent. "If you strike me down, I shall become more angry than you can possibly imagine. You won't like me when I'm angry."

"Less blathering, more fighting," Alabaster said.

The bikers fell upon them.

Sam broke the cue over a charging biker. He reversed his grip and clubbed the next. "Sam bash!"

They came at Sam and Alabaster in waves of ones and threes. Between the wall and each other, the two beat down the bikers until only broken furniture and a single biker remained.

The last biker crawled behind the bar, rising back up with a shotgun in hand.

Alabaster ripped the shirt sleeve from his right arm, the hammer transforming into a glowing energy weapon. He pointed it at the wide-eyed biker.

Sam adopted an Australian accent and inclined his head at the dwarf. "That's a gun."

The biker raised the weapon's barrel toward the ceiling and set it slowly onto the bar. "I'll just have a seat back here while you finish your drinks then?"

Sam nodded.

The biker disappeared. A moment later he crawled from behind the bar and out the front door. Steff emerged from the kitchen. An otherwise bald man with reddish-grey mutton chops held a cleaver behind her.

Sam wiped blood from his face. "Dinner ready?"

"Get out," Chops said.

"You Miley? Great place you've got here." He scanned the wreckage. "Had here. You take plastic?"

Chops nodded.

Sam offered his charge card for a pair of wrapped meals and the dented asteroids machine. Near him, Alabaster eyed their unconscious opponents.

Steff placed the card onto the machine, covered it with a receipt and ran the clacker arm back and forth over it to take an impression. Sam signed the receipt, wincing at the huge number in the cost line. He pushed the arcade game toward the door on a hand truck Sam'd picked up at headquarters to replace his malfunctioning grav-lift.

"Good fight, Bridger." Alabaster slapped Sam's shoulder. "Very relaxing."

12: Stowaway

Sam Bridger

Sam and Alabaster entered the world of Netaol during the dead of its night. Like in Dorsun, a team of realistic looking horses pulled them onto a tightly cobbled road braced by elms and oaks. The rig resembled an ornate stagecoach, typical of the world's magical craftsmanship. A gibbous moon rode high between the branches, casting silver upon them.

Sam glanced at the dwarf. "There's a rest area a mile up the road. Can we stop?"

"We have several pickups some distance apart in this universe. I fear we'll have little choice."

Sam rubbed his neck and yawned. "Glad to hear it."

He pulled the rig off of the cobbled road into a roadside privy, parking the truck next to a small corral. Alcoves offered well designed campsites, one of which sported a trio of tents.

Sam glanced over at Alabaster. "I'm going to use the facilities. Be right back."

He dismounted the covered wagon and crossed the medieval rest area. A small girl frowned sleepily at him. A ruby glinted on her left cheek beneath bed-tousled dark curls.

Sam stopped. "Evening, little miss."

"You should untie your team and see to them before yourself," she said.

Sam chuckled. "Is that so? As it happens, my team prefers to stay hitched up."

She glared. "*Buckwart.*"

"Pardon?"

"You're a Buckwart."

Sam's brows bent. "And that is?"

She threw up her hands. "Everyone knows that."

"I don't."

"Because you *are* a Buckwart, big, mean and *stupid*."

Sam stuck his tongue out at the little girl.

A woman in her late twenties appeared. Cream embroidery threaded her emerald robe with fanciful designs. A cat of yellow crystal walked at her side, tail flirting in the air.

"What's this, Tabitha?" she asked.

"This Buckwart was using the privy without taking care of his horses, Mistress."

The woman frowned at Sam and Tabitha in equal measure. "You'll keep a civil tongue, child."

"Yes, Mistress."

"I don't take kindly to animal abuse, sir," the magus said.

"Neither do I. That's why I don't have any."

The magus gestured toward his rig. "What do you call those?"

Sam pointed at the cat. "What do you call her?"

Confusion danced along the woman's features. Her eyes widened. "They're not foci. A conjuring?"

Sam inclined his head.

She curtseyed. "My apologies for my tear's actions, magus. The way you're dressed I thought you were a woodsman."

Sam beamed. "Adorable little tyke."

"Where is your circle?"

"Don't have one, just me and the dwarf."

The cat darted off.

She stiffened. She flipped her wrist to bring a mote of swirling electricity to hand. "Where?"

Sam chuckled. "Can't say he isn't a mean cuss on occasion, but he's not a danger."

"All dwarves are subject to execution."

"Wrong kind of dwarf, babe. This one's okay."

Her expression suggested she might use the lightning ball on Sam. Her eyes flashed out and back into focus. "My foci agrees with you. Just the same, I'll check this out for myself."

Sam pantomimed shooting her. "Knock yourself out, doll."

He disengaged himself and rushed to the privy to do his business. He returned to find Alabaster settling into a bedroll next to a small fire pit.

Sam gestured at a small carriage compartment just behind the driver seat. "You can sleep in there if you want. Forgot they don't like dwarves hereabouts."

The dwarf rose onto one elbow. "I've enjoyed many a night bivouacked, wayman. Go ahead. It's yours anyway."

"What about that sexy mage?"

"We've settled any possible disagreement. You can use the sleeper assured I'll haunt you in flesh rather than spirit."

Sam chuckled. "Sleeping in it makes me nervous, never know when she'll have a mood swing and drive me God knows where."

"He," Alabaster corrected. "That wouldn't be a fear if you read the manual."

"I know all about spiders. They still scare the bejesus out of me."

Alabaster frowned, shook his head, and laid back down.

Sam glanced at the sleeper.

The dwarf chuckled. "He isn't going to drag you off a cliff with me here. Go ahead."

Sam climbed into the small bedroom. The large soft mattress dominated the carriage inside, footprints on one end.

A flash of movement seized Sam's attention. He narrowed his eyes, rubbing his neck. *Do I own a second pillow?*

He picked it up, turning it over in his hands. With a shrug, he ducked out the door and tossed it to the dwarf. "Guess Ren likes you."

Alabaster punched a suitable dent for his head and settled down onto it.

The sound of laughing children drew Sam from his bed the next morning. He emerged from the sleeper bathed in the first rays of dawn. He glanced over to see the dwarf's pillow bent over his head to hold off noise. An aroma of bacon caressed Sam's nose, drawing him toward a communal pavilion.

He glanced at Alabaster, wondering if he should wake the dwarf. The pillow blinked at him.

Sam rubbed his eyes for the three steps it took to close the distance. He bent down and studied the now-eyeless pillow. He shook his head.

Been working too hard.

Alabaster snorted and flopped over to his other side, putting the pillow back under his head. He yawned and turned one red eye upon Sam.

"Morning already?" Alabaster rose and rolled up his bedroll. "Best be on our way."

Sam gestured at the pavilion. "Don't you smell that?"

"Of course I do, unwashed children and fried pork fat. What of it?"

"Bacon."

"Yes?"

"This is a socialist society."

"Right."

"That means they'll share their bacon."

Alabaster frowned. "You're not part of their society."

"They don't know that."

"Get on the truck, Bridger."

Sam narrowed his eyes at the pillow, his nose laboring to drag him to the pavilion. "We have to eat."

"You could do to miss a meal or two. Builds character."

"Rather have the bacon."

They rode away from a tower resembling an enormous ivory and gold candlestick complete with candle-like towers atop its upper arms. A city with apartment tenements to rival Detroit clung to its feet, surrounded by a greenbelt that took days to cross.

Magus traveled on foot or by wagon along the road, each equipped with a small crystal companion and a half dozen children to superpower their magic.

Sam watched another magus circle pass them. "You ever wonder about these medieval worlds?"

"What about them?"

"Bob says Netaol's been like this for thousands of years, relying on magic and never growing up."

Alabaster harrumphed. "Look who's talking."

"I mean they don't seem to evolve technologically."

"Netaol's gone through quite a history, but their system works for them. They live better than many places with far more technology."

"Cobbled roads, no electricity, no movies," Sam said.

"With a specialized socialism bolstered by magical craftsmanship which provides for every need, I doubt they think they have a problem. Happiness is more important than creature comfort."

Sam snorted. "Ruskies probably don't think they could live a better life, either."

Alabaster shook his head. "You don't live a better life; you live a more wasteful one."

Guess I shouldn't argue, Sam thought. He's been almost civil since the brawl. Better to leave him ignorant if it keeps him amenable.

Netaol's Masters, leaders in their communities, proved happy to deliver their goods to the dwarf. With a full belly and three of their five pickups complete, Sam contented himself with watching countryside and the occasional passing sorceress.

Tiar Netalin, once capital of the six kingdoms, remained a ruin of walled circles - testament to the first uprising against the villainous Masters in their past. Tiar Trillarian floated above the original capitol, dwarfing it in size. Passage to and from the flying city's byways required transit through a gateway similar to a crossway.

Bob still hasn't had a chance to come study them. I'd bring her along, but... Sam rubbed his neck. Having her close for that long might cause problems. She sure does want to figure out whether or not they were waygate predecessors though.

"Base, twenty-three, get Bob for me."

Bob's voice came to the communicator broken and out of breath. "Sam? Are you all right? You're not hurt, are you?"

"No, calm down, Bob. I'm fine, girl."

"Why're you calling? Is the auditor dead?"

Sam chuckled. "No, just snoring."

Bob's voice lowered to a harsh whisper. "Sam, you can't make a personal comm call with an auditor in your rig."

"This isn't personal."

Bob's tone fell flat. "Oh. What do you want, Bridger?"

"Dwarf's got me running all over the ten worlds, but I don't have anything on my itinerary. Can you check if the system is receiving?"

"It's fine."

"You checked that fast?"

"No."

"Bob, are you all right, love?"

"I'm not your love," Bob snapped. "If there's nothing else, I have work to do."

"You're sure nothing's wrong?"

"Your equipment is just fine. Bob out."

Sam frowned at the communicator.

Alabaster cleared his throat. "All of your tasks are being routed through me rather than your passport."

"Why?"

"Because that's the order I issued."

Sam pulled his team to the right and approached a Mageway arch. A young magus barely at the end of his teens waved at him.

"I think he wants you to stop, Bridger."

Sam shrugged but didn't slow the team.

"Bridger," Warning filled the dwarf's tone.

Sam flicked the reins for more speed.

Alabaster chirped at the passport.

An energy net materialized across the gateway.

The horses skidded to a stop; their limbs planted forward to arrest the loaded rig's momentum.

Sam flew from his seat, over the first pair of horses to tumble to a stop between the front pair. Blood ran down his chin from a re-opened cut. He dusted himself off and charged the magus. "What's the meaning of stopping me?"

"Cargo deliveries are not permitted through this gate. It is for--"

Sam decked the young magus. The children serving as his circle rose to their feet in uproar. Sam stepped over the groggy wizard and slammed a fist into his face, finalizing the punches on his ticket to take him to dreamland.

To Sam's right, the energy net vanished.

Guards swarmed Sam. He knelt, hands up and gave them an almost guileless expression. When they seized his arms, he blinked at them. "I don't know what happened."

"You assaulted a magus," one said.

"I know, but I would never--"

"Right," the guard said. "The devil made you do it."

Sam smiled and jerked a thumb over his shoulder. "Might've been the dwarf."

Alabaster

Alabaster paced back and forth a prison cell, glaring at Sam's lounging form on each turn. "Our last pickup and you've got to pull a stunt. I clearly underestimated your idiocy."

Sam shrugged, rose, and approached the bars. "Guard!"

A guard appeared a moment later. He wore medieval style chainmail. Crystal-edged armor plates covered the chain's chest, biceps, and thighs. "What?"

"What are you doing?" Alabaster asked.

"I'm hungry," Sam told the guard.

"You just ate."

"Netaol society prides itself on no one going without, right?"

Alabaster growled. "Bridger."

The guard drew out the word. "Yes."

"I'm without, and I'm hungry."

"Fine." The guard stomped away.

"Bring me some bacon!"

Alabaster slapped a hand over his face. "Has it escaped your notice that I'm an auditor, Bridger?"

"Nope."

"You're violating protocols right in front of me."

"I'm hungry. There's a protocol against being fed?"

"Against misuse of knowledge derived by association with Crossways Transportation and the UPO."

Sam blinked at him. "So I have to starve when on Netaol, but I can eat in any other universe?"

"You pay for the food in the other worlds," Alabaster said.

"They don't let you pay here."

"Here their labor pays for their food."

Sam rounded on Alabaster. "What exactly do you think I'm doing here? Taking a vacation in this tidy stone prison?"

"You don't work for Netaol."

"Do so."

"No, Bridger, you don't."

"Yes, I do. I work for the barons and aristocrats in their upper caste. I bring them what they want, carry trade goods to places they can't and facilitate obtaining resources—usually for personal need rather than public."

Alabaster opened his mouth, but the retort died on his lips. "I suppose you have a point."

"Good," Sam smiled. "I want some bacon."

Magus Vyse Helios of Netaol

Vyse strolled the busy streets of Tiar Trillarian, footsore and sick of the crowds. Both his boots and robes were worn, but not so much that he felt the need to seek out replacements.

<A magus should comport himself better.>

Vyse sighed, weary of repeating the familiar argument with his symbiote. *There're magus everywhere, Byron. Let them be an example.*

<This is precisely the attitude that got you thrown from the guild.>

Vyse shrugged. They never appreciated me anyway.

<Your specialty is hardly useful in everyday life.>

Not my fault. I can do other work.

<But you don't.>

Vyse stepped around a gaggle of children all marked on their right cheeks with a magus's rune. An older tear kept an adult eye on them while a youthful grin fought to emerge.

A sad smile caressed Vyse's lips.

<What if you apologized?>

Wouldn't do any good.

<Begged?>

No.

<We were nearly a master.>

And now we're nothing.

He stepped from the busy market street into one designed for carriage travel. He walked its length, watching more affluent individuals come and go along the street. Byron's tiny feet tickled beneath his robe as the foci collected - transforming from a quarter dozen mice to a walking staff.

"Can I help you, magus?" a young woman rose from her seat beside the Mageway gate, leaving her bored circle guessing shapes in the clouds.

"We're going down," Vyse said.

"There's a pedestrian gate a few streets over."

Vyse ran a hand through wild, grey hair, mussing it further. "I'm tired, young lady. Can I please use this one?"

A soft smile grew beneath pity-filled eyes. "Yes, magus."

"Thank you," Vyse stepped through the gate, appearing on a cobbled byway far beneath his departure point.

Crossways

He glanced around, hoping for one of the stagecoaches that ran from city to city. None were visible, but an ornate cargo wagon parked to one side of the road, its team unusually still.
<What are you thinking?>
You know as well as I do.
<Why?>
I just want to go somewhere, Byron, anywhere.
<Where you go, I follow.>
A smile turned Vyse's lips up. *You're a good friend.*
Vyse opened a small passenger compartment behind the driver's seats. A down mattress filled the compartment, drawing a bigger smile from the old magus.
"Perfect."
He climbed aboard, laid his head on a pillow, and rolled onto his side. A cat stared at him from the corner. Vyse reached out and stroked its fur a few times before falling asleep.

13: Done with Idiots

Sam Bridger

A note sat in the driver's seat beneath a small, towel-wrapped bundle. Sam read it. "Instructs me to deliver my current to an address in Buenos Aires."

"Give me that." Alabaster snatched the note, running a red laser scan down the locally produced parchment.

Sam shrugged and opened the bundle, revealing a selection of iced muffins. He raised one to his lips. The creamy cool icing tantalized his taste buds, complimented by a sharp sweet berry in the moist cake.

Sam moaned with pleasure.

Alabaster slapped the muffin from his hand as Sam raised it to his lips for a second bite.

"Hey!"

"Are you out of your mind?" the dwarf demanded. "It could be poisoned."

Sam's brow wrinkled. "Why would someone leave me a note with poisoned muffins?"

Alabaster folded his arms. "You just shouldn't eat things when you don't know where they come from."

"It was left for me."

"Still."

Sam cradled the other muffins, turning his back so he could enjoy another without the dwarf snatching it away.

"If you die of poison, I'm going to laugh at you."

Sam rolled his eyes in pleasure. "These would so be worth dying for."

"Idiot."

Sam spoke through a mouthful of muffin. "I think I'd prefer you call me Happy Fool."

"Idiot," Alabaster said with absolute finality.

Alabaster

They followed the passport's directions through a series of waygates to a small church on the outskirts of Buenos Aires proper.

If this idiot wayman moans about more muffins one more time I'm clubbing him over the head for some damned silence.

His cybernetic eye ran an infrared scan over the church, then switched modes and scanned for explosives. When he verified no imminent threats, Alabaster turned to the wayman. "Stay here, Bridger."

"You're going to unload for me? Cool beans."

Alabaster modulated his voice to hide thinning patience. "I'm going to check the place out before you unload."

"Lighten up, Al. It's just a church."

Alabaster narrowed his normal eye. "It doesn't trouble you that we've brought all of these things to a church in the middle of nowhere? Goods from a completely different universe?"

Sam laughed. "I do that every day. You UPO guys squirrel away things you want no one knowing about in the crappiest rental location like that'll keep your junk safe."

Alabaster's brow rose. "What?"
Sam shrugged.
"Just stay with the rig, Bridger."
Sam snorted. "Someone going to steal it?"
Alabaster gritted his teeth. "Stay."
"Woof."

Sam Bridger

Sam strolled around to the truck's trailer. He donned his back brace. A flash of movement inside drew him up short.

"Look, if any of you crates has eyes, just keep them shut and we won't have any problems."

Alabaster appeared at the rear of the trailer, his arm transforming from energy weapon to a hand. "What are you doing?"

"Talking to the cargo."

The dwarf rolled his eye. "It's all clear, you can unload."

Sam moved cargo crate by crate into the church. Alabaster contented himself by counting the crates and tinkering with the damaged grav-lift.

Halfway through the unloading, Alabaster pushed the repaired lift into Sam's hands.

"Thanks."

Alabaster shrugged. "Got tired of waiting on you."

"Could've helped."

"I'm supervising."

The lift sped the unloading process. Alabaster's grim expression became a full-fledged scowl as Sam drew the last load from the trailer. He pushed the unloaded lift back to its dock.

Alabaster waylaid him. "What did you do?"

"I unloaded the truck."

"There're two extra crates."

Sam felt his neck heat. "Are you accusing me of something?"

"You're smuggling, helping her."

"Her who?"

"You know."

"No, damnit, I have no idea who you're talking about."

"You loaded extra crates I didn't know about into the trailer," Alabaster said.

Sam goggled. "When?"

"What?"

"When did I do all this? You insisted someone else handle all loading. You haven't left me alone this whole trip."

"You've had several chances to smuggle things into the truck," Alabaster said.

Sam checked the coast clear, leaning in. "I admit it. I plotted the end of the world in the privy."

Alabaster's arm changed to an energy weapon and swung toward Sam. "Traitor."

Sam's hands shot up in submission. "Whoa there, cowboy. I was just kidding."

"This isn't a laughing matter, Bridger."

"No, it isn't. If you don't lower that weapon, I'm going to have to beat you down. That can't be good for my audit."

A robed man dismounted the truck, scanning their surroundings with a confused expression. "What's going on here?"

Sam and Alabaster spoke at the same time. "Who're you?"

"Magus Vyse Helios."

"Again, Bridger?" Alabaster roared.

Sam blinked. "What? I didn't know he was there."

"Just like you didn't load the extra cargo?"

"I didn't."

"Confess or I'll have to shoot," Alabaster said.

"I can't let you harm a Netaolian citizen," Vyse said.

"This is none of your business, sir," Alabaster said. "I'll return you to your world once I've finished here."

"World?" Vyse asked.

"Confess!"

"I didn't do anything."

Vyse threw his hands forward as Alabaster fired. Sam dove out of the way a moment before the energy blast crashed through a cellophane thick shield.

Vyse stared at his staff, mouthing words that had no volume.

Sam rolled to one side behind a metal trash can, scooped up the lid and threw it at Alabaster. An energy blast sent it flying at an oblique angle.

"Come on, Al. I didn't do anything."

"You're trying to tell me you're not a smuggler?" Alabaster said.

Sam rubbed his neck. "I didn't add anything to this load except the Asteroid machine and I paid for that."

Vyse threw another shield spell, but it materialized as weak as his previous attempt. Sweat dampened the old man's forehead. "You there, throw another of those things, but at that wall there."

"What good will that do?" Sam asked.

"Confess your part in things, Bridger. I'll see they go light on you."

Sam cursed. "I don't know what you're talking about."

Alabaster fired another shot, this one melting the cans and incinerating their trash.

Sam scooped up a trash can lid, careful not to touch its glowing metal edges. He hurled it at the wall. It hit with more force than he expected, bounced off a light pole, the curb, the trailer and finally slammed into Alabaster's head behind his left ear.

The dwarf went down.

Sam stood. "What the hell. That's impossible."

Vyse wiped sweat from his face and crossed the distance between them. "Improbable, but within the bounds of possibility."

"You?" Sam asked.

"Yes."

"Thank you?"

"You can thank me by telling me why my magic doesn't work."

"This isn't Netaol."

Vyse gestured at the semi. "I gathered."

"There isn't any magic here."

"There must be. I can feel it, though it's very faint."

"Maybe from...never mind. I'm not allowed to talk about it."

"Can you take me home?" Vyse asked.

"Yes, but first I have to deal with him."

"Very well, kill your foe and we can be on our way."

"Actually, I like the angry little bastard."

Sam retrieved his shotgun from the rig and a trashcan lid full of water from the church. He put the shotgun beneath Alabaster's chin and doused him.

The two met each other's gaze.

"I didn't do whatever it is you think I did. Sam Bridger may have a number of faults, but disloyalty isn't one of them."

Sam cracked open the shotgun, dumping unspent rounds to the ground. He handed it over and offered Alabaster his hand.

Alabaster's red light passed over Sam's hand and then across the rest of his body. He nodded to himself, took Sam's hand, and regained his feet. "You could have killed me."

"I know," Sam said.

"Or let him."

"Yes."

"Why didn't you?" Alabaster asked.

"I like you, Al, and murdering an auditor has to be bad for your score."

"You're an idiot."

"So you've said."

"But maybe not a traitor."

"Sorry to disappoint you?"

Sam pulled his rig into a Union 76 truck stop, stopping next to the gas pumps. He glanced at Vyse in the second row of seats. "Be just a moment."

"What is this place?" Vyse asked.

Alabaster's tone demanded caution. "Bridger."

"Roadside privy."

"Excellent," Vyse said. "I've need to make water."

Sam glanced at Alabaster.

"Keep him from trouble, wayman."

"Why don't you do it?"

"I'm guarding the truck while I make a call."

Sam rubbed his neck. "Fill her up while you do?"

Alabaster regarded Sam.

"Right. That'd be too much to expect." Sam helped Vyse out of the rig. He glanced at the magus's outfit. "You can leave the staff behind."

"I may need it," Vyse countered.

"Thing is, walking around with a big crystal staff will draw attention, make people nervous."

The staff flared with light a moment, then broke apart into a small swarm of mice which darted beneath Vyse's robes.

"Awesome, but doesn't that tickle?"

Vyse shrugged. "A little."

Out of Alabaster's earshot - at least so Sam hoped - he answered Vyse's questions about automobiles, neon lights, gas stations and various other trivial items. *I know the dwarf'd have a hissy fit, but I just don't see the harm.* He led Vyse into the diner area of the truck stop, hit with the warm wonderful smells of brown, greasy spoon food at its best.

Vyse's stomach growled.

Sam chuckled. "We'll grab some food on the way out."

He led the magus through the driver lounge. He noticed Vyse fall behind and went back to pull him away from a selection of slot machines. Inside the lavatory, Vyse stopped once more, gazing at the somewhat clean porcelain urinals.

Sam gestured at one. "For making water. Sink's over there to wash your hands after."

Vyse approached a urinal, and Sam moved deeper into the bathroom.

"Where are you going?"

"Got to make some water myself."

"Why not use these?"

"Bigger job."

Vyse's brow creased, a moment later he inclined his head and returned his attention to the urinal.

Sam completed his business, washed his hands, and glanced around for the magus. He exited the bathroom, expecting to find Vyse just outside or back in the driver's lounge.

He wasn't in either.

Sam rubbed his neck, glancing at the showers and the women's restroom. A small pang of regret washed over him as he turned away from the showers.

Vyse's voice drew Sam. "Unhand me, knave, by what right do you accost a magus?"

"You can't just eat stuff and walk away," another voice said.

"I hunger."

"I don't care. You have to pay for it first."

"Pay?" Vyse asked. "No one pays for food."

Sam ran toward the altercation, weaving in and out of aisles and forcing his way through a small crowd of spectators.

"Crazy vagrant bastard," the cashier said. "Bev, Sheriff's in the diner. Fetch him for me."

"Good," Vyse said. "He'll see you punished for disparaging a magus's lineage."

Sam interceded. "Bev, doll, no need for all that. Just a misunderstanding. My friend here's from...Canada."

Heads around Sam nodded, and a soft murmur swam the crowd.

"I'll pay for whatever he ate."

"What is this insanity? True trade is appropriate for luxuries, but this swill can't be considered thus."

Sam patted Vyse on the back. "Don't worry, I'll explain it to you later. Just let me pay."

"Who pays for food? I just don't understand."

"It's called capitalism, you dirty communist," another trucker said.

Vyse opened his mouth to retort. Sam dropped a twenty on the counter and slapped a hand around Vyse's mouth. "Easy, brother, just keep your peace, and we'll get out of this without a tussle."

Sam's hand muffled whatever Vyse said.

Sam addressed the cashier. "Any change?"

The man glared but rang up the items taken and handed over the remaining money.

"Thanks, brother."

Sam led Vyse back to the rig and helped him climb inside.

"I do not understand, Sam Bridger."

"I know."

"I didn't mean you trouble."

"I know."

"What trouble? Bridger, what have you done?"

Sam opened his mouth, closed it, and opened it again. "Watch him. I've got to pay for the fuel. You want any food?"

"From this sty?" Alabaster asked.

"No," Sam snapped. "The sewage treatment plant next door."

14: For the Little People

Taleh

Taleh glanced at the stooped, age-shrunken figure that was Mite. She patted his hand. "Stay here. I can handle this."

"But, Mistress," Mite rasped.

"It'll be fine."

"The dwarf may have left traps or surveillance."

She offered what she hoped was a reassuring smile. "And he'll see the face I present, no matter."

"What of tracking devices?"

"My agent will have removed them while in transit."

Mite's brows rose. "Pardon, Mistress, but you have mentioned this agent before. Can you tell me more?"

"Rest, my friend, don't fret."

"What if the dwarf left tracking devices after they unloaded?"

Taleh left him without an answer. *I didn't think of that.*

A frown grew upon her illusionary face. She picked up the shipping manifest left upon the delivery, scanning the items requested from Netaol. She wondered what the UPO thought of the strange list - strangest on the list was a dozen orders of Rappetan Fire Squid cooked and magically sealed against spoilage. She *loved* that squid so much!

Several of the items were unnecessary—such as the aforementioned seafood. Others served as passable substitutions for items she needed rather than genuine articles which might feed the UPO clues as to her real intentions.

Taleh picked through the crates, nibbling her squid snacks. She dug through a crate of wooden toys that would serve in her endeavor and removed a small, painted horse that came alive when the name painted on its harness was spoken.

She set it aside for her niece and continued checking the items. Two camouflaged crates held key items obtained and clandestinely loaded by her agent. In case the auditor left behind a set of eyes, she resisted opening them.

A work crew arrived a bit late with several cargo vans. The locals didn't speak English, but a handsome man with grey edging into his hair saw the cargo loaded.

She returned to their rental and led the trucks into the nearby city. They stopped outside of an orphanage. She enlisted the man's help distributing the extra toys included in her delivery. Several bundles of Netaolian flowers and mage-crafted candies delighted the orphans. She left them bolts of cloth and gardening tools as well, allowing her to consolidate the essential cargo into a single van.

She returned to the rental and led the van through the busy streets.

"You fancy him, Mistress?"

She smiled. "He's handsome enough, for a human."

"I could enlist him for you."

Taleh set a hand upon his gnarled knot of fingers. "Thank you, Mite, but that isn't necessary."

"My replacement should be on Mars awaiting you by now."

"I'm sorry to see you go. You've done so much for me."

He nodded. "Some of us are very sick, Mistress. Despite this universe's hypoallergenic nature, constant expenditure of energy required to help you on this world drains us."

"Kills you, you mean."

"We are honored to serve your efforts to save your people."

"Our people."

An airy laughter bubbled from him, almost the high-pitched giggle she knew as his norm. "Yes, of course."

They exited the city, driving into the country to a small farmstead. Mite exited the car with effort. "I will pay the man while his people unload."

She measured his strength by the way his illusion moved. "Thank you."

Mite offered her a weak smile, lowering into a formal bow.

Realization struck. A tear rolled down her cheek. "You're not coming with me?"

"No, Mistress. It is my time to take my leave of you."

She rushed forward and embraced him. "Thank you for everything, Mite."

"Fear not." He wiped the tear from her face. "My replacement will serve you as well as I would."

A lump formed in her throat, leaving her only to nod.

"Go. Let me take care of this last task for you."

Taleh nodded and headed into the farmhouse. She glanced back as Mite hobbled toward the workers. She committed him to memory. When their people were safe, she'd see a monument raised in his honor on Mars.

Elmeddi the Conqueror

Elmeddi watched Taleh go out of the corner of Mite's eye. He forced Mite's stolen body. He forced Mite's shriveled limbs to carry Elmeddi across the distance to the workers. The men shifted crates from the van onto a metallic replica of an old-fashioned wagon.

Elmeddi took a moment to recall the local language and shambled over to the man in charge. "You have our thanks."

"Just doing our job," he said. "Your daughter was very generous to the children."

Mite smiled. "She's like that. She's left you and your workers a case of beer in thanks. She asked me to request your name, so she can commend you to your supervisors."

"Varian," he smiled.

Elmeddi checked the workers otherwise occupied and extended Mite's hand. "A pleasure, Varian."

Varian took the old man's hand. Instead of a simple handshake, Elmeddi drew Varian into a hug. The man resisted for a moment but relented to let the old man embrace him.

Elmeddi's claw tore his way out through Mite's chest. Blood ran down Mite's torso. Varian saw it, eyes widening with fear. He opened his mouth to cry out, but Elmeddi shoved Mite's hand into the man's mouth.

Varian bit down, but Elmeddi ignored Mite's pain.

Elmeddi's claws tore an opening in Varian's torso. The man gurgled, drooling blood around Mite's wrinkled hand. The small crystalline being crawled from Mite's body Varian's. The Brazilian worker collapsed. Mite's body fell like a marionette with its strings cut.

Varian

Varian struggled against the thing writhing inside of him. Images bombarded his mind, places and horrors that he couldn't comprehend.

Elmeddi's thoughts careened around Varian's head. *<Submit, Varian.>*

No.

<I'll win anyway, save yourself the pain.>

You won't win.

<I've never failed before.>

God, save me.

<There is no God, Varian, and if there were, He wouldn't intervene.>

You're a demon.

A giggle emerged from Varian's throat. *<Not a demon, a Linurian.>*

What do you want with me?

<Your body.>

Why?

<Your flesh will protect me from your world and feed me your life's energy.>

You are a demon.

<No, I'm Elmeddi the Conqueror, and no accident of sentience will stop me from ruling the eleven universes.>

15: Back at Base

Sam Bridger

Sam enlisted a pair of warehouse workers to assist him in unloading the Asteroids machine. They set it up beside the Pac-Man game. He gave them a handful of quarters. "Get a head start, boys. I'll have SOB on that high score in no time."

Beatrice blocked his exit. "What the hell is that?"

"It's called an arcade game."

She glowered at him. "Why would you bring that thing in here? Isn't it bad enough you left that one in here to remind me that a game was more important to you than me?"

The warehouse workers pointedly looked anywhere else.

"I brought Pac-man here because you left me with nothing. I had no other place to put it. As for this one, Alabaster damaged it, so I had to buy it. Figured bringing it here might entertain the boys and ease expensing it back to the company."

"This company is on the edge of bankruptcy. Neither them nor you need more ways to avoid working." She shook her head. "You've got a place now. Just take them home."

"Pleasure's in the sharing, not to mention friendly competition – builds team unity."

She rolled her eyes. "Now I know you're talking out of your ass. Who's that?"

Sam glanced over his shoulder to find a soaked Vyse dripping on the yellowing floor. "That's Vyse, an Netaolian magus."

"You stole *another* citizen?"

"Stowaway," Sam pinched his nose. "Just introduced him to the shower."

"A wonderful concept, enclosed waterfalls," Vyse said.

"You're taking him back right now before Auditor Roxx finds out," Beatrice said.

"The dwarf was there."

She pinched the bridge of her nose. "You're going to jail."

"I look good in stripes." Sam chuckled.

"Grow up." Beatrice glowered, stomping one heel. "*This* is serious. You can't keep treating life like some sort of game."

Sam's grin widened. "But life is a game. You're just sore because you can't figure out the rules."

"No. This is serious; life is serious."

A high-pitched trill escaped Sam's throat. He pitched his voice to match. "That is why you are so grumpy."

"God, Sam, you can't even quote a movie right." Beatrice closed nose to nose with him, stabbing a finger into his chest. "Stop living like you're some Muppet on Sesame Street. People are counting on you to..."

Sam snorted, continuing the imitation. "In need of counseling, they are."

Running feet neared, charging through the opposite door. Bob shoved Vyse out of the way.

The magus grunted.

Sam sighed. "Are you here to lecture me--"

Bob tackled him, wrapping her arms around him. "Thank God you're safe."

I could get used to this. He glanced at Beatrice's scowl and sobered. His heart ached to see Beatrice's pain. He looked down at Bob, keeping the maelstrom of feelings clear of his face. There was a lot to like about spunky, intelligent Bob. Even if he accepted that she might like him more than he wanted to admit to himself, pursuing her would hurt Beatrice and jeopardize Sam's friendship with Bob. *No. It's just friendship and even if she has a crush on me, I can't risk hurting both.*

Sam forced a smile and waggled his eyebrows. He resumed his imitation. "Happy to see me, you seem."

Bob slugged him in the stomach.

"Don't ever do that again, you stupid son-of-a--"

Beatrice's voice dripped venom. "Shouldn't you be repairing something?"

The two women locked gazes over Sam's shoulder. Bob's tan cheeks flushed umber. "I-I, there is a lot of work, I mean, but...."

"Go," Beatrice snapped.

Bob fled.

Irritation narrowed Sam's eyes. He'd only just made a decision based on protecting Beatrice, and his ex attacked Bob. He tightened his jaw. "Why're you being mean to Bob?"

Could she have feelings deeper than jealousy?

"She hit you."

"So? What do you care?"

"It's inappropriate."

"I'd think you of all people would support the random pummeling of my person."

Beatrice spun on her heel. "She violated our company code of conduct."

Sam frowned at the vacated doorframe. "Never stopped you."

Vyse sidled up to Sam. "They war for your affections."

Sam laughed out loud. "You obviously don't know anything about women."

"I've shared many a heart."

"Then women are different where you come from. Beatrice left me, and Bob...well, everyone loves Sam Bridger. It's probably nothing. Even if it is more, I'd rather not indulge a crush that could ruin a good friendship."
"They are different. Mine throw fire."
"Mine too."

Alabaster glared. "You understand?"
Sam barely paid the dwarf any mind. He'd repeated Sam's orders six hundred times. Instead Sam studied Beatrice. She loomed in the background with her lip beneath her teeth.
Bea only chews her lip when she's fretting over something serious...never when she's jealous. What's going on around here?
"Are you listening to me, Bridger?"
"Yeah, take Vyse home, force Niri back to Dorsun, and then radio in. I'll head out as soon as the rig's paintjob sets."
Bea's been too serious lately, and I'd swear she was about to tell me something earlier. The last time... His stomach bottomed out. He forced the memory of that conversation back into hiding. Her tears. Her miscarrying a pregnancy they hadn't even known about. He never wanted to think about it ever again.
"Don't dawdle," Alabaster said. "There are things to do."
Sam flashed the dwarf a wide grin, deciding to test the waters. "You've heard of time off, right?"
"Keep your primitive mythologies to yourself."

Sam's smile widened. He marched from the room, pausing to pitch his voice just for Beatrice. "You okay?"

Beatrice's hard expression wavered. "Do what he says, Sam. People are counting on you...to get a good score on the audit."

Alabaster cleared his throat.

"You know me."

"That's what worries me, Sam. Fetch that princess and get back on the job."

Sam pantomimed shooting her. "You got it, babe."

No way I'm forcing Niri to do anything she doesn't want, but a little Sam Bridger charm might just do the trick, in more ways than one. His daydreams about the desert beauty wavered, shifting to Beatrice and then to Bob. He pushed his fantasies away from dangerous waters. Niri might stab him, but even so represented a lesser danger. While Sam distracted himself, Vyse stared at the cars and surrounding countryside.

"It's a good world you have," Vyse said at last, "though it would be better if you gave up this barbarism."

"What?"

"Capitalism. As you explain it, you pit your people against one another, like some vast arena battle."

"Hey, brother, it isn't like that. Not like they're cutting each other's heads off."

"No, merely edging one another out to the point of starvation."

"Maybe in concept, but that's not really what happens. People look out for each other."

Vyse shrugged. "Byron and I still think it's a poor system."

Sam shrugged. "Free country."

They fell into silence.

Sam tried to examine life in the States from Vyse's perspective. The ten worlds enjoyed different styles of governance and different technological levels. Some differences might benefit his world, but UPO watched those who knew the truth closely. One wayman had been jailed for trying to originate an idea involving phones with no wires of all things.

The UPO hadn't meant to create humanity, hadn't meant for echoes from the other ten worlds to so permeate Sam's world. It'd been an uncomfortable revelation, learning his species lived at the sufferance of others who decided killing humanity would be less convenient than enlisting them as a workforce to haul their cargo. Beatrice and the others knew it in concept.

They haven't faced it at gunpoint like I have.

His thoughts returned to Beatrice's accusations in the breakroom. She didn't know how deeply she'd stung him, how her words lingered over the miles. She hadn't known him before she came to Crossways Transportation. She never saw him as the young earnest go getter, just as bright-eyed, dedicated, and hard-working as Kenneth. Beatrice met the man he'd become after the ten universes abused him, after the tragedy, the carefree persona he'd created to bury his guilt.

She fell in love with him as a man embracing life for every moment, every pleasure, and every adventure. When they miscarried, he'd wrapped himself even deeper into the persona. When Sam went the opposite way Beatrice needed, when he grew more childish instead of growing up like she thought he should, she distressed of all those things that first attracted her.

She'd never have left the younger me, before I... Sam chuckled. *She'd never have liked younger me in the first place.*

Irony played a dirty game.

16: Foolhardy Wagers

Sam Bridger

Sam glanced over at his passenger. "Hungry, Vyse?"

"Food would be welcome."

"Great, we're only a little way outside of Vegas." Sam licked his lips. "They've got incredible buffets. Cheap, too."

"So long as it isn't poisonous."

Sam scrutinized Vyse in glances. "That common in Netaol?"

"No, but I don't dwell in barbarism."

Sam's neck warmed. "Now, look here--"

Vyse chuckled. "You're a truly gullible young man."

Sam blinked. "You were putting me on?"

"Indeed." Vyse watched the road pass. "Where does your cat go when your carriage takes this shape?"

"What cat?"

Vyse watched him.

Must be another joke.

A semi raced passed Sam's rig. He glanced in his mirrors. Another several with similarly painted cabs paced the first. Sam rubbed his neck.

"You boys are too near Vegas for that kind of speed," Sam mumbled under his breath. "What's the hurry?"

"What did you say?"

Sam gestured. "Vegas cops live for stupid tourists and speeding truckers. These guys should know that."

The first truck cut into Sam's lane barely a car-length ahead. Brake lights blazed red.

Sam cursed, hit his brakes, and snatched up the CB. "What the hell, brother? Watch your spacing."

He checked his mirror, preparing to pass the idiot. Two more trucks raced up alongside and settled into position. A fourth rode his bumper.

A gruff voice came over the CB. "Pull over, Bridger."

The door decal on the truck to his left read ELT Shipping.

"I need HQ on handsfree right now, buddy." The communicator lit green. "HQ, Twenty-three, I've got a problem here."

"HQ," Beatrice said. "You drive into someone's pool?"

"Pull over, Bridger, or we'll force you off the road."

"You hear that?" Sam asked.

"What did you do to them?"

"Not everything is my fault, Bea."

"Damn near."

Both rigs to Sam's left edged closer. The forward truck's trailer swung wide, crashing into Sam's cab. His rig jolted right with the impact.

Sam fought the wheel. "I just had that painted!"

Alabaster snapped a command over the rapid thud, thud, thud of roadside warning ridges. "Don't pull over, Bridger."

Metal scrapped against metal. An explosive pop startled Sam, trailer tire shards thrown against his windows.

"Great idea, Al, just not sure they'll give me a choice."

The truck in front of Sam's pumped its brakes. The trailer smashed Sam's cab with a windshield-splintering impact.

"We don't need you alive, Bridger." Mister Gruff added. "We only want your rig."

Sam turned to Vyse. "Holy hijackers, Magicman."

"Shall I immolate them?" Vyse asked.

"What?" Sam asked. "No, we'll be all right."

"Surrender, Bridger."

"Don't push me, boys," Sam barked into the CB.

The trucks beside him slammed into Sam's rig, forcing tires onto the roadside. Sam jammed his brakes. The truck behind Sam slammed into his trailer. It braked hard, leaving Sam's trailer bouncing wildly. Sam swerved right then left, bludgeoning another attacker with his trailer.

Ren-2-3 beeped at him.

"You got that right, bud." Sam laughed. "Damn good thing that's not a normal trailer hitch, huh?"

"Bridger, report." Alabaster said.

Sam floored the gas, accelerating before the truck in front of him could take advantage of Sam's sudden deceleration. His left hand cranked down the driver side window then seized the wheel. Whipping his shotgun free, he propped it on the sill and blasted the attacking cab with both barrels as he sped by.

Sam thumbed the lock, broke open the weapon and dumped spent shells to the cab floor. He passed the gun. "Shells are in the drawer under your seat. Reload me."

"It's permitted to hurl thunder at your foes but not for me to summon fire?"

"Trying to scare them off, not torch them."

"To hedrin with scaring them off," Alabaster said. "If they strike at you, send their remains to their fictitious deities."

"Not helping here, Al."

Sam checked Vyse's progress in fits and glances. "No, other way. Good. Now fold it closed and hand—"

Vyse reached the shotgun across Sam and pulled the trigger. Fire, light and thunder enveloped Sam as the shells tore through the rig's doorframe. His face crisped as propellant burned his nose and flash incinerated nose and eyebrow hair.

The ear that could hear rang like a Vatican City celebration. Blood ran down his neck from the other.

Sam blinked away phantasms, shouting at top volume. "Hey, watch it!"

The blasted truck slammed into his sideways, driving Sam's wheels all the way off onto the soft shoulder. He jerked the wheel back out of reflex. Their impact sent the other truck off the far side of the highway.

Vyse reloaded the shotgun. "This sorcery is surprisingly easy to wield."

Sam shouted. "Don't wield it in my face, would you?!"

Vyse laid a hand on Sam, face screwed up. Fiery agony enveloped Sam's head and fatigue washed through him. Sound returned to normal and the sunburn on his skin faded. A quick check discovered regrown eyebrows. "You didn't have any Tylenol spells you could cast first?"

"Tile-what?"

Bob's voice reached through the fading bells. "Sam?"

"Bridger's Party line, bad guys and bombshells, no waiting."

"Hold on, Sam, I'm going to get you clear," Bob said.

"I'm good." Sam accepted a loaded shotgun from Vyse, pointed it out his window and blasted the nearest tires.

"Listen to the woman, Bridger. *She's* competent."

"Ryalox controls on three," Bob said.

Sam's head shot around. "Say what?"

His steering wheel transformed into the throttle and flight controls used when delivering goods to Alabaster's intergalactic government. He cursed the sky blue. "Damn it, Bob, how do you expect me to drive?"

"Not drive, fly."

"This is Nevada, darling, not Space Mountain."

Bob ignored him. "Transformation in five, four, three..."

"Crap! Feet up in the stirrups, Vyse, now!"

Without the pedal down, Sam's rig slowed. The two alongside semis slammed into Sam, muscling him off the road. Mileage markers and highway signs slammed into his nose, but the rig somehow held together without losing speed.

The change field enveloped the truck, bleeding over into the shoving trucks. Wheels along the near side transformed into a hundred Rockette legs, sprinting in ruby heels and taking turns kicking Sam's rig.

Sam's tires became maglev repulsors, smoothing out the borderline off-roading he was doing. A blast of repulsor thrust launched Sam's rig skyward. The resulting pressure wave catapulted the two leftward trucks into the median—one flailing its shapely legs. The legless truck's nose hit hard, flipping both cab and trailer into an end over end.

While the lead truck disintegrated, the second caught a concrete barrier. The impact disintegrated the stone and whipped the rig into a wild spin.

The truck behind him took less of the blast, but the rig in front slammed its brakes bringing the two together with metal smashing zeal.

"Are you clear?" Bob asked. "Sam, answer me."

"Yahoo!" Sam exclaimed. "Better than a flying Winnebago."

Beside Sam, Vyse pressed back into his seat, eyes wide with terror. He touched the magus's arm. "Be just fine, brother. Hold out a few more minutes and we'll have terra firma beneath us once more."

"Ren-2-3," Alabaster said. "Engage light bending matrix."

Sam's eyes widened. He stuck his head out the damaged window, tearing up with wind and joy. "Holy crap, I've got a Roman cloaking device?!"

"You mean Romulan," Bob said.

"Oh, baby, you're so sexy right now."

"Cybriean," Alabaster corrected. "Mate on your personal time, Bridger.

"I thought personal time was a myth," Sam said.

"It is, bringing great joy for humanity's future. Now, land so Ren-2-3 can convert you back to normal."

"Were they cargo jackers?" Bob asked.

"No, they wanted my rig. Referred to me by name too."

Beatrice's voice was all vinegar. "You mean like how it's painted on the truck's door next to the word operator, idiot?"

Vyse looked over, his skin returning to its normal color. "At war, Sam Bridger."

Sam led Vyse along the Las Vegas strip, amused that the magus wasn't the weirdest sight on the sidewalks. "We should hit a show before I take you back."

Vyse studied his surroundings, his tone distracted. "Aren't you in a hurry?"

Sam shrugged and his voice adopted a sing-song quality. "A little nonsense now and then is relished by wise guys everywhere."

"I'm not sure I understand."

"All work and no play makes for a dull Sam?"

Vyse cocked his head. "What about your life is dull?"

"Being this exciting while still looking good takes a lot of work," Sam said.

"Work harder," Mister Gruff shoved a revolver into Sam's back. "But don't move."

"Vyse, get away."

A pair of burly truckers seized Vyse's arms.

"He's not going anywhere," Mister Gruff said.

A calm yet smarmy voice made Sam cringe. "Let the Netaolian go. He's not our concern."

Sam groaned. "Ah hell, not *you*."

The approaching man oozed confidence. Equally broad chested and a couple fingers taller than Sam, his easy grin spilled menace. Short blue-black hair with a single curl on his forehead framed sun-bronzed skin and dark eyes. "Nice to see you too, Bridger."

"Who's this man, and how does he know whence I come?"

Before Sam answered, Eugene Lazarus performed a formal bow of Netaolian aristocracy. "A pleasure to meet you, magus. My name's Laz, like Taz."

Sam let his contempt show. "His first name's Eugene."

A few pedestrians stopped, watching the altercation as if it were a stage show.

Vyse remained nonplused. "If you know I'm a magus, you know that if your men don't release me this moment, I'll conjure acid beneath their skins."

"Sadly, magus, so little magic remains in Eleventh World that your spells are of little affect. Where's your rig?"

He managed to heal me. Sam looked thoughtful. "Could be up your ass. No? Oh, right, no room left."

"Charming. How's Beatrice? I hear she left you."

"Still smart enough not to fall for your bull."

"How does this man know how my magic works?" Vyse asked.

"He used to be a wayman," Sam said.

"I still am," Laz said.

"Bullshit, your rig was..."

"Stolen?" Laz smiled. "And right before they drummed me out, such an unfortunate coincidence."

The crowd grew. A few tourists wearing lederhosen took snapshots, light from the flash cubes bright even in daylight.

Sam smiled at the tourists, posing as he added, "For gross misconduct."

Laz chuckled. "I suppose you've never smuggled anything to pay for that little paintjob fetish of yours? Or brought denizens of another world here?"

"He's a stowaway," Sam said.

"You're an idiot."

Vyse raised an eyebrow. "That does seem to be a common misconception."

"Trust me, it's all too true," Laz said. "Your rig, Bridger, or he shoots."

"Too cowardly to do it yourself?"

Laz extended a hand. "The gun, please."

Mister Gruff extended the gun. Sam head-butted Gruff, knocked the gun from his grip, and dove at Laz. "Vyse, run."

Byron formed a crystalline staff in Vyse's extended hand.

The crowd offered a smattering of applause.

Laz's claims that Vyse couldn't do magic hadn't satisfied his hired muscle. One drew a T. J. Hooker Colt revolver and pointed it at the magus. A shimmering energy barrier appeared, weak and thin much as it had when he'd tried to protect Sam. Vyse summoned a sphere of crackling electricity.

Several watchers oohed.

The thug frowned at the witnesses but shot the magus before he could attack.

A bullet ripped through the shield into Vyse's leg.

"You only have so much life force to expend, magus," Laz ducked Sam's fist. "Especially now. Surrender and you'll be taken home."

Sam blocked Laz's left hook and jabbed the man's midsection. "He was a liar ten years ago, brother, I doubt he's joined a priesthood."

Sam and Laz fought, even in strength and pugilistic skill. Both landed occasional blows, blocking or dodging the other's strikes.

Vyse's staff transformed into a scythe, sweeping toward the man who shot him. The glowing blade slid through his foe's head and shoulders without slowing. Blood flew everywhere as the four pieces tumbled to the ground.

A few startled cries punctuated the otherwise overwhelming roar of approval from the crowd.

A tourist gasped. "Wow, these special affects..."

"Dude, totally awesome!"

Mister Gruff scrambled for his pistol. Another thug fired at Vyse. Despite pulling the trigger over and over in blind terror, the bullets improbably missed every one of the man's point-blank shots.

Sirens raced closer.

"You have to go, Vyse. Run, please."

Laz's fist broke Sam's nose. The familiar pain blinded Sam. Blood flooded his face, flecking onto Laz with each heavy exhale. Laz dodged Sam's counterstrikes.

"Cops," Laz said. "Clear out."

"But what about Paul?" Mister Gruff demanded.

"Paul's been humpty-dumptied—unless you've got a lot of Superglue," Sam said.

"He's right, nothing we can do." Laz said. "This isn't over, Bridger."

"Bring it on, brother."

They bolted into a storefront, shoving people out of the way. The audience, morbid or confused, shouted objections. Sam considered fleeing, but the sirens' proximity, his aching face and quickly worsening headache teamed up to dissuade him.

Sam flopped to the bloody pavement, panting through still trickling blood. Lightheadedness slowed his thoughts. *Cops'll...they'll sort this out then I can track down Vyse.*

A beefy policeman with a thick mustache appeared above him.

"Glad you're here, brother. They--"

"Cuff him."

17: Truth and Circuses

Sam Bridger

Sam sat in a tiny room. Handcuffs bound him to a ring set in a scarred and stained old table. Tape and gauze forced breath through his mouth. His chair lacked one caster, forcing him to teeter back and forth trying to discover the perfect balance point. A long mirror with a y-shaped crack hung opposite him. He made faces at it.

The door opened. Sam turned his head—eyes still scrunched and tongue hanging lopsided from his lips. Two men entered. The first glowered at Sam with considerable effort. The tall, black glowerer wore impeccably pressed slacks, shirt, and sports jacket. A crucifix tie-tack held a boringly plain tie. He leaned up against the mirror with his arms crossed.

The second man barely cleared five feet. He had long, fine brown hair, two-day's stubble and khaki Bermuda shorts. He pulled the chair opposite Sam, folding one leg beneath him as he sat. Intelligent blue eyes examined everything and everyone.

Good cop.

His partner deposited a folder on the table and stepped back to the mirror.

And here's bad cop.

Good cop ignored the folder. Instead he picked at a dried glob of red jam camouflaged by his wrinkled Hawaiian shirt.

Sam watched him. "Does the jelly stain mean you've got a spare donut? Your guys arrested me on the way to lunch."

Good cop glanced at bad cop. Bad cop shook his head. Good cop turned back to Sam. "Sorry."

Sam shrugged.

"I'm Detective Errol King," good cop said, "This is my partner Erik Scarecrow."

Sam raised one brow at King. "Does that make you Scarecrow's missus?"

"*Detective* Scarecrow," bad cop snapped.

King shrugged, flipping open the folder. "You are?"

Sam pointed. "Right there on the top."

King chuckled. "Didn't see it there."

Sam shared a companionable smile. "Can't imagine you've seen too many of these forms."

King's amiable smile faltered. "You know governments, always changing the paperwork."

Sam laughed. "Got that straight."

Scarecrow slapped the table. "Why'd you kill him?"

"Good looking corpse, ancient Chinese secret?" Sam asked.

"Not my partner, that trucker," Scarecrow said.

Sam let out his breath. "Oh, that makes more sense, because your partner doesn't look that dead, and it's daylight so I'm guessing he's not a vampire. Could be a werewolf, I suppose, but they aren't actually dead. When's the next full moon? Should he be restrained?"

Scarecrow slammed a fist into the table. "Why?"

"Werewolves are dangerous, though not as dangerous as weretrees. I mean you wouldn't think it, but a weretree's bark really is more dangerous than a werewolf's bite."

"Shut up, and answer my question," Scarecrow said.

Sam opened his mouth but closed it again. He raised his hands as much as he could considering the cuffs and gesticulated.

King raised his brows. "What are you doing?"

Sam glanced at Scarecrow.

"You may speak," King said.

"I was using sign language to answer his question."

"It didn't look like sign language."

"You know sign language?"

King nodded.

"Cool, mind teaching me in case he tells me to shut up again?" Sam asked.

"You were answering me in sign language that you don't know?" Scarecrow asked.

Sam inclined his head. "Figured I'd wing it."

Scarecrow rounded the table, glowering down at Sam. "Witness report your friend killed that man with a crystalline scythe. You're going to tell me why."

"They have active imaginations?" Sam said.

"No, why'd he kill him?"

"If it wasn't a magic show, I imagine self-defense."

"Where's your friend? Where's the murder weapon, and where'd he get it?"

"No idea where he Houdini'd off to. There's no murder weapon as there was no murder and," Sam grinned. "Magic."

"You expect me to buy that?" Scarecrow asked.

Sam smirked. "We are in Vegas. Besides, where, exactly, do you think he could've concealed a scythe? Up his butt?"

A knock cut off any response. Scarecrow opened the door to reveal one man dressed in a clown suit and another in a roman centurion's outfit. The clown addressed the Roman. "Wait here."

The Roman nodded and took a seat in chairs lining the hall.

"Who are you?" Scarecrow asked.

"Ronald Went, Mister Bridger's attorney." The clown walked into the room; each footfall accompanied by a squeak.

"You're joking," Scarecrow said.

"Do I look like I'm joking?" Went sat next to Sam.

"What's with the getup?" Sam asked.

"I changed careers. I do children's parties these days."

"And Sparticus?" Sam asked.

"He gave me a ride," Went said. "Hard to drive in these shoes."

Sam grinned. "Man, if my hands weren't cuffed."

King's brow rose.

"I *really* want to squeeze the nose to see if it squeaks."

"It does," Went said. "What are the charges?"

"Accessory to murder," Scarecrow said.

Went glanced at Sam, brows high on his white forehead.

"Got jumped," Sam said.

"So you killed someone?" Went asked.

"No, brother, dudes jumped us, shot my passenger. He took it badly, summoned a scythe and cut the other guy into chunks."

"You're serious?"

"I so want to squeak that nose."

"Which brings us back to our question," Scarecrow said. "Where was your accomplice hiding the weapon?"

"He wasn't my accomplice, I barely know the guy, and where could he hide a scythe, really?"

"It could have been telescoping or modular," King said. "Or even hidden nearby in preparation to jump those men."

Sam gave King a sidelong look. "They jumped us, brother. I've got a couple dozen witnesses."

"Sam," Went said. "Maybe we should discuss this in private before you answer any more questions."

"I'm hungry, Ronnie. I haven't done anything wrong, and the only way out of here is to answer their questions."

Went frowned. "Don't incriminate yourself."

"How could I? I'm the victim...well, a victim."

"Witnesses say you struck first," Scarecrow said.

"Mister Gruff pulled--"

"Who is Mister Gruff?" King scribbled on a pad, never taking his eyes off Sam.

Sam shrugged. "Called him that cause of his voice. Gruff handed the gun he had in my back over to Laz--"

"Who's Laz?" King asked.

"Eugene Lazarus," Sam said. "Laz ordered Gruff to kill me, but I called him chicken. He demanded Gruff's gun so he could shoot me."

"So you knew this Mister Lazarus?" King asked.

"Unfortunately. Bastard tried to steal my wife...ex-wife."

"Sam," Went said.

"That's why you wanted to kill him and his associates?" Scarecrow asked.

"I didn't kill anyone, whether I wanted to or not."

"So you do want to kill Mister Lazarus," Scarecrow said.

Went's warning tone intensified. "Sam."

Sam snorted. "Sam Bridger's a lover, brother, not a killer. Bastard can skinny dip in battery acid or blue whipped cream like a goddamned maraschino cherry for all I care."

"How do you know Paul Stratford's killer?" King asked.

"He stowed away in my rig," Sam said.

"So you're a trucker?" King asked.

"You've seen my licenses, kind of pointless paying for the extra if I'm puttering around in a Gremlin."

"Why would you let a stowaway continue riding with you?" Scarecrow asked.

"I was taking him home," Sam said.

Disdain dripped from Scarecrow's lips. "What a good Samaritan you are."

"Be careful, Detective," Went said.

"Did he mention his name or where he came from while in your presence?" King asked.

"Name's Vyse. He's an alien."

Went tried to whisper in Sam's ear, but he waved Went off.

Disdain soured to contempt. "As in outer space?"

"Alternate universe," Sam said.

"You expect us to believe this killer is from another universe?" Scarecrow asked.

"He ain't from Tijuana, brother."

"Just how stupid do you think we are?"

"What's the scale?"

"God created one universe, this universe."

Sam chuckled. "You got that from him in person?"

"This isn't a laughing matter." Scarecrow seized Sam's head and forced him to look up into his face. "A man is dead, and you're telling us fairy tales."

Went leapt to his feet, bringing two squeaks from his long red shoes. "Unhand my client this instant."

"Erik," King said in a warning tone.

Scarecrow released Sam.

"Brother, you've got no idea how wrong you are."

"Fine, talk, straighten me out," Scarecrow said.

"God didn't create Earth. Our whole universe was a political stunt. Humanity, we're an accident."

"Is that so?" King asked.

"Yeah, the whole thing was cooked up by a bunch of self-serving assholes. Think twice before worshiping them, they're insufferable enough."

Scarecrow mimicked him. "You got this from them in person?"

"I work for them."

"You've met the creators of Earth?" Scarecrow scoffed. "How do you explain centuries of history?"

Sam shrugged. "Eleventh World's original creators died long before I was hired. I just work for the current jerks."

"Sam, maybe we should discuss this in private," Went said.

"This is all bullshit," Scarecrow said.

Sam turned his cuffed hands palm up. "Believe me or not, but when they told me it made sense."

"Who told you, your cult?" Scarecrow asked.

Sam glanced at King. "What's with him? It makes sense. Look how screwed up Eleventh World is. Nobody can screw up a project like ten self-interested politicians."

"Eleventh World?" King jotted down notes.

"Right," Sam said.

"Suggesting there are at least ten other worlds."

"Universes, really, but referring to Earth as eleventh universe is harder to say and some of the others make you sound like a leaky snake. Just better to say world."

Scarecrow paced, shaking his head.

"You said we were an accident? Like we crashed here and were abandoned by the galaxy's other space men?"

"Nah, brother, we're it. Nobody else out there."

"No intelligent life elsewhere in the universe?"

"What do you mean elsewhere?" Sam laughed. "Sorry, nothing but empty space."

"Mars?"

"The Taurons tinkered around with it a few thousand years ago, but I'm told the project lost funding."

"We just sprung into being then?" Scarecrow asked. "Poof?"

"Look I wasn't there, but one way or another we're the result of the universe's broken condom. You know how that is."

Scarecrow rounded the table and seized Sam. "I don't have to take your shit."

"Detective, unhand my client. This is my last warning," Went said. "Any more physical abuse, and I'll have your badge."

"Sorry to break it to you, altar boy, but the UPO never meant to create sentient life here."

"What the hell is a UPO?" Scarecrow asked.

"Opposite of a Down-O?" Sam asked.

"Bastard," Scarecrow said.

"Cool down, Erik," King said.

"No! A family man was chopped up on a busy sidewalk and this bastard's spewing bullshit to cement an insanity defense!"

"Insanity? Try self-defense. Now, I've tried to cooperate. I surrendered, endured your abuse, even told you shit that'll probably get all our minds wiped. Assuming Alabaster doesn't just shoot me."

"Who?" King asked.

"Grumpy dwarf who's auditing me."

Scarecrow threw up his hands. "Snow White now, see what I mean?"

"If our universe is empty, why is it so big?" King asked.

"Future expansion? Love nests for their mistresses?" Sam shrugged. "Something to do with positioning for new gates?"

"Gates to hell?" Scarecrow asked.

Sam glanced at his attorney. "Could we get another bad cop, he's starting to piss me off."

"You have to admit, Mister Bridger, this really does all smack of a bad joke," King said.

"That isn't my fault. Eleventh World - Earth - was created by committee and generally considered in hindsight as a colossal waste of tech and magic."

"Fine, this isn't an insanity defense, that you want to help us," Scarecrow said.

"Yup."

"Then you'll help us find this Vyse."

"Sure, dwarf wants me to take him home anyway."

"To another universe," King added.

Sam leaned back as much as he could. "You got it."

"So," Ronald said. "You've got witnesses that my client was defending himself. He's willing to help. I expect you to drop these ridiculous charges."

Scarecrow stared at the clown. "He's a crackpot with a clown for a lawyer. This whole thing is the biggest line of bullshit I've ever heard."

"I've told you all I know. If I find him, I'll be happy to turn him over to you. What more do you want?"

Scarecrow licked his lips.

"Sorry, brother, I don't kiss dudes."

18: Phone Home

Taleh

Taleh stared at her communicator. Kept off to prevent tracking, she only turned it on to check for messages. A recording waited beneath the image of Ambassador Hullis of Vuria. Dread filled her.

"Problem, Miss?" Varian asked

Taleh hesitated. "Maybe. Got a message from my older sister."

"Family is important."

She smiled. "True, but we don't always see eye to eye."

"You'll call her back?"

"I can't, not while I'm in Eleventh World.

"This is difficult?"

Taleh stared out at the dull red horizon beyond the atmospheric dome. After a time, she directed his attention to the large archway stretching two stories beneath the central dome. Missing plates and open access panels dotted the half-block long tunnel's sides. Unknown runes glowed strange throbbing light along its exterior.

"If the gate worked, leaving would be easy. Then again, if it did, I'd have no reason to dread the reason for her call."

"What is the hold up?"

She sighed. "Mite's replacement hasn't arrived. I don't have the technical knowhow to proceed without their assistance."

"Could I help?"

She laughed and patted his hand. "No, your efforts have been commendable, but this is a whole lot more complicated than just unloading cargo."

His expression grew odd.

"Oh, Varian, I'm sorry. I didn't mean it the way it came out."

"You do not respect me. Are you not attracted to me?"

"Yes, but we're from different worlds."

He gestured. "You are from Mars, I am from Earth, but we are both human."

"No, Varian, I'm not."

Shock darkened Varian's expression.

"I'm sorry. Perhaps I should return you to Earth."

Varian refused to look at her. "Maybe."

"Get your things, I can be ready in half an hour."

"As you wish." Varian walked away, dejected.

Taleh shook her head. This whole thing comes at such a terrible price. I can only hope it's worthwhile in the end.

Elmeddi

Elmeddi nodded his satisfaction. He'd thought to glean more information from Taleh in the attractive human body. Instead he'd suffered humiliation and forced labor. Continuously feigning ignorance nauseated him.

He'd forced the conflict, so she'd return him to Earth.

Elmeddi needed another body. Varian's flesh, already old, withered faster than expected under his energy drain. He'd managed to keep the evidence beneath the skin but knew the man's body would age horribly very soon.

The host also fought more than any other. Most bodies Elmeddi stole fought a little at first. Their wills faded to sleep and never woke again. Varian fought, constantly fighting back from odd angles and unexpected places.

Elmeddi needed a large body to extend its service, preferably one with weak willpower. The Guru of Sweating collected such people. The guru himself might've served, but his charges offered ample service. Besides, the curly-haired guru's voice made Elmeddi's crystal crawl.

Taleh

Taleh got the distinct impression the rogue wayman was flirting with her. His reputation painted him as a scoundrel, and not just with women. The smuggler had known contacts among villains in every UPO world.

Laz brushed fingers through his hair flashed a brilliant smile. "We ship your crate to Vuria. Two days later, we fetch it from the drop off point."

"Yes."

"Let's have dinner to celebrate. Perhaps you'll convince me to offer a discount."

"The price is fine as long as you don't open the crate."

He shrugged. "Ship whatever. You've paid for discretion."

Taleh offered her hand. "Deal."

"How'd a Vurian end up here without a passport?" Laz asked.

Taleh's breath caught. *How does he know I'm shipping myself?*

Laz's grin made her insides slither. "Only one crate, about the right size, and I noticed your illusion stutter when you came in."

"My business is my own."

Laz shrugged. "Have it your way."

Unbeknownst to Taleh, Laz left her crate not far from where her wink had watched Sam offer a small Vurian a doll. She'd turned down his offer to ride up front. The crate was uncomfortable, but a necessary sacrifice to ensure no one saw her with a wayman—disgraced or otherwise.

She didn't exit the crate right away either. When she did, Taleh rushed across the detritus of a ruined neighborhood, down a side street, and around a corner. Hidden in a cavity of a destroyed home, she removed her illusion.

Once more appearing native, she wove through a dying world to a preselected safehouse. The surrounding ruins wrung tears from her eyes. Her vision blurred enough she had to duck into cover just short of an intersection.

She wasn't alone.

No children played on lawns or in playgrounds. No adolescents flirted outside their regular hangouts. Instead, faces appeared and vanished behind curtains and corners.

The normality from her childhood departed with the incident, never returning to the poisoned world. Instead, her people suffered constant storms, terror, and death.

Propelled by the tadpole-like tail, she sped toward the four-story building awaiting her. A stiff wind fought her, but she floated up three stories to the ajar front door.

The single-family home presented a ruin of panicked haste. Plates of a long-desiccated home-cooked meal surrounded serving dishes and dead flowers.

Hopefully you reached an evac center before being contaminated and summarily exiled to a slow death by poison. She chewed her lip. Maybe a mercy compared to starving to death.

A pile of varied geometrically shaped plastic blocks rested on the carpet. Tears welled in Taleh's eyes. She had to leave, and to leave she first had to make a call. She powered her communicator, finding another message from Hullis.

She keyed a callback.

Hullis's voice snapped like a whip. "Where are you?"

"Does it matter?"

A sound of opening and closing doors filtered through the communicator, replaced by rushing wind. "It does if you've done what I think you have."

"Where are you?" Taleh asked. I'm not going to like her answer.

"On my way to you now."

"I won't be here when you arrive."

"Why couldn't you just trust me, Taleh? I told you the UPO would help our people."

Heat permeated Taleh's voice. "When? After half of us are dead? More? Three-quarters?"

"These things take time, little sister."

"It's been decades. Our world is dying."

"And that makes it all right to destroy another?"

"No idea what you're talking about."

"You will when we get you under questioning."

"You'd let people interrogate your innocent sister?"

"I recognized your voice, Taleh. Technicians confirmed it. You're the one holding Earth hostage."

Taleh scanned the home. "Our people need help now."

"They'll have to wait while the request is properly deliberated."

"Not if I have anything to say about it."

"You're only making things worse, Taleh."

"How? Even if what you say were true, it's your theory. No one else has any idea who's behind the threat or even why."

"You know a lot for an uninvolved innocent." Hullis sighed. "It doesn't matter. Once you're in custody, they'll know."

Taleh laughed. "If I'm the villain, you won't capture me."

"You always were too sure of yourself."

A flier buzzed Taleh's safehouse. The rounded structure shook. Taleh keyed her communicator to destroy itself, set it among the dinner plates, stepped into a corner and pretended to be furniture.

Armed Vurians rushed inside, Hullis right behind them. She floated in the room's middle while security scoured the place.

"Nothing but a burned-out communicator, Ambassador. Maybe she used a relay."

The soldiers withered under Hullis's scowl. "Search the surrounding area for anything suspicious, hiding places, whatever."

They saluted and floated out the door in a rush.

Hullis paced the room. "You may have learned guile, sister, but this can only end badly."

Taleh's stunning beam knocked Hullis from the air. She approached her unconscious sister. "Seems arrogance is a family trait. Objects are easier to disguise with illusion, sister, and can be large enough to cover two."

Taleh moved her sister to the corner she'd occupied and resumed her disguise. When security returned, they called out to Hullis before departing in search of the Ambassador.

Maintaining the illusion long enough for them to call off the search drove nails into Taleh's head, but she held on. When the coast was clear, Taleh squeezed Hullis and herself into the crate and waited for pickup.

Now I've got a UPO Ambassador. She bit her lip. *When did I become someone who thinks of her own sister as leverage?*

She sighed.

I'll save my people, no matter what it costs me personally. Besides, trussing up Hullis as leverage is a better way to prove I am serious than killing thousands.

19: Don't Blink

The Wink, Taleh's Agent

The wink tired of being a pillow. Waiting in Sam's vacant truck in an impound yard wasn't fulfilling its mistress's mission. So long as Sam Bridger remained incarcerated, the wink was failing.

It'd taken a day of waiting before something the locals called detectives came, looked around, and impounded the truck. They, like all humans, remained blind to the wink. The argument over Sam's fate served a helpful distractor.

A human named Erik insisted they keep Sam indefinitely.

This won't do. Must obey.

Erik's hand touched the wink. Instinctually, it memorized the human. The wink had no idea why or how it absorbed the thoughts, memories, and appearances.

The wink was. That sufficed.

The detectives abandoned searching to procure sustenance.

The wink concentrated on Erik. Its skin writhed in a thousand directions painlessly. Limbs budded. Hair sprouted. Outer skin replicated clothing while remaining anchored to the wink's core mass. The wink became Detective Erik Scarecrow.

Adopting the subject's gait, it strolled into the police precinct holding Sam Bridger. Things within the Erik Mind conflicted, confusing the wink's simple mind. Detective Erik Scarecrow believed itself a superior creature but downplayed his massive advantage for dubious reasons.

Why lie? Why be as you aren't?

The wink was.

It entered, noticing devices and people. The wink studied a large image writer of some kind, noting the simple key interface for possible use.

"Detective Scarecrow?" a blue uniformed human asked.

The wink emulated Erik's voice. "Yes?"

"Did you need something?"

"Release Sam Bridger."

"Weren't you still investigating?"

"Detective King is correct."

The blue uniformed man blinked. "What did you say, sir?"

"The wayman is not at fault and should be released without further delay."

"Wayman?"

"Trucker."

The officer chuckled.

A man in a moth-eaten suit approached both of them. "You finally came to your senses?"

"I don't know about sense, Mister Went, but for now, Detective Scarecrow has decided your client has sufficiently established his innocence."

"Wonderful," Went said. "How long will it take to process his release? I have a birthday party at seven."

The officer chewed his lip. "It might take a--"

"Sam Bridger must be released without delay," the wink said.

"Paperwork'll take a while," the officer glanced toward the captain's office. "And I'll need Cap's approval."

The wink assumed Scarecrow's sour disposition. "Wait here."

The wink strode across and into the captain's office. A plump, balding man glanced up from his phone. An airy voice emerged from it. "Tell me what you'll do to me next, honey."

The wink cleared Scarecrow's throat.

"Hold on a moment, Desire," the captain covered the phone's receiver. "What the hell's the matter with you, Erik? How many times have I told you people not to enter without knocking?"

The wink glanced at a desk nameplate. "Captain Frank Holt, I need you to approve the release of Sam Bridger."

"You said Bridger was dirty."

"I changed my mind."

"Your partner still agrees?" Holt asked.

The wink nodded.

"I need to hear it from him."

"He is fetching sustenance."

Captain Holt narrowed his gaze. "Well, come back when he returns, and knock next time."

The wink laid a hand on Holt's shoulder. "I need your approval now."

Holt lifted the phone back to his ear. "I'm busy."

"Would your spouse approve of this phone call? Or Jessica in dispatch?"

Holt purpled. "Get out of my office before I demote you to parking meter reader."

"Reading is fundamental."

"Out!"

The wink exited, winking forms from one step to the next. It approached Went and the other officer. "I talked to Scarecrow. Release Sam Bridger immediately."

"I'm still working on the paperwork, Cap."

"Get it done before I demote you to parking meter reader."

Crossways

The officer stared at Captain Holt as if he might be kidding. "Are you wearing platform shoes, sir?"

The wink increased Captain Holt's frown angle. "Pardon?"

"You look taller somehow."

"Finish that paperwork." The wink watched the room. The moment all attention focused elsewhere, he winked back to Scarecrow's shape. "Is the release ready yet?"

Went did a double take. "Didn't see you return, detective. I'd like to thank you. I know Sam can be difficult, but there's not an evil bone in his body. He's actually quite naïve."

Scarecrow's face smiled. "We know. He is perfect that way."

20: Fish Out of Water

Sam Bridger

Sam shook Went's hand on the front steps. "Thanks, Ronnie."

"Stay out of trouble, eh, Sam?" Went handed over some paperwork. "This releases your truck from impound. Keep your release paperwork against misunderstandings."

"Why?"

Went shrugged. "Arrests get sent around to other agencies. Releases get less priority. Just best to keep a copy."

"You'll keep one on file too?"

"Sam, I'm not a lawyer anymore."

"You weren't disbarred, were you?"

"No."

Sam grinned. "Then you're the only clown I want between me and the electric chair."

Went cradled his face, shook his head, and groaned.

"Later, brother, just send me a bill."

"How about I don't bill you, and you don't call me again?"

"We both know it won't work out that way." Sam chuckled. "What do I owe you?"

Crossways

Sam drove up and down the strip looking for Vyse and a large enough parking spot for his rig. Once parked, he started his search in the nearest Vegas buffet. Despite thoroughly exploring three lobsters, several slabs of prime rib and a slew of side dishes, he found Vyse nowhere—not even in the desserts.

Fed, Sam headed back to his truck to resume searching the strip. Laz's people slunk around his rig.

Sam shouted at the top of his lungs. "Stop! Thief!"

The truckers turned hijackers bolted for the shadows.

Sam chuckled, strolled up to his rig and drove off.

"Bridger, answer already," Alabaster said.

"Hey there, Al."

"Where the hedrin have you been?"

"I got arrested, thanks for not answering the phone when I called for help by the way."

"That will be addressed. Why were you incarcerated?"

"Eugene Lazerus and his goons accosted us, the same guys that tried to hijack my rig. Vyse cut one into thug chunks. Cops showed up, saw the mess and arrested yours truly."

"Did they capture the magus?"

"Nope, he vanished."

"Do you know where he is?"

"Been searching, but so far I've got no clue."

"Stop looking. I need you working. Get to Quiss, take princess pain-in-the-butt home and report in."

"But I can't just leave Vyse alone--"

"Do what I tell you!"

Sam sighed. "You got it, chief."

It took some time for Sam to make his way across the country to the nearest Quiss crossway. Sleep weighed down his eyes. His blinks got longer and longer.

"Sam."

He shook himself awake. His eyes closed again.

"Sam!"

He bolted upright. He checked the comm, but the incoming message light was off. "Thought I heard, must be dreaming, right bud—"

Bob's head projected over the passport's surface.

"Now I know I'm dreaming."

"You're not," Bob said. "Now shut up and listen."

Sam made sure he was still in his lane before addressing Bob's head. "Are you my father? Am I from an alien planet destro—"

"Mother f—," Bob stopped herself. "*Shut up,* Sam! This is important."

Sam snorted. "That would've been, too."

Bob's expression forewarned of impending metal mastication. Her voice was pleading. "You don't have anything to do with what's going on, do you?"

"What're we talking about?"

"You wouldn't say, hypothetically, destroy Earth?"

"We could probably do without the IRS...maybe aerobics instructors, I swear the anorexic things are one missed meal away from cannibalism, but no, not the whole planet."

"Then look, we're not supposed to—"

Alabaster's voice boomed in the background. "Miss Zephyr, what are you doing?"

Bob's eyes fixed on Sam's, probably conveying something. Her image blinked out without transferring understanding.

Sam pulled off at the next truck stop. He caught a couple hours sleep and showered. Still a little groggy, he stocked up on heat-lamp burgers, drinks, fuel, and caffeine pills.

The silence in his cab became oppressive. He reached for his CB, broadcasting his opinion on things to the open airwaves.

A thick southern California accent belonging to a trucker with the handle Beach Babe replied. "Like, I don't get what you mean, Bridger."

"Come on, BB, you have to see it."

"Oh my god, there's no way Reagan's a robot."

"His hair never changes."

A gruff tenor crackled over the CB. "You better pick your next words real careful there, paco. I won't have you maligning our president?"

"Who's that?" Sam asked.

"Rolling Soldier."

"You've got it all wrong, RS. Sam Bridger *is* a patriot, serving the greater good while you're all drowning in suds. He doesn't have anything against good old Ray Gun Ron."

"You suggested he's inhuman, paco, and you're portraying American voters as stupid enough to elect a machine."

"Like, there was this one guy they re-elected even though he was dead," Beach Babe said.

"No, guys, hear old Bridger out on this. Our big cheese being Ronnie the Robot is a good thing."

"Like, totally not getting how."

"Better impress us if you know what's good for you, paco."

"A robotic president would be fair and impartial, right? Above being bribed. I mean, how could people manipulate him?"

"Watch who you accuse of being bought, paco."

"But see, being a robot makes him incorruptible. No biases...except maybe regarding the price of oil."

"You've, like, lost me again."

"Well, he wouldn't want to get tin-manned. Sam Bridger's rule number one for productive government, elect robots."

"Thanks, but I vote for holding off Skynet as long as we can," a woman said.

"Hey, hey, I know that beautiful voice. That you, Lil Beaver?" Sam asked.

"One and only, slick talker."

"How're you doing, babe?"

"Just thanking my stars you aren't in charge."

"But think about all the love, baby doll."

"With robots?" Lil Beaver asked.

"Kinky, girl, but not what I meant." Sam said.

"Oh my god, sex robots? Like a man who never stops and only cares about me? Totally awesome."

"They all screw like machines anyway," Lil Beaver said. "Leastwise on batteries they'd keep going and going."

"Sam Bridger can be counted on to take care of his ladies."

"That's not how I remember it," Lil Beaver said.

"Lies. Slander." Sam exaggerated a scandalized tone. "You wound me, LB, and without ever offering Old Sam Bridger a chance to prove his amorous work ethic."

Lil Beaver's playful laugh filled the CB waves.

"Can't speak knowledgeably about robo-dudes, BB," Sam said, "but babe-bots kiss like a machine press and smell of 10w-40."

"What're you doing going French with a machine press?" Lil Beaver asked.

"Machine's need love too," Sam said.

"Ugh, like, grody to the max."

Lil Beaver laughed again. "You're too much, Bridger."

"And *that's* what you should remember about Sam Bridger's service to the ladies."

Sam's daffodil submersible fell into formation with a pod of creatures winged like rays but otherwise shaped like rhino-sized swordfish.

"You can do that shape, right, bud?"

Ren-2-3 didn't reply.

"Party pooper," Sam yawned.

Sam passed a convoy of aircraft carrier sized whales serving the Quissians by towing the huge seaweed bulbs used for buildings. Their work song permeated his hull, invoking another yawn. Sam got Ren-2-3 to sideline to the nearest way station. He edged through the other cargo submersibles and smaller aquatic species used for transporting crates floating around the parking area. Once docked, he grabbed a nap in the drivers' lounge, drifting off beneath an episode of Sharkhunter. Spicy suckerfish in a roll served as breakfast.

Rather have chili dogs, but it's close.

As a world, Quiss had a lot going for it. Their fair, peace-loving people made democratic governance look efficient in ways the United States never managed. That wasn't to say they didn't go to war. They had their selfish squids and negative neons just like any other sentient species.

Give or take vibrant colored hair and all of the water, Quissians reminded Sam of Australians. Always wondered if they evolved from sea monkeys instead of fish. His gut knotted. Better not let them know how many I let die as a kid.

Meeting the Quissian Ambassador settled Sam's guilt. Some Quissians definitely descended from sharks.

Sam arrived at Perudathe late in their evening, though neither bioluminescence nor electric lights ever dimmed. He docked inside Laris's loading bay, glad to be off his backside. He stretched, leaning back against his hands while trying not to teeter on the flexible plant-floor beneath his feet.

A Quissian woman with orange hair rather than the usual blue or green smiled at him. "You're the wayman, Sam Bridger?"

"That's me, beautiful."

"I've heard much about you."

Sam smiled. "Hope some of it was good."

An extra sway attached itself to her hips with each step. "Oh, Laris went on and on about how generous and kind and giving you were."

"That's me, candidate for sainthood. How long have you worked with Laris?"

"Not long." She stopped outside arm's reach and twirled a finger in her hair. "So handsome, too."

Sam's chest did an imitation of a puffer fish, absent the spikes. "Little butter on your tongue, darling."

"Want a taste?"

Tempting, but this fish doesn't smell fresh. "Surely, Laris mentioned fixing me up with his sister-in-law."

"I'd like you to help me, wayman."

"Call me Sam."

"Help me, Sam." She batted her lashes. "You're my only hope."

"Big blinding light and widespread homelessness in your near future?"

"What?"

"What's the problem, doll?"

She pouted and posed, becoming more vulnerable and more desirable at the same time. "There's this man."

"You want old Bridger to teach him a few lessons," Sam raised clenched fists. "Balboa style?"

She closed the distance, stumbling and falling into his arms. "No, just take me away—somewhere he can't find me."

"I'm not really supposed to take passengers."

"Please, Sam Bridger."

He rubbed his neck. "I'll talk with her warshipfulness, she might let you sit in the back with Phred until we can drop you at another city. Let me fetch my abductor and get a load from Laris. Then we'll--"

She pressed her lips against his in a rush, bringing to mind Laris's apron. Her fingers caressed the back of his head, descending tingles washing away thoughts of clothing.

"Take me to your world."

"Not supposed—"

"You have a wife waiting at home? A woman in every port awaiting manly Sam Bridger?"

"Sam Bridger's a free agent, baby doll, never again to shackle down."

"So sad. It's in your eyes, knowing what it's like to be with someone but feel so very alone."

She kissed him.

"What's your name, doll? I usually prefer not to make out with strangers."

"Rayelynn."

Sam licked the taste of her from his lips, but she pressed her mouth to his again. "No strings, just passion shared between two wounded souls. Please, take me where he can never follow."

She's hurting, afraid. I know I shouldn't, but someone needs to help her.

Laris often tried to fix Sam up with Vella, and Laris wasn't the type to want his sister-in-law in an impossible relationship. Sam swore he'd never chance foisting another disastrous accident on an innocent woman. Vella's overtures had tempted him, but nowhere near as much as this Rayelynn.

It's been so long.

Her fingertips ran down his back. "Please save me. You won't regret it."

"Not sure you've thought this through. Nobody in my world has green skin, and you'd have a hard time getting medical care when they don't know Quissians even exist."

"Everyone in your world is ignorant of us?"

"Not everyone, but almost."

She raised wide eyes to his. "Is there nowhere you could take me?"

Sam opened his mouth. Several Ryaloxian water worlds sprang to mind. The Feirinese were different, but she could probably survive there, universes away from whomever she fled.

And neither of us would end up hurt.

"Might be a place—if you're not ill suited to the other universe."

"I trust you."

"Alright, babe, let me think it through while I get my order." Sam strode toward the office.

Rayelynn grabbed his arm. "Don't...don't leave me. I'm frightened."

"Come along then, I'm only going up to the office."

"No, take me away, please!"

Sam frowned. "Don't you need to get your things first?"

She shook her head. "I'm afraid to return to my quarters. He might seek me there."

"I'll go with you."

"No, please, Sam Bridger." She traced kisses up his neck. "Take me away right this moment. I promise reward."

Sam rubbed his neck. "Guess her worrisomeness will be sleeping. Let me place my order, and we'll go."

"I'll do it." She hesitated. "I work here, after all."

Sam shrugged. "Okay, I need a hundred disguised barrels."

Rayelynn glanced at his rig. "Do you have an aiathynn waiting outside?"

Sam chuckled. "It'll fit, trust me."

With a last rigward glance, she disappeared into Laris's office. Sam opened up his passenger door and tidied up the seat. He turned to find her nearly atop of him.

"Order's placed."

"Great, did you need my card?" Sam asked.

"You can pay when you return."

"Okay. All aboard."

She entered the submersible and Sam strolled across the fluid floor to his door.

"Sam Bridger," Laris called.

Sam stopped. "Evening, Laris. How's the wife?"

"You must stop where you are, Sam Bridger."

Sam cocked his head. "Why?"

"You're in grave danger."

Sam looked down at the floor. None of the plant had withdrawn to offer a sudden plunge, and he was a good swimmer in any case. He bounced up and down on the floor to check its stability.

"Feels okay to me."

"This is not the danger I mean, Sam Bridger."

Sam opened his mouth when he felt two cold metal barrels press against the back of his head. Sam sucked in a sharp breath and tried to glance behind him. "Really, Niri? Again?"

Rayelynn answered. "Get in the sub, wayman."

Genuine fear in Laris's expression made Sam's stomach slither. "What's going on, Rayelynn?"

She knocked him in the head with the barrels and pressed his shotgun into his back. "In."

"She doesn't work for you?"

"No, Sam Bridger."

"So her whole act, the whole seduction, was a con? Again?"

Rayelynn's breath felt hot on his neck. "And you fell for it, my big, strong hero. What a boob."

Niri appeared behind Laris, swords in hand. "Release the wayman, villain."

Phred followed, his small blowgun cradled close to his body as he edged sideways for a shot.

Sam raised his hands with exaggerated slowness. "Nobody does anything rash."

Rayelynn bopped him with the shotgun barrel again, seized his collar and pulled him against the barrels. She positioned him between her and the others. "Boob's right. No sudden moves or we'll all need a new ride."

Niri's voice was steel. "You'll not harm this man or--"

Rayelynn hit Sam again, dragging him toward the driver's side. "Oh, I'm sorry, you were saying?"

"It's okay." Sam offered Phred a significant look. "No need for violence. I'll go peacefully for a *change*."

Niri took three steps forward, causing Rayelynn to bow Sam's back against the gun. "Stop or he dies, and you get the next shot in the face, desert bitch."

Phred grabbed Niri's arm, cowering beneath an angry glare turned against him. He whispered apologies and explanations that narrowed her glare. She sheathed her blades. "Take him. I care not, just go."

"So very generous of you. In, wayman."

Sam climbed into the truck. For a moment, he considered kicking her from the higher ground, but decided to let her take position behind him as originally planned. She settled into position as Phred once had.

Sam piloted his rig at gunpoint. Really going to miss granddaddy's shotgun.

He returned a short time later. Sam turned over a creature to Laris. She was mostly neon platypus with a bit of ant and boulder spliced in at random angles but no brightly lit boobs.

21: A Good Deed Repaid

Sam Bridger

Sam's rig emerged from the Quiss waygate pulling a double trailer. It pulled out of the second waygate with three barrel-laden wagon beds.

"You're a harder man than I knew, wayman," Niri said. "But equally generous."

Sam tried to summon his best smile, but grief weighed down the corners of his mouth. "She killed those men."

"And you served honor and justice."

His smile kindled. "You didn't feel that way when I did it to Phred."

"You restored Phred and might have restored the girl."

"If they hadn't..." Sam shuddered.

The sharks hadn't cared what her shape had been.

"You came back for us armed with honor rather than force, and obtained water for my tribe, despite your short nemesis."

"Al's not that bad."

"I'll see to it the slave Corlan and your UPO are notified of your generosity."

Sam laughed. "Thanks, but, telling them I'm breaking rules isn't likely to help me."

"No one will know you purchased the water as collateral until I sent back the earth."

"That wasn't my intention."

"But it is how it resolved, bearer. My mother shall grant you half the profits of any earth you return to Quiss on our behalf for perpetuity."

"Helping me get a pregrowth geonode would be thanks enough."

Phred sucked in breath.

Sam glanced back. "Did I say something wrong?"

"Such things are valuable and well-guarded," Niri said. "Why would you need your own kingdom on Dorsun?"

Sam rubbed his neck. "Nothing like that, princess. The UPO charged me to pick one up, but Ambassador Corlan--"

"Slave Corlan," she corrected.

"Right. Well, he stopped us from picking it up. Alabaster was furious."

"By what right did he refuse?"

"He claimed it wasn't in Dorsun's best interest."

Niri glanced back at the massive load. "He is male, and ignorant."

Sam glanced at her. "Princess, with respect, that he's male doesn't make him ignorant. I don't think he is, either. He was playing his own game."

"You'll take us to him," Niri commanded.

"Any chance I've earned a please?"

Her expression suggested he'd shoved her mouth full of Zotts fizzing candies. "Please, wayman."

Sam bowed. "Your wish is my command, Princess Niri."

The flicker of a smile played at the corners of her lips.

There, I've finally cracked her candy shell. A few more trips on her behalf I might score a dinner date, maybe a movie, with the perfect woman – one that'd never take me to bed.

Corlan looked down his nose at Niri. "With respect, Princess Niri, you're unaware of the true circumstances."

Sam sucked in a breath.

Niri bristled. "Then explain them, slave, in small words a Sun Cavalier might understand."

Corlan leveled furious eyes on Sam but smiled at Niri. "This wayman has deceived you. His world is bluffing the UPO to acquire concessions they don't deserve."

"What're you talking about, dude?"

"You're not permitted this knowledge," Corlan said.

"You shall forbid me, as well?" Niri asked.

A spider couldn't have offered a creepier smile. "You're not a tribal leader, Lady."

"You'll deliver us the geonode the wayman requires."

"I won't," Corlan snapped, adding, "for the good of Dorsun."

"I'll see your mistress."

"No."

Niri scowled. "Phred."

Any doubts Sam might have had about the manservant's skills evaporated as he leapt to action. He took hold of Corlan and levered him to a kneeling position in front of his mistress. Just as quick as Phred, Corlan reversed the grip.

Corlan's retinue stepped up, hesitating when Niri turned imperious eyes upon them. They seized Phred and pinned him to the ground beneath their blades.

Corlan rose, dusting his brown aba. "You have attacked the Dorsun representative to the UPO. Your mistress will be notified through channels. I won't have you imprisoned in the meantime out of deference to a Sun Cavalier. You have my mistress's leave to depart."

Niri closed, their noses almost touching. "I'll see you whipped for this, slave...or drowned."

"This meeting is over," Corlan said.

Sam laid a hand on Niri's arm. She snatched it away, but he persisted. "Princess, a lady of your caliber shouldn't soil your hands with such a bastard."

Corlan darkened, opening his mouth. Sam's fist bloodied the open target, sending the desert warrior to the ground, absent a tooth.

"You take her ladyship to your leader nice and proper, or I'll knock your teeth out and embed them in your forehead."

"You've just signed your death sentence, wayman."

"Got a pen? I'll autograph it for you." Sam slammed another fist into Corlan as he rose. The Dorsun man went down again. "Dear Caroline, best wishes on your trip to the dentist, love and kisses your friend Sam."

Phred snorted.

Corlan sprang to his feet, but Sam swept his first leg as soon as he put his weight on it and brought another fist down into the man's face. "Apologize to her ladyship."

"Let me regain my feet and fight me fair."

"Why? I look like a knight to you? Round these parts they have to have breasts."

"Seize him!"

"We'd have to release the manservant," one of the guards said.

"Think hard about your next decision, Carol." Sam hummed game show theme music.

Corlan rose.

Sam ducked in for another hit but reversed it into a feint which drew out Corlan's retaliation. Sam dodged to one side and drove a fist into Corlan's face again. "Oh! The kid takes him down again and the crowd goes wild! Apologize, creep."

Corlan spat blood. "You'll die for this."

"He will not," Niri said. "Sam Bridger, I charge you in the name of the house Hivrus, execute this slave."

"Sorry, your womanliness, beating down jerks I can do, but I don't do executions. Why not just do it with those blades?"

"She can't," Phred said. "Much as he's insulted her, she's not allowed to slay another mistress's slaves without leave."

"But she can have me do it?" Sam asked.

"You're a water bearer," Phred said. "Immune to many laws and shielded from others, even so--"

"Phred," Niri snapped.

"Yes, Mistress."

"If you don't slay him, he will hunt and kill you, wayman."

"Like to see him catch me." Sam bounced around making high pitched woohoo noises. The others stared at him.

Corlan wiped blood from his mouth as he rose.

Sam let him.

He spat blood on Sam's boots.

Sam darkened. "Apologize, butt face."

"I owe her no apology for performing my duties."

"Naw, man, you soiled my boots," Sam said.

"The dead deserve no remorse."

"Oh, I've had just about enough of you. One more comment like that and I'm going back to my truck."

"Flee your fate, coward, if you think you can."

Sam stomped toward the exit.

"You would flee, wayman?" Niri asked.

"Flee, hell, I'm getting my tire iron."

"You said you wouldn't execute him," Niri said.

"I won't, but I'm feeling real flexible on the subject of kneecaps and genitals."

Sam returned to find Corlan reinforced with a dozen more guards. He rubbed his neck and debated returning to ask Ren for another. He took up position next to Niri and slapped the iron against his palm. "Alright, boys, who wants a career in midget opera?"

22: A Desert Gift

Niri

Niri assessed the tableau, analyzing attack scenarios and strangling back rage on the brink of shattering her calm façade. The wayman fought well, if sloppily. Unfortunately, primitive sensibilities hampered him. Phred would prove a harder opponent than most expected of a small slave but held and guarded by four men limited his options.

She met Corlan's eye. He'd denied her an audience, defied her commands. Before her eye-opening trip to Quiss and Phred's relations of life on Earth, she'd not have questioned their loyalty. Now, there seemed little reason to expect his men to be any less disloyal.

Killing Corlan outright seems the best tactic. She sighed. The world was simpler when neither males nor slaves exhibited minds of their own.

Sam Bridger evidenced the flaw in her dogma. He was loyal without a lash or collar. True he originated from a different world and culture, but even so his influence had infected Phred with growing independence.

I'd chastise him if his new strength wasn't oddly heartening.

If not kill Corlan, her next best tactic involved charging Phred's captors. The attack would be expected, sacrificing much. Niri's question escaped her mouth before she could restrain it. "Does your mistress still live?"

"Of course," Corlan's haughty expression remained unreadable. His guards weren't as schooled. Fear herded blood from their faces.

"Release my manservant and we'll be on our way—my word as a Cavalier."

Corlan's smirk practically demanded she hurl her sword into his gut. "Of course, Lady. I'll let you go. I trust your word."

Sam scowled. "Why?"

"Wayman, please," Niri said.

"Fear not, fool, I'll explain before killing you if she does not."

Niri seized Phred's robe the moment he was up. Her manservant resisted; eyes fixed on Corlan.

"Slave," Niri snapped.

Everyone but Sam and Corlan tensed.

"We're leaving," Niri said.

She caught his expression when Phred obeyed. Fury, contempt and Corlan's certain death filled him. Either he remained ignorant of their peril or uncaring.

Sam marked her expression. Anticipation drained from him. "Always invited to the ball, but never get to dance."

Niri suppressed a smile. Giving in might fuel his growing interest. She led them back to the wayman's wagon, taking in breath once outside his city.

"Where to, your highfalootinness?"

"My mother, with all haste."

"Sure, but if there's a convenient waygate along the way, I need to stop for...," Sam grinned. "essentials."

"Your claims are ridiculous, child," Lady Hivrus said.

"I assure you, mother, it is true."

"You've seen her body?"

Niri counted to ten. Her mother's arrogant attitude raised ire and frustration at the best of times. After dealing with Corlan, Niri's limit grew dangerously close. "I saw it in their eyes, mother."

"I'll not say a foe's eyes cannot reveal murderous intent, but you're talking about males. Men do only as they're told."

Sam snorted.

Phred hushed him.

Hivrus darkened. "You *will* be silent, water bearer."

"Yeah, that'll happen," Sam scoffed.

Phred paled.

Hivrus's voice rose. "What did you say to me, male?"

Sam ripped aside his face cloth. "Maybe you can understand better without this ridiculous thing."

"You dare bare your face in a lady's presence?!"

Niri cringed. The wayman's actions jeopardized everything. Once Lady Hivrus planted her feet, she didn't budge.

"Wayman," Niri warned.

"You're familiar with this man? You know his name?" Hivrus's tone struck Niri as false. *Fear? Of what?*

"Cool your jets, babe. Wayman's my title. Name's Sam."

"Guards!" Lady Hivrus covered her ears. "Cast this male into the pits!"

Guards rushed Sam.

"Whoa, hold up there." Sam darkened, drawing a shotgun from his aba's folds. "Look, baby doll, I've had just about enough of this male crap."

Shock enveloped the expression Hivrus turned on Niri. "Your slave is addressing me. Remove its head."

"Jesus, lady, don't you get it? Forgetting for one moment slavery is wrong, Corlan's traveled to another universe, experienced life without chains. He tasted power. He won't just relinquish it because you tell him," Sam adopted a falsetto. "'I've got boobs, and you don't, so surrender your power.'"

Blood fled Niri's face.

Hivrus's voice turned shrill. "We will not hear these things. Silence him! Silence him now!"

Sam frowned.

Charging guards broke his concentration. The wayman pointed his replacement thunder stick and flexed a finger. Smoke and fire exploded out of the weapon, doing the job of a hundred moths to the expensive rug.

"Back off, boys." Sam shifted targets. "As for you, stop playing the blushing virgin. You're not ignorant of the UPO."

Sam's disrespect mortified Niri, and the damage to the beloved rug she'd toddled on made her physically ill. "Wayman."

"We don't have time for all this. You've got a murdering usurper to deal with, and I've got a pickup to make."

"Sam, be silent," Phred whispered.

"You said I was basically immune," Sam shot back.

Niri interposed herself. If she can't see the wayman, perhaps she'll forget and dismiss him.

"You'd protect this creature from me?" Hivrus asked.

"You from him, mother." Niri squared her shoulders. "Disliking the messenger doesn't invalidate the message."

"His claims of mindful traitorous males are less credible from his lips, not more. I'll hear no more of this. I command you to depart and take this trash for execution."

"He saved me, mother, brought us the grow water, enabled our tribe to thrive like no other. We're in his debt."

Lady Hivrus glared down her nose. "Fine. Eject this diseased mongrel from our lands—our debt paid in sparing him."

"Mother." Niri took a deep breath. "His debt isn't so easily discharged."

"I have spoken, *child*. Do as you're told."

Niri bristled. The fight was over. The word 'child' reduced her from knight and heir to a little girl at her mother's hems. Her mother would hear nothing more. Niri seized Sam's bicep and led him toward the door.

Sam resisted at the doorway, offering his odd grin. "Lady, you seriously need to get laid."

Lady Hivrus stared at him, brows pushed together.

Sam pushed his shotgun barrel in and out of a ring of fingers and waggled his eyebrows.

Niri's eyes widened in shock. She forced Sam out before her mother realized his meaning. They wound out of the stone, cold palace, into surrounding buildings both temporary and permanent.

"This should be lost enough." Niri rounded on Sam. "That was dangerous, even for you."

Sam shrugged. "Sometimes the truth has to slap you in the face before you'll accept it."

"She could execute you."

"Your tribes got Quissian water which increased your farming output. Small tribes became big ones." Sam held her gaze. "I'd guess you need more water each year as the population continues to grow."

"My mother might well kill you before she realizes doing so would destroy our tribe."

Sam laughed. "Wonder where she gets that?"

"This is serious."

"Yup, but she and Corlan are your issue. I've brought you home. I'm leaving."

"You can't."

Sam flashed a smile. "Would you miss me, baby?"

Niri couldn't believe a single male could be so infuriating. "I owe you a debt. If it takes raiding the mines, you'll have that geonode."

"Mistress, there may be no avoiding bloodshed," Phred said.

Niri set her shoulders. "Then we'll water the desert."

Niri, Sam and Phred crouched just over the rise from an open pit mined for geonodes. Countless slaves dug the depression deeper. Odd beehive-shaped mounds dotted the exposed slopes.

Niri hollowed out the ground, drawing around it with her knife. Each time she extended a hand, Phred placed a pebble in her palm. She placed each to represent guards.

She assessed her creation, making small adjustments. Satisfied, she pointed. "This path will mean only killing four or five males to reach this incubator. We seize the geonode and return along the same path."

"Do not endanger yourself, Mistress. Let your lowly servant shoulder the risks."

Sam frowned. "Stow that horse crap."

"I wish only to protect my mistress."

Niri squeezed Phred's shoulder. Inwardly, she shuddered. I'm comforting a male servant. Mother would execute Phred on the spot if she saw. His death would sadden me.

"No, Phred, I need you here to support our retreat if an alarm is raised."

"Sounds to me like she respects your skills, my not-so-lowly brother."

"I respect the investment Mother made in his training." Niri snapped. "Nothing more."

Sam winked. "Whatever helps you sleep at night."

Niri gritted her teeth. "If an alarm is raised, we'll move to this exit."

"That'll bring baddies at us from either side," Sam said.

"True, wayman, but the terrain I chose is better suited for a fighting retreat."

Sam studied the map, rose on his haunches, and peered over the ridge. He rubbed his neck.

Niri watched him, wondering what thoughts brought his nervous tell to the surface.

"What's the name of Corlan's mistress?"

"Lady Shindra," Niri answered.

Sam marched over the hill, and threw a thick, halting accent over his shoulder. "Be right back."

When she recovered from surprise, she lurched forward to pursue. He crested the hill into plain view before she could. Niri settled along the rise's edge. Sam strolled into the pit as if heading to market. Phred took position on her right, blowgun and hand crossbow readied.

"I hate him," Niri spat. "He's going to ruin everything."

Phred gave her a sidelong look, a sad smile on his face. "He's an amicable fellow, Mistress, with pervasive charm."

"I have no such feelings for the reckless barbarian."

"Of course, Mistress, just as well."

Sam approached the mine's entrance.

"Speak, Phred. Why is it so?"

"Many women war for his affections." Phred smirked. "What hope would a Dorsun Princess have against the blacksmith or his former lover?"

Niri glared. "You've learned bad habits in his world, slave."

Phred pointed. "He's inside."

Niri weighed different plans for rescuing the moronic wayman. Her jaw dropped as he strolled into view with another male and two guards. They chatted animatedly and crossed to the nearest incubator.

The worker extracted and examined a pregrowth geonode before handing it over.

"Unbelievable," Niri whispered.

Phred chuckled. "Be glad he has no desire to rule."

"What man of his world wouldn't crave power?"

Phred gestured. "Sam Bridger."

Sam disappeared back inside the mining camp. He emerged some time later burdened with a satchel and two handfuls of meat kabobs. With a backward wave, Sam strolled back up the rise, tearing meat from sharpened sticks.

Niri and Phred stared up at him.

He offered his other kabobs. "Hungry?"

"Impossible," Niri whispered.

Sam grinned. "Why, thank you."

"Not you. There's no way you should've been able to walk into that mine and return with a PGN," Niri said.

Sam offered a kabob to Phred. "Not impossible, not even improbable really."

Niri's mind whirled. *It's impossible. He cannot have retrieved such a priceless treasure.*

"Show it to me, wayman. I must know if you were cheated."

Sam handed off his food and slid his satchel off. He removed a head-sized stone sphere. Light played about the surface where Sam's hands touched. The stone lit to Niri's touch as well. A euphoric rush like physical pleasure filled her.

"It is true," Niri gasped. "How?"

"I asked for it."

Phred choked on kabob.

The ramifications dizzied her. "No. Impossible."

"I told them Mistress Shindra commanded me, Corlan, to retrieve a geonode." Sam smiled. "Males do only what they are told. A male acting on his own is unthinkable."

Phred's choking transformed into full-fledged laughter. "He's right, Mistress. Lady Hivrus said so herself."

Slowly, subtly laughter filled Niri accompanied by a warm glow akin to basking in the morning sun. "My mother would be quite distressed for instructing your theft."

Sam shrugged. "I won't tell her if you won't."

23: Red Tape Vortex

Alabaster

Alabaster stood imperiously over a group of grey-haired old biddies and a nineteen-year-old blonde whose personnel file listed her from the San Fernando Valley. They lacked urgency and showed him even less respect. The older women stared placidly in his general direction and the blonde stared at nothing, too simple to fear him as she should.

Biometric readings confirmed them alive, but unimpressed.

"Don't you understand? Your world's survival depends on locating that shipment," Alabaster said.

The closest old woman smiled at him. "That's nice, dear."

The next nearest turned to the first. "What did he say?"

"The turtle's arrival depends on our singing, Wendy."

Wendy frowned. "We want a turtle here?"

A third elder patted Wendy on the back. "Might be turtle soup."

"I don't want turtle soup, Marge." Wendy turned to the first woman. "Did you order soup, Helen?"

"Rather have a cup of tea," Helen said. "Don't trust those foreign foods."

"There isn't any turtle soup," Alabaster snapped.

The blonde focused on him. "You are, like, such a bully, and holding their dinner hostage is like totally bogus."

"Your world will *end* if we don't find those records!"

"Calm down, sonny," Helen said. "You'll work yourself into a fit."

"She's right," Marge said. "Whatever snarled your shorts, it isn't the end of the world."

"Yes, it is," Alabaster said.

"Youngsters, always so melodramatic," Wendy said. "Maybe you *should* have some soup—calm you down."

"Or tea." Helen addressed the blond. "Bubbles, fetch some tea, would you?"

"Look, you old crones. We have to figure out how, when and where a bomb was shipped into this world."

Bubbles scowled. "Oh my god, I am not old."

"Did he say there were scones?" Marge asked.

"Don't cotton to foreign foods," Helen said.

"Might have blueberries," Wendy said. "Blueberries are very American."

"Strawberries too," Marge said. "With whipped cream."

"That's an American dessert, strawberries, cream and blueberries," Wendy said. "Red, white and blue like our flag."

"French flag is blue, white and red," Bubbles said.

"No it's not." Marge said. "They can't steal our colors."

"It is, actually," Alabaster said.

"They eat their dessert backwards?" Helen asked. "Damned unnatural foreigners."

Alabaster resisted the urge to euthanize the lot. "We need to search shipping records."

"What are we looking for?" Marge asked.

"A bomb," Alabaster said.

Marge halted midmotion, heart rate rose despite her calm exterior. She stood slowly. "Come with me, girls."

The others regarded her.

"Come on, we need to move to the break room," Marge said.

"Time for tea?" Helen asked.

"No, dear, someone hid a bomb in here," Marge said.

The other older women rose.

Bubbles's eyes widened. She leapt to her feet, voice screeching. "Like a bomb, bomb? Oh-my-god, oh-my-god, we're going to die."

Alabaster blocked the door.

Wendy pointed her cane. "Nice of you to shield us from the bomb, sonny, but you're supposed to block the door after we leave. Otherwise we'll be buried alive."

"Buried in jive?" Helen gasped. "Lordy, lordy, has disco made a comeback?"

"The bomb isn't in here," he said.

Marge planted gnarled hands on her hips. "Then why are you telling us to look for one?"

Alabaster took a deep breath, instructing his attachments to lower his heart rate. "The shipping records hold the information we need to find the bomb and defuse it."

"Why do we care about a bomb that isn't here?" Helen asked.

"Perhaps it got lost in shipping," Marge said.

"It could destroy the world," Alabaster said.

Bubbles returned to panicked babbling.

Helen frowned then shrugged. "World's had a good run."

"What I want to know is whose idea was turtle soup for a last meal?" Wendy said.

"I don't want soup for a last meal," Helen said. "Or anything foreign."

"Sit!"

Wendy pointed her cane. "Watch the blood pressure, sonny."

"He needs some tea," Helen said.

Alabaster balled his fists, his right creaking under the pressure. "We have to find the shipping manifest. That will tell us where the bomb is, enabling us to defuse it and save your worthless species."

Helen beamed. "He's our hero."

"Rotten attitude for a hero," Wendy said.

"Could we trade him in?" Marge asked.

Bubbles offered a dreamy smile. "Like for Harrison Ford?"

"Oh, excellent choice," Wendy said. "Solid hero material."

Marge pointed at Alabaster. "He looks pretty solid."

Helen sighed. "And oh, what a tushie."

Bubbles scowled, motioning toward Alabaster. "Him?"

"No, dearie, Ford," Helen said.

Wendy eyed Alabaster up and down. "Not that your tush is too bad."

"Wendy," Marge whispered in scandalized tones. "He's half your age."

Wendy shrugged. "World's ending."

"It won't if we find that bomb first," Alabaster said.

Helen straightened. "We'd be heroes."

"Still rather have Ford," Bubbles pouted.

"You and I both," Helen said.

Wendy pointed her cane. "To the records room."

The three old women led a geriatric charge to the room's rear. Marge dipped a hand deep into her neckline, fumbling around for several moments before triumphantly holding up a key.

"Whoa," Alabaster indicated their desktop computers. "Why aren't the shipping records on your computers?"

Marge frowned. "In that little box?

Helen opened the door to reveal a warehouse maze of filing cabinets. "How would it hold them all?"

Papers poked out of drawer edges, littered the floor and stacked Pisa-esque atop cabinets of every size and color.

Despite himself, Alabaster goggled. He scanned the visible cabinets, estimated record counts climbing across his HUD. "Computers were issued to you for digitizing company records, enabling faster and more efficient access."

Wendy patted Bubbles. "We hired Bubbles for the fancy typewriter work."

"Still don't see how they'd all fit," Helen said.

"Is there a filing system at least?" Alabaster asked.

"I like the white and blue ones," Helen said. "Very American."

"Won't use the black ones." Helen wrinkled her nose.

"Filing cabinets?" Alabaster said.

"Nothing wrong with the black ones," Wendy said.

"I rather like them, all big and shiny," Marge said.

"So there's not a system?" Alabaster asked.

"Sure there is," Helen beamed. "We put the ones we spilled tea on in the back row nearest the heater. Dries them faster."

His feeling of impending doom grew as Alabaster turned to Bubbles. "Please tell me you've entered all of these into the computer."

She smiled at him.

Alabaster took a cleansing breath. "Yes?"

She beamed. "Totally. It's just—"

His growing smile faltered. "Just?"

"The records, like, vanish when I turn the computer off."

Alabaster cradled his head. "Do you know how to save?"

"Of course," Bubbles said. "I'm a Baptist."

Alabaster slammed open the repair bay doors and stomped inside. Bob looked up from the engine she was bent over. He picked up previously uninspected tools. Several bore designs that violated information restrictions forbidding advanced technologies to immature societies.

He marched over to Bob's tool cart. Scowling, Alabaster turned each tool over in his hands as he scanned them.

Bob snatched one from his grip. "Mitts off my tools."

"You admit ownership then?"

"Of course I do."

"Who's guilty of smuggling them here?"

Her thin brows scrunched together. "No one. I made them."

"Botracl," Alabaster cursed. "These tools are clearly early Ryaloxian designs that Earth is not permitted."

Bob brandished her tool. "Every one of these is my own design, built and cast with materials *I* purchased. They don't belong to Crossways Transportation, the UPO or *you*."

"Inconceivable."

Bob scowled. "What, a woman isn't smart enough?"

"A human."

Bob collected and tucked away her tools. Alabaster reclaimed those he hadn't scanned. Increasing magnification, small inconsistencies from standardized norms became apparent. It seemed she'd developed alternate methodologies to achieve Ryaloxian equivalents.

"You made these?"

Bob released an exasperated sigh. "Didn't I just say so?"

"Why?"

She blinked at him. "Why? Why were the best old-world inheritances the craftsman's custom tools?"

"I don't see how your gifting rituals are pertinent here."

She rolled her eyes. "Skilled craftsmen build special tools over their working lifetime. I did the same."

"The UPO sees to it--"

Bob's pulse rate shot up and thermal readings of her neck and ears flared. "The UPO foists crap on us to repair garbage parts. We get bottom of the barrel rejects, yet we're expected to keep waymen on the road."

Alabaster circled the engine between them, performing a slow thorough scan. Several components resembled UPO issued stock, but material compositions marked them as local goods.

Alabaster gestured at the engine. "Will it run?"

"When I'm done, this baby will run better than a new one."

"I'd like to test that."

"Go ahead."

He scanned a nearby rig. The more data he compiled, the more modified components he found. Climbing beneath the truck, he found expert weld points, elegant redesigns of mediocre components, and respect he'd thought unwarranted for any human.

Alabaster rose. "I'd like to see more of your work."

Bob's wrench gestured around the bay. "Get your jollies."

"Unfortunately, it will have to wait. It's imperative I find a man named Ian."

She raised a brow. "Why're you looking for three-eyes?"

"Your records department requires significant training in computer use. Such is his job. I have a bomb to find."

"Yet you took time to criticize my tools."

Alabaster's fast exhalation swayed his mustache. "I may owe you an apology, Miss Zephyr. My frustrations biased me to finding fault. Instead, you've shown yourself to be no less capable than a Ryaloxian trained apprentice."

She bristled. "Apprentice?"

Alabaster offered her a smile. "No less than."

Bob pursed her lips. "That way, turn right at Buford and left at the power junction boxes. The door's labeled janitor."

"Buford?"

"The change field restoration chamber."

"Which you call Buford, why?"

She smiled. "No idea."

"This have something to do with Bridger?"

Her smile vanished. She dropped her gaze. "No idea."

Biometric readings and body language revealed the lie. He considered pursuing the matter, but other issues took precedence. He inclined his head and charged toward his destination. Heavy footfalls echoed clunk, thud, clunk, thud across the concrete.

Alabaster found the door locked.

Inside a robotic voice cried out. "Intruder alert! Intruder Alert! Death to the intruder."

Alabaster knocked.

A man's voice replied. "Busy testing systems, come back later."

"Open this door, now."

"Go away."

"Open this door or I will destroy it and dock the replacement from your pay."

"Who the hell?"

"Auditor Roxx."

The man behind the door cursed. Metal scraped across concrete. His response sounded strained. "Just a moment."

The door opened, revealing a lanky, bespectacled youth with wispy facial hair which yearned to be called whiskers. "Yes?"

"Why did you make me wait?"

"Securing sensitive materials."

Alabaster scanned the small room. A quarter arc of scrape marks led to one wall section not quite flush with the rest. Beside where the wall would stand when opened, four computer servers more powerful than the combined computational power of the planet rested on a steel rack. Barcode scans revealed them to be fifty-two generations obsolete by current Ryaloxian standards.

He turned his scanners onto the boy. The wannabe beatnik appeared at least one generation too new for his position.

"Identify yourself."

"Ian Ives the IT Guy." Ian extended a hand. "Call me three-eye."

Alabaster scanned the offered hand. "That appendage requires washing."

Ian blinked several times.

"Are bespectacled youths normally called four-eyes?"

"What? Oh, glasses," Ian chuckled. "That'd make me seven-eye, sounds like a bad sci-fi killer."

"I require you to perform your duties."

"Um, what duties?"

"You were trained to use the desktop and server computers entrusted to your care?" Alabaster asked, knowing the answer.

"Yeah, that's what makes me the IT guy."

"Your role was to train records department personnel. I need that training completed immediately.

Ian ran a hand through his hair. "Yeah, see, here's the thing. The ladies weren't interested in learning...," Ian's fingers made air quotes, "fancy typewriters."

"Including Bubbles Sugarhill?"

Ian blushed, absently kicking the doorframe. "Yeah, well, no, I mean I taught her how to input the forms."

Alabaster scowled. "But not how to save them?"

A bemused expression overtook Ian. "Every time I tried, she started talking about religion."

Alabaster folded his arms. "Fictitious deities make you uncomfortable?"

"Nah. Mama taught me never to discuss politics or religious stuff with coworkers."

"So you left her ignorant."

Ian shrugged.

"And possibly doomed all life on Earth to destruction."

"Yeah. Wait, what?!"

"There's a bomb - a bomb which you're forbidden from discussing with Sam Bridger. This device will destroy your entire universe if we don't find it—a task made nearly impossible without digital records."

He shook his head. "Oh, no, you aren't pinning this on me."

"You didn't teach her to save her work."

"No, I programmed the system to do it for her."

"She said when she turned her system back on all the work she'd done was gone."

"Of course," Ian said. "It just confused her."

Alabaster considered a moment, then nodded. "Her work is housed on the servers."

"Yes."

Alabaster clapped Ian on the shoulder. "Seems I won't have to execute you after all. Can I access it here?"

"Sorry, they didn't give us local monitoring equipment. We can access the servers from records."

"Lead the way."

Ian led Alabaster to the records room's back corner, shying away from Bubbles who watched him with absent fascination. He signed into the computer, opened a simple menu, and launched a database client.

Alabaster pushed him from the way and laid his arm next to the computer. A small cable snaked from his cybernetics to plug itself into the computer. He entered UPO master access sequence and followed it with a record search string.

The computer hummed to life. It beeped. Grinding noises preceded copious grey smoke. The computer burst into flames.

Ian yanked the power cable from the outlet. "Um, cool arm and all, but might be a bit advanced for this gear."

Bubbles stepped close, sniffing the air and staring. "It just, like, burst into flame, spondiferous, like, combustiness."

"Told you those things were from the devil," Wendy said.

"That's worse than being foreign," Helen said.

"There was like a devil inside?"

Alabaster gave her a flat glare. "Yes, but it fled with the magic smoke. You're safe now."

Ian opened his mouth to speak, met her eye and froze.

"Thank you." Bubbles turned then shrieked. "Oh-my-god, oh-my-god, exorcize this one, and that one, and that one."

Alabaster glared at Ian.

"What?" Ian asked.

The dwarf turned to Wendy. "Why don't you take Miss Sugarhill for some tea?"

"You heard him, ladies," Wendy said. "Let's go to the break room while they light the rest of the typewriters on fire."

"They shouldn't do that, should they?" Marge asked.

"Probably an insurance thing," Wendy said. "None of our affair."

Helen glowered at Alabaster. "Foreigner."

24: Bobcat

Tayanita "Bob" Zephyr

Bob sat in the break room, mulling over an untouched spinach salad. Her thoughts roamed universes from the end of her fork, gallivanting around trying to get himself killed.

The heavy clunk, thud, clunk of Auditor Roxx entered behind her. She didn't turn. The auditor wasn't her problem.

Sam is. Somehow, I need to protect him from Roxx...and himself.

The dwarf's presence lent a sort of pressure to her back. He loomed in silence, probably hoping he'd unnerve her. When she'd ignored him long enough, he spoke. "I have questions."

She shrugged. "I'm eating."

"Not from appearances. In any case, your lunch period ended three minutes fourteen seconds ago."

"Dock me."

"I already have."

Bob snapped her head around and glared.

Alabaster's good eye narrowed. The pinprick of red light in the other shrank. "There is a warrior spirit in you after all."

Bob fled his gaze.

"Your friend won't fare well after my report is filed."

Lava flared up in her stomach. Its heat erupted upward, rebounding off her shoulders to flow down into tightly clenched fists. "Why tell me? Don't you have records to find?"

"Your pitiful systems are being rebooted once more. I'd repair them, but that would allow your..." Alabaster cleared his throat. "...tech expert to play video games rather than work."

Bob swallowed rising bile. "What do you want from me?"

"I have questions."

"Ask them already."

"Why call yourself Bob?"

Bob's gut knotted. She'd expected him grill her about Sam, wheedling secrets out of her that might hurt him. She'd never expected that question. "Kind of a long story."

Alabaster glanced at her salad. "We appear to have time."

"Your world's doubtless more evolved, but here we've got very few women mechanics."

"Your evaluations show you to be an exemplary employee. Though your skills are primitive compared to a Ryaloxian, you've proven to be exceptionally competent."

"Thanks," Bob said. "I think."

"You do, a rare quality in your species."

Bob stood. "I've had about enough of your insults."

Alabaster smiled. "Yes, I see you have."

Bob poked the dwarf with her index finger. "The way you talk about humans is exactly the way men treated me. 'Thanks for answering the phone, sweetheart, grab the mechanic and let the boys talk this out.'

"'Got parts here for your boss, can you fetch me a cup of coffee, darling?' They'd refuse to explain their engine's problems or detail part variations because I'm female. Part suppliers assumed I was a ditz and tried to cheat me."

"Wouldn't most of your parts come from the UPO?"

"Right, prejudiced against for my species rather than not having a hose between my legs to do my thinking."

Alabaster listened.

"I got fed up. I was complaining to Sam." Bob's eyes grew wistful. "He clapped my shoulder, not condescendingly but like he really understood. 'You're the best mechanic there is, doll. When they treat you like that, you just show those morons what a bobcat you are with a wrench. If outshining doesn't work, beat them with it when they treat you bad.'"

The dwarf nodded. "You began using Bob on forms and requisitions, either used a voice modulator or played the dumb female calling for your boss."

Recalling the sudden attitude changes brought a bittersweet smile to her lips. Bob got respect where Tayanita didn't. The former warmed her, while the other remained disheartening. "Couple of times I hit rough spots when someone learned the truth, but for the most part they adapted."

"According to my records there was one male who did not."

The warmth in Bob's chest waned, doused by a sudden chill. Something rekindled the flame to a radiant glow twice as hot. "Yes, there was. Sam beat the hell out of him."

"Was this when your affection for Bridger emerged?"

Bob's stomach dropped through the floor. A plague of butterflies swarmed the emptiness left behind. "No, I mean he's a great guy, for an inconsiderate...idiot, like you said."

"My biosensors belie your words, Miss Zephyr."

Bob fell back into her seat. She fixed the dwarf with pleading eyes. "Don't tell him them, please. No one else knows."

Alabaster's laughter caught her off guard. For a moment she thought he was taunting her, but realized his tone wasn't teasing. "Your secret isn't one. Ever noticed the way Ms. Bridger treats you?"

Bob shrugged. "She's a bit prickly. That's just her way."

Alabaster shook his head. "No. You make her uncomfortable. She's jealous of you."

Bob's mind ran around, taking turns doing a spirit dance, jumping for joy, and wringing its hands. "She's beautiful. Sam loves her. Why be jealous of me? I'm just...me."

"She fears you'll claim him."

"But she divorced him. She doesn't even like him anymore."

"Yet she doesn't wish you to have him," Alabaster walked to the door. "She needn't fear the mouse, but perhaps the bobcat?"

She stared at his back.

"Please resume work, Miss Zephyr. I've arranged a delivery of replacement components for the countless overdue repairs."

25: Useful at Last

Vyse

Vyse wandered the streets, distancing himself from the bright lights and crowds. Older, quieter neighborhoods lurked only a few avenues away from shops, shows and other hubbub. Fading show posters covered alleyways' brick façades. Filth, strays, and vagabonds similar to himself filled their byways.

Disgusting.

<Here is where they hide the flaw in their system.>

Our way is definitely better.

Vyse scrutinized the huddled people. Dirty, hairy, and dressed in drab greens, they cradled paper-wrapped containers or the occasional stray.

One reached for Vyse's robes. Sunlight glinted off his outstretched left hand. "Please, some spare change, sir."

"I'm afraid I have none of what you call money."

He tugged Vyse's hems. "Come on. Just a little change."

"I sympathize, however, I insist you release me at once."

The vagabond scrambled to his feet coming nose to nose with Vyse. Unwashed body and pungent intoxicant bombarded the magus's nostrils. A dirty finger stabbed Vyse's chest. "You have any idea who I am... or used to be?"

"None."

"I was a captain of industry. My wife modeled for the best magazines. My children attended the finest schools."

Vyse frowned. "Why are you here?"

"Th-those blasted casinos stole everything."

<They stole his wife?>

Heat blossomed in Vyse's chest. His hands tightened until the nails bit into his palms. "Where have they taken your family? I shall assist in their rescue."

"What?" he asked. "No, they didn't take them take them."

"Then where are they and why don't you return to them?"

"They're still there, well, no, probably not. I lost everything. Perhaps with family, maybe friends."

"Return to them."

The man hung his head, twisting the ring on his hand. "I couldn't, not after so long, not after what I did to them."

"Time with loved ones is a fleeting treasure."

The wayward man's voice dropped to a tortured whisper. "No, forget it. Just give me some change."

"I have no moneys, but perhaps I can find what you're after, food, yes?"

He nodded, then shook his head. "No, not really. The buffets don't lock their dumpsters. "

"Then why?"

A gleam kindled in the man's eyes. "One coin. One quarter in the right machine, in the right moment I can have it all back, all of it. I could go home."

"You could go home now."

"Give me a coin. Just a coin. Everyone's got some change."

Vyse marched away. He met others' gazes, wondering how many more matched the first.

<I'm not sure capitalism can be blamed for that.>

Perhaps not, or perhaps it is the root.

Vyse wandered through sweltering days and frigid nights reminiscent of Rapetta's Eastern Barrens. Hunger ravaged him. He came upon an open-air tavern just as a strangely dressed serving wench placed food before a trio.

He drew upon his symbiote and their remaining power. Vyse had never been a powerhouse, cursed as he was with a specialty that had little to no use in Netaol.

<Are we to become thieves now, Magus?>

You may not require food, but I do.

As with all magus, working spells outside his specialty required a much higher cost. In his home country, he could've drawn on a circle of children for more power or townspeople in need of some service.

Vyse hadn't been able to rebuild his initially assigned circle. None had been willing to commit their children to a magus with such a useless power. He focused on the trio, pushing waning strength through Byron.

A large man with egg yolk on his chin stumbled into the man Vyse chose. The larger apologized to the diner, rushing away without noticing the scraps of parchment that fluttered from his pocket to land beside the table.

The second returned to his conversation, taking an excruciating few minutes to notice the rectangular scraps. He frowned, bent down and brought up the refuse. Eyes widening, his attention shifted to his wide, black bracelet. An avaricious smile preceded an urgent, whispered conversation. One woman shook her head, but excitement brightened the other. She convinced the contrary woman and the table's occupants bolted to their feet. The contrary woman discarded colored paper onto their table before they all rushed away.

<Improbable. The longer view would've been to obtain and sell whatever it was they discovered.>

Get off my back, Byron. I'm hungry.

<You used our magic to rob that man of his possessions.>

I did.

<Thieving like a common bandit.>

Vyse hurried to the abandoned table and seated himself in front of a steaming basket of yellow tubers topped with a meat-bean mixture and orange goat's cheese. The hot, if strange, food drowned Byron's rebukes.

Good as filling his stomach felt, the meal failed to assuage his guilt. His magic had stolen some valued possession. The people of this world struggled daily, fighting against their insane governance to clothe themselves and fill their bellies

And my theft robbed the man of his hard-won harvest.

Vyse needed sustenance no less than they.

A shadow fell over him. Vyse looked up to find a massive man with pinched features glowering down at him.

"That's my food, weirdo," he said. "And where are my companions?"

Vyse counted the place setting.

Four...not three.

He cursed inwardly. "They left, abandoning interest in the meal."

<And their friend.>

"Since they didn't want it anymore—"

"Of course, we wanted it. Why would we have ordered it if we hadn't?"

Vyse offered no argument.

"Put our food down and walk away. Otherwise I'm calling a cop." The large man caught the attention of the passing wench. "We're going to need to-go containers for all this."

She nodded.

"You intend to eat all this food?" Vyse eyed the huge man's bulk. "All by yourself?"

"Not that it's any of your business, but why wouldn't I?" The large man gestured at the abandoned paper. "We paid for it after all."

Vyse's brows knit together. "Are you saying capitalism caused your obesity?"

"What are you talking about?" His pinched face reddened. "Never mind, get lost. I'm warning you."

<Let him have it, magus. Can't you see he's about to faint from malnourishment?>

Before Vyse objected to either, the flutter of robes lifted his spirits. Three robed individuals walked the roadways opposite side. Each held ornate mage staves.

Vyse leapt up, knocking over his chair. He rushed past the man and his petulant vulgarities. He ran into the street. Cars screeched to a halt left and right of him. Horns blared. Insults bombarded him.

He ignored all in his haste. He summoned Byron into staff form and hurried up the sidewalk in pursuit.

Shabby robes of grey sackcloth garbed the rearmost. He turned at Vyse's approach. "Whoa, Dude, gnarly staff. who were you supposed to be?"

The other two magus stopped. Delight filled their expressions.

"I'm Vyse Cloudstriker. Guild magus of Rapetta."

Crossways

The mage wearing blue robes dotted with silver stars and moons spoke. His voice seemed far too youthful considering his long white beard. "Is that like Skywalker?"

Vyse scowled. "No."

"I'm Merlin." Their senior, blue robed leader gestured to a surprisingly youthful magus garbed in shiny, swirling pastels. Five fingered leaves dotted robes suggesting him a nature magus. "This here is Waldo, Wizard of the Weed. You've already met old Stormcrow."

Waldo looked Vyse up and down. "You attending the convention, man?"

"A meeting of this world's magus?" Vyse asked.

"Sure." Stormcrow said.

Waldo leaned in close to Vyse's staff. "Man, I think his wood just made a face at me."

Vyse scolded Byron in his thoughts.

Merlin snickered. "Stay away from his wood, you homo, and lighten up on the marinated weed."

Stormcrow shook his head. "Come on, guys, we've got to get to the casino before we miss all the good stuff."

The three rushed off, leaving Vyse to watch them go. Stormcrow stopped. "You coming?"

"I've heard casinos are evil."

"Nah, man. Casino's just a place. Money's the root of all evil."

"You got that all wrong," Merlin said. "If you've got money everything's nice. Showgirls are really nice."

"And if you don't have it?" Vyse asked.

Stormcrow shrugged. "Babeless starvation?"

Merlin cuffed Stormcrow, knocking the long gray hair askew. "No. You get a job. Make something of yourself. That way you're not making costumes out of sackcloth."

Stormcrow shrugged. He turned to Vyse. "You hear lots of things about casinos. Some of it's true, some of it's ridiculous rumors. What I can tell you is they hand out free drinks."

"Why would casinos give free beverages in a capitalist society?" Vyse asked.

"Keeps you inside their walls," Merlin said. "The longer you stay the more likely you are to gamble."

Things Sam told him about capitalism contradicted with their claims. "Are these beverages inexpensive?"

"They're not top shelf, Dude, but they ain't rot gut."

Stormcrow's answer confused things further. "The goal is to assemble riches. How do they do this offering free beverages and honest games of chance?

"Nah, man, games are rigged. The house always wins."

Vyse's brows tighten. "This is true? They cheat people?"

Merlin and Stormcrow shrugged.

"The house does tend to win," Merlin said.

<Are you thinking what I'm thinking?>

I believe I am. Vyse looked at his new companions. "Do these games revolve around monies?"

Merlin nodded.

"Yeah, dude," Stormcrow said.

"Would any of you have the smallest amount that I might use in these games?" Vyse asked. "I promise you'll get it back."

Waldo took turns staring at Vyse and Vyse's staff. "You got a system man?"

Vyse smiled. "Better. Magic."

Waldo beamed. "Righteous."

Vyse studied the slot machine's face. Beside him, Merlin looked skeptical over his crossed arms. Waldo stared dreamily. Stormcrow entered the row smiling and holding a sweating glass.

<I've never seen anything like this.>

No, but Merlin explained it is based on probabilities.

<How very convenient.>

Vyse chuckled.

An elderly woman to his left shoved coins into a slot. She pulled back on a lever. Independent dials spun beneath the machine's window, stopping one at a time. As the last one locked into place, the woman rolled her eyes and groaned.

"Pardon me, Madam, but how do you play this game?"

The woman interrupted the smooth motion her hands made from coin bucket to coin slot long enough to tap a small image on the machine's right-hand side. Vyse leaned in close, his chin over her bucket of coins.

She backhanded him in the face. "Look at your own."

Vyse studied his machine's diagram. It showed the winning combinations and payout ratios. He turned toward Merlin, brows raised. "Might I have those monies?"

Merlin unfolded his arms, reached into a pocket, and produced a shining coin. "You're sure that there is no way that you can lose?"

Vyse smiled. "I suppose there is always a chance. But it seems unlikely this device is protected from magical manipulation."

"Relax, man. It's only a quarter."

<You could test the spell on the lady's machine.>

I'm weary, Byron.

<Suit yourself, but if you lose, how will you repay him?>

Vyse accepted a quarter. He studied the woman a moment more. Readying his coin, he double-checked the chart, chose his desired combination, and focused his magic. He inserted the coin and pulled back on the lever.

Power surged, and fatigue filled him. The other three pressed closer, eyes intent on the spinning wheels. The first one dropped into place: Jackpot.

Skepticism filled Merlin's voice. "Coincidence."

The second wheel fell into position: Jackpot.

"No way," Merlin said.

"Dude."

"I believe, man."

The last wheel fell into place. Flashing lights and bells erupted from the machine. Coins streamed into the catch tray.

The woman next to him froze spitting curses vehement enough to curdle dairy. She glared. "Twenty-three years. In twenty-three years I've never got three jackpots."

Vyse retrieved two coins. He returned the first to Merlin, drawing energy from the man when their fingers touched. He repeated his draw as he passed her a coin. "Perhaps, your life is about to change."

She looked at the coin skeptically.

Vyse nodded his encouragement.

Crossing fingers of her offhand, she inserted the coin and pulled back on the lever.

Vyse focused his borrowed power.

Merlin gaped. "No way in hell."

"Dude, are you seeing this?"

Crossways

"Man, it really is magic."

Vyse exhaled as the jackpot erupted from the old woman's slot machine. She turned bodily to stare at Vyse. Her mouth moved but no sound came out. A tear ran down one cheek. She licked her lips. She tried once more to speak, gave up and handed over one coin from her overflowing tray. "For luck."

Vyse beamed. "Yes, for luck."

The crowd around the craps table cheered once more. A scantily clad brunette clung to Vyse's right side. A second cupped his buttocks, but otherwise out of the way of his dice throwing. Three more women clung to his fellow Magus, the last with a hand on his shoulder, completing the circuit.

Vyse collected another stack of chips and another sip of the group's vitality. He stacked chips on the table.

Stormcrow, Merlin and Waldo placed bets to match his own.

Vyse focused through a heady whirling sensation, called on the magic, and tossed the dice. They rolled down the table. One stopped displaying four pips. The other spun on a corner. Vyse urged it to tip over the right way. His grip felt slippery. Another sip pushed the die over to display three pips.

Cheers ran around the table.

"Dude, you're the greatest."

Waldo giggled. "Yeah, man, it's almost like magic."

Merlin cuffed Waldo.

A cocktail waitress removed Vyse's empty glass and sat down a fourth drink. Vyse brought the drink to his lips.

<Perhaps you should slow down considering that last throw.>

Winning again had used far more magic. *You might be right.*

A man in a suit walked up to the Magus bracketed by two large men. "You seem to be having a good evening, Mr. Vyse."

Vyse inclined his head. His balance waivered. A third beefy man collected the table's dice and handed them to a smaller man with a jeweler's glass for examination.

Vyse focused on the man in the suit. "Yes, but I think it's time for us to take a break."

"Are you staying here in the hotel?"

Vyse shook his head. The floor wobbled. "No, I'm not staying anywhere yet."

He smiled and held out a key. "Allow me to offer you and your friends accommodations free of charge and perhaps tickets to a show here in the hotel."

"That would be very welcome." Vyse took the key.

The woman pressed to Vyse's right bounced up and down providing delightful sensations. "Sinatra? Could we see Sinatra?"

Mister Suit smiled. "I believe he's just returned from Reagan's campaign. I could arrange tickets if you like."

The woman seized Vyse kissing and babbling high-speed at him. "Please, please, please-please-please."

Vyse inclined his head.

The woman squealed and kissed him full in the mouth. The heady sensation of alcohol and the blazing warmth of her arms redoubled his vertigo. Her tongue slipped between his lips, caressing his while hands roamed inappropriately for a public setting. She released him just before he ran out of air.

Vyse turned toward the others. "This is acceptable?"

"Hell yeah, dude, everybody adores Sinatra." Stormcrow said.

26: Revelations

Sam Bridger

"Where the hedrin have you been?" Alabaster shouted over the communicator.

Sam pulled rein, slowing so the caravan ahead of his didn't overhear the loud bodiless voice. "Just out and about, returning princesses, uncovering insidious plots, storming castles and retrieving one PGN."

Silence.

"Al? Still there, buddy?"

"I'm not your buddy." Alabaster said. "You actually got the pregrowth geonode?"

Sam patted the cloth ball. "Yeah, ain't I the hero?"

"Have you gotten a delivery instruction for it yet?"

"Conversation with Ren-2-3's a bit wooden." Sam laughed at his own joke. "But he hasn't indicated any new destinations."

"Might not come over the passport. Don't forget the written instructions you got on Netaol."

"Thought you left that on the seat."

"Anything been left in your truck telling you where to go?"

"It's not under my bench. I could head home and check under the bed covers."

"Seems unlikely they'd leave it there. Hold onto the PGN. You've got another pickup. Your mate will hand off the details."

"Who is this sexy beast, and will I find *her* under my bed covers?"

Acid laced Beatrice's voice. "Not in this lifetime."

Sam sighed, shaking his head. "You mind telling him we're not mates?"

"He listens about as well as you do. Updating your passport now. Head to crossway two-six-two."

An involuntary shiver gripped Sam. He glanced at his aba. "I hate Siberia."

"I know," she said with a smile in her voice. "Have fun."

"Just for that, I'm seducing some elf maiden."

"Oddly appropriate world for you and your delusional fantasies. Maybe some insane old fairy will warm to your charms and enthrall you for a few centuries."

"You liked my charms once."

"I was young and stupid." Beatrice hesitated. "Sam, stay away from the fairies on this trip. Seriously."

Mischief twisted the corners of his mouth. "How's Bob?"

"HQ out."

A laugh warmed Sam, unwelcome in the deserts of Dorsun, but a good hedge against Siberian cold. He flicked the reins, anxious to finish the pending assignment. He raced around the next caravan. The woman at its head snarled something at him.

Sam waved.

He changed routes, heading for an alternate waygate several geonations to the up-north-east. Without a working radio, batteries for his boombox or rock-n-roll stations to pick up, Sam contented himself with thinking.

When he stopped for a meal, a Sun Cavalier forced him to sit on the hard ground at the edge of the restaurant's yard with other males. He didn't mind the company, nor their silence. He chatted amiably about nothing in particular and chose not to notice the glaring women.

Alabaster's arrival and the subsequent changes troubled him. Something was off. It chewed at him, like assassin gnats that attacked whenever he wasn't looking. The dwarf, who'd claimed to be running his itinerary, hadn't left the Netaolian shipment's delivery instructions. As was appropriate in Netaol, they'd been handwritten on local parchment.

Netaol, like the other nine universes, contained several Crossways Transportation offices. The assignments were mostly plush administrative posts with small warehouses staffed by locals in the know. Not as clandestine and less subject to tech restrictions, they were better funded and equipped. They also employed insufferable locals Sam preferred to avoid.

Netaol's staff included minor magus whose private knowledge of the Crossways let her feel superior to more powerful magus. In the wrong place at the wrong time, Sam had been forced into attending a ball with them once. The food had been spectacular, but otherwise the experience left him with nightmares and a formal injunction against future attendance.

Sam couldn't imagine any of the spoiled local dandies hand delivering the instruction - magic notwithstanding.

He reviewed his memory of Dorsun offices. He recalled three, though felt he should remember more. The closest resided in Corlan's geonation. The UPO Ambassador wouldn't be pleased to learn he, himself, had picked up a PGN.

Won't take him long to pin it on old Sam Bridger.

Sam chuckled. "Best to keep a bit of road between us, don't you think, darling - I mean dude." Sam sighed. "Why couldn't you be a chick? Then we wouldn't have this problem."

Crossways

The other two offices weren't connected to the local geonation maze - unless through one of the lakes. Sam couldn't travel across Dorsun just to check for a delivery sheet.

Sam shrugged the problem away. It belonged to the dwarf. He'd just keep the extremely rare and valuable geonode, resist playing with it or accidentally creating a new geonation.

The local star dimmed.

Sam glanced up. He hadn't even noticed the soft flares it gave off when warning of impending night.

Sam rubbed his neck. He was only a few hours from the closest waygate. He drove on, missing his headlights and thinking about Beatrice. She'd seemed more serious lately, layering honest concern under her normal scorn. Sam couldn't figure out why. The dwarf's audit seemed over.

A soft glow escaping the seat's slats drew Sam's eye. He pulled rein, stood, and stretched. His back popped. Sam lifted the seat. Inside the compartment, the PGN had become unwrapped. He lifted it out, warmth and joy flooding into him.

Sam closed his eyes and soaked it in. A moment later he realized what a wonderful profile he and the glowing, unguarded PGN offered bandit archers. Wrapping the orb in haste, he blinked back his night sight and flicked the reins.

Sam drove. He rubbed his neck. He glanced at his passport. His thoughts drifted. He checked his calculator watch and drove another half hour. Sam looked down at his passport once more. "Ren-2-3 huh? Not a bad name. Too short for people to shorten it and make fun of you."

Ren-2-3 didn't reply.

Sam drove.

Desert passed; the night grew deeper. Calls of predators and prey floated through the cool night air. Something growled nearby, perhaps intent to spook Sam's horses. They never flicked an ear. Still, Sam pulled his shotgun and sent whatever it was into the night with a nice big boom.

"Ren, bud, get me HQ on the communicator." His passport offered a triplet of beeps. "Twenty-three to base."

A man's voice replied. "HQ dispatch. How can I help you, twenty-three?"

"Who's this?"

"Kenneth," Kenneth said.

It took Sam a moment to recall. "Oh, the new guy. What're you doing answering?"

"According to Auditor Roxx, all waymen must learn HQ positions their first three weeks. This training ensures they understand how the company mechanism functions."

Sam laughed. "You're putting me on."

Kenneth's tone confirmed he wasn't. "No."

"Either someone is pulling your leg, or I got seriously gypped. My trainer said, 'here's a truck, that's your passport, read the manual, mount up, and deliver stuff. Don't let the natives into your rig and don't dawdle.'"

"I haven't read the manual yet."

"Me either." Sam chuckled. "Bob around by any chance?"

"Let me check."

Sam drove on in silence, waiting for the new kid to return. Bob always seemed to be there when he called in for assistance, no matter the hour. She worked as hard as he did but loved her job more. He didn't think she'd ever even taken a night off for a date.

"Sam?" Bob asked.

"Yeah, glad you're still around."

"Something wrong?"

"Yes and no." Sam rubbed his neck, his thoughts a tangle. "You single? Alone, I meant alone."

"Just me and Kenneth in here."

"Give the kid some quarters and send him to the break room."

"Why?"

"I'd like to talk to you without anyone else listening." Sam imagined an interchange between the two of them and wondered if the new guy would leave or insist upon sticking by his post.

A queer note flavored Bob's return. "He's gone. What is it, Sam?"

"That's what I can't figure out," Sam said. "Something's going on with us."

Bob sounded unnerved. "We're just coworkers."

Sam's brows pressed together. Still, considering what he intended to ask, he decided to let it go. "We're more than that, babe. You're the best friend I've got."

"What are you saying?"

"I think you know. We're of a kind, Bob, feel the same way about things."

Bob stuttered a rapid reply, her volume rising. "I-I never thought you even n-noticed, I mean I hoped, but I didn't want, well I did, but--"

"Of course I noticed. Strange conversations, odd silences, secret glances and of course Beatrice's change in attitude."

"You noticed that, too? I never realized until Alabaster pointed it out."

"Did he yell at her for it?"

"Not that I know of, just...oh Sam. I'm so relieved you finally noticed."

"Guess a blind hog finds an acorn once in a while, huh?"

"You're so much more than that. I know the others say, I mean, you just have your own way of seeing things."

"The others what?" Sam smiled. "Think I'm an idiot?"

"That too, but mostly that you're a heartless womanizer," Bob's words accelerated. "I knew you cared more than that, that Bea hurt you. That's why I helped you in Florida. I figured if I showed you how much I cared and waited--"

"Womanizer?"

"Yes," Bob said.

"What's womanizing got to do with this conversation?"

"Well, I told you I never believed it."

"Right..."

"But you know how people are. They said you'd never settle down with a woman again, never consider marriage or a real relationship. I knew they were wrong, knew if I just waited..."

"Honey, I'm not sure what you're talking about."

Bob's pitch rose. "What are *you* talking about?"

"The weird orders since Alabaster showed up. Something's going on that they're not telling me. I hoped you'd know."

Her voice grew hollow. "You said I was your best friend."

"You are, best there is. I know you're a damned sight smarter than me. Figured you'd noticed things going on there at HQ. It took me a while to figure out you were trying to let me in on the secret the other night."

Vitriol slammed into Sam's ears. "As opposed to you, who wouldn't notice a good thing if it sat in your lap."

Several images flashed across his mind, summoning a grin. "Well, if she sat in my lap I'd hope--"

"You're a hopeless, idiotic bastard, Sam Bridger, and I don't want you to talk to me again as long as I live."

The communicator signal went dead.

Crossways

The reins fell from Sam's hands. He stared at his passport "What just happened?"

His passport growled beeps and chirps.

"Hey, bud, I like Bob as much as anyone. I didn't mean to upset her."

Its chirps and noises became a snarl.

"You can translate other languages, why can't you use the translator circuit so I can understand you?" Sam demanded.

Ren-2-3 spat a single word fueled with intense hatred. "*Buckwart.*"

Sam's lip curled but relaxed almost at once as the word brought Vyse to his thoughts.

<These women war for your affections.>

A hollow formed in Sam's gut, its edges icing over. He cursed, slamming a fist into his forehead repeatedly.

Oh, shit. Sam, you stupid son-of-a-bitch. Vyse was right. It isn't just some schoolgirl crush. She's got real feelings for you.

His gut knotted.

Oh, double shit. That conversation. Everything she said. Sam Bridger, she thought you were confessing your love. You led her right along only to humpty dumpty her heart off a cliff.

Blood turned cold in his veins.

You did it again. Sam Bridger hurt, no destroyed, someone he cares about. You've, no I've ruined my second chance, shoved away the second woman I called a best friend. I did this.

I.

Me.

Sam Bridger, super jackass.

27: Hijack

Sam Bridger

J ust inside Nebraska, Sam pulled off into a roadside bar. He parked next to several other rigs and trudged across a dimly lit lot. He entered the bar with an uncharacteristic frown.

Neon brand names tinged the brightly lit interior. Rotating ceiling fans huffed and whined, thinning the cigarette haze. Varied clientele clumped together in three areas of the bar. Truckers, bikers, and locals huddled separately with little interaction between them.

A trio of women in cutoff shorts and cowgirl boots slipped casually through the crowds avoiding friendly hands. A brunette in a pink checkered blouse unbuttoned low enough to show off a red satin bra strolled up to Sam. "Looking for somebody, honey?"

Sam opened his mouth, then shook his head. "No."

He sidled up to the bar, perching on a stool. The barman approached. Sam pointed behind him. "That bottle of whiskey."

Before the bartender could say anything, Sam set three twenties on the surface. He received his selected bottle of whiskey and a glass with a nod. "Thanks, brother."

A man next to him glanced at Sam. "There's a liquor store a couple blocks down, be cheaper."

"Spend enough time alone."

A bark of laughter drew Sam's attention behind him to an obese biker. "Know that look. Some little girl sucker-punched you in the nads. What happen, you knock her up or the mailman?"

Sam drained then filled his glass. "Mailman's not my type."

The biker's expression clouded. Sam drank more whiskey.

Pinky appeared at his unoccupied elbow. "You want anything from the kitchen, honey?"

Sam shook his head, satisfied by the way the room moved in slow motion. "Don't want anything between me and the bottle, baby doll."

"How're you going to get home like that?"

Sam shrugged. "Home's parked in the lot."

Pinky sighed, action doing delightful things to her chest.

Sam concentrated on the bottle. He drank, refilled, and drank again. The cheap whiskey burned each time, a steady stream of all too deserved punishment until the bottle was empty. *Where'd it all go?*

Sam's words slurred together. "Barkeep, another."

The bartender and his two twins frowned at Sam.

Sam slapped money down and shoved the bottle forward.

The barman caught the empty. "Haven't you had enough?"

Sam blinked, tapped the twenties, and shook his head.

"Sorry, bud. How about you take a break, get some food."

"I'm fine," Sam slurred.

"I doubt you could make it to the door, let alone your vehicle," the bartender said.

Sam turned to his neighbor. "Where was that liquor store?"

The man rattled off the directions.

Sam shook his head. "Can you take me?"

"Sorry, no." He pulled a pen from a shirt pocket and started scribbling on a cocktail napkin.

"What're you doing?" Sam asked.

"Drawing you a map."

"Don't read maps."

"But you're a trucker."

Sam shrugged. "Don't read them. Don't need to."

"Bullshit, you'd have to use maps."

Sam shook his head again. "No, my dash has this thing. Used to think it was a woman, but it tells me where to turn."

"Sounds like a woman," a man further down the bar said.

"You let a machine tell you where to go?"

Sam nodded, pitching forward, and striking his head on the bar. He rubbed the knot and beamed at the man next to him. "My little buddy takes me anywhere in eleven universes."

"Get him to take you to the liquor store then."

Sam glowered. He pointed at the man. A lopsided grin replaced his glower. "You've got a good point."

"You'd really let some device tell you where to turn?"

Sam nodded.

"You're nuts."

Sam stumbled across the bar, colliding with chairs, a table, and Pinky. He reached the door and stuck his tongue out at the bartender. He threw open the door, stepped over the threshold and got clobbered by the rebounded door.

Cold struck Sam first. His absurd position followed. Wedged between bed and driver's seat, Sam's legs draped over his seat. Throbbing pounded his head in time with his rig's tires crossing concrete highway seams.

Crossways

Sam groaned, struggling to upright himself. "Where are we, baby?"

The rig swerved hard left, then right. Sam slammed into the side wall.

"Buddy, I meant, buddy."

Sam climbed out of the sleeper. Everything hurt, but nothing more than his skull. He eased into the driver's seat. Bleak, snow-flanked highway stretched out before him. A drab green engine compartment bulged from the front of his truck.

Sam rubbed his neck. "Russia?"

Ren-2-3 said nothing.

Sam cranked up the heater, folded his arms and nestled deeper into his seat. He yawned. "Well, if you've taken it upon yourself to move us to a different continent, then you can drive us the rest of the way while I nap."

Sam closed his eyes. Their sedate ride turned rough as the right wheels edged off of the roadway proper. Sam cracked an eye. The rig raced toward a road sign Sam couldn't read. Her jerked the steering wheel, missing the sign by mere inches.

"What the hell, brother?"

His passport chirped a lullaby.

"Yeah, that's helping."

It played it again, this time dimming its lights.

"You're kidding, right? You don't nap."

The lights on the passport blinked out.

"How am I supposed to know where to turn?"

Ren-2-3 didn't reply.

Sam yawned, muttering under his breath. He scanned the horizon. Nothing in sight seemed to offer a toilet or place to grab food. He drove on, fighting his eyelids for territory.

Sam jerked awake.

The rig veered toward the left edge.

Sam shook his head, slapping his face. "Robot's going to kill me."

He stopped on the shoulder, climbed out and stretched. He worked out the kinks in his legs, circling the truck. Rather than the hard sided trailer normal on Earth, a canvas top covered its empty interior. Unfamiliar symbols decorated the truck's door.

Looks like the troop transport from Raiders.

A thud inside the trailer drew Sam's attention. He peeked into the back. A single bench occupied the far end.

Sam rubbed his neck, shaking phantoms from his brain. Unsure what else to do, Sam wrote in the snow.

A man snapped at him in Russian.

Sam whirled around, failing to halt his previous activity.

The soldier leapt back; eyes widened. He snarled something two parts threat and three parts command.

Some kind of sergeant?

The sergeant gestured. Soldiers stood up around Sam, dislodging fresh snow caught in their camouflage.

Sam goggled.

Sergeant Soviet growled at him.

Sam hit his palm to his ear, pointed at it and shrugged.

The sergeant grumbled something and rolled his eyes. He closed to a hand's breadth from Sam and repeated the words at full volume.

Sam's ears rang.

Sergeant Soviet's next orders sent soldiers scurrying up into Sam's trailer. Sam watched. *How do I dissuade them without getting executed as a spy?*

The sergeant pointed at Sam's pants.

Sam glanced down and zipped up. "Thanks, brother."

Sergeant Soviet's eyes widened. He whipped up his rifle.

Sam decked him, turned heel, and sprinted up to his cab. Cranking up the engine, He gunned the accelerator. The sudden lurch through dismounting soldiers to the ground.

Weapons opened fire. Bullets perforated the cab's rear wall, executing fluffy dice hung where a rearview mirror might otherwise reside. Sam swerved right. His lower side mirror shattered. He swerved left, right foot slammed to the floor. Gunfire dwindled, and Sam exhaled his pent breath. He gave his passport a disgusted look. "Lot of help you were."

Movement caught Sam's eye. Soldiers were visible in his right mirror, edging their way along the trailer's side. The remains of his other mirror showed more soldiers making their way toward him.

Sam rolled down his window. "I'm not an archeologist!"

A gunshot whizzed by his ear.

Ahead, the roadway offered no way to scrape off the soldiers. "At least they're not Nazis. Come on, bud, wake up."

Sam leaned left and kicked the passport "Ren?"

Ren-2-3 remained off.

Sam snatched up the communicator headset and shoved it over his ears. "Base, this is twenty-three. Get me Bob and hurry."

Beatrice's voice replied. "Don't you think you've hurt that girl enough?"

"I've got an emergency."

"Where are you?"

"Somewhere en route to my Feyrth pickup."

"Somewhere?"

"I was asleep; Ren was driving."

"Then get your passport to help," Beatrice said. "HQ out."

"He's asleep!"

"Samuel Oswald Bridger, you are the worst liar in history. What did you do, shoot it?"

"I swear, I didn't do anything. I need Bob to wake it up in a hurry."

"Why?"

A man appeared in Sam's left window and wrenched the door open. Sam whipped his shotgun out and shot him. "I'm being attacked by Russian Nazis."

"Was that gunfire?" Concern Sam hadn't heard in a while filled Beatrice's voice. "Sam, are you all right?"

Another soldier leapt into Sam's passenger seat. Sam kicked him, sending him swinging on the still open right door.

"Russian." Sam kicked him again. "Nazis."

"Hold on, I'll find Alabaster."

"Why? So he can audit my fight?"

"Bob's helping him with...something."

Sam turned away and shot his side window. Glass, shot, and a ginger-headed Russian went flying. Sam cracked open his shotgun, dropped it between the seats and leaned toward the under passenger seat drawer, his left hand anchored low on the steering wheel.

Got to find a better place for these.

A soldier tackled him, pinning Sam's face to the passenger seat. The assault drove Sam's hand down and right. The wheel jerked right, turning rig hard left. The truck hit the road's edge and plowed into the snow. A rise launched them into the air. The almost immediate landing dislodged several soldiers and slammed the head of the soldier atop Sam into the cab roof.

Sam scooped up his gun and jabbed the soldier in the genitals. He swept the barrel up into the man's jaw. The soldier tumbled out. Another replaced him before Sam grabbed any shells.

Boots shoved Sam into his attacker and both of them out of the truck. Sam caught the door but lost his shotgun. His handhold swung out to its limit and rebounded back to slam Sam into the door frame. It swung back open, Sam's combat boots dangling over dead winter foliage.

A soldier clinging to the cab's edge pulled a revolver. Sam kicked, not managing to disarm his adversary but causing the man to miss.

"What the hell is wrong, Bridger?" Bob asked.

"Oh, Bob, thank god. Help me!"

"Why should I?"

Sam kicked at the gun as it went off again. "If you don't, these Russian Nazis are going to make me their girlfriend."

"I hope they're happy with you."

"Bob, please, wake up Ren-2-3. He's asleep."

"Passports don't sleep," Bob snapped.

"Under normal..." Sam jerked his attacker close and head-butted him. "...circumstances I'd agree. Please, Bob, I'm sorry. I'll do anything."

"You'll quit."

Sam caught hold of the frame and dragged himself on top of the cab. "What?"

The driving soldier fired at Sam. The bullet pierced Sam's left arm. He jerked the limb back, losing his grip.

"You'll quit Crossways. You'll move away, and I'll never have to talk to you again."

The soldier swerved.

Sam slid across and off the roof, grabbing the passenger door at the last moment. "That's not fair, Bob."

Another bullet barely missed him.

"That's my condition. You promise to quit."

Sam swung feet first into the truck, driving the driver toward the other doorway and yanking the glove compartment open. He snatched up his replacement squirt gun and fired red water into the recovering driver's face. Water went up the Russian's nostrils. Sam took advantage of the distraction. He smashed the soldier's nose, knocked his gun to the floor, and shoved the Russian out the far door.

Alabaster's voice exploded in the background. "What in hedrin is going on here? What did Bridger do now?"

Sam slammed his foot down on the accelerator, weaving back toward the road. The truck leapt and wobbled.

"Thank God, Al, please make them wake my passport."

"Are you drunk, Bridger? Passports don't sleep."

"Please!" Sam pleaded. "If you don't wake him up, these Russian Nazis are going to kill me."

"Is he serious? Are you serious?"

Soldiers appeared on either side, holding tight against the rough ride. Sam seized the stray revolver and shot both in the face. "You're goddamned right I'm serious!"

The truck leapt another small rise onto the highway. Sam jerked the rig straight, glancing in his mirrors.

"Passports don't sleep, Bridger."

Bob shouted over the dwarf. "Are you going to keep your promise or not?"

"Promise?" Alabaster asked.

"To quit if she helps him," Beatrice said.

Alabaster sounded pleased. "Really?"

Sam slammed on the brakes, dislodging the last two soldiers. He leapt from the cab, kicked one in the face and turned his revolver on the other. "Freeze, cowboy."

The soldier went for the submachine gun slung over his shoulder.

Sam shot him.

"Bridger?"

Sam stomped to his rig's passenger door and pointed the revolver at Ren-2-3. "Passports don't sleep, they tell me."

His passport's lights flickering back on. It let out a sorrowful moan.

"I'd shoot you if I knew how to escape Russia alone."

"Bridger?" Alabaster asked. "What's going on?"

"You can all go to hell!" Sam ripped off the headset and threw it to the floorboards. "Thanks a lot for nothing."

28: Broken Trojans

Sam Bridger

Sam's truck coughed and jerked unsteadily from the waygate. Both truck and trailer still had wheels as well as spider-like walker legs curled up on either side. They weren't on a high forest treeway, and the immediate terrain wasn't rough, so Sam didn't engage them. A cherry wood grain covered the truck's exterior, highlighting gems alongside gold and silver filigree.

The normal beauty of the form was charred and pitted after his encounter in Siberia—about as battered as Sam felt.

Feyrth usually raised Sam's spirits. The world remained his favorite among the ten, perhaps because Feyrth's geography inspired Earth's own. Centuries before, the universe suffered under rule of insane fairy nobles. A worldwide uprising had splintered its people, leaving a world of magic and technology at constant war with itself.

A checkpoint stopped Sam less than a hundred yards from the waygate.

Two elf-driven mecha constructed of hardwoods and precious metals towered five stories over him. Jewel clusters glowed with destructive magical energies beside miniguns and rocket launchers. Another four patrolled in the distance, still close enough to ambush anything unwanted arriving via waygate.

A homely elven woman - merely beauty contestant runner up material on Earth - approached in a befuddling camouflage uniform. The colors on the jumpsuit and accompanying body armor shifted in slow subtle mimicry of the surrounding forest.

"Identification, wayman?" she said.

Sam presented his ID, taking a moment to wipe someone's blood from his picture.

"Are you injured?"

"Rough crossing."

She stepped back from him and scrutinized his vehicle. "I can't let you journey through the wood in this condition."

Sam's jaw tightened. "Listen, sweetheart, I've got a pickup. I've had enough drama for one day. I'm not going--"

The elf woman swept Sam's leg out from under him without warning. She grabbed one of his wrists, turning Sam as he fell so that he hit face first. One hand between his shoulders pressed him down while her other hand pulled the very sharp edge of a bronze, leaf-bladed combat knife backward against his throat. "What did you call me?"

"Sweetheart, on account of you looking like a warm and giving woman – despite your murderous rages."

A menacing smile lit her face. "You're not familiar with me, wayman. Most women don't appreciate a man treating them familiar when they're not."

"Look, I didn't mean no ha—"

"Captain Haeli."

"What?"

She glanced at his badge. "Say it, Sam, Captain Haeli."

"Uh, Captain Haeli?"

She smiled. "Now we're familiar, handsome. Pick me up for dinner at seven."

"I've really got to deliver—"

She spoke over him, her tone silver-steel. "You will move your vehicle as directed to the portable gnomearage and then accompany me to the healer's tents prior to continuing on your way."

"You're going to fix me up?"

"For the prescribed rate," she said. "Need you in tip top shape, wayman."

"Look, beautiful, I don't have--"

"We'll bill it to your company."

Sam smiled. "Damned right you will."

Dinner with Captain Haeli left a smile on Sam's face. The delightfully forward young elf flirted a good game but in a bout of universal irony turned out to be old fashioned about first date sex.

The one time I might've just gone with it.

Sam kissed her cheek before departing. He left with a spring in his step, an appetite for a dessert not on the menu, and a promise for dinner some other evening.

A few centuries too old for me, but you wouldn't know it.

Sam returned to the gnomearage to find the crew still going over his rig. The woman supervising the work almost came up to his belly button. She wore a bright jumpsuit inundated with pockets and tools as well as the same look of adoration for Sam's rig Bob usually wore.

A pang of guilt tickled his stomach.

She turned toward him. Brown hair clipped to a short bob framed her dimpled smile. "Evening, wayman."

"How's she looking?"

"You've got a solid vehicle, though your passport had quite a bit to say about you."

"Does everyone but me speak beep?" Sam groused.

"Apparently." She chuckled. "Actually, passports are a hobby of mine."

Sam nodded.

"Like I said earlier. We'll have her ready by morning."

Sam didn't recall asking, but he'd enjoyed quite a bit of the elf wine Haeli served. "You have my thanks, Miss."

"Just call me Alex. Everyone does."

Sam extended his hand. "Thanks, Alex."

She shook his hand and Sam turned away to find accommodations for the night.

"We'll have the cargo you requested loaded by then too."

Sam gave her an uncertain smile. "Okay. Good. Thanks."

Sam spider-walked his rig sideways along the treeway, making good time but not pushing himself to work the levers and pedals too fast. Another of his favorite things about Feyrth, treewalking presented a delightful challenge while exercising all of his limbs.

His focus lay so entirely upon his progress that the first explosion nearly tumbled them from the trees. Sam scanned the dense forest, trying to figure where the skirmish he'd bumbled into originated.

Something slammed into the tree beneath several of his legs, splintering the arbor to sawdust and flame.

Sam whipped his controls through a stunt he'd never fully perfected, effectively cartwheeling his rig along the sides of several trees. He reversed his motions for three short steps, then continued his rotation.

The stunt move revealed another rig in close pursuit. The other rig differed in only one obvious way - weapons.

Sam reached for the communicator. He stopped mid-reach. "Ren, we need guns."

Ren-2-3 chirped a defiant note.

Another tree exploded just as Sam left it. He increased the pace until he reached the point where arms and legs barely managed each bound without missing anchor points.

Machine gun fire peppered his rig's posterior.

"I don't care if it's allowed or not!"

His passport refused once more.

"He's going to destroy you," Sam said.

Laz's voice filled Sam's cab. "Surrender, Bridger."

"Not likely. We're one on one this time."

"And you're as unarmed as you would be in a battle of wits," Laz said.

"I'll take my nice big Johnson over your oversized brain anytime, you dickless son-of-a bitch."

"Charming."

Sam scanned the off-kilter horizon. He let go of his holds just as Laz launched another rocket. Sam's rig fell toward the ground. Occasional grabs of the surrounding trees controlled his descent. He clamped down one leg claw and rather than releasing it before moving on, he dragged the thick branch along. It snapped from its tree. Sam cartwheeled his rig and hurled the branch. It smashed into the nose of Laz's vehicle.

"Sticks and stones, Bridger."

"Will beat your pompous ass bloody."

Machine gun fire shattered one of Sam's spider legs. "I just had that fixed!"

"As if I care."

"You better. If you take my rig, it's going to cost you more to repair."

"Touché."

Sam climbed the treeway and continued throwing branches at Laz. He hoped neither the elves nor any druids came down on him for the destruction.

A rocket disintegrated the top thirty feet of a tree Sam intended to latch onto next. His rig teetered. Sam released his other holds and latched onto another set lower and to the right of Laz's truck - putting thick trees between them.

Laz adjusted course to match, firing rockets and bullets.

Sam felt short of breath, moving arms and legs as fast as he could. "How're you keeping up and firing too?"

"They're called friends, Bridger."

Sam glared at Ren-2-3. "Wish I had some."

"Pity your magus friend isn't here. He'd find the magic available here quite to his liking."

"Who says he isn't?"

"The singular lack of retaliatory lightning bolts."

Sam scowled. "Look, Ren, you won't make weapons, will you at least change the CB so I can call for help?"

In answer, the CB reshaped itself. Sam snatched it up and thumbed the button. "Mayday, this is wayman twenty-three, I'm under attack and in need of assistance."

"Wayman twenty-three, this is a restricted channel, if you have a genuine emergency--"

"Genuine?! Look, you pointy eared bureaucrat, I'm not ordering hot cocoa here. Some guy is attacking me and blowing up *your* forest in the process."

The cab filled with a pregnant pause. The radio crackled back to life. "State your location."

"Following treeway six-twelve three miles north of Gailus."

"Support forces dispatched to your location."

"Thank you," Sam shifted his attention to Ren-2-3. "Thank you too."

His passport chirped.

Sam shook his head. "Freaking prima donna."

Sam dodged, running and panting with all of his ability. Laz's weapons tore into Sam's rig. A half dozen massive eagles soared over the fight. They circled back, transforming mid-flight into angelic bird-headed mecha. The plummeted toward the treeway. Taloned feet grabbed passing trees as they bounded along in pursuit. Spell weapons launched tiny spheres of swirling blue-white electricity.

"You asked for lightning, wish granted."

The spells raked Laz's rig, ripping its superstructure and scrambling his equipment. Laz's voice stuttered over a squelching signal. "Thi...long w...ov...idger."

Laz turned his weapons on the patrol in a fighting retreat.

Sam slowed, descending to a stop on the forest floor. He heaved a huge sigh of relief. The elves would return, and he wanted to seem calm and cooperative when they did.

He passed a hand over his face. "I seriously need a beer."

A squadron of dwarves in spec-ops battle suits popped out of the surrounding foliage like daisies and trained weapons on him. "Hold, wayman, we're taking you prisoner."

"Well, hi, ho, call me Snow." Sam flashed them a weak smile. "Don't suppose prisoners warrant a dwarf mead?"

"You'll smuggle us through a waygate behind their lines," young Lieutenant Toss said.

Sam sipped his mead, pausing to rub his neck. "You know this isn't going to work, right?"

"They trust waymen. It'll work."

Sam snorted. "They don't, and I'll get executed—at best."

A dwarf marked as a lance corporal frowned. "What's worst?"

"I lose wayman rights to Feyrth for everyone."

The corporal shrugged. "Might have already done so."

Toss offered a fierce grin. "Corporal Drull might be right. Points don't take kindly to blowing up their trees."

Sam shook his head. "I sent out a distress call. They know I was being attacked."

"They know you said you were being attacked," Toss said. "Then you disappeared."

"And whose fault is that?"

"I'm not planning on telling them." Toss pointed his gun at Sam. "Neither are you."

Sam took a long draw from his mead. "Nope, can't help you."

"If you don't, we'll just shoot you and take your rig."

Sam shrugged, collapsed to the ground, and folded his arms. "I'll just sit here until you do."

"Do what?" Toss scowled.

"Shoot me. After the week I've had, it'd be a kindness."

"You want us to shoot you?" Drull said.

Sam scowled. "No, I want *him* to shoot me. Being killed by a dwarf isn't great, but it's a higher honor being snuffed by an officer rather than a grunt. Besides, it'll improve his stats. You guys probably hog all the kills."

"You want to be shot," Toss said.

"Want? Hell no. If I don't, you kill me. If I do sneak you guys in, they splatter me. I prefer the low effort death."

"What if we just left you here?" Toss said.

Sam sighed and replied weary and dejected. "Leave me to die, kill me, whatever."

Toss sat next to Sam, wrapping an arm around his shoulder. "It's not all that bad. Maybe I can leave a guard with you."

"It won't matter."

"Why's that?"

Sam snatched Toss's pistol from his belt and pressed it to the dwarf's neck. "Because you're my prisoner. Tell your men to drop their weapons."

Drull glanced at the other dwarves as he set his weapons on the ground. "Told you he wouldn't live to be a captain."

Something pushed into Sam's back. The weapon buzzed, an electrical jolt scrambling Sam's thoughts about a potentially sneaky dwarf silently getting the drop on him.

Sam's head lolled around; his speech slurred. "Stealthy."

Sam awoke strapped to his steering wheel. Multiple weapons pointed at his throbbing head. His upper back felt sunburnt.

"What happened to shooting me?"

"Your vehicle exceeds you in stubbornness," Toss said.

Sam laughed. "That's my little buddy."

"You'll drive us twelve clicks north. There we'll exit Feyrth, travel across your New Hampshire, and return to Feyrth just outside Lovell, Maine."

"Got it all figured out, do you?"

"I believe so."

Sam shrugged. A twinge pinched the skin between his shoulder blades. "You're the boss."

They approached the waygate to New Hampshire in silence.

Transforming ignorant locals is becoming a hobby. Maybe I should install cameras and sell the VHS's.

They drove into the waygate. Sam awaited their tortured cries. When silence reigned, he glanced around.

Toss showed his teeth. "Keyed our suits to resist the change field while you were unconscious."

Sam bit back a curse and drove the dwarf attack squad across the states. They entered Maine to a long concert of gurgles from Sam's empty gut. He gnashed his teeth in silence.

Sam spoke as they approached the next gate. "You realize this will drop us a long way from where you were on Feyrth, right? Nowhere near whatever your objective was."

Toss smiled. "Indeed, a fortunate opportunity."

"You know where this gate drops you?"

"Within the elf capital city, right?" Drull asked.

"Absolutely," Sam said.

Sam's rig emerged onto a military parade ground complete with a parade. The waygate's exit was cordoned off against a rig emerging from Eleventh World by encircling elf mecha. Their drivers turned weapons on Sam and his hijackers.

Sam raised his voice. "I'm tied here, so I can't raise my hands, but I surrender."

"Sir?" Drull said.

Toss closed his eyes and lowered his weapon. "We surrender, too."

"All bow before the mighty Trojans." Sam smiled. "You guys are so screwed."

29: Blood

Taleh

Taleh looked at her older sister, tied to a chair under the watchful eye of her new helper: Tyrone McGlip. McGlip's arrival heralded good things and the jolly soul kept Taleh's spirits high with his optimistic attitude.

"Word's just come from my agent," Taleh said. "The wayman's finally made his second delivery."

McGlip offered her a lopsided grin and clapped his hands. "We will soon have the waygate repaired and our people on their way to their new home."

Taleh avoided her sister's glowering eye while resisting the urge to gloat. "Wonderful news, McGlip."

"Shall we depart for the pickup?"

"Someone has to watch over my sister."

McGlip's expression flickered as if the large illusion taxed his abilities. "Shall I fetch our goods, Mistress?"

"Perhaps I should go. It can't be easy to move around such a bulky disguise."

"It gets easier," McGlip said.

She eyed her sister. No reason to distrust him, but I'm not sure about leaving Hullis in someone else's care.

"Please, fetch the shipment."

Elmeddi

Elmeddi the Conqueror sweated like a pig in an oven. The surrounding desert shimmered with heat. Despite his claims, Tyrone McGlip's clumsy body proved a troublesome vehicle. Not for the first time, he wished he could move about without Earth flesh to protect him.

Dunes stretched in lazy waves from horizon to horizon to horizon with only the far-off mountains behind him breaking up the golden monotony. Digital imaging binoculars allowed McGlip's feeble human eyes to follow wide tracks across the sand to a camouflaged pavilion nestled in a depression.

Elmeddi would've circled a third time to preclude ambush. Unfortunately, the heat damaged his host more than his presence. He knelt and vibrated within his host, sending out a clear tone. A moment later several pony-sized crystalline creatures rose out of the sand. The beasts resembled crossbred offspring of a scorpion and a trapdoor spider.

"Anything?"

A single tone chimed simultaneously from them all.

"Very good. Keep an eye out and stay close to me."

They emitted an interrogative tone.

"In case I need to be carried."

He trudged across the dunes. A cloth wiped beading sweat from his face, but desert heat drank it away first.

If only it were so between my host's buttocks cheeks.

The pavilion contained his cargo and no ambush. As with the last delivery, crates held unneeded items and passable substitutions. Elmeddi searched crate by crate, verifying no tracers had been included in the packaging.

What does Taleh intend with all of these extras?

He sighed.

Knowing the girl, she intended some philanthropic gesture, easing her conscience and delaying his ambitions.

A smile stretched his pudgy face.

He summoned burrowers and ordered them to fetch the vehicles. The creatures weren't as capable as higher Linurian species. They could control the worthless humans, but not hide within them.

Elmeddi found the pregrowth geonode while he waited, wrapped in a desert aba at the bottom of a crate of Feyrth ice bursters. He unwrapped it gingerly. Unnatural light lit his host's eye to match the sphere's glow. It brightened at his touch. The excitement of impending victory and a vibration akin to successful mating rushed through him.

Three trucks arrived. A Linurian burrower rode each driver like an odd backpack, appendages thrust into its shoulder blades to control the dying puppets. Special enzymes delayed the host's death until the burrower ate it - a slow agonizing deterioration which ended in a crunch.

Elmeddi directed the loading, culling the needed parts to two trucks. Burrowers moved cargo while he stroked the PGN, enraptured by the euphoric sensation. Elmeddi licked his host's lips. Pressing the sphere against his bulbous torso, he dug his true hand out through layers of fat to touch the PGN.

He hesitated, savoring the sensation felt through his host and anticipating the pleasure touching would give him directly.

Touching the sphere lit it brighter than the desert sun and filled Elmeddi with pleasure so potent he didn't recognize the danger. The PGN's vibration reached its apex. The orb blasted Elmeddi's crystalline body out the back of his host. The tiny crystal marionette tumbled end over end across sand and stone. He lay dazed.

The burrowers froze, oriented on him, and dropped their puppets. Mandibles rubbed together producing an eager trill.

Elmeddi climbed to his feet. "Continue loading."

The burrowers skittered toward him.

"Load!"

They froze, watching him with hungry intensity. Their mandibles rubbed against one another, emitting a siren song like crystal violins.

Elmeddi cursed and raced for McGlip's body. Burrowers charged his direction, intent to feed on the higher Linurian's pure energy. He dodged grasping pincers and clicking mandibles. As a pack, they would've shared Elmeddi's energies. Instead, they fouled one another's attacks, allowing him to plunge into McGlip's all but ruined flesh.

He absorbed the obese flesh and poured personal energy into the wasted body to rebuild its spike and essential organs. Fat and skin flowed like liquid, filling in torn flesh. The repairs cost McGlip a hundred pounds—an otherwise major accomplishment the Guru of Sweating would've applauded.

Elmeddi chimed another command from within the human meat shield. The burrowers, hardly intuitive thinkers, recognized the command while simultaneously being unable to determine the hiding place of their prey. They reclaimed their puppets and returned to work, leaving Elmeddi exhausted within the ravenous cacophony of his host's stomach.

Elmeddi delivered the truck of spare goods at the nearest refugee center. Once his other trucks were long gone, he detonated the acquired explosives. Drone cameras caught the massive explosion that leveled the block and sent a plume of wreckage, body parts, and dust soaring into the air.

Bridging his advanced tech into a VCR, he transferred the proof to VHS tape and paid a man to send copies to Eleventh World news outlets.

He chuckled.

Human news would replay the event sufficiently for Taleh to bear witness, encouraging the girl to fall into line.

Once the cargo has been loaded onto his spacecraft, Elmeddi released the burrowers to consume their puppets. He launched while they lunched. Burrowers were easy enough to acquire, and their hunger would plague the region until breeding season.

A mix of mirth and his host's growing insanity bubbled from McGlip's lips.

A half dozen years after their pathetic humans thought the monsters were gone, their desert would overflow with little burrowers undeterred by their natural enemies.

Taleh

Taleh couldn't believe her eyes.

"I am sorry, Mistress."

She stared at the live broadcast from Earth's Middle East. She felt light-headed, her chest hollowed out and filled with ice. "How could they?"

"They meant to kill you, Mistress," McGlip said.

Taleh collapsed. Wild, incoherent thought cascaded through her mind. Disbelief warred with the evidence before her. She rounded on her sister. "Did you know about this? Did you sanction it?"

Hullis shook her head. "No."

"I know not this woman," McGlip said, "but how could one of the council not know they intended this betrayal?"

"I've been your prisoner, remember?" Hullis said.

"The UPO doesn't decide things so quickly," McGlip said.

"They might if they felt threatened," Hullis said. "I don't know how that might have come about."

Taleh pointed at the screen. "Most of you may think humans are unwanted vermin, but they're sentient, feeling beings."

"Beings you're threatening to exterminate," Hullis countered.

Taleh's rebuttal died unspoken. She couldn't refute the accusation to either McGlip or her sister.

A giggle escaped McGlip. "There's more bad news, I am afraid, Mistress."

"Bad, funny?"

"No, forgive me. A nervous habit, the stress we're under. You understand."

Taleh inclined her head.

"I believe the PGN was damaged, perhaps by the explosion though I was fortunately just outside the blast radius."

"Thank the Auris for that, McGlip. Thank the Auris."

"We will need another."

Taleh found a chair before collapsing. She buried her head in her hands as tears besieged her.

McGlip wrapped an arm around her. "All will be well. We must persevere, Mistress."

"How can we?!" Taleh snapped. "How can we countenance such death and destruction, even for our people?"

A queer expression crossed McGlip's face, worry and anger mixed beneath a lopsided grin. "How can we not? How can we let so many die in vain just to let our peoples die too?"

Taleh searched his face, seeking hope, or faith, or something that would strengthen her resolve. She glimpsed the fury and something like betrayal simmering beneath his calm.

Both troubled her, but less than her own tumultuous emotions. Stress and prolonged holding of her illusion wore on her. Guilt plagued her, robbing her sleep for days.

Do I have the strength to finish this?

McGlip studied her, a queer light in his eyes.

"What is it, McGlip? More bad news?"

He closed his eyes and nodded at the floor. "I hate to burden my mistress more. Perhaps another time."

"Tell me."

"All the men who helped us in Brazil were slain."

"Varian?"

"Dead as well. Helping you led to his execution."

Taleh refused to look at McGlip. She found instead her sister's gaze, but within it dwelt neither pity nor love nor understanding—just contempt.

"You started this war," Hullis said.

Taleh leapt to her feet. "Then you'll help me quell it. McGlip, prepare the transport and any parts we need. We're going to have a little chat with the UPO."

Taleh glowered down at the assembled UPO representatives. "Such violent betrayals will not be countenanced."

"You put the humans in harm's way," Corlan said.

"And it was this body who killed innocents in a quest to destroy me," Taleh said.

Onklus snorted. "What're a few humans more or less?"

"An uneducated perspective," Leahna said.

"But our honored Tauron ambassador is right," Corlan said. "Who cares if we squash bugs while exterminating the rodents?"

"I thwarted your assassination attempt and hold the coordinator behind your attempted double-cross." Taleh swung the vid to show Hullis gagged, trussed up and heavily bruised.

Felisian rose. "By what right do you hold one of us hostage?"

"War," Taleh said. "If you don't accede to my demands in a timely manner, I will carve pieces from her in front of you."

"Our auditor is riding herd over the hapless buffoon of a wayman you chose," the blue haired Gramoard said.

"Your explosives damaged my PGN, not the wayman."

"What—"

Corlan shouted over the squeaky little Tuweine ambassador. "What PGN? Dorsun gave none."

Taleh reached to the edge of the screen and pulled a PGN into view, half its surface blackened. "This one, delivered with goods from Feyrth two days ago."

She watched the dark-complected desert ambassador purple. He whispered growls to an aide, who paled to unhealthy levels before running from the room

"What do you mean, Dorsun gave none?" Taleh asked.

Gramoard folded muscled arms over his beard. "I'd like to know this as well."

"My mistress commanded we not give in to this terrorist," Corlan said. "I suggest this honored body follow her wisdom."

A pixie rose from behind the Feyrth tables. High pitched chatter poured from his lips. "Has your mistress, who never troubles herself to attend, bothered to consider the damage losing Eleventh World would cause the rest of us? Assuming the world's mere destruction doesn't catastrophically damage areas - including populated cities - where waygates are situated?"

Felisian inclined her head. "I'm forced to agree with Ambassador Plix."

Corlan folded his arms. "My mistress has surely considered this situation with deathly seriousness."

Gramoard strode to within striking distance of Corlan, flanked by several dwarves and Audorians. "Dorsun will provide a replacement PGN, or I will personally see it sanctioned to within an inch of extinction."

A general murmur of assent ran behind him.

"Dorsun will not replace what was obviously stolen," Corlan said.

"No Ryaloxian auditor would have stolen your PGN unless forced to do so in protection of the Ten," Leahna said.

"My mistress turned away Auditor Roxx," Corlan said. "He left Dorsun empty handed. If there's a thief, it's that traitorous wayman."

"Debate on your own time," Taleh said. "You've received an updated list of my needs. Please fulfill it so I don't have to kill your fellow ambassador or annihilate your way of life."

Corlan sidestepped the besieging crowd to address Taleh directly. "Kill her. Destroy Eleventh World. Dorsun will not enable terrorists."

The explosive uproar let Taleh disconnect unnoticed.

30: Desert Revenge

Sam Bridger

Sam Bridger enjoyed the muscle soothing warmth of a Bedouin camp hot spring not far from his Middle East drop off.

The communicator headset under his headwrap beeped.

Why the hell did I wear the stupid thing?

"Sam?"

"I'm not talking to you, Bea."

"So, no big change. Just listen, Sam."

"Not doing that either. Go away."

"Listen, you meat-headed Neanderthal, this is important."

"Don't care."

"People will die if you don't—"

Shouting over her drew others' gazes. "You mean like being shot by Russian Nazis? Attacked? Incarcerated? Abducted? Oh, right. None of you give a goddamn about that, do you? You just want old Sam to grin off the blood and the bullets and drop off your Christmas presents. Well the world can go boom for all I care. Stop the world. Sam Bridger's getting off. Now, go. Away."

He ripped the wrap from his head and shoved the communicator into the water. Leaning against spring's edge, he cradled his head. "Sweet silence."

Niri

In a rare moment of inter-universal conflux, while Sam enjoyed the Bedouin camp pool, Niri lounged in a cool spring in her mother's palace—a pleasure she'd heretofore avoided.

Niri missed Quiss's ready waters and friendly colorful people. She even missed the intolerable wayman despite his last encounter with her mother haunting Niri daily.

A short distance away, Phred's expression seemed far away. The half dozen other guards positioned out of sight around the spring remained uncorrupted and fully alert.

"Far away thoughts, Phred?"

Phred started. He bowed low. "Apologies, Mistress. How shall I punish myself for this egregious lapse of duty?"

"Ten lashes with a barbed whip."

Phred blanched but bowed again. "At once."

"After the lashes, bathe your wounds in citrus juices."

"Yes, Mistress."

"Then don one of my gowns and skip around the palace pretending to ride a horse like a little girl."

Phred's eyes widened. "Mistress?"

"Then change out of my dress and repeat the punishment six more times."

"Yes, Mistress, you are, uh, ever merciful." Phred turned to go.

"Phred?"

He spun back around.

"A jest, my loyal friend." She laughed. "Fetch me a cool drink and then seek refreshment for yourself."

Phred gaped.

She made a shooing motion. "Go on, I thirst."

Phred bowed once more and jogged from her presence, shaking his head as he went.

Phred

Phred returned, setting his Mistress's beverage at hand for her enjoyment. "Anything else before I depart for repast?"

"Send a maid by to keep my drink full in your absence."

"As you wish," Phred bowed. Her wistful expression delayed his departure, but after a moment he tore himself away.

A writhing sensation dwelt in his gut, dwindling the desire for food. His beautiful mistress seemed to miss the wayman as much as he, though doubtless for different reasons. Despite being a cursed infidel doomed to eternal darkness for not worshiping the Sun, Sam Bridger was a good man. Time forbad them from enjoying the promised movie, but he imagined the wayman would keep his word when next they met.

An honorable infidel.

He glanced back toward his mistress, still barely visible through the spring's concealing foliage. Melancholy clung to her lithe curves.

Stop. You mustn't think of her in such a manner. Such thoughts mean execution, and who will watch her as well as you? Phred's eyes ran down the long leg she slid from the water. Earth has infected my mind, spread warrior courage to places it must not go.

His chest ached.

I'd do much to have the infidels' magic, to ensorcell Lady Niri's heart. She'd never find a more loyal concubine.

Ladies of his mistress's rank were normally allowed to choose their concubines. Lady Hivrus forbad Niri a choice until she'd birthed two heirs from royal studs.

They don't deserve to lie with her. Only I, and I alone, certainly not the wayman. He already has two women while Dorsun men are lucky to share even one, assuming they're chosen at all.

Phred entered the kitchens, a sigh on his lips.

The head cook pinned him in the doorway. "Your mistress requires something, manservant?"

"No, Master," Phred granted the kitchen head the title in the only place a Dorsun man might earn it. "I was sent for my own refreshment."

The cook pointed to a corner table. "Lunch scraps are over there. Be mindful not to be selfish."

Phred inclined his head. He assessed the table's compliment of stale food, yearning for the fresh meals he'd enjoyed in Quiss and Eleventh World. He stuffed flat bread with lean meat sitting in congealed fat, wilted greens and pried uneaten remains of hot peppers from their bitten stems.

His position allowed for a second portion, but Phred didn't wish another manservant to go hungry. He strolled from the kitchens, climbed a slow spiral of stone steps toward a balcony from which he could gaze upon his soaking mistress.

His nibbled food tumbled to the tiles.

The guards, a maid and three other servants lay dead. Their pooling blood dyed the spring scarlet. One of his mistress's swords protruded from an unknown body. Another lay dead beneath the impaled corpse.

Panic and dread overwhelmed Phred.

Instead of sounding the alarm to summon manor guards as was proper, he leapt from his high place, using transplanted foliage and decorations to safely descend the distance.

He raced to his mistress's blade and rolled the dead man over. A dead maid rather than Niri lay beneath.

Relief and terror warred inside him as he searched. The spring offered two exits. He chose one and raced his thoughts toward it.

Mistress is an accomplished swordswoman even with a single blade. She won't go down easily.

Phred stepped into the street, coming upon another slaughtered stranger. Bloody footprints surrounded the corpse but ended only a short way into the road.

A wagon. It'd have to be enclosed; else she'd be seen.

Phred raced after them down heavily trafficked streets. He wove through travelers, citizens, and merchants about the day's business. He darted from group to group in hurried steps, using each as camouflage while seeking signs of their passing. A covered wagon moved with unseemly haste in the daylight heat.

Phred double-checked for any other likely target before pursuing the wagon. He bulled through the throng, heedless of drawing attention. He buffeted women of standing and dodged several lashes swung at him a moment too slow.

The wagon disappeared down an alleyway shadowed by close buildings. Phred bolted toward the nearest shop, leaping to a handhold, and then launched himself further up with only his arms. Feet found purchase upon hot clay tiles. He raced across rooftops, dodging laundry lines, small potted oases and young girls playing younger boys off one another.

At alley's edge, arguing camel herders fouled the wagon's escape. His heart leapt. He charged. Knives flashed from his hands. The nearest guard fell before the second knew there was trouble. Phred cut the shout from the second's throat before it escaped. He dove through the wagon's curtains, bloodied knives at the ready.

A shocked and mostly naked mistress too impatient to reach her bower before being pleasured screamed, clutching concubines to her to cover herself.

Phred scoured the wagon but decided with little hesitation that his mistress wasn't hidden beneath their pillows. He fled, grateful for once that his face was covered. He scaled the nearest wall. Two guards pursued almost as fast. He sent them back to the alley floor and a death less definite than that dispensed by his knives.

He backtracked as fast as his feet would take him, leaping rooftop to rooftop in hopes he might catch his mistress's kidnappers. An hour later he trudged back into his mistress's keep, exhausted and defeated all the way down to his spirit. Guards at either side of the entrance seized him.

"What is this? I must help my mistress."

"Lady Hivrus decreed all who let her daughter be taken are to be executed," the guard said.

Phred's pulse quickened. "She's returned? She freed herself?"

"Seven men guarded her. Six lie dead in her defense."

"My mistress sent me from her."

"Better you'd died in service than what the Lady has planned for you."

Phred crumpled forward, letting the guards bear his weight. They adjusted their grip. He drove blowgun darts into their thighs. The knockout drug took effect before they realized the tiny pinpricks represented a danger. They collapsed, losing Phred in the process.

Phred scoured them for coin purses and stripped one's aba as a disguise. Guilt seized his chest, squeezing his heart.

These two will die for my escape, but neither would throw himself into hell itself to recover my mistress.

Phred eased their pace as the geonation's star flared to life, resting his fourth stolen mount. The tan mare needed replacing, though her night ride had been less arduous than the daylight rides which nearly killed her three predecessors.

He'd hoped to cross paths with a water bearer, but the Sun hadn't blessed him with a wayman. His escape from the Taite geonation hadn't been the ordeal he expected.

Once mistress is rescued and risen to tribal head, I shall speak to her about improving security.

Phred scanned the sky, estimating the current geonode's diameter. He'd guarded Niri's youngest sister during her early lessons, learning the fancy arithmetic she disdained. The numbers estimated his distance to Unati geonation's entrance. His thoughts lingered on that school room; simple days before he'd become a manservant, before the blood guilt. He loved serving his mistress, but children's laughter and schooling observed from the room's edge didn't haunt his sleep.

The mare failed before he reached the next town, forcing Phred to leave her to the desert predators. He bought food and a local aba. He ate in the corner of a yard beside other locals, peering through his lashes at women and listening to everything. News of his lady's abduction didn't cross a single tongue.

How has Lady Hivrus silenced news of Niri's abduction? Shouldn't fury and outcry fill the streets? He chastised himself for thinking her name. Mistress or Princess Hivrus. I am not familiar. I was unworthy to think her name before I failed her, now, I can be no lower carrion.

Phred slept in a communal bed chamber among tired workers. None asked after him or struck up a conversation. The others passed overheard news one to the other, every tidbit treated as if it were a state secret. Their trifle gossip brought no word of his mistress. Eventually, he shut them out in favor of rest.

He rose after a few hours, just as the geonation's light dimmed. He strode into a stable closing up for the night as if he were mission sent or, perhaps more accurately, Sam Bridger. "I require a horse."

The stableman's head shot up. "Do you now?"

Phred hesitated. The stableman should have acquiesced without comment. Phred took a deep breath, hoping to inhale some of Bridger's magic. "My mistress has dispatched me with an urgent message."

"Your mark?"

"Do you question all messengers thus?" Phred demanded.

"I do when I've lost most of my horses to unfulfilled promises of payment or return."

Phred noted most of the stalls stood empty.

"I, too, answer to a mistress, messenger. She commands I give service to any Sun Cavalier or their representative, but she expects me to account for my beasts."

Phred opened his aba, exposing the flesh beneath his right arm. A brand depicted both the Taite dynasty and Lady Niri in his flesh. "I'm on the business of High Princess Hivrus and command your discretion, excepting in matters of recompense."

"Long way from home, and that isn't Taite garb."

"I trust you recognize the authenticity of my mark."

"Yes, and the reason for your garb. I want no part in your business. Take a horse, leave your mark and be gone," the stableman exited, abandoning Phred with the remaining animals.

Phred saddled a sorrel to his liking and entered the stableman's office to leave his mark. He hadn't intended to identify himself, trusting in the logic which won Sam a PGN without a fight. Even so, he was on his mistress's business.

And Lady Hivrus can only execute me once.

Another mark caught his eye. He examined the loose papers. A crude number ten lay beside Lady Shindra of the Unati's mark.

Phred shuddered with elation and dread. I'd hoped the trail led beyond Unati. Thinking of Mistress in the hands of Slave Corlan's agent fills me with terror. If only I'd crossed paths with a wayman to enlist Sam Bridger.

Phred regretted the death of the unnamed Unati which provided his disguise. Dressing the Unati in the previous geonation's robes, he hoped the Unati would grant a dead stranger a decent burning.

Walking casually rather than sneaking through Lady Shindra's household took supreme will. He inclined his head as he passed a pair of servants in the hall. They fled to the hall's edges as he passed, as if they saw their countryman's blood on Phred's hands. A backward glance saw them flee. Phred double-checked his aba free of blood.

The next man he passed reacted much the same. Phred checked the hall for watchful eyes then seized the man. "Explain why you treat me so?"

"F-Forgiveness, Sand P-Puma. I meant only deference."

"Why do you think one man should cower to another as a sign of respect?" Phred asked.

"Lord Corlan commanded all Sand Pumas be treated as knights."

"Men? Treated as Sun Cavalier?"

"No, mighty Sand Puma. You are greater than any female."

Phred released the man, secure that the terrified man would keep his tongue still. Changing his mind, he grabbed the servant and yanked away his face covering. "The desert princess recently brought here, where is she?"

"Lord Corlan's newest concubine?"

Heat rose in Phred's chest. His hands tightened around the man's robes. "Yes, where does *Lord* Corlan keep his concubines?"

"I don't know."

Phred removed a knife from his belt.

"Auris's truth, Sand Puma! Once he marks them, they're taken to his secret palace."

Phred's words fought to escape. "He slave marks them?"

The man nodded.

"Awake?"

"Not in this case, Sand Puma. She was a spirited one."

Phred forced his knife away and pried his fingers loose. "You've served Lord Corlan well. Be on your way in peace."

Disbelief flooded the man's features.

Phred nodded. "Go."

He departed with worried backward glances, breaking into a run the moment the next door presented itself.

Phred stalked the hallways, no longer concerned about servants' reactions. His mind had room for only two things: Corlan and devising him the most agonizing end possible.

He stopped a servant. "Know you Lord Corlan's whereabouts?"

"The yard, Sand Puma."

Phred found the yard.

Corlan sat atop a steed on the yard's far end, flanked by a half dozen hulking Sand Puma. Between Phred and Corlan, another twelve knelt on one knee, curved knives held to their breasts.

"This scion of Auris shall lead you to a new world of evils and temptations, a place unlike any you've seen," Corlan said. "In this corrupted land you'll find a man, a thief who wishes to steal all I've given you. Find him. Kill him."

A cold washed over Phred. His eyes settled onto the silvery disc, recognizing it from Bridger's vehicle: a passport.

"What shall you do?"

They rose as one. "Find him. Kill him."

"Kill who?"

"Sam Bridger," they answered.

31: Holiday Entertainment

Sam Bridger

Sam watched the cheery gnome tinker at his workbench, trying not to loom despite his interest. Having been lambasted for drinking near the workbench earlier, Sam retreated a few steps for a swig of elf wine.

The wine had almost drowned out Beatrice's and Alabaster's echoing demands. They'd yelled and cajoled. Bea'd even begged.

Some nonsense that only I could return to Dorsun for a PGN.

He swayed into a wall. He gave it what for until it let him lean against it without remark.

Should've told me while I was there. Why's everyone acting like Chicken Little? I've done nothing but work and work and for what? Death by Russian Nazi, that's what. Well, I'm taking a day off...maybe a week. Let some other mule go get it.

The gnome turned toward him, a gleam in his eyes almost as bright as the silver-steel barrels of Sam's new shotgun. "It is done, wayman, just as you asked."

"And it'll work in my world or any other?"

The gnome's smile faded. "You question my work?"

"Well, you know, not all worlds work well together."

"This is state of the art techgnomology."

Sam wished the gnome would stop swaying. "But if I have a problem?"

"Bring it back—if you survive."

Sam did a double take, vertigo nearly bringing him to the gnome's level.

"A drunk man who wants a weapon like this? He's headed for danger, isn't he?"

Laughter bubbled up to Sam's lips, carrying with it the scent of elf wine. "More than my share."

"Why seek out danger, wayman?"

"I haven't. Isn't that odd?" Sam scowled, rubbing his neck. "I've been behaving myself. No wine, women or song...well, some wine...mostly no women. God, don't get me started about women."

"Perhaps the fates have need of you."

"Then fate can tell it to my answering service." Sam chuckled. "I'm not taking calls."

The gnome handed Sam a shoulder holster and satchel of ammunition. "Best not to ignore fate when She comes calling."

Sam scoffed. "I've got a date. Fate'll just have to understand."

Birds awoke, filling the predawn with sweet music, accompanied by the whir of Sam's fly rod. He cast, drew, and then reeled in his fly with mechanical bliss, repeating the simple motions in the otherwise still morning. A slowly emptying case of beer sat atop his yet empty cooler.

Sam's stomach grumbled. He'd brought food, but he'd left it in the rig. The hundred yards was too much effort for chips or hoagies. He reached for his beer instead.

A hungry fish hit his line, costing Sam some beer. Eyes intent and smile eager, Sam played out his line to ensure the bass thought itself free before he snapped the rod back hard. The fish fought him. Sam reveled in the win or lose contest.

Sand Puma 13

Shadows on the opposite bank from Sam Bridger darkened.
The wayman didn't notice.
They shifted.
Sam missed it, focused on his sport.
Thirteen Sand Pumas burst from the brush along the opposite bank and onto the bridge leading across the waterway, curved knives to hand.
Sam blinked at them, still fighting the fish on his line. He growled, snatched a knife from his boot and cut the fish free. "Yo, Fate, gone fishing Bitch!"
The first Sand Puma across the bridge wore a strange silver backpack with spindly straps. Sam whipped the attacker's face with the fishing stick, cutting his covered cheek and driving him into the water. He cast the combat knife's pummel into the face of the second, snapped up his half-drained bottle and hurled it at a third. He grabbed the cooler's handle, spilling beer cans to the ground.

Sam brandished his cooler as a clumsy shield and bludgeon. Rod whipped out at the Sand Pumas as they dove at Sam, slashing like they intended to cut down harvest wheat.

Sam Bridger

A mad scientist Sam Bridger wasn't, but addition and subtraction were well within his grasp. Thirteen on one, or ten as the new odds stood, didn't figure into Sam's likely victories - regardless of ego.

He fought backward, using trees and terrain foreign to the likely desert warriors to his advantage. He whipped branches into faces and kicked pinecones beneath their feet.

"Tell Lady Hivrus that when I told her to get laid, I didn't mean with yours truly!"

Nothing? Another abduction happy princess then?

Despite a bulging bag of low cunning, their blades found pieces of Sam Bridger to cut. A stray branch brought Sam to his end, leaving both buttocks' cheeks stinging.

A desert assassin sped in for the kill, his brother close enough for a piggyback ride.

Sam gasped. "Oh my god, it's Mistress Shindra!"

The whole group wrenched their heads around.

Corlan.

Sam slammed a combat boot into the man's genitals—Sam hoped it was a man and had genitals—before scrambling to his feet.

The second Sand Puma pressed the attack. Sam blocked with the offending branch but got a deep cut across his forearm. Sam took out the second in time for the first's recovery and for several reinforcements to arrive. They came at him in a slow half circle, having learned the price of a careless rush.

Sam backed toward his rig, hands held up but ready. "I don't know what this is about, but surely it's nothing some beer and a trip to a chicken ranch can't cure."

They pursued in silence.

"You boys ever had your own woman? Come on, thirteen ladies of negotiable virtue on old Sam Bridger."

"Twelve," one of his attackers snarled.

"Sorry about ruining the mood for you, brother."

"Sand Puma *never* travel as thirteen."

Sam blinked at him, counting those around him and those he'd dropped. "Why not?"

"An unholy number."

"Anyone ever teach you counting? There's thirteen of you."

"You won't distract us again, thief."

Sam straightened. "Sam Bridger is many things, but he's no thief."

"You stole a geonode from Lord Corlan."

"*Lord* Curly is it, now?" Sam laughed. "Guess he doesn't like you because there's definitely thirteen of you."

The Sand Puma wearing what Sam recognized as a passport spoke. "One."

"Two," the next Sand Puma said.

The others counted off until the thirteenth Sand Puma said, "Thirteen."

Sam imitated the vampire Muppet. "Thirteen, bwua-hah-hah!"

Confusion slowed them a moment. The lead Sand Puma shook his head. "It matters not, you die. We're victorious."

"But thirteen is unholy, means unlucky, doesn't it?"

"Very," the thirteenth said. He slashed the two closest throats and locked eyes with Sam. "Good to see you, wayman."

"Phred!" Sam whipped open his truck door in the momentary distraction and pulled out a gleaming silver shotgun. "Nice to see you, too, brother."

Sand Pumas turned back-to-back, split between sides facing Sam or Phred. The closest lunged at Sam, losing his upper third in a colossal wave of thunder and flame.

"Thunder stick, brothers, newly improved. Next idiot who attacks Phred or me gets to be a matched set with stumpy there."

"We're not so uneducated, wayman," Passport said. "We know you wield a weapon that can only strike twice."

Sam pointed the shotgun at him. "You volunteering to go down so the others can jump me?"

He straightened. "I'll gladly die for Lord Corlan."

Sam sighed, offering Phred a companionable grin. "Zealots."

A different Sand Puma charged Sam first, followed closely by a second. Sam sidestepped, lined them both up and fired. "Buy one, get one half off!"

More Sand Pumas charged him, but he didn't bother trying to reload. The next attacker got a truck door to the face and the one behind a combat boot to the knee. Sam flourished his wrist, flipping the shotgun in a tight circle. Much like Alabaster's cybernetic arm, gnomish nangnome-robotics transformed the shotgun into a long silver steel rod.

Sam spat curses through his grin. "He *told* me to read the manual. Ah, well. Batter up!"

The next Sand Puma lunged at Sam. Sam swept the metal baton up like a golf club, taking the Sand Puma in the teeth. His knife missed a dastardly blow to plunge into Sam's torso.

Sam fell backward against his rig, grunting in agony. "I'm no longer amused."

Phred shot a glance over at him. "This is amusing?"

"Not anymore. You should duck." Sam flipped his wrist once more. The silver submachine gun in Sam's hand unleashed a barrage of energy bolts. Sam choked his way through a Cagney imitation. "You dirty cats. You dirty cats."

The remaining Sand Pumas fled before his energy weapon, cursing the techgnomologic sorcery which gave them extra sets of heels to flee on.

Sam slid to the ground, a queer grin twisting the corners of his mouth. "Sometimes I'm such a stinker."

Phred knelt beside Sam. "What can I do?"

"You know doctoring?"

"No."

"Healing magic?"

Phred shook his head.

Sam cursed. "Guess we have to call for help, then."

"Who am I to call?"

"Ghostbu--" Sam dissolved into choking gasps. "Bob...call Bo--"

Bob

Bob leaned deeper into the engine compartment for better leverage. She adjusted the last spark plug, careful to align it to her stricter personal specifications. A touch on her thigh brought her up fast. She ducked the engine cover at the last moment, whirled around, snapped up a spanning wrench and held it ready to educate someone about personal space.

It was Kenneth. The trainee wayman wrung his hands. "I'm really sorry, Miss Zephyr. I called your name a few times, but I guess you didn't hear me."

She took a breath and tried not to sound like an incontinent badger. "What can I do for you, Kenneth?"

"Someone on the communicator says he must speak to you."

Heat brimmed her voice. "It'd better not be Sam Bridger. I wouldn't talk to that worthless jerk if he were dying."

"Um, no. Someone named Fred?"

Bob frowned. None of the wayman were named Fred, but the name seemed familiar. "Fred?"

"Yes."

"Fred."

"Yes," Kenneth repeated.

"Phred!" Bob jogged across the garage to her communicator, acknowledging Auditor Roxx's entrance with a tiny nod. "This is Bob. Phred, how did you get a communicator?"

"What's going on?" Alabaster asked.

Kenneth shrugged.

Bob held up a hand while she waited.

"I, uh, used the one in the truck. Can you hear me?"

"I read you fine."

"If that idiot wayman brought another--" Alabaster began.

Bob held up her hand, adding the weight of her glower to quiet the auditor. "Whose truck?"

"Sam Bridger's."

"That's it, after this crisis ends, Bridger's gone."

The heat returned, beating at her chest like a bored gorilla with a new drum. She vented the sudden fury on the auditor. "Will you shut up so I can find out what's going on?"

Alabaster's features tightened, but he held his tongue.

"Thank you. Phred, why're you on Sam's communicator?"

"He told me to call you."

"Then he'd better be dead," Bob snapped.

"I think he might be."

The fury building inside Bob flushed itself out through her feet, leaving a sudden vacuum which kept her from breathing.

"Hello? Hello, Bob?"

Alabaster stepped forward, prying the communicator from Bob's hand. His words sounded far off. "What's happened?"

"Lord, I mean, Ambassador Corlan abducted my lady. He sent a dozen assassins into your world to kill Sam Bridger."

"Preposterous, Dorsun warriors couldn't enter Eleventh World without a passport."

"They carry one."

"How do you know of this plot, Phred?"

"I infiltrated Corlan's usurped palace to find my mistress. I witnessed his order to the assassins. I didn't know where he'd hidden my mistress, so I infiltrated their number in hopes of enlisting Sam Bridger's aid."

"UPO regulations restrict employees from interfering with local--"

A shriek escaped Bob's throat, driving Alabaster and Kenneth a few steps back. "Shut up!"

She snatched the communicator's cord, whipping it out of the dwarf's hand. "What happened to Sam?"

"He's been stabbed and cut many times."

The cold which had stolen her breath returned with malicious intent, held back only by a heat bubbling from the smelter in her gut. "Are you near any waygates?"

"I'm not sure, we came some way cross country."

A vice tightened Bob's chest, squeezing tears to the very edge of tumbling. Sam had hurt her. The incompetent buffoon had offered Bob her dearest wish and snatched it away without a moment's care. She hated him. She'd told him so, demanded he quit. Now he was dying and that thought closed the world in around her.

No. He's not dying until I hand his handsome, oblivious ass the beating he deserves.

She spun toward her consoles, fingers flying over keys. Vehement curses lashed the system, driving it to function at greater speed. "What the hell was he doing way the hell out there?"

"I cannot answer, Sam's Heart."

The world froze once more, gravity giving her a pass. A whirlwind of noise and color clouded her lightheaded brain.

Alabaster stepped closer to the communicator. "Was the blade pois--"

"Poison is possible." Phred said. "He's fades rapidly."

"Everyone just shut up and let me think!" Bob closed her eyes and took a deep breath. She knew what had to be done just as she knew she didn't care about Alabaster's objections. "Get him in the truck, Phred."

"Miss Zephyr, might I inquire--"

"No, you may not," Bob forced the snarl out past the heart lodged in her throat. Her fingers danced across an open window, The cryptic characters of the Ryaloxian programming language lining up like alien ships on an arcade screen. "Phred, put him in the sleeper."

"I already have."

Bob finished the script and pushed the commit button.

"Something's happening," Phred said over a sudden roar. "The truck is shaking."

"Keep your feet up. The truck will do all the work."

"May I now ask where you're sending him?" Alabaster said.

"As it happens, to the finest medical resources in the Ten. They were closest in any event."

"I note you said ten rather than eleven."

Bob bundled all her anger and terror into a glare meant to burn. "Have I done something to make you question my IQ?"

"You programmed a passport to use an unauthorized mode to fly a wayman you reportedly despise across several population centers without any kind of stealth technology to shield it from detection."

Bob's thoughts, already an unlikely maelstrom, raced through the responses she really wanted to give the dwarf. In the end, she settled for a simple retort. "Bite me."

Sam Bridger

Sam awoke beneath bright, overlarge pastel lights in a room decorated by most every color in the visible spectrum. A machine off to his right sounded a slide whistle synched to the pulse throbbing in his ears. A machine the size of a refrigerator hung over his left side. Outsized monitors covered its near surface. Vibrantly colored lines displayed his vital statistics, a small man-shaped figure leaping and swan diving on each as his readings varied.

"Tuweine," Sam moaned.

Phred's face appeared, somehow subdued compared to the bright colors around him. "Sam Bridger, you're awake."

"No."

"No?"

"I'm a figment of your imagination."

Phred shook his head. "My imagination is not so large."

"You saved my neck, brother. Isn't it about time you just called me Sam?"

"I thought your name was Sam Bridger."

"It is, but Sam's my first name - what my friends call me."

Phred licked his lips. "Do you not speak of yourself as Sam Bridger?"

"Now and again."

"But you wish me to call you just Sam."

"Now you've got it."

"Confusing, though not as much as this place."

A doctor in a paisley lab coat entered Sam's line of sight, black stethoscope bouncing about his neck. A headlamp was strapped around his bulbous forehead and plastic-stiff hair. He was human...ish, in a part real, part surreal way.

Nodding made Sam wish he hadn't. "Tuweine."

"Welcome to Nudel Medical Center, Mister Bridger." The doctor showed off perfect marble white teeth. "You can call me Doctor Wright."

"What do other people call you?"

Doctor Wright studied Sam, his smile not faltering. "We've run into a bit of trouble, haven't we?"

"Someone stab you too, Doc?"

Doctor Wright checked his own chest. His answer brimmed with optimism if not conviction. "I don't believe so."

Sam reached up to cradle his face, but found his hands restrained by cuffs as wide as his thighs. He looked at the Tuweinie doctor, the man's over-large hands and head,

Considering how disproportionate what I can see is, are his feet huge too? Dollars to donuts I'd make a killing smuggling in used clown shoes.

While Feyrth served as Sam's favorite world, Tuweine gave him headaches. Bright colors, primary and pastel, painted everything. Shapes refused to maintain proportion, shrunken or enlarged by whim - or worse, perfectly normal save one warped aspect. The people, the objects, the animals, even the clouds always struck him as creations of a mad animator twisted with power - like Darth Disney.

"Am I well?"

"Your wound is nearly gone," Doctor Wright said.

"Run out of giant erasers before finishing?"

Doctor Wright's brows rose, threatening the limits of his head. "I'm afraid I don't understand."

Sam shook his head. "Nothing. Can I get out of here?"

"I'd prefer if you allowed us a bit more recovery time. I can have the nurse administer pain medication if needed."

An image of a syringe the size of a bazooka flashed through Sam's thoughts. Another bazooka firing body-swallowing ooze followed. He tried to bolt upright, but the straps prevented it.

"Mister Bridger?" Doctor Wright asked.

"That's okay, Doc, no injections needed."

Doctor Wright smiled. "I had pills in mind actually."

"I'd probably choke to death," Sam mumbled.

"Maybe all you need is some rest," Doctor Wright chuckled. "Nurse, something to help the patient sleep."

Sam met Phred's eyes. "If she brings in a huge mallet, promise me you'll get us out of here."

32: Reunion

Taleh

Taleh scrutinized her helper, a feeling of dread hard in her stomach. McGlip's skin had turned sallow and sweat sheeted off of him even in the cooled chambers. His clothes hung baggy from his limbs and his smile cast a shadow of former warmth.

"I'm sorry, Mistress, some of the waygate's components were damaged though my predecessor didn't see it."

"What does that mean?"

"More parts, some for the things we didn't know were broken, more to replace parts we've received that damaged components destroyed via malfunction."

More parts.

Taleh hid her disappointment. She didn't wish him to believe his efforts were the reason for her displeasure. *I hate going back to those people for more, even if I did prepare the them for the possibility.* The Dorsuns had been ready to sacrifice Earth over a simple item which grew naturally in their universe – rare though it might be. *I hate them. I hate their greed. I hate their...faces.*

Disgust welled up in her almost as strong as what she'd felt in the UPOs presence. She felt small, childish. She couldn't even hate them in an adult manner.

But I can't abandon my people, not now.

She cast her eyes past the waygate to a small environment bubble where Hullis rested if not comfortably, at least unrestrained. Mars didn't have enough atmosphere for her sister to leave the bubble for any length of time.

Words tumbled from her. "I'm going to have to hurt people."

A giggle escaped her helper. "Perhaps if we merely ask...."

Taleh shook her head. "I've asked too many times without proof of my resolve. Each time it gets harder."

"Perhaps beat the ambassador?"

"No."

"Exploding a bomb in an entertainment center--"

Taleh shook her head.

"Lay waste to a school--"

"No."

"Destroying a small city--"

"McGlip!"

He bowed low, swaying on his feet when he straightened. "My apologies, I only meant to help. If we only knew why things don't go smoothly…"

"There are too many people involved with this."

"Nothing can be done about the UPO."

"Not the UPO, the wayman!" Taleh regretted raising her voice at McGlip. "My agent reports he goes here and there, a cadre of passengers preying upon his attentions and delaying him from doing our bidding."

"He'd risk his world?"

"Not intentionally. That's the problem. Someone in the UPO is interfering. They've prevented the wayman from learning my demands or the stakes involved."

"Have they saddled the wayman with these extra people? Are they spies seeking us out through him?"

"The auditor for certain, but a Dorsun princess? Her manservant? A Netaolian magus?"

McGlip tensed visibly.

"Something?"

McGlip stared into space.

"McGlip?"

He shook cobwebs from his head. "The princess, could she be the mistress which refuses you?"

Taleh laughed. "Believe it or not, she helped the wayman steal the PGN."

"Perhaps if you let me see these reports or speak to your agent--"

"No, just fix the waygate and rest. I fear you'll not be with me much longer as is." Taleh regretted speaking her fears, twice so when McGlip's expression hardened. She placed a hand on his arm. "Rest first. I'll deliver the new list to the UPO."

Elmeddi

Elmeddi searched the last delivery once more, unable to find any means by which an agent communicated with Taleh.

She must receive messages some other way.

He waited until she left for Earth, resting often and gorging himself more so.

McGlip's body hadn't recovered as well as he thought. Somehow, forcing the body to surrender so much in repairing it from the PGN blast left it locked in a destructive cycle. Heady energy levels had distracted him at first until the danger of his host body devouring itself became apparent.

He strolled with a casual gait from the launch pad, having seen Taleh off on her errand like a good servant. That her lodgings were locked didn't surprise him. She'd played many things close to her breast in a way he approved.

It took moments to hack the lock, using resonant tones to drain its energies rather than more traditional security overrides. It was during this that McGlip's brain flickered back into focus. As McGlip made no effort to wrest control, Elmeddi let him watch—though the Linurian didn't understand the fierce hunger leaking from the human's mind.

Elmeddi broke through the security on her portable computer next, eliciting excited mental fluttering from the otherwise quiet captive. Memories arose with the ticklish fluttering. The crowding memories and rising greed suggested that Elmeddi's host yearned for such espionage skill earlier in his life.

Most traces of the messages from her agent had been expertly removed, something that surprised him. What remained told him the messages had been moved elsewhere.

"What are you doing?" Hullis said.

Elmeddi turned McGlip's head around. "Checking messages for my mistress."

Hullis's features tightened, disdain and disbelief prominent in the mixed landscape of his face.

"Do you require something?" Elmeddi asked.

"My freedom."

"Next on my agenda." Elmeddi sneered with McGlip's mouth.

"Primitive." Hullis strode away.

Elmeddi expanded his search until he finally found a digital diary on a small pad. Simple security hardly slowed him, and soon he was skimming through comprehensive reports on the agent's activities, along with detailed accounts of the wayman's actions and those of his companions.

Elmeddi shook his head. He couldn't believe the misfortune that had befallen them in being saddled with the spectacular idiot named Sam Bridger. His incredulity grew when he found notes pointing to Bridger as Taleh's chosen.

He thought back to Taleh's first call with the UPO. She had said something about the wayman. He'd been tracking the bomb and hadn't paid close attention. Despite learning what he sought, he delved into her diaries. Galactically proportioned disgust seized him. Repulsion grew the more he learned of her intentions.

He left her quarters as they were, crossed the complex and strangled Hullis. Feeling more centered, he arranged her body to suggest suicide by hanging.

Upon Taleh's return, he reported on waygate progress then returned to work without mention of the Vurian. Taleh would find her sister's body when it suited her to look.

Elmeddi settled the spacecraft in a junkyard just outside Las Vegas, hiding it in detritus of casinos and stage shows. He rose from the command seat and nearly crumpled to the floor. Loose skin hung from his body, jiggled by shaking limbs.

Taleh blamed him for allowing Hullis's suicide and drove him from Mars in her fury. Considering his failing host, her eventual apology would be too late for McGlip. Elmeddi would return in a fresh host to 'serve' her cause.

Before McGlip fell to pieces, Elmeddi had a mission to accomplish. He braced himself against an oversized plastic showgirl and focused his strength into a subharmonic vibration.

An answer came back high and clear accompanied by the baying of hounds. He got a cab outside the junkyard and had the driver take him toward the signal. Short pulses replied each time he sent another query and at last he directed the driver to a casino entrance.

A man stood in the doorway, old but not frail. He was garbed in a suit and hat dissimilar to the formal attire of affluent gamblers coming in and out of the doors. He leaned on a cane of yellow crystal which to Elmeddi's shock he recognized as the Linurian he sought - unprotected by flesh.

Elmeddi strode up to the man and vibrated a customary greeting. The cane vibrated in reply, though the reply was antiquated to the point of almost being unrecognizable.

"You are?" the man asked.

"El-McGlip," Elmeddi said.

The man inclined his head. "Vyse Cloudstriker. Shall we go inside?"

"Please."

Vyse led the way to an elevator and then to a penthouse suite. Pictures on the walls of the suite resembled the magus's dress, though the face differed in both appearance and in several by age. Elmeddi gestured to the pictures. "A relative?"

Vyse opened the door to the suite. "Role model."

He led the way to a large sectional couch, tossed the crystal cane onto it and dropped into a recline beside a sweat-beaded silver carafe. "Cocktail?"

Elmeddi chimed a series of tones equivalent to a document of lineage and pedigree. He pointed at the cane. "I am here to speak with him."

Vyse blinked at him. "Byron?"

The cane shifted forms through several it knew well coming to rest as a marionette without strings. It folded its hands together and waited.

There seemed no reason to pull punches. "You betrayed us."

"What's this about?" Vyse asked.

"Be silent." Elmeddi turned back to Byron. "Have you anything to say for yourself?"

Byron watched in silence a moment more before answering. "The Linurian scouts sent to Netaol found a world better than that they left. They found power. Easy life and endless riches. While I am not one of their original company, it seems hard to blame them for not returning to a life as indentured minor Linurians."

Elmeddi stared. He let the words pass over his memory once more. "You are not sorry."

Byron laughed. "Neither are they."

"You will show respect, serve me, and obey my every command," Elmeddi thundered, McGlip's voice backed by his own vibrations.

Byron's laugh intensified. "The Masters broke your strings long ago."

A scowl settled onto McGlip's face. His flesh shook, with rage more than illness. "You are a mere scout."

"I'm a meister, a second generation foci born of a master's seed, evolved in power, ability and protected by magus bond from this environment. Now, what do you want?"

"Our world is dying."

"Used up is how the Masters told it."

"When our scouts were lost in the universe you call Netaol, we tried to send more to an additional world we discovered. The two worlds did not interact well."

"How'd the other world make out?" Vyse asked.

Elmeddi glowered. "Will you silence this monkey?"

"Byron and I are friends, partners."

McGlip's eyebrows rose.

Byron shrugged. "He's been a friend a long time."

"I require your help with the wayman."

Byron sat forward. "How does that work with Linuria's destruction?"

"We have the opportunity to save our people by taking an unused planet here in Eleventh World. A plot is afoot to make an exodus to that world possible, but only if Sam Bridger delivers the cargo we have requested."

"Sam Bridger seems like an honest man, loyal and hard-working," Vyse said.

"If you were my host, I would have you slap yourself silent," Elmeddi snapped.

Vyse's expression darkened. "I know a spell to destroy your kind in an agonizing flash."

Byron nodded. "Standard training these days. Not a nice way to go, either."

"I need you to keep the wayman on task. Make sure he does his job. Help him if need be. Is that so much to ask?"

"What happens to Earth?" Byron asked.

"What do you mean?"

"The history of our race is one of ever-expanding conquest. What happens when all of your empty planet is consumed?"

"Perhaps another empty."

"Perhaps Earth?" Vyse asked.

"Perhaps," Elmeddi admitted. "It is not my choice."

"We won't help you," Vyse said. "Flawed though they may be these people have a right to their lives."

"It doesn't seem much to ask," Byron said.

"They'll kill the earthlings," Vyse said.

"That could happen, but I can't say I want my race to die either," Byron said.

"There are many more back on Netaol," Vyse countered.

"Not many Linurians left among the foci, most were born from the Change."

"Even so, Byron. We won't help them slaughter Earth."

Elmeddi saw the tension rise between them. He resisted the grin that threatened his cheeks. A war of wills crackled silently across the couch's length. Byron shifted shapes as they warred, finally settling into the shape of a giant crystal head glowering down at Vyse. "We *will* do this thing, Magus."

33: Pop Goes the Evidence

Sam Bridger

"That was an odd world," Phred said. "But the same."

Sam glanced over. "How do you mean?"

"They treated me like the mistresses of my world, making efforts not to see me."

Sam frowned. "People are people. I just don't like that world."

"They've wronged you?"

"Nah, wonderful people. The shapes overheat my primitive human brain."

"I maintain you're not as simple as you pretend."

Sam fought the smile but failed. "Keep that kind of thinking to yourself."

They drove in silence. A young boy caught Sam's attention and received honks in return.

"Are you going to tell me how you ended up on the pajama patrol?"

"Corlan has taken Princess Niri."

Sam tightened his grip on the steering wheel.

"She was stolen away, branded as his concubine, and taken I know not where."

Sam's knuckles went white. "And you need old Sam Bridger to aid your rescue?"

"I learned of Corlan's plot to slay you. My mistress will geld him before he has pleasure from her."

Sam kept the disappointment from his voice. "So you don't need me."

"Your thunder stick would be a welcome addition."

Sam glanced at Phred. *He saved you Bridger. You can always buy another.* He nodded. "I'll teach you how to use it."

"I think if you and your weapon came to speak with Corlan, he might give up my mistress without bloodshed."

"He just tried to kill me."

"You might needs raise your voice."

"I might needs kick his balls so high they jingle when he sneezes."

Phred grinned. "Would this shed blood?"

"He got more of those Sand Puma bastards?"

"I believe he has been training many warriors."

Sam pulled his truck down an offramp and then brought it back up going the other direction.

"You're taking me back to Dorsun?"

Sam shook his head. "I'm headed for some real food. Hospital food is never good, but on Tuweine I'm always worried the Jell-O will open its eyes and complain about the way I'm eating it."

"Once we've eaten?"

"We're going to find a friend of mine who owes me a favor."

The rig made it to Vegas in record time. Between Sam's network of trucker friends, the truck's ability to change colors when spotted by highway patrol and a few choice shortcuts through waygates, the speedometer seldom fell below ninety.

Sam and Phred talked about everything and nothing. Most of the nothings pertained to skirts—plenty of the everythings, too.

"Will we see the movie you have promised?"

"I'd love to, brother, but I thought there was a reason we were tearing up asphalt to rescue your sexy mistress."

"How long do these things take, movies?"

"Couple of hours."

"Why can't we watch them while we drive?"

Sam chuckled. "Movies in a car? That'd be the day - probably cause plenty of accidents - but we don't have that kind of technology. Might never have it."

"Quiss had something like it."

Sam sighed. "Yeah, but the UPO doesn't let us steal technology from the Ten. Doesn't let worlds like Dorsun have it, either, for that matter.

"I wouldn't scream from the mountain tops about not being able to import video games that fit in your hands, but there's plenty, like medical stuff, that would save lives."

"Dorsun would benefit from many things I've seen."

Sam laughed and chucked Phred in the shoulder. "I'll bet, like strip clubs and not having to wear face wraps."

"Being able to speak to a woman without fear of her cutting your tongue out."

Several sidelong glances passed between them before Sam spoke. "Just so you know, there's women here that'd do that too. Of course, the law wouldn't let them get away with it."

"Is Beatrice one to cut things from a man?"

Sam's grin vanished. His tone hardened. "I'd take it as a kindness if you'd leave Beatrice out of our conversations."

"Bob as well?"

Sam rubbed his neck. "I ain't figured Bob out yet. Might be best to leave her aside too."

"I should like very much to court a woman of Bob's beauty."

Sam went from calm to volcanic. "You just leave..."

He caught the small smile on Phred's face and knew he'd been had. He cursed.

"As I said, Sam Bridger, you're not too simple."

"Sneaky bastard."

"Fear not, Sam. I know Bob is your heart."

Sam gave Phred a side-eye. "Just don't say shit like that where she can hear you."

"I shall not."

Phred stared wide-eyed at the nightlights of the Las Vegas strip. "So many people, so many buildings."

"Surrounded by desert no less."

"A weak desert compared to the burning sands of Dorsun."

Sam grinned. "Right, a wussy desert any woman could cross."

Phred's face clouded. "You agree to its inferiority, but then proclaim it a knight's challenge?"

"Speaking about our babes, not yours."

Mirth cleared Phred's expression. "Without a sword, my mistress might find Beatrice or Bob a worthy challenger."

"Don't tell her worship that you think she's gone soft."

Phred laughed. "You neither."

They cruised the strip a few times. Sam scanned the crowds. He considered expanding the search into quieter neighborhoods, but the strip was magical.

Where else would a wizard wander?

Sam brought the rig to a sudden stop, whipping into a parking place pursued by angry horns.

"You've seen your friend?"

"Nope, next best thing."

Sam slipped his shotgun from its place behind his seat and into the new shoulder holster. Donning his bomber jacket over the holster still left a sizable bulge sure to attract attention. With the way things had been going, Sam'd rather have the shotgun ready for party action, but scaring tourists or getting arrested again wasn't going to help. He drew the weapon and flipped his wrist until it was a shotgun handle with the silver-steel baton. He collapsed all the way down and holstered it once more.

Better.

Sam moved through the crowd with an ease the desert manservant had trouble duplicating. Size accounted for less of the ability than Sam's presence. He raced across a busy street, laughing at those throwing curses in his teeth. When he reached the opposite side, Sam laid his hand on a man robed in rainbows and marijuana leaves. "Pardon me, brother."

"Man, don't wrinkle the threads."

His two robed companions faced Sam, eyeing him and Phred.

"I'm Sam. You guys are part of a fantasy convention, right?"

"Yeah, man," Waldo said. "Call me Waldo."

"Glad I found you. Have you seen more wizards, maybe one with a crystal staff that can do neat tricks?"

A man dressed as Merlin from Sword in the Stone narrowed his eyes. "Maybe, you got a name?"

A third rolled his eyes. "Come on, dude, you know he means Vyse."

Sam lit up. "Thank God, you've seen him."

"Course we have, man," Waldo said. "We're all staying in the penthouse they comped him."

Sam let out a pent-up breath. His relief faded under a deluge of questions. "Hold the phone, you're sure some casino comped Vyse a room? Dude's a socialist and he had no money. How'd he manage that? Don't they only comp high rollers?"

"Dude's a slot machine wizard, man."

Hands seized Sam. He reached into his jacket for his weapon.

"Freeze. Sam Bridger, you're under arrest."

"Man," Waldo said. "Busted."

Phred tensed to strike, but Sam shook his head.

"What's this?" Detective Scarecrow nearly crowed as he pulled the weapon from Sam's holster. "A concealed--"

"Presentation pointer," Sam said. "Perfect for real estate presentations and anatomy lessons with naughty catholic college girls."

Scarecrow turned it over in his hands, eventually getting it fully extended. "Looks more like a club."

"Yeah, because a bent grip is just the thing for easy fencing."

"Man, that would be epic for tamping down a huge--"

"Waldo," Merlin snapped.

Errol King pulled Sam's left hand behind his back, Mirandizing him from memory.

Scarecrow scrutinized the other four men. "ID's, gentlemen."

"What's this about? Why're you arresting me?"

"Fleeing incarceration." King secured the second cuff.

"I got release papers." Sam pointed at Scarecrow with his chin. "Bad cop signed them."

Scarecrow looked up from the driver's licenses in his hand. "I certainly did not."

"I got a copy in my truck a couple blocks up."

"You, ID," Scarecrow said to Phred.

"He doesn't have any."

Scarecrow scowled at Phred, gesturing at Sam. "He speak for you?"

"Sam's a good man," Phred said.

"You're not helping yourself," Scarecrow said. "Show me your ID."

"He hasn't got any, leave him alone."

"You going to tell me he doesn't have ID because he's an alien from another universe?"

"He doesn't have a driver's license 'cause he can't drive. Nothing illegal about that."

"He's right," King said.

"Oh, so this one isn't an alien?" Scarecrow snarled. "What about the others?"

"You already checked their ID's." King said.

"I do come from another universe," Phred said.

Sam cringed.

Scarecrow seized Phred. "You're going to tell me God doesn't exist, that he didn't create us?"

"Of course God exists. Auris shines every morning, lighting the day."

Scarecrow adjusted his grip. He glanced down at Phred's outfit, peeling open the black aba. "What's this?"

Sam's hopes fell.

Scarecrow removed a knife. He pulled free another. A blow gun came next, followed by a small crossbow. "What are you doing with the--is this blood?"

Phred shrugged. "Fantasy convention."

Sam forced a laugh. "Pretty realistic, huh? We all thought so, too. Didn't we, fellas?"

Waldo nodded, grinning. Merlin didn't, but after a time the shabby third wizard did, too.

"I can prove I was released legally. This is a wrongful arrest, and I'll sue you both into the stone age if you take me to jail without allowing me to prove my innocence."

King stared at Sam as if he'd transformed into a new and fantastical creature. "Erik, might be worth the time."

Scarecrow met Sam's gaze, chewing his lip absently. "Fine."

King looked at the three wizards. "We bringing them?"

Scarecrow watched them. "No, I've got their names."

"And him?" King gestured at Phred.

"I think he needs to come along with us for the moment," Scarecrow said.

"On what charge?" Sam asked.

Scarecrow looked down at the assorted weapons in his hands. "This knife is outside the lawful length to carry in public and the stains are suspicious."

Sam sucked in his breath. "Brother, I hope you've got a real good attorney."

"He's no clown," Scarecrow said.

Detective King turned the papers over once more. He shook his head. "These are legitimate."

"I never signed that," Scarecrow said.

King shrugged and handed them over once more. "Captain witnessed your signature and everything."

"Forgeries," Scarecrow said. "We take them in."

"We haven't time for this, Sam."

King frowned.

"We were hitting a show later. It'll be fine, Phred. We'll get there."

They took Sam and Phred into the precinct. The paperwork Sam provided matched that filed at the precinct itself, much to the consternation of Scarecrow and the Captain. Neither remembered signing the documents.

"Are they a match?" Sam asked.

King nodded.

"Witnessed by my attorney and signed by me on release?"

"Yes," King said.

A dangerous note entered Sam's voice. "Then I suggest you release me." He glanced at Scarecrow. "With an apology."

"I'm telling you, he's guilty. This is all some sort of elaborate conspiracy." Scarecrow waved Sam's weapon.

It changed into an energy blaster.

The surrounding officers stared at it. A smile bloomed on Scarecrow's face. "Explain this, why don't you?"

Sam shrugged. "It's a toy, but just to be safe, don't hit the orange button and pull the trigger."

"Don't, huh, to be safe?" Scarecrow asked.
Warning filled Sam's tone. "I'm serious. Don't do it."
Scarecrow did it.
A low hum rose from it, rising to a whine. Officers around the room turned toward the noise. It vibrated in Scarecrow's hand while the detective eyed it with growing concern. A glow emerged from the silver-steel. Others edged away from Scarecrow. He flung it away as if it were a live grenade. It skittered across the floor to land beneath a desk. A tiny pop proceeded a miniscule wisp of smoke. A scent akin to the smell of a heater when first lit for the winter filled the room.
"Chinese trick...firework...toy...gun." Sam flashed a confident smile. "Now, about our release?"

34: Picking Up the Pieces

Sam Bridger

A man entered the precinct dressed in a fine suit. "What's going on here?"

Captain Holt inclined his head. "Nothing to concern yourself about, sir."

"Who's this?" Sam asked.

"District Attorney Patrick Cica," the man said.

"Great. I'm being railroaded here. If someone doesn't let me go, I'm going to sue."

Captain Holt led DA Cica away, conversing with him in low voices. He showed the documents to the DA. They returned moments later.

"The DA says we're letting him go," Captain Holt said.

Sam offered an insufferable grin.

"He's a criminal," Scarecrow said. "You saw that weapon."

Captain Holt sighed. "I saw something that looked like a silver gun from a B-grade sci-fi flick, and you destroyed it."

Sam waggled his eyebrows. "Told you not to, silly guy."

Scarecrow gestured toward Phred. "What about him?"

"We got anything on him?"

"Weapons."

"Like Mister Bridger's?"

Scarecrow opened his mouth, but hesitated.

Captain Holt scowled. "You and your friend are free to go."

"Am I free to get taxi service back to where you abducted me?"

King stepped between Sam and the others. "I'll take him."

Crossways

Detective King dropped Sam and Phred off at the rig. Sam turned to go.

"Mister Bridger, you promised to assist us in finding your stowaway," King said.

"I honestly haven't seen him since you first arrested me. I will say this: I'm not sure why I should help if you intend to ramrod me every time I come to town."

"You escaped custody."

"All evidence to the contrary."

Sam climbed up into his rig, unlocking the opposite door for Phred. He sat behind the wheel, his stomach grumbling.

"For what do we wait, Sam?"

"I've got a hunch the good detective is going to sit on us for a while. Just verifying it."

"Your law enforcers display odd choices in torture."

Sam turned toward the Dorsunian. "What?"

"You don't find sitting upon us an odd torture?"

Sam snorted. "Depends on the officer, I guess."

Sam's stomach grumbled once more.

"Shall we see to a meal before finding your friend?"

"I'd rather grab him and hit the road."

"Yet, we wait here."

Sam nodded, but he didn't reply. He scanned the pedestrians, taking an occasional glance out of his mirrors to see Detective King parked behind him, but not moving. Sam climbed out of his seat and did an inspection round of his truck and trailer. He inclined his head toward Detective King. When he felt certain no vehicular violations would offer Detective King an excuse to arrest him once more, he drove to a pay lot.

"Why the short distance?" Phred asked.

"Just want it parked all nice and legal. I don't trust these cops."

Sam caught sight of a multicolored robe out of the corner of his eye. He locked the truck and hurried after with Phred on his heel. Waldo, Wizard of Weed, meandered through the crowds, purchasing tidbits from food vendors along his path. At long last he entered a hotel, burdened by consumables.

Sam stepped up next to him and hit the elevator button. "Allow me."

"Thanks, man.”

Sam and Phred entered the elevator with Waldo.

"Penthouse?"

"Wow, man, you like a mind reader?"

Sam smiled. "I don't know, let me try."

He scrunched up his face, placing both index fingers in his ears. He swayed a moment and pointed at Waldo. "I've found you. You're Waldo."

"Was I lost?" Astonishment filled Waldo's face. It turned to confusion a moment later as Waldo tried to figure out how to clap with full hands. The elevator door opened, relieving him of his dilemma. He exited into a short, plush shag carpeted hall.

Sam exited the elevator. "Let me get that door for you."

"Thanks, man, you're a real sam...samar..."

"Got it." Sam knocked on the penthouse door. He glanced at varied portraits featuring Frank Sinatra on the walls.

A grey-haired Frank Sinatra that strongly resembled Vyse answered the door - complete with suit, hat and crystal cane.

"Snazzy hat, brother."

Vyse's eyes widened. "Sam Bridger."

"That's my name, don't wear it out."

"You survived."

"Yeah. Vyse, this is Phred. Phred, Vyse. Vyse is a magus from Netaol. Phred's a manservant assassin for a smoking hot princess. So, why all gussied up?"

"We were going to dinner," Vyse said.

"We?"

Vyse led Sam inside.

Sam stopped dead. The opulence of the penthouse - filled as it was with Sinatra paraphernalia - brought a tear to Sam's eye. But it was the eight women dressed in slinky evening dresses lounging everywhere that gave Sam pause.

Vyse pointed at two of the women with his cane. They rose, sashayed across the living room, and clung to either side of the elder magus.

"Wow. Just wow."

"You've introduced me to your friend. Allow me to introduce mine." Vyse gestured as he went round the room. "That's Andi with an I there next to Stormcrow. Next are Francine and Nan, then Merlin, Ashley and I think you've met Waldo. That's Kelli, also with an I, and Lauren. This is Mindy and Cindy." Vyse gave the two brunettes on his arms a shove toward Sam. "Girls, this is my very good if heartbroken and lonely friend, Sam Bridger."

Mindy and Cindy curled around Sam.

"I didn't get you anything."

"You brought me to this wonderful place."

Sam ran his eyes up and down the women on his arms. He licked his lips. "Mindy, darling, this here is Phred. He might be a virgin."

Phred opened his mouth. Mindy tittered and flitted from Sam's arm to Phred's. Phred closed his mouth and Sam gave him an approving nod.

Cindy whispered words into Sam's ears that he hadn't heard in far too long. Sam let out a low whistle. "Hold that thought, baby doll. Need a moment with Vyse in private."

Vyse's brows shot up.

Sam took him by the arm to one corner of the room. "First off, thank you, thank you, thank you. Second, cops are searching for you - for cutting up that trucker."

Vyse shrugged. "A benefit of your system as I understand it is the ability to purchase the authorities."

"Corrupt cops aren't a guarantee, particularly for a murder charge."

"I'll take caution, then."

"I need a favor which may actually help you out a bit."

Vyse looked back at the women lounging throughout the room. "Which one?"

Sam rubbed his neck. "No, I need to rescue a princess in a different universe. I could sure use some magical back up. It'd get you out of the cops' reach."

"Sam Bridger, I'm not sure we should spend too much ti--" Vyse's whole body tensed. His grip on the top of his cane turned white-knuckled. Something about his tone fell upon Sam's ears slightly out of tune. "We'll be happy to accompany you, wayman."

Sam scrutinized Vyse. "Yeah?"

Vyse returned a stiff nod. "But in the morning."

Sam glanced at Cindy. A smile filled his face. "Morning's fine. You say something about dinner?"

"Yes."

"Sam?" Phred asked.

Sam sidled up to Phred's free ear, whispering possibilities into the assassin's ear. Phred's eyes widened.

"We good for a little delay, brother?"

Phred swallowed, glanced at Mindy and nodded.

"Great. Let me move my truck and I'll be ready for dinner."

Vyse relaxed. "We can have the concierge do that."

Sam raised his brows. He glanced around at the penthouse suite. "Guess you can. Can you get him to take it in for a fresh paint job too?"

"They'll do almost anything with a big enough tip."

"All hail capitalism."

Sam led the other two men from the limo to the auto detailing office. He presented a charge card for clacker treatment and signed the receipt. Sam's rig rolled out of the bay, glossy red with a horizontal white stripe around its midsection and blue detailing on the rear wheel housings.

Sam thrust out his chest and beamed. "Gorgeous."

"May we go and rescue my mistress, now?" Phred asked.

"Just one or two quick stops."

He stopped the truck in front of the hotel holding the fantasy convention but didn't stop the engine. "Be right back."

He reappeared a few minutes later with a small plastic bag and a huge grin. They pulled away from the hotel only to stop at a convenience store on the edge of Las Vegas. Sam ran in once more.

When he emerged, he stepped to the front of his truck, ripping a package open with his teeth. Sam tucked a tube of crazy glue between his lips and dug the convention bag from his pocket. Vyse and Phred exited the truck to watch him. After a few moments juggling items in and out of his hands, he stepped back from his rig with a wide grin.

"Perfection."

"Is this the symbol of your religion?" Phred asked.

A hurt look covered Sam. "That's the Autobot symbol."

"Which means what?" Vyse asked.

"Autobots are vehicles that can transform into robots. They are the heroes of justice, protectors of the weak."

"And you wish your carriage identified with them for this reason?" Vyse asked.

"Can we enlist these Autobots in our cause since you are now one of them?" Phred asked.

Sam turned to each man in turn. "No and no."

"Then why?" Phred asked.

"Cause it looks *freaking awesome*."

Alabaster snarled through the communicator. "I told you--"

"Man saved my life, Al. I owe him a soldier's debt. I'd think you of all people would understand that."

"There's work for you to do."

"That I know, but what I don't know is, what gives?"

Silence filled the cab for a few moments. "I'm afraid my translation circuits can make nothing of your last comment."

"Don't go all Robby on me again, brother. I'm not as stupid as you seem to think."

"I couldn't estimate your intelligence at much higher than single-celled organisms," Alabaster snapped.

Sam threw his hands up. "Fine, then call it base primate instincts. Something's going on that you aren't telling me."

"The number of things you aren't told rivals the number of things you couldn't possibly understand."

Sam glowered at the communicator. He glanced at Phred and Vyse, mumbling so only they could hear. "See, that's the problem with playing the fool. People never take you seriously when you want them to."

"Are you going to abandon this plan of yours and do the work I've assigned you or not, Bridger?"

"I'm headed to Dorsun for a PGN and I'm not only inviting you along to supervise, but to join a throw down. Come on, Al. Let's kick some skulls together."

"I told you before, assaulting the Dorsun Ambassador--"

"So what was different then about abducting Niri?"

"We weren't attacking her."

"You did."

Silence.

"You want me to pick you up or not, Al?"

Frustration leaked through the communicator in the dwarf's voice. "Bridger, I've got a job to do, and so do you. Abandon this nonsense, get the new PGN and head to Tuweine for a pickup."

"Fine. Twenty-three out."

Sam used highway ramps to turn his rig back around. He glanced at his passengers, grumbling beneath his breath. "Try and be nice to a guy."

"How long to Dorsun?" Phred asked.

"Nearest Dorsun gate is local. Just wish we had time to swing by Feyrth."

"Why?" Vyse asked.
"I had to self-destruct my cool new thunder stick."

35: Imperiled in Luxury

Niri

Niri paced a pleasure pit, garbed in only three sheer veils, and surrounded by women wearing even less. Small tables set with food or drink filled the cool room. Silvered glass covered one wall. Bathing pools behind silk curtains dominated the opposite end. Plush cushions dotted the room, piled thickly next to the mirrored wall.

She refused to sit upon the many cushions. She refused to lay upon the couches. When she allowed herself to sleep, she slept in corners of bare tile.

Her stomach rumbled, but she ignored it.

Fresh fruit or nuts hadn't been included on the serving dishes. She wouldn't have trusted them if they had. Pitchers and decanters offered juices, wines, and cool water.

None of it trustworthy.

The women around her, once warriors or noblewomen like herself, lounged in a haze, all of them inured to their nudity. Several fondled themselves openly, without even the shyness of young girls discovering their libido.

"We must rise. We must fight," Niri repeated.

They watched her behind slow blinks and bemused smiles.

Disgust tightened Niri's stomach until it ached. *Drugged and weak, all of them.*

She'd maintain vigil against the food and drink lest she'd wind up like them.

Crossways

The slave pretender Corlan entered, flanked by guards. Women surged toward him. Rather than in a concerted attack, they fell to his feet, begging him to be pleasured.

Niri dug her nails into her palms.

Corlan met her gaze, smiling over the heads of kneeling women kissing his feet. Niri's attention went from Corlan to his guards. Large and bulky with muscles, they resembled gladiators more than bodyguards.

She ceased her scrutiny to find Corlan still beaming at her. "You might slay one. Two if we weren't on our guard against you. I can replace them easily." Corlan gestured at the women at his feet. "Using up your strength only hastens your fate."

"Force me to bed and you'll become as close to a woman of power as might be."

"Why would I force you when I have them? I can be patient. You must drink eventually."

"I'll die first."

He shrugged. "You'll weaken enough for my purposes before you perish."

Corlan turned his back to her, crossing the room to a mound of cushions followed by the other women. She tensed to strike but found him watching via the reflective wall. Women who should've beaten Corlan to death, disrobed him instead.

She turned her back on their baselessness, folding her arms across her body. Her fingers brushed the still raw branding wound. Pain erupted along it, kindling a rising firestorm. She wanted to cool it in the bathing pools, or at least clean the scent of sweat from her limbs.

Niri feared the pool and hated herself for that fear.

Death by water no longer plagues me, but I trust not the waters. The pretender has access to magic I cannot fathom and wouldn't have believed before the wayman. Drowning beneath that slave's treachery, bowing to him drugged or otherwise is a fate worse than even what I intend for him.

36: Second Thoughts

Alabaster

Alabaster cradled his head in his hands, trying to ignore the sounds emanating from the two arcade games in the break room. A tiny throb pulsed behind his eyes, deadened by drugs injected by his components to let him ignore pain and continue working.

He'd been shot. He'd been critically injured, even losing limbs in battle. He'd never been so thwarted as he felt within the offices of Crossways Transportation.

A very real possibility of failure loomed.

I've always gotten the job done, and by the book. Curse Bridger and this whole world.

Despite his efforts on Eleventh World, the book might as well have not existed. The wayman, Sam Bridger, ignored orders, doing whatever he thought best. Alabaster couldn't fire him, because the terrorists insisted he be their deliveryman - a demand that baffled the dwarf.

Why would they hang the fate of their efforts on the hapless boob?

It irked him to consider some blame for current events. He'd determined — as best as was possible under the circumstances — that Bridger wasn't part of the threat. He could've rescinded the order not to explain the reality of their situation to the wayman. Not knowing his world's impending peril enabled Bridger's quixotic heroism for a desert Lady clearly beyond the wayman's romantic aspirations.

"Hard day?" Bob asked.

Alabaster looked up. A sardonic chuckle escaped his lips. The grease smudged mechanic standing before him should've been beyond Bridger too.

If she didn't adore him to unreasonable levels. He frowned at her. What does she see in him? Have I missed something?

"The records department and three-eye continue being troublesome," Alabaster admitted after a moment. "Manual search continues, but hope dwindles."

"You've learned nothing?"

"Word came from the UPO suggesting the terrorist of Vurian origin, but the records here are so hopelessly disordered that we may never find the critical shipping manifest. I begin to wonder some other method brought the bomb here."

"So... we're all going to die."

"Unless I can convince Bridger to make the deliveries demanded by the terrorist, we may indeed."

"I meant humanity."

"It's my duty to continue the search until the last moment. I'll likely perish with the rest of you."

"Why not just tell Sam?"

"I was considering that, but I fear his complicity."

Bob's tone hardened. "I thought you'd decided he was a harmless idiot."

"I'm forced to wonder.... "

"About?"

"Your loyalties."

Bob bristled. "I'm no traitor."

Alabaster shook his head. "No, your loyalty to Bridger. You're a smart woman - for a human. The longer I observe you, the harder it becomes to believe you'd pin your loyalty on an imbecile."

Bob sat opposite the dwarf. "I don't think I understand."

"What if Bridger is smarter than I believe?"

She laughed. "He couldn't be dumber than you've suggested."

"Precisely, what if it's all a ruse to throw off suspicions?"

"It is." Beatrice's hard tone came from the doorway. "Just not for the reasons you assume."

Alabaster glanced at Bob then gestured for Beatrice to sit down. "Would you care to elaborate?"

Beatrice eyed Bob as she sat. "Sam *seems* like a free spirit. He's been that way since I met him, but there are shackles hidden beneath his cavalier womanizing ways.

"Something happened to him before we met. I never learned what, but whatever it was must have been really bad for him to even hide it from his wife. I always thought I could break his facade, bring him back to what he was in his early evals."

"You've seen Bridger's records?" Alabaster asked.

Beatrice nodded. "And before you ask, yes I know it's a violation of policy."

"You can't 'break' Sam." A dreamy expression slid onto Bob's face. "He has an indomitable spirit, a zest for life that holds the jaded cynical nature of reality at bay."

A quiet laugh escaped Beatrice. "I thought so too, once."

"None of this saves your world."

Beatrice fixed the dwarf with a steely glare. "Tell Sam. He'll save the world for us."

Alabaster couldn't help the snort that escaped him.

"Doubt all you want. He might not look it, but Sam's the kind of hero that nothing can stop."

"Preposterous," Alabaster said.

"I believe in him," Beatrice said.

"Then why did you leave him?" Bob asked.

The tension in the room skyrocketed, but toward its apex turned back to crash on the rocks below.

"Because he wanted–no, needed to be left. We had a miscarriage. After that, he went out of his way to give me reasons - whether or not he did so on purpose, I don't know."

Alabaster scanned through Bridger's personnel file. "There may be something to what you say. His records indicate a consistent resistance to restrictions."

Bob frowned.

Alabaster nodded. "To someone like him, commitment would appear as the ultimate restriction"

"There's more to it than that. Sam loves the idea of commitment, marriage, but something about it also terrifies him," Beatrice said.

Bob stared at the table in silence. Her lips curled into a pert smile. "Then I know how to solve all this."

Alabaster raised his brow.

"Tell Sam the truth," Bob beamed. "Then forbid him from saving the world."

37: Dressing for War

Sam Bridger

Phred and Vyse employed spy craft and magic until they learned the location of Corlan's secret palace. They returned to find Sam practicing with a mysteriously acquired crossbow.

His shot went wide of the sparsely bolt-peppered cactus. Far more littered the sand surrounding the cactus. He looked up at their approach. "Good news?"

"Phred regards it as bad, though we've discovered his location," Vyse said.

Sam turned raised brows upon Phred.

"You'll never believe this, but Corlan traveled to the PGN mines some time back."

"Where'd Carol stow it?"

"He created a kingdom with it," Phred said.

Sam cursed. "He used my pickup to set himself up?"

"In a way," Vyse said. "My divinations indicate he gave the UPO an excuse, but too long ago for the PGN to have been meant for you."

"So, where is it?" Sam asked.

"The way is at the back of Lady Shindra's geonation, beneath the lake," Phred said.

Sam crossed to the cactus, plucking bolts before marching back to his wagon. "Let's go."

"It's beneath the water," Phred said.

"Not a problem." They rode through the desert, three men with their faces covered and no lady to direct their movements. Several knights eyed them, but only one stopped them. Sam's amulet bought their freedom.

They camped each night, staying out of villages owned by Corlan save when forced to pass through. Phred complained about the food. Vyse complained about the accommodations, and Sam bemoaned the loss of his new gun. Dorsun had never suffered three motleyer, less likely heroes.

Phred brought down a night flier during his watch, augmenting a desert night chilled breakfast of Pop Tarts with enough meat for two meals. They skirted villages when terrain demanded it.

"Man, it'd be so much easier if we could cut this short with a montage," Sam groused.

"A what?" the other two asked.

"Nothing."

A silent tension lingered near population centers. Women with cast down eyes performed tasks normally reserved for man-slaves, flinching away from the slightest attention.

Vyse scowled at them. "My people's monarchies are patriarchal, but our women are content. They don't fear men as these do."

"Yours is a lush world. And the way I heard it, you had your own taskmasters not too long ago."

"The Masters, vile cre--" Vyse froze mid spit. "virtuous creators slighted for their purpose and vision. Your Earth will do well beneath such leadership."

Sam chuckled. "I know our languages are similar, but I think you meant would rather than will."

"Yes. The Masters would have done well for your world."

Sam rubbed his neck. "Well, old Sam Bridger wasn't there, so he can only say what he's heard."

"Best you stick to what you know, wayman," Vyse said.

"What happened to these Masters?" Phred asked.

"A child." A hardness usurped Vyse's faraway expression. His voice followed suit. "A so-called savior."

Sam knew something was wrong long before they reached their destination - not by the terrified women, but by the vast expanse of squared fields. Quissian water offered the only explanation for such waste. Employed with the waters of a geonation, crops grew strong and plentiful. To grow crops on Quissian water alone represented an unprecedented expenditure of wealth.

A small lake rested in a sheltered depression. Trod and brown fields surrounded it. A dock built of grey plastics offered moorage to twin barges at home on Earth but too advanced for Dorsun. An island floated at the center, hugging a capped tube that reminded Sam of an Audorian elevator.

"Somebody seriously needs a visit from a friendly neighborhood UPO auditor," Sam said.

"If Phred's description of geonations holds true, wouldn't the platform they're loading be upside down when it arrived below?" Vyse asked.

Sam shook his head. "I've seen similar. The elevator will rotate around in a gravitational null point."

Phred drew his dagger. "Shall we swim or obtain a boat?"

"Let's go with none of the above." Sam flicked the reins, rousing his team to speed. "All right, Ren, it's time to see what these babies can really do."

Guards shouted at Sam to stop. A few peppered his horses with crossbow bolts. Sam flicked the reins harder.

Vyse seized Sam's shoulders with a death grip. Phred's own knuckles held the wooden wagon bench with bloodless strength. Mad laughter bubbled from Sam's lips. He stood, working the reins hard enough to have permanently injured live horses.

The wagon and its three passengers mounted the dock, knocking guards and a ferryman into the water. It crashed into the lake, Sam's laughter echoing off its surface. They sank without a single swimmer returning to the top.

Wet and red faced, Phred and Vyse glared dripping faces at Sam within the confines of the metal submersible.

"You could've said," Phred said.

"Agreed."

Sam grinned at both of them. "Where's the fun in that? Besides, at least one of you has visited Quiss and should have known what I was doing."

"The sentries will report our approach," Vyse said.

"Doubtful, Vyse."

"Why would they not?"

"They bore crossbows."

Vyse's forehead wrinkled.

Phred whipped around to face the magus. "They're ignorant of Corlan's knowledge, else they'd carry more advanced weapons."

"Perhaps they're only armed thus not to arouse local suspicions," Vyse said.

"You mean like the dock and the boats would?"

"I lack some essential element to your stratagem, Sam Bridger."

"We drowned."

Phred nodded. "The lakes are deep, going to the next geonation. In this case, Corlan's hidden fiefdom. Things that fall into the lake seldom come out the other end."

"I imagine it happens once in a blue moon."

"Just often enough to have established among our people that they connect geonations."

Vyse nodded. "We drowned."

The submersible glided through the water, following the thick elevator shaft. Sam wondered after its construction but supposed nangnome-robotics had been used to construct it rather than the parts being brought one by one into Dorsun somehow. Even with nangnome-robotics to explain the elevator, the materials for the dock and the barges themselves seemed troublesome evidence that Corlan had some sort of way to move goods without Crossways Transportation or UPO sanction.

Sam keyed the communicator.

"What're you doing?" Phred asked.

Sam smirked, adopting a childish voice, and stretched out his last word. "I'm telling..."

"HQ. Is that you, twenty-three?" Beatrice asked.

"Hey, hey, busy Bea. This is twenty-three."

"Grow up and tell me what you want"

"Get the big bad dwarf, would you?"

"He's busy."

"Too busy to bust a creep for about a dozen major UPO violations?"

"Yes."

Sam scowled at the communicator. "What aren't you telling me, Bea?"

"Plenty, none of it your business."

Heat rose in Sam's neck until his ears burned. He ran a hand down the back of his head. "I'm getting pretty sick of your attitude, Bea."

"Finally, we agree on something. If you don't have Crossways business, then stop wasting company money."

"I'm reporting a UPO violation, in compliance with Crossways Transportation employee rules and responsibility documentation, to include notification of ruling governance council or committee of gross misuse or appropriation of UPO technologies nonindigenous to a given universe's evolution."

Silence filled the cab.

"Where in the hell did that come from, Sam?"

"Employee manuals."

"But-but you don't read them."

"All Crossways employees are required to sign off acknowledgement of the manuals, swearing they have read and accepted the updated version each year." A smirk lit Sam's face. "Sam Bridger is a lot of things, but he's not a liar."

More silence.

"Look, if you're not going to take my report, I'll have Ren-2-3 transmit all..." Sam trailed off, staring at a wide side channel in the lake's null gravity center.

"Sam?"

"I'll get back to you."

Beatrice's tone bristled. "You called us!"

Sam ignored her, turning his rig into the passage. "It could connect them all."

"How will this help us?" Phred asked.

Sam sighed, letting a pouty expression surface. "It won't, but I'd really like to know where this goes. I mean, beyond the adventure, how cool does Sam Bridger, Multiverse Explorer sound?"

"Another time?" Vyse asked.

"Yeah," Sam turned the rig around.

He exited the water channel, taking a lap around the elevator to verify his bearings. Another water passage occupied the opposite side.

Sam rubbed his neck. "It must run through the whole world. Phred, have they ever found evidence that the lakes connect to more than two geonations?"

"Never," Phred said.

Sam sighed. "A mystery for another day."

They rode through the water until the surface drew close. Sam kept the rig beneath the lake's surface, rising only once he'd gone to the opposite end of the lake from a matching dock to the one in Lady Shindra's geonation.

A palace to turn Cinderella jealous rose at the lake's edge. Rather than cool colors meant to suffer desert heat, the walls were stained black and edged with great swaths of blood red. Guards patrolled the structure's exterior, armed with swords but dressed in body armor outstretching the best the US Military had in service.

Phred swore, gesticulating through his entire repertoire of deific wardings.

Sam drew back on the controls and cast the manservant a long look. "Something the matter, brother?"

Phred shook his head. "He uses valuable growing land for a palace not designed to withstand siege. He rings it with flesh rather than stone."

"He was a gladiator."

Phred spat.

"Hey, not in the truck!"

Phred apologized.

"What now?" Vyse asked.

"Storm the castle, rescue the princess, clobber the bad guy, limp off into the sunset," Sam said.

"Limp?" Vyse asked.

"Because rescuing this princess is more likely to get us a kick in the balls than thank us with a kiss."

"Why would she do this?" Vyse asked.

Sam shrugged. "She wants to rescue herself?"

Vyse frowned. "I'd think she'd be grateful."

"You haven't met Niri."

Phred cleared his throat.

"Sorry, you haven't met *Princess* Niri," Sam amended.

"Better," Phred said.

"How do we proceed?" Vyse asked.

"We could stroll up to the door and knock," Sam said.

Phred smiled. "I somehow doubt a man who wants you dead will open the door and let you in."

"What if he thinks I'm selling Girl Scout cookies?" Sam glanced at the other two. "No comments? Here I thought the little terrors were a universal thing."

"I believe I could nova that star," Vyse said.

"Good finale," Sam said, "but let's not lead with it."

"Your passport will not arm us?" Phred asked.

Sam shook his head. The three sat in silence for several moments. Sam sucked in a deep breath.

"How about we sneak up from behind, where no one is supposed to be?" Sam asked.

"And if they notice us?" Vyse asked.

"I play the meat shield, Phred flanks, and you cover us with your magic," Sam said.

The other two nodded.

Sam glanced down at his red flannel shirt, mumbling under his breath. "Crap, wish we had a cleric."

"You feel the need for a blessing upon our venture?" Vyse asked.

"Nah, just someone to make with the healing magic so I don't end the way of most red-shirted meat shields."

"I can work healing magic, though without a circle to draw from, it will be limited," Vyse said.

"Yay for cross-classing! Just vamp any guards we come across for extra juice."

"Vamp?" Vyse asked

"Leech?" Sam asked.

"Ah."

"You two mind waiting outside while I button up?"

The other two exited the rig without a backward glance.

The three of them snuck a wide circle from the far end of the lake to the back of the palace. They kept low where they could, ducking behind buildings and wagons. The terrain around the lake had been grown for use as farmland, leaving them without geography suitable for concealing an invading force.

They made it around to the side before a pair of guards caught them. "Halt in the name of Lord Corlan."

Sam straightened, the other two eyeing him. He set down his crossbow, raised his hands, and strolled toward them. "I'm sorry, brother, in whose name did you say?"

"Lord Corlan," the first said. "Halt right there."

Sam pointed at the ground. "Right here?"

"Yes," the guard said.

Sam pointed behind him. "Not back there."

"Where you are," the guard said.

Sam turned his back to them. "It really wouldn't be any kind of bother to go back to where I was when you shouted."

They rushed up to him, swords in hand. "Halt right where you are. Now."

Sam stopped, back still to them. "Now, you said Lord Carol?"

"Corlan," the second guard snapped.

"Really?" Sam cursed. "We were looking for a Lady Googoo."

"Who?" the first guard asked.

"Googoo," Sam looked at Phred and Vyse, still eyeing him as if he'd lost his sanity. "Looks like we stormed the wrong castle, fellas."

"Shut up," the second guard pressed his sword to Sam's back.

"You guys couldn't help a brother out? Give us directions to the castle of the other despot in the region?"

The first guard approached Phred and Vyse. "Lord Corlan is the only...hey!"

"Didn't mean anything personal about--Ow, ow, owie," Sam lowered one hand, but the sword in his back pressed harder.

"Don't move."

"I'm trying, but I've got a wicked cramp. Give a brother a break. Either let me rub it away or chop off my head."

"That is a cruel fate," Phred said. "Not being able to treat a cramp."

"Silence, you." The second guard pointed his sword at Phred.

Sam bent to rub his leg.

The sword came back to poke a hole in Sam's flannel. "I didn't say you could move."

"Maybe you should let him rub it, Malek," the first guard said. "Go ahead."

"Don't move."

Sam froze half bent over. "Hey, make up your minds."

"Least you could do," Phred said.

Malek pointed at Phred once more. "Shut--"

Sam's fist came from near the ground to land the blow beneath Malek's chin. He fell to the ground, sprawled spread eagle.

The first guard turned to rush Sam, but his eyes rolled into his head. He flopped to the ground.

Sam lunged forward with a follow-up blow, but Malek didn't move. Sam chuckled. "Men with glass jaws should stay out of the bullying business."

"You're a sly one, if a few muffins shy of a basket," Vyse said.

Sam shrugged. "Nice bit of magic."

Vyse pointed at Phred.

Sam smiled, nodding. "Nice one, Phred."

"Shall I immolate them?" Vyse asked.

"I'd rather not kill them for making a poor choice. Hell, where would that leave me? Anyway, I want out of this red shirt before I end up Kirked."

They took a few moments to strip the two guards and truss them up. Phred kept the Sand Puma garb he'd stolen. Vyse redressed in Malek's armor. Sam struggled to don the other guard's armor but was too big for either guard's attire.

Vyse pressed a hand to Malek's bare chest and extended his other toward Sam.

Sam's and the guard's clothes whirled around him, unraveling at the seams, and recombining around his limbs. He dropped his hands to his waist. "Leave the skivvies, brother."

They settled a moment later a mix of red and tan.

"Do you have a color preference?" Vyse asked.

"Black," Sam said.

"In this heat?" Phred asked.

"Never go wrong with black," Sam said.

Vyse released the spell, garbing Sam head to toe in black.

Phred shook his head. "If Corlan doesn't kill you, your fashion sense will."

Sam puffed out his chest. "A real man will always give his life in the name of style. Sam Bridger is just such a man."

Vyse made a stirring motion with his staff.

Sam's clothes were augmented by peacock feathers highlighted with blues, greens, and violets.

Phred snorted.

Sam glanced down. "We're not going to a Netaolian ball."

"Yet it seems so fitting," Vyse said.

Sam strutted a circle glancing himself over. "Perhaps a lesser man couldn't pull it off, but it looks good on Sam Bridger."

"You're really going to make him assault a fortress in that?" Phred asked. "I thought we were trying to blend in."

"The black didn't blend in any case, and he seems pleased."

"The guards will laugh themselves to defeat," Phred said.

"All part of a good strategy," Sam glanced down at his clothes. "Vyse, can you make those great muffins?"

"Which muffins? A magus I may be, but I cannot create the ones you're missing from your basket."

"When I was at Tiar Trillarian, and I got...you know what, let's worry about it later."

"When we're not sneaking through enemy territory to storm a castle?" Phred asked.

"Right, but in my defense, they were *really* good muffins."

38: Storming the Castle

Sam Bridger

They encountered a second set of guards before they reached the rear castle entrance. Both went down staring at Sam with disbelieving expressions - though it was Phred's darts which knocked them out.

The closer they got, the more the castle fit Sam's vision of a fairytale at odds with the surrounding desert. He pressed his back to the black castle stone.

Surprised icing isn't dripping on my feathers.

They entered a kitchen garden resembling a prison yard. The plant life flourished, perhaps due to Quissian water, but the maids seeking a moment's rest wilted visibly when the men entered.

Sam planted a fist on either hip. "Never fear, dear ladies, we're here to rescue you."

Phred whispered. "We're here to rescue my mistress."

"I won't leave a damsel in distress."

"Most of these women would execute for talking to them."

"Perhaps, before they were press-ganged."

Vyse stepped in front of his companions. "Women of Dorsun, while we attempt to bring justice to this keep, please stay out of harm's way."

"Just as well we stay out of this," an older woman said. "We've worked for two days to set Lord Corlan's feast."

Sam beamed. "A fitting reward for victory."

She shrugged. "If you win, sure. You lose, it'd be best if he gets his feast undisturbed."

"Will you be punished for letting us pass?" Vyse asked.

The older woman sized them up. "Never saw you."

"Especially not him." A younger brunette with dark circles beneath her eyes tittered at Sam.

Sam strutted through the garden, swinging his hips a bit to flourish the tail of peacock feathers. Several kitchen maids giggled. He stepped inside and turned to Vyse. "Enough's enough. Take off the feathers."

"I thought you looked darling out there," Vyse said. "A delight to those poor tired eyes."

"What's going on here?"

Sam turned to find a trio of guards with a trio of submachine guns. He glanced at Phred, clearing his throat. "My guards were just bringing me inside from a bit of air."

"Who're you?" the lead gunman asked.

"Entertainment," Sam swiveled his hips to show them his tail. "For the feast."

The gunmen glanced at one another then Phred. "This is true, Sand Puma?"

"True as his lordship's greatness," Phred said.

Their leader nodded. "Very well."

Sam led the way past the guards, ignoring their smirks. He stopped within arm's reach and raised an eyebrow at the weapon in their hands. "That some kind of new crossbow?"

"It's none of your business. Get back to the performer quarters."

Sam bowed. "You're right. In this heat, I could really use a nap."

The guard kicked Sam, ruffling feathers. "On with you."

Dizziness assaulted Sam as the guards wavered on their feet. A huge yawn broke his face. He hit the floor with the guards.

Vyse

Vyse scowled at Sam's limp figure.

Phred dropped to his knees next to Sam. "What happened?"

<What indeed.>

A miscalculation.

<Not like you. I'm given to wonder if you're trying to get the wayman to distrust us.>

He shouldn't. Vyse thought. "I miscalculated the spell. I'm still acclimatizing to your local magic."

"Can you wake him?"

"Yes, move him from the others so they remain asleep," Vyse knelt next to the sleeping guards, placing a hand on each to draw power until it pressed uncomfortably against his skin.

He wove an awakening spell, then regarded the guards. Despite the wayman's gentle sensibilities, leaving guards tied up every time they encountered them was hardly a sound way to avoid defeat.

Sam stepped up beside him, groggy and yawning once more. "What gives?"

"A mistake. Please accept our apologies," Vyse said.

"We all make them. What're you doing with Cory's minions there?"

"I was just pondering that."

Sam rifled through the bodies, taking the guns, utility belts and extra magazines. He checked the guns to make sure they were loaded and offered a gun and belt to Phred. He offered a second to Vyse, but the magus refused. Sam strapped one belt around his waist and the second over his chest. He hefted the guns, one per hand with a wide grin. "Let's tie up these puma kittens and get moving."

Vyse smiled, picking the right intonations from his memory to transform the guards. "I'll see to it and catch up."

Sam exited the kitchen with Phred on his heel. Vyse followed them a moment later, leaving a trio of kittens snoring on the tiles.

Sam Bridger

While Vyse dealt with the three newly downed guards, Sam kicked in the door to the concubine chamber. He swung his guns in lazy arcs, firing high to riddle art and artistic frescos with bullets.

"Honey, I'm home..." His voice faltered from Cuban to New Jersey. "And I brought some little friends."

Dozens of women stared at him.

Phred rushed around Sam and his accompanying cloud of gun smoke. "Mistress, Mistress?!"

Heads snapped toward him.

"Yo! Niri, babe, we're here to rescue you," Sam shouted.

Phred glared.

"Right. Yo! *Princess* Niri, babe, we're here to rescue you."

"She's not here." A woman's hurt expression crept into her voice. "Lord Corlan took *her* to the feast."

Sam sighed. "Okay, well, we're here to rescue you too. Get your things. We're going."

"Why?" A naked woman rolled over in the cushions to Sam's right, her limbs laid at a distracting angle. A purr escaped her. "We have everything we want here."

Another, this one wearing veils too sheer to have much point, licked her lips. "Well, except you. We haven't had you."

"I've seen something like this before," Vyse said.

Sam adjusted his trousers. "Me too, but not awake."

"These women have been subjected to a euphoria inducing magic," Vyse said.

"We have no magus," Phred said. "But I've seen pleasure houses where the males act this way."

"Do they pay well?" Sam asked.

Phred's brows met in the middle.

"The pleasure houses, what do they pay their men?"

"They're slaves," Phred said.

"So not much point in putting in a resume?" Sam asked.

"Focus, wayman," Vyse snapped. "What causes this in your world, Phred?"

"Drugs," Phred said.

Sam adopted a falsetto. "Don't say yes."

The two men blinked at him.

"Forget it. You two get the babes, I mean their high holy and mighty bitchinesses sorted out. I'll crash the feast."

"I should come with you," Phred said.

Sam shook his head. "Stay here and watch out for Vyse."

Vyse raised both hands, his staff breaking into a swarm of hummingbirds which flitted circles around the heads of the women.

"Sam?" Phred said.

"Bring you back a sandwich?" Sam asked.

"Be cautious."
Sam offered a bright smile. "Always."
"With my mistress. She may be drugged too."
"I wouldn't hurt or anything else with her, not drugged."
"Take care she doesn't regret hurting you."

Sam encountered no one during his journey back downstairs. He considered entering the feast as an entertainer but figured the submachine guns might belie his efforts.

A door at the foot of the rear stair opened up onto a sight that took Sam's breath away. An arsenal of weapons originating from many of the eleven worlds packed the room. Sam cherry picked items from the racks, filling his belt and stuffing pockets with ammo and grenades.

He continued down the hall to find a massive pair of closed doors, the sounds of a cafeteria slipping to him beneath them. He pushed one open enough to peek through. A wide path stretched up the hall, bracketed by tables filled with men laughing, eating, and grabbing serving women in ways which anywhere else on Dorsun would cost them limbs. Corlan sat on a throne at the hall's head, raised a few steps above the others. Naked women stood around him with palm fans, pitchers, platters, and his goblet.

Niri lay on her side at his feet, dressed in too sheer veils, and chained to his throne. Her scowl offered clear evidence that she wasn't under Corlan's influence.

"Holy Hutts, talk about déjà vu," Sam mumbled. "Wish Phred was here to ask whether Dorsun has big lobster-spider things."

Sam watched the feast for another moment, weighing his options. He was fresh out of robots to gift as a distraction and men on the inside to help him escape if he got captured. He glanced at the guns, then returned to the armory.

Once inside, he set the submachine guns down. He stripped out of his top, ripped a strip of cloth from his hems and tied it around his forehead. He bent for his weapons, but as an afterthought strapped the Kevlar back on before he did so.

He traded his submachine guns for a pair of assault rifles, but a rack of thirty caliber machine guns caught his eye.

Sam discarded the assault rifles and pulled two of the machine guns from their place and set them at his feet then draped extra ammunition chains across his chest. He bent to lift the machine guns but found them impossible to lift singlehanded no matter what Sly movies told him.

Sam scowled, rubbing his neck. An idea brought a grin to his lips. He worked for several minutes, rigging a harness which hung the heavy guns from his shoulders. He adjusted it several times until, though a heavy load, the guns could be wielded with relative ease in each hand.

Sam returned to the doors. He peeked through them once more to check everyone's position.

Corlan rose from his throne, extending his hands. "This is just the beginning. One geonation at a time, we will restore the natural order. Women will bow and beg to serve our every whim. As it is in other worlds, it shall be so here."

The assembled men cheered.

"Once Eleventh World is destroyed, no one will have access to Dorsun unless we grant it. No one will learn of the things we've brought in from other worlds. No one will come to stop us until it is far too late."

Sam figured he wouldn't get a better straight line. He kicked the door open and sauntered inside. "Someone order an ass-kicking with extra cheese?"

Corlan spat one word. "Wayman."

Niri's face lit up. "Bridger."

"Everyone stay right where you are. All I want is the princess in sex slave attire."

Niri growled. "Bridger."

"Give her up, and you can return to your regularly scheduled megalomaniacal freak feast."

"Always in the wrong place for the wrong reasons," Laz said. "Not to mention inappropriately dressed."

"Eugene!" Sam grinned toward the former wayman, stepping around the room's edge toward the buffet table. The shift put his back to a wall rather than the open doorway. "You don't like my party dress?"

"No."

"Kind of shocked to see you here. However could you have gotten involved with a bunch of power-hungry, sociopathic...you know what. Forget I asked."

"How did *you* get here?" Corlan asked.

"By way of your armory. Nice toys there. Pity I rigged it to blow." Sam kicked himself for not coming up with the idea earlier, but he hoped they bought his bluff.

"You'd die too," Corlan said.

"The hero never dies, besides, I'm too pretty. Death wouldn't take me."

"We can fix that," Corlan said. "Mutilate his face, then kill him."

Benches scraped the floor.

"Whoa there, boys, mindless minion doesn't have a whole lot of job security. You're really going to let him send you into the business ends of my two friends? Pretty sure Sly and Chuck here are going to leave you needing of a whole lot of corks."

"He's bluffing," Laz said. "Bridger hasn't got the balls to kill."

Corlan's soldiers charged.

Sam opened fire, shouting over the massive noise. "Big. Beautiful. Burly. And brass."

Blood and bodies littered floor, tables, and benches.

Several guards drew handguns. Shots impacted against the Kevlar. A round hit him in the left shoulder, a second and third in the same arm.

Sam's guns locked back, breeches open and out of shells.

Sam dropped to one knee behind the buffet table. He struggled through pain of his injured left arm to get an ammo chain off his shoulder. It caught on the other. "How in the hell do they manage this so fast in the movies?"

"They get a cut," Laz shouted. "Surrender, or I put a bullet in the woman's skull."

"I want her alive," Corlan said.

"We don't always get what we want," Laz said.

"You don't rule here," Corlan said.

"Give him another minute to reload and neither do you."

Sam managed to get one chain loaded while they argued.

"Bridger, up where I can see you or she's dead. You know I'm not bluffing."

Sam let the machine guns hang. The weight on his left shoulder was excruciating. A cold sensation filtered through the pain, spreading out from his wounds. He reached for a pair of grenades, but his left couldn't feel them.

Sam stood, a pinless grenade in his right hand.

"Hands, Bridger," Laz said.

"Can't lift my left."

"Lift it anyway."

"Seize him," Corlan said.

Guards scrambled over bodies to rush Sam.

Sam lifted his hands, one grenade visible.

Guards froze.

"Drop it," Laz said.

"Can't. No pin."

"Then she's dead," Laz said.

Sam eyed Corlan. "Come on, Carol, you've got a whole room full of babes upstairs. I know you want me for taking those two PGNs using your name."

Corlan purpled. "Two?"

Sam shrugged. It was agony. "Let her go and I'll surrender."

"Why should I?" Corlan asked.

"I'm not a soldier, but I'm pretty sure if the grenade here goes off it will chain react with all the others hanging off my belt. If that doesn't do it, the timer on the charge in your armory ought to finish you off if you're still here fighting with me."

"Go check," Corlan said.

"I wouldn't. Door's rigged with a claymore."

Corlan narrowed his eyes. "For not being a soldier, you seem pretty skilled."

Sam resisted the urge to shrug again. The cold in his shoulder crept toward his chest. "I like things that go boom. Let her go. My arm's getting tired from holding up this grenade."

"Hardly an effort," Laz said.

"After these damn monsters, even marshmallows would be heavy. Come on, Carol. Let her go. Once she runs from the room, I'll surrender. You can always chase her. What've you got to lose?"

"If you call me Carol one more time, I'll kill her myself."

Sam sighed, blinking away black spots creeping into his vision.

"Let her go. He's right," Laz said.

Corlan drew a key from around his neck, tossing it to Laz.

"Great," Sam said. "Send one of your boys over here to take this hot potato, would you?"

Chains dropped from Niri. She met Sam's gaze. He nodded and gestured toward the door with his eyes. She ran.

Sam handed the grenade to a guard. The others seized him, stripped him out of his harness and removed his grenade belt.

"Bring her back," Corlan ordered. "You wasted your efforts. She can't escape here without my leave."

Sam smiled. "I got here, didn't I?"

"How?"

"Trade secret, Carol."

Corlan thundered up to Sam. "Tell me how."

"His rig," Laz said. "Changed into a submarine if I'd guess."

Corlan glanced away from Sam. "Excellent."

Sam fixed a grin on his face to meet Corlan's returning gaze. "You've underestimated me and the element of the pies!"

Before anyone could react, Sam snatched a pie from the buffet table and slammed it into Corlan's face. He snatched his grenade belt from the guard holding it, bulled him over and sprinted for the doors.

Shouts and gunfire followed him into the palace halls. A few impacted on the back of his Kevlar, knocking him forward and off balance. He considered backtracking through a few rooms and dropping a grenade into the armory, but he wasn't sure if Phred and Vyse were safely away, not to mention him surviving long enough to escape. He made it down the front steps, sprinting past four startled guards. Lights popped before his face and his limbs grew heavier.

Phred might have criticized Corlan for planting his palace at the edge of the lake, but the shortened distance to the dock made Sam ecstatic.

Sam leapt onto one of the barges, ducking into the telephone booth-sized control room to dodge more gunfire. He cranked the ignition and shoved the boat to full speed. It leapt forward, only to jerk backward.

Sam cursed. He raced for the mooring ropes.

A guard leapt onto the boat.

Sam pointed over his shoulder. "One eyed, one horned, flying polka dot cookie monster!"

The guard looked, and Sam's fist sent him into the water.

Sam jerked his combat knife from his boot and cut the mooring line. The boat jolted forward, throwing him to the deck. The blow to the back of his head served as a rave invitation to any pixie lights that hadn't already collected around his throbbing head.

He crawled to the controls. He'd have told anyone who asked that he did so to avoid gunfire, but only to save his pride.

He used the controls to climb up high enough to see. Corlan had stolen the sports model - of course he had eleven universes to shop. The elevator platform rushed toward him. Guards on it leveled weapons at the boat, but crossbow bolts had nothing on modern hull materials. Sam crawled to the bow, staying low to avoid an allergic reaction to bolts suddenly introduced into his flesh.

He positioned himself as best as he could for the collision. The barge hit the landing with a massive sound of crumpling plastic and tearing barge. The impact threw Sam forward as planned.

He didn't land well, but he managed his feet before the guards regained theirs and realized he was past him. He stumbled through the elevator entrance.

He pushed the button.

It buzzed at him, flashing red light on the keypad summoning several curses.

Sam pulled a pin and dropped the grenade belt.

Staggering from the elevator, Sam tumbled gracelessly into the water.

Just have to swim far enough—

The elevator exploded.

A massive concussion wave slammed Sam before the words 'no fair' could form in his mind.

39: From the Beyond

Niri

The sound of running feet demanded Niri's attention. She wrenched captured swords from the bodies of their previous owners and whipped around.

Phred rushed to a stop and fell to his knees. "Mistress. My direst apologies."

She caught her breath as she eyed the oddly dressed man leading a line of women up Phred's wake.

She lifted her blades to a guard.

"No, Mistress, they're with us."

"On your feet, Phred. We'll discuss my abduction once we're safe. Where's Bridger?"

"I don't know. His vehicle is this way."

"I doubt a wagon will help us escape. We'll use the slave's transport tube."

"Sam's vehicle swam us here, Mistress."

A rush of incredulity filled Niri's thoughts. Of course a vehicle that could sail infinite seas would have no issue navigating a Dorsun lake. "Lead on."

Phred leveled an uncertain expression. He tightened his jaw and rushed forward toward the rig. Niri followed in his wake. "How is it you got the other women to come?"

"Magus Vyse cleared the drugs from their systems," Phred said. "After his magic, they were eager to depart."

"You'll tell me later of this magus and how he did this."

"Yes, Mistress."

Crossways

Bridger's yellow submersible rose into view in the distance. The last time she'd seen it, only the cockpit bore windows. Small square windows ran its length above black letters reading: Walkerville Elementary. A large door opened, releasing a symphonic sound wave of some bracing music she'd never heard. A ramp lowered to the bank to allow multiple women to ascend at once.

Niri gestured toward the vehicle. "Everyone inside."

Several of the women bristled, but all followed her direction. Niri entered first, moving left up an aisle between the seats to take the copilot chair. A glowing blue specter of Sam Bridger appeared over the silver disk at the front of the vehicle. It spoke with the wayman's voice.

"Princess Niri. If you are seeing this message, I've become a blue glowie and joined my fellow practitioners of the forc--" the image broke down laughing. "Sorry. Anyway, obviously, I didn't make it, but I hope you appreciated the reception I programmed. I ask that you don't fault Phred for your abduction. The rescue was his idea. He crossed worlds to summon help to free you. He's your good and loyal *friend*. You should treat him so.

"Ren-2-3 will take you back through the lake. From there it can take you wherever you need to go. If the opportunity presents itself, use the communicator to tell Bob I'm sorry I didn't keep my promise. Good luck, beautiful."

Niri stared at the image, an odd lump forming in her throat. She glanced back to see Phred staring in horror at the fading hologram.

"I'm sorry, Mistress, I didn't--"

Niri placed a hand on his arm. "The wayman's right, Phred. You're free. I release you, my loyal friend."

A green tint colored Phred's bronze skin. "Does that mean I have to leave?"

She offered him her best smile. "I'd rather you didn't, particularly here. Is everyone inside?"

Phred swallowed hard and nodded.

Niri turned forward. "Ren-2-3, take us from this place."

Many of the women in the seats lining the walls gasped as the vehicle dropped beneath the waters. She ignored their shock, working out plans to return with a force of men, assault Corlan and free the wayman if he yet lived. The rig came abreast of the side tunnel.

"Do we use that passage?" Niri asked.

Phred shook his head. "No, Mistress."

"Where does it go?" she asked.

"Sam thought it might go to the source of the water, or that it might connect all geonations."

"An exploration would benefit us if that's the case, but another time."

"Yes, Mistress."

Niri cradled his hand between hers. "Phred. You may call me Niri."

A few gasps reached them from the other passengers. Phred glanced nervously behind them. "Thank you, Miss-Niri."

The rig surfaced inside Lady Shindra's geonation. A few guards objected to its use of the dock, but the ladies onboard dispatched the men in short order, seizing their weapons.

Niri addressed them. "Go to your geonations. Tell your matriarchs what you've seen. Convince them to march here."

"What of us?" Vyse asked.

"You're the wayman's friend?" Niri asked.

"More or less," Vyse said.

"We must plan for an assault. Tell me you ski--"

The elevator exploded. Fire jetted out of its shaft followed by water, showering metal for hundreds of yards in all directions.

A weight materialized inside Niri's empty gut. "Dear Auris, the wayman."

"It seems neither Sam nor your enemy will be able to escape that geonation for some time," Vyse said.

"A small comfort," Niri said.

Niri asked Phred and Vyse to step outside the vehicle. In her life, many men she'd known had died in battle - they were only males after all. The wayman had been something more, something larger. An ache squeezed her chest, startling in its intensity.

She stared at the silver disk before her, unsure despite Phred's instructions on how to operate the communicator. The wayman asked her only to convey an apology, but something told her the task meant more.

She keyed the communicator. "Hello?"

A woman's voice responded. "This is HQ, please identify yourself."

"Princess Niri Hivrus of the second Taite dynasty. Who speaks to me?"

"Beatrice. What did Sam do now?"

"I care not for your tone," Niri snapped.

"This is an official Crossways Transportation channel, an expensive one. If you don't have official business, then I'd ask you--"

"It was Sam Bridger's last wish I speak to a man named Bob."

The woman on the other end of the communication sounded as if someone wrapped a garrote around her throat. "Last wish? He asked for *Bob*?"

"You will fetch this Bob, that I might speak to him."

"Bob is a her, and I don't work for you," Beatrice snapped.

Anger warmed Niri while a chill worked its way up from her feet. The person the wayman had intended the apology for was a *woman?* Heat and cold met in her midsection, joined by a queasy twist of her gut.

"Is this Bob a blacksmith?"

"A mechanic, but for a primitive like you, I suppose a blacksmith is close."

Niri fought her fury. Were the woman before her, she'd already be on her knees with a blade to her throat. She mastered herself. "Have I wronged you in some way, that you speak to me thus?"

"The way I hear it, you're a rich, spoiled, over-privileged bitch. You call here, making demands, telling me my Sam--"

The woman broke off, a sob cut off before it could complete transmission. Understanding nudged Niri. "You're the wayman's former lover."

"I was his wife."

Her shrill voice was replaced by a deep baritone Niri recognized in an instant. "What is going here? Who is this?"

Niri introduced herself once more.

"For what reason are you using this channel, your highness?" Alabaster asked. "And what've you done that Missus Bridger raced from her post in tears?"

"I'm charged to deliver a message to the blacksmith Bob."

"From whom...oh," A somber expression overtook the dwarf's features. His body snapped to attention, eyes staring into the middle distance as a silent litany escaped his lip. When he returned to the present a moment later, Alabaster acted as if nothing had happened. "Did he die well?"

"Like a Sun Cavalier."

"I've sent for Bob. I'm afraid I must ask after the disposition of his truck. You're in it, yes?"

"It is undamaged, though it is the only transport which can reach the slave Corlan's hiding place at present."

"I'll have to recall it. Regulations are quite firm."

"I need it."

"It isn't yours."

"Bridger gave it over for my use."

"It wasn't his to give."

Another woman's voice joined the conversation. Its melodic quality didn't fit Niri's preconceptions of a blacksmith. "This is Bob, how can I help you?"

"Before anything else happens, Miss Zephyr, I must remind you of the rules and regulations involved in your employment. You're instructed not to give out any restricted information to unauthorized persons, regardless of their position in foreign governments."

"What? You got me on the line for a lecture? Why not just come into the garage?"

Niri cleared her throat but found the lump there resistant to being dislodged. When she managed her first words, a squeak accompanied them to her embarrassment. "You're Bob?"

"Who's this?"

"Princess Niri Hivrus of the second Taite dynasty, of Dorsun," she added as an afterthought.

Bob's words emerged slowly, each reluctant to follow its predecessor. "Hello, your highness. What's this about?"

"I've been asked to convey a message," Niri paused, gooseflesh running rampant across her skin. "From Sam Bridger,"

Bob's word came with a squeak as well. "Yes?"

"He asked I convey to you an apology for breaking his promise."

"Where is he?" Bob asked.

"Where are his remains?" Alabaster amended.

"I do not know."

"Where was he when you spoke to him?" Bob asked.

"I didn't. He left a message for me in his vehicle."

"Hold on, calling it up now."

Sam's voice floated through the communicator. A sob mixed with a laugh followed it partway through, though Niri wasn't sure why the woman should laugh. Both were replaced by a litany of curses in a tongue Niri didn't understand.

"Miss Zephyr," Alabaster snapped. "That kind of language is inappropriate on company--"

"What I say in a language no one but me can understand is my business, and I wasn't talking into the communicator," Bob scolded.

"Miss Zephyr--"

Bob spoke over him. "Thank you for relaying the message, Princess Niri."

Crossways

"You have my sincerest apologies." The earnestness of her own words surprised Niri. "He was a great man."
"Thank you," Bob said. "Goodbye."

40: SOB-2-0

Bob

Bob keyed off the communicator and fell back into her chair. She missed, bringing herself hard to the concrete floor. Furious tears welled in the corners of her eyes.

The insufferable lout had tricked her into revealing feelings he hadn't shared, leaving her mortified and furious. When she wanted nothing more than to hit him over the head with her biggest wrench, he'd gone and gotten himself stabbed.

Alabaster had fined her and put an official warning in her record for her reprogramming of Ren-2-3, adding to her anger.

She'd barely realized most of her anger had been at herself.

Now he's gone and gotten himself killed...helping...helping another woman.

"If you weren't already dead, I'd kill you mys—" Sobs overwhelmed her. Tears flowed free down her cheeks.

An ache in her chest rose. She rose with it, the question of how Sam had died burning through her thoughts. She linked into Ren-2-3 from her console once more. The passport offered up its feed. Bob watched it in spurts. She rewound recorded video logs, played them back, and rewound further.

She watched the incredibly beautiful Niri sit in Sam's rig, wrestling with her thoughts prior to calling HQ. It made Bob's stomach slither into knots.

The explosion left her heart in her throat.

Niri's proclamation to rescue Sam left Bob cold.

She found the end of Sam making the recording.

"If they come back, you've got to play Flight of the Valkyries then take them out of here," Sam told Ren-2-3.

A giggle escaped Bob's lips.

He rose to leave. The passport chirped at him, displaying a hologram of Bob's face. Sam fell back into his seat.

"No, I can't. I've hurt her enough."

Ren-2-3 made several rude noises.

"Look, what good would it do? I'm sending her a message before I know whether or not I'm coming back. Do you really think telling her will help her? I took too long to realize what she means to me. I've hurt her enough."

The passport replied in firm tones.

"I asked Niri to handle it, didn't I? I'm not confessing my...well, love to Bob on my way out the door to save another woman – particularly since I left a message in case I die."

Bob went cold all over.

Sam's expression grew stern. "I know you probably don't feel you owe me anything, but I know you passports love Bob. You owe her. So you'd better erase these video logs, all of them. I don't want her seeing this."

Bob wasn't sure whether she wanted to bless Ren-2-3 or disassemble him.

Sam exited the truck and the three men disappeared. Bob stared at the empty cab's video, warmth creeping back into her.

Alabaster's thud, clunk, thud, clunk heralded his arrival. He stopped feet away, scowling at the video. "I need you to recall Bridger's rig."

Bob punched up the current view of the cab. "She's still inside."

"Have Ren-2-3 eject her." Alabaster cursed. "If I'd gone with him then reclaiming the rig wouldn't be a problem."

"Yeah, you could've just thrown his corpse out for the buzzards and brought back the truck yourself."

"That's not what I meant, and you know it. If I could've gone, I might have been able to make a difference, but regulations forbid me from being there to save that man from his own idiocy."

Bob cast her eyes to the floor, her hair becoming a curtain to hide her expression.

"Blast it to Welor, I didn't mean it quite like that either."

She nodded up at him, a lock of hair between her teeth.

"What're you planning?" Alabaster asked.

Bob lowered her eyes once more, hair muffling her mumbles. "Who says I'm planning anything?"

"You chew your hair when you're anxious. Under the circumstances, I can only assume you're considering something illicit."

Bob tugged the hair she hadn't realized she was chewing from her mouth. She hadn't been consciously planning anything.

"It's no use sneaking off to Dorsun. Bridger's gone."

Butterflies fluttered around her stomach. She set her hands on the controls. "Right, programming Ren-2-3 to eject the princess and return to base."

"Good. How long does it estimate until it returns?"

"I'll instruct it to run the calculations and report them once figured. If you'll excuse me, I need to use the little girl's room."

She fled Alabaster's presence, unconcerned with any objection he might have. She'd done as the dwarf asked, though he'd no doubt be irritated to learn she'd inserted a seventy-two-hour delay.

It'd take her at least that long to get there.

Bob stayed in the bathroom long after her allotted three-minute bathroom break. When she emerged, the garage was empty. She crossed to her station and withdrew a desk drawer. Crouching low, she removed a memory stick taped to the underside.

She turned it over in her hands, chewing on a lock of hair. She glanced across the garage at her white Volkswagen Thing.

Indecision kept her poised over the intercom button for what felt like an eternity. She hit the button for Percival Wiggin's office.

"Wiggins."

"Percy, I'm not feeling too well."

"I understand. It's been a hard day for all of us."

"Mind if I head home?"

"All our critical repairs are complete?"

"Yes."

"Feel better, Bob. Don't know what we'd do without you."

"Let's hope we don't have to find out." She crossed to her car, pausing only to check its tire chains in place before keying open the garage door. She drove into the winter weather without haste, navigating salt and slush covered roads with care until she merged onto the highway. Once she was on a clear straightaway, she pulled over to the shoulder. Bob leaned over and opened the glove compartment. She removed a headband composed of twin copper rings joined at the back by a small box filled with circuitry. Slipping the headset on, Bob reached toward the tiny switch only to hesitate.

Her fingers refused to touch it.

Bob hadn't used the neural link to her passport since she'd decided to force Sam out of her life. She hadn't had time to reprogram the passport's AI. She wasn't sure how her passport would change when it once more scanned her subconscious for its evolutionary sync to an ideally compatible personality. All she knew was that she couldn't bear for the current identity to remain any longer than necessary.

Bob wiped itchy eyes and flipped the switch.

Sam Bridger's voice filled her thoughts. <Evening, beautiful. You mad at me or something?>

Bob struggled to restrain a sob.

<What's wrong, babe? Did I do something?>

She flipped off the makeshift neural link.

When the passport became Sam, I feared I might secretly be some kind of creepy stalker. Time and research proved the AI became who it had due to the high degree of compatibility between her and Sam - at least the Sam living in her thoughts. She gasped air, holding back more sobs. *Maybe I shouldn't reprogram it, this may be all I have left of Sam.*

Her car speakers crackled to life. "What's going on, babe?"

Bob wiped her eyes and flipped the link back on. *You might be dead. The other you.*

<Sam Bridger's a lot of things, but dead?>

Bob chuckled despite herself. We need to find out. Open up your data port.

A section of dashboard retracted to reveal a matte black passport. A smaller door on its surface opened a data port. Bob removed the data stick from her pocket, turning it over in her fingers.

<That for me? Here and I haven't even gotten you a Christmas present yet.>

Bob chewed on her hair. Prepare sectioned memory location, acknowledge command.

<Your wish is my command, baby doll.>

The data from this is to be moved only into the new memory location, to be deleted upon my death or completion of this mission. Acknowledge command.

<You're the boss.>

Bob plugged the data strip into the recessed port. Lights flashed in and out of sight on the passport's surface.

The passport let out a low whistle. <Wicked, cool beans. Weapons, lots of weapons.>

You're only to adopt these weapons on my direct instruction. Acknowledge command.

<Sam-2-0, armed to the teeth at your briefest whim.>

This is serious. Acknowledge command.

<Yavol, Mon Capitan.>

Sam.

A sullen note colored his reply. <*Command acknowledged.*>

Bob checked her mirror for other traffic. The late hour would've seen the roads clear, if it weren't for last minute Christmas shopping. She pulled out onto the highway, continuing down the highway until finally alone well outside the city.

Fighter configuration, stealth mode engaged.

A change field enveloped her Volkswagen Thing. A moment later, the boxy, homely vehicle transformed into a sleek white aircraft with red pinstriping.

A girl's voice crackled from the radio. "Stage fright, go away. This is my..."

The vehicle lifted higher off the road and rocketed southwest - silent except a celebratory whoop heard only in Bob's thoughts as it vanished into evening sky.

41: Misplaced Trust

Taleh

Taleh slumped in her desk chair, a feat considering her propensity to float. McGlip's report dealt her a crushing blow. She hadn't seen her assistant in some time, but received regular reports, all cautioning her to remain outside the repair area.

The universe conspired against her attempt to save her people. She threatened the UPO, and they inched forward. She got her deliveries, only to have parts provided arrive in a damaged condition. The list of needed parts grew daily. It felt as if she were trying to build a dozen waygates rather than just repair and redirect one.

Her latest demands had gone more poorly than most. She nearly dissolved to tears when she told them their inaction had cost them Hullis's life. If anything, sending them Hullis's body as proof slowed them.

It became ever clearer that Eleventh World didn't hold the importance she thought it should.

Threatening an entire universe, not to mention the UPO's trade crossroads, should've garnered results.

As an organization, the UPO was moved to action, but as individuals its representatives looked upon humanity as an expendable nuisance.

They wouldn't feel that way if they spent time among them...or at least I hope they wouldn't. If only I could make that a demand they'd take seriously.

She'd chosen the wrong threat just as she'd chosen the wrong wayman. Her chance encounter with the earnest wayman had made him the obvious choice to take care of shipments. Her wink's reports supposed her decision. Sam Bridger had stopped to give a Vurian child candy and a toy. Only someone with such empathy could be trusted to protect his world.

I just don't understand why such a man doesn't take my threats more seriously.

Of all the humans she'd met, Sam Bridger seemed the stuff of heroes - a man to sacrifice himself for the good of others.

Taleh took one of the ships back to Earth, landing at night not far from her RV in a place called New Mexico. She opened the communications channel to find the UPO assembly chamber empty save for a single representative.

Leahna and her crystalline owl looked up from her papers.

"Where're the others?" Taleh asked.

"Your sister's funeral," Leahna said. "Should I assume you have more demands? Perhaps another relative's body to deliver?"

Taleh's skin prickled. "How did you know?"

Leahna arched a grey eyebrow. "I'm an old magus, Taleh, but hardly senile."

Taleh felt sick, but she'd known from the beginning she might have to sacrifice herself to save her people. "Is there a manhunt for me now? Is that why I've not seen my next delivery?"

"Your delivery has been delayed by the death of your wayman. Tell me, was he an accomplice?"

Taleh shook her head. "Just a good man I once met."

"You've put him in a crucible by choosing him, though that hardly matters now."

"How was he killed?"

"Ambassador Corlan," Her owl screeched. Leahna nodded. "Seems he is the villain you aspire to be."

"What happens now?"

"You choose another wayman or let us choose for you," Leahna said.

"You're not going to turn me in?" Taleh said.

"Netaol has supported help for your people from the start," Leahna said. "How close are you to your goal?"

"Not as close as I'd like. Many of the deliveries have been damaged."

Leahna turned back to her paperwork. "I assume you have a new list for us?"

"Yes."

"Send it along, I'll update Auditor Roxx so that you get it as soon as possible."

Taleh felt a surge of gratitude she wasn't sure how to express. She prepared to sign off when she remembered her list wasn't complete. "I'll need for a single wayman to be assigned, and I'll need to know who."

Leahna glanced at her owl. The two stared eye to eye. The old woman nodded. "I'll see you're notified. You have my condolences. It's a hard thing to kill your own blood."

Taleh opened her mouth to reveal her sister's suicide but closed it once more. "Good night."

Leahna returned to her papers.

Taleh closed off communications, feeling hopeful and relieved. Things were looking up at last.

She sent a message to her wink, instructing the shape shifter to hide at Crossways HQ and await notification of the replacement wayman.

Elmeddi

"You see?" Elmeddi asked.

Leahna turned toward the room's deepest shadows, able to see through her symbiote's owl eyes. "You were right. She is close to giving up."

A handsome, muscular figure emerged from the shadows. "I need one of your magus, preferably young and weak-willed."

"I'll arrange a suitable apprentice," Leahna said. "Though many apprentices still die in the Change."

"Then bring me two, our conquest of Earth is too important to risk," Elmeddi said. "Once Eleventh World is ours, we'll deal with Netaol in a way no girl child can undo."

42: Forgot the Sunscreen

Sam Bridger

Being alive came as a great, painful shock to Sam Bridger.

He hung from the ceiling, tied hand and foot to a wide disk of stained glass. His shoulders and legs ached. His skin burned and felt pulled tight across his bones. Hunger gnawed his gut.

Beneath him the waters of the concubine bath taunted him with cool kisses upon a soft breeze.

"Enjoying the view?" Laz asked.

Sam tried to chuckle but found his throat too dry. "Just hanging around. Though some of those concubines would improve the decor."

"I'm sure they'll be glad to know being recaptured and once more enslaved makes you happy."

Sam frowned. He'd meant the whole thing as playful banter. Maybe Laz took what Sam'd said to mean he considered the freed women were property, or Laz just sucked at banter. Accidental or on purpose, Laz's interpretation didn't sit right. Sam'd freed them because people shouldn't be enslaved.

They shouldn't be treated like decor either.

"Thanks for your rig. I'd worried about losing some of your passport's stored data when I wiped its memory, but it seems you never bound to it."

Bound to Ren? What's this jackass talking about? Realizing his furrowed brow might reveal his own confusion, he threw out a question meant to chum the waters. "Thought Carol claimed it."

Laz shrugged. He knelt, running his fingers through the water. "I managed to convince him my possession of it was in his best interest."

"Where is Carol?"

"He'll be along soon. I wanted to say my final goodbyes."

"You retiring?"

"One of us is."

"Not me, brother. I'm fit as a fiddle."

Laz laughed. "I have to admit, I've always admired your indomitable innocence. How you regained it after everything you did to poor Theophanie, I've never known."

Hunger vanished, replaced by a long-suffering ache. "Theophanie wasn't my--"

"Don't bullshit me, Sam. I was there, remember?"

Sam struggled against his bonds, grinding teeth together.

"Shall I give Beatrice anything for you? A baby, perhaps?"

"If you touch Bea, I'll peel your skin off while you scream," Sam snarled.

Corlan strode into the room. "I'm afraid you won't be in much condition to do anything of the sort...though I'm curious which of you would triumph in the ring."

"Throw us in, Carol. Let's find out."

Corlan circled the pool, laughing up toward Sam. "I need Lazarus to fetch more nangnome-robotics to repair my elevator."

"When he gets back then."

"This sudden, if surprising, vindictiveness suits you." Corlan stopped beside a pillar anchoring a thick rope. "Unfortunately, you won't be in any shape to fight by then."

He untied it, pulling hard on the rope. The disk of stained glass with Sam tied to it flipped over, exposing Sam to the geonation's tiny sun high overhead.

43: Bob Sunk His Battleship

Bob

Bob thundered across the desert on a four-legged locomotive, hair whipping behind her. The white steed galloped tirelessly beneath her. Bob hadn't ridden horseback since she was a teen. Her body remembered how to move with the steed, but her muscles were no longer used to the motion.

She pushed her discomfort away, though she knew she'd probably crumple to the ground if she tried to stand. Luckily, as long as she had her Thing, she wouldn't need to stand.

Her passport had changed her clothes while transitioning to Dorsun. She'd never entered a waygate, let alone experienced the change field. The former enraptured her, making her never wish to leave. The latter had tickled like mad, but her passport had changed her clothes without changing her.

Sam-2-0 hadn't dressed her like a desert princess, but rather in doe leathers with Cherokee tribal markings. She rather liked the overall affect, except the neckline pressed her breasts up and together in immodest ways

<I still say you look, like, totally awesome hot.>

"How much further?"

<Ren-2-3's signal is just ahead.>

A massive explosion threw smoke and debris skyward, almost throwing Bob from her mount as well. They paused for her to steady herself and then resumed their gallop.

"They're not supposed to have explosives in this world."

<Dirty cheaters, we were supposed to be the ones with the phenomenal cosmic firepower.>

Bob galloped around the last rise into view of a clear blue lake. A silver chimney in its center spewed dark smoke. At its edge, Sam's rig was defended by a handful of basically naked swordswomen.

<Hell yeah, now this is what I call a reception.>

A miniature U.S. destroyer floated in a small lake, blasting the shore with energy weapons. The women fired back with crossbows and a smattering of simple gunfire.

<Damsels in distress, can I use the weapons now, please, please, please?>

Scan the attack craft.

Her passport adopted a gravelly baritone. <I'm a stallion, not a science officer.>

Bob glowered.

Sam-2-0's tone flattened, becoming serious. <Scanning. Sensor readings indicate the craft is of Federation make.>

Sam!

<The vehicle responded with identity codes when I polled it. Its designation is Pim-1-4.>

It's a Crossways rig? Bob gasped. But it has weapons.

Her horse whinnied, rearing to paw the air with its huge hooves. <*So do I.*>

You're not technically Crossways property anymore. Open a communication channel back to HQ.

<Hailing frequencies open.>

"Crossways HQ, who is this?" Kenneth asked.

"Ken, it's Bob. Could I get you to run a records check?"

"Can I?" Kenneth asked.

Before Bob could ask what he meant, Beatrice's voice joined the channel. "Where are you, Bob? Alabaster's going nuts."

"Doesn't matter, I need a records check for a passport, Pim-1-4."

Beatrice cursed.

"HQ?" Bob asked.

"I don't have to check, that's Eugene Lazarus's passport."

"He's a wayman?" Bob asked. "I don't recognize the name."

"He was drummed out shortly after his rig was stolen. Why?"

"I've got a rig with that passport signature right in front of me."

"Shouldn't be, after his rig was stolen, they sent a disable command to the passport."

"Looks pretty active to me," Sam-2-0 said.

"Sam?" Beatrice gasped.

"No, not Sam. Thanks. Bob out." She cut the connection and addressed Sam-2–0. "Do you have any data on this ex-wayman?"

<I know Laz is the kind of bastard the devil reserves for his special hell.> A man's face projected overtop of the passport. Vitriol filled Sam-2-0's voice as he holographically added a mustache and devil horns. *<Useless, rich, pretty boy.>*

Bob rode to the lake's edge, coming up on the battle from the side. She cupped hands around her mouth and shouted to be heard over the water. "Pim-1-4, I order you to stand down. Authorization code CT-Omega4."

A handsome man matching the pre-graffitied holographic image stepped onto the deck of the boat, a transparent shell growing up to shield him from attack as he did so. "Who're you?"

"It doesn't matter. Surrender the passport."

Laz laughed.

"I'm warning you."

"Yeah, thanks for that, but I'm not really interested in anything but how you obtained that code. You work for Crossways Transport?"

"I do."

"That horse have a passport too?"

"It does."

Bolts continued to bounce off the transparent wall between them.

"Want a job? I need more waymen, not to mention passports."

"Not a wayman, I'm a mechanic."

"Even better. You must be the famous Bob. If you join me, you'll be well paid, and the benefits are incredible."

Phred flitted across the battlefield from cover to cover. He raised his voice from behind the smoking remains of several crates. "Bob?"

Bob glanced down.

"This is the man responsible for Sam's fate," Phred said.

"Oh," Bob said.

"So, you want the job, honey?"

"You killed Sam Bridger?"

"A service to women in all universes."

Bob's skin tingled in a way it hadn't ever before. A heat bloomed beneath it, pressing hard from the inside out until she thought fire might burst from her limbs.

One word wrenched itself free of her clenched teeth. "Surrender."

"So that's a no?"

"Or we'll kill you."

"Arrows against a battleship?" Laz laughed. "You should read your history."

"Ever heard of Custer?" Bob asked.

"Of course, but he didn't have the weapons I do. Afraid if you don't want the job, I'm going to have to demand you hand over your passport."

"No."

"You don't have a choice, honey. You're defenseless."

"Why's that?" Bob asked.

A bullet impact shot up a plume of sand from the feet of Bob's horse. "Because I said please."

"You answered the wrong question," Bob snarled. "And picked on the wrong Indian."

Bob's horse transformed around her, adopting the form of a white, winged robot thirty feet tall and edged with red. Power pulsed from beneath its feet, raising it into the air.

"Impressive, but hardly threatening."

Laser cannons grew into the robot's hands. They raked the ship with blue plasma energy.

Laz gaped.

Sam-2-0's shoulder pauldrons opened up. A flurry of small missiles fired out in a haphazard cloud. They picked up the target an instant later and all bee-lined straight for the rig.

Laz dove headlong back into his ship as rockets ripped up his hull and shattered the transparent shield the bolts hadn't scratched.

A cheer rose up from the swordswomen near Sam's rig.

Bob darted over the water, her robot quick and agile. She raked the ship with laser fire once more, unleashing another salvo of rockets.

Cannons on the ship tracked her and fired. Lances of light cut through the sky, missing her by the barest margins.

Bob flew past the boat at full speed. Her weapons struck the stationary target with ease.

A rear cannon on Laz's ship transformed and released a salvo of homing missiles.

She rolled, Sam-2-0 transforming the robot into a sleek fighter with a smaller cross section. It dodged most of the missiles, but a pair slammed into one wing, turning the roll into a wild spin.

Fighter returned to robotic battle suit. It pirouetted in midair. Wheel-shaped turrets grew from knee and elbow joints. They spat out laser fire at high speed, cutting down a second rocket salvo.

The ship projected an energy barrier just as Bob's main guns lanced plasma. It reshaped itself into a mecha but began to sink before the transformation was completed.

<She sunk his battleship!>

Keep firing until we know for sure.

<You got it, one order of ass kicking with a side of sexy beefcake...er steelcake coming up!>

Sam-2-0 lobbed a stream of depth charges into the water around the sinking rig, sending lake and metal chunks spraying in all directions.

Laz's rig vanished beneath the water.

Sun Cavaliers along the lake cheered once more.

Bob scoured the water with digital sensors. She repositioned to an angle that could fire anywhere on the lake should Laz and his rig emerge.

She waited.

In the silent tension, the smell of damaged components reached her. The throb of her pulse sent stabs of pain through her head. She reached up to massage her temple, bringing back bloody fingers.

Sam, scan my injuries.

<Superficial, babe, you're still the fairest of them all.>

Bob laughed, wishing the real Sam said things like that to her. *Could they be waiting for us to go in?*

<Could be, he's a wascally wabbit.>

Hit the lake with another set of depth charges, vary trigger depth.

<She cannae take much more, Captain Great Breasts.>

Explain.

<Well, they're a good size, pert, and if I had hands-->

Explain why you can't fire more charges.

<Going to need to collect some mass first. Energy weapons are one thing, but rockets and depth charges have to be made out of something.>

Right, I should have remembered that. Water do?

<You won't make friends with the natives.>

Bob nodded. Right, set us down on the far side of the lake from where he last saw us.

<How about catty-corner from that? Opposite might be too obvious.>

Okay.

Sam-2-0 landed. The ground touching his change field shimmered, melted, and flowed into it - slowly digging a divot in the sandy ground. It collected around her like a heavy set of armor augmented with missile pods and depth charge launchers. They took to the air once more, peppering the lake with charges.

Wreckage didn't float to the top.

Laz didn't emerge.

Guess he's waiting in another geonation.

Sam-2-0 shrugged the battle suit's shoulders.

A delegation met Bob as she dismounted the battle suit. The familiar looking woman at the lead had Phred at her side and could only be Princess Niri. Bob's legs crumpled, but Sam-2-0 caught her. She blushed before the beautiful, muscular woman, cringing inside.

No wonder Sam likes her. I'm not even an ugly duckling compared to that.

Even her voice was lovely. "You're Bob?"

Bob chewed a lock of hair. "Yeah."

Niri flourished her sword. "I salute you, one warrior to another."

Bob blinked.

"You've come for Sam Bridger's vehicle?"

"No, for Sam himself."

"The explosion was horrible." A hint of regret underpinned Niri's tone. "He couldn't have survived."

Bob shook her head. "Let me tell you one thing about Sam Bridger. He has uncanny luck, both good and bad."

A man in a tan aba approached, a crystalline hawk on his shoulder. "There is a minor probability he is alive."

"You're the Netaolian I saw at HQ. Vyse, right?" Bob asked.

"Indeed."

"I could use your help."

"I'll assist in any search and rescue for Sam Bridger."

Bob looked at the crowd of warrior women. "Anyone else?"

"The weapons at Slave Corlan's disposal are superior to our own," a woman said. "Suicide is foolish, particularly for the sake of a male."

Bob bristled. She turned toward Phred. "What about you?"

Phred glanced at Niri. He stepped forward. "I'll come."

Bob turned back toward her vehicle. "Adjust configuration for two additional gunners."

Niri placed a hand upon Bob's arm. "I couldn't return and hope to succeed with the wayman's vehicle as it bears no armaments, but I would gladly join you if you'll have me."

Bob turned back to her Thing. "Make that three."

The change field enveloped the rig. Ground around the truck shimmered, melting into it as it transformed into a larger, more heavily armored battle mecha.

Sam-2-0's voice crackled from his external speaker. "One more and you get the full set of lions."

"Sam?" Phred asked.

"Not really," Bob said.

The change field stopped, and the mecha turned in a circle with hands on its hips. "Does all this armor make me look fat?"

Sam Bridger

Sam wrenched his head toward the first explosion. His sunburnt skin pulled painfully. A flying white robot vaguely resembling a Valkyrie darted left and right, slamming Corlan's dainty palace with heavy weapons fire.

Gunfire responded.

Rounds ricocheted off its armor, tiny motes of light like pixie dust.

A dry chuckle emerged from his throat, devolving into wracking coughs. "Sorry, Carol. My ride's here."

The Valkyrie's head rose toward him. It darted across the intervening space, pausing only to deflect a ground-launched proton missile and kill its user.

Sam blinked.

He opened his eyes to find the vaguely familiar robot hovering over him. Its massive hands slammed into the ring surrounding the stained glass on which he was chained.

Sam heard the metal tear away from stone.

He blinked.

Bob's face hovered over him, bent by worry yet more beautiful than he remembered. "Must be heaven."

He heard Bob's voice float toward him over the sounds of continued battle. "Stay still. Vyse is healing you."

Sam blinked.

Niri and Bob were lowering Sam into Snow White's coffin inside a floating submersible. A half dome shimmered over them, concentric circles rippling from weapons fire.

"No," Sam croaked. "I'm not--"

"We know you're not dead. It's a Ryaloxian healing bed."

"No," Sam struggled to rise and wrench his weak limbs from their hold.

"Sam, calm down. It's okay," Bob said.

"No. I refuse--"

"Shall I knock him cold?" Niri asked.

Bob glowered at Niri over Sam's body.

Sam shook his head. "I won't be rescued--"

"Oh, it's fine for you to rescue the damsel, but you have a problem when she saves your bacon?" Bob asked.

"Bacon?" Sam's stomach rumbled.

Bob laughed. "He's seriously out of it."

Sam locked eyes on Bob. "I won't be rescued. Not until someone tells me the truth of what's going on."

"What?" Bob said.

"We're under attack here, wayman," Niri said. "This isn't the time to be irrationally male."

"Promise me," Sam said.

"Fine. I'll tell you everything, but we have to go."

Sam smiled and ceased his struggles. "Okay, I'm ready for my bedtime story, mommy."

Bob rolled her eyes. They set him into the healing chamber.

Bob

"Vyse, he's in. Let's go," Bob said.

"What of these?" Vyse asked.

"We'll return and pay them blood for blood," Niri said.

"We have a faster way," Vyse said.

Byron, don't do this.

<They've earned it.>

They have servants, innocents.

<Collaborators.>

No, I won't let you. This is wrong.

<I'm sorry, old friend, you've no choice.>

Vyse raised his staff. A light lanced from its tip to the star high above. Light flared around it.

It grew.

It bent.

It shrank.

It distorted.

Flares shot out, scorching the ground.

"Now would be a good time to leave." Vyse settled into his seat.

"What did you do to it?" Niri asked.

"It will supernova in minutes," Vyse said.

Niri stared at him without comprehension, but all color drained from Bob's face.

"Sam, get us out of here," Bob said.

Sam's voice crackled through the healing bed's speakers. "I thought I was getting a story."

"We're a flash in the night, a streak among the stars, we are out of here," Sam-2-0 said.

A dreamy tone escaped Sam's lips. "Very poetic, aren't I?"

44: Fool's Bet

Sam Bridger

Sam charged from Bob's stretched Thing, slamming the door. "Why the hell didn't you tell me?"

He scanned the lake shore, eyes locking on where a swarm of concubines stood between his rig and the shore. They stared aghast into the churning waters.

"They...they destroyed a geonode," one said.

We did?

Bob scrambled to keep up with his breakneck stride. "Alabaster insisted we keep it from you, and slow down, you were only in the healing bed for a few hours."

Vyse, Niri, and Phred trailed behind them.

"Damn it, Sam, where are you going?"

"I'm going back to punch both those bastards in the nuts!"

"They're not there, Sam. They're either dead or they escaped before the geonation collapsed."

Sam shot her a dirty look, desperate for something—though not Bob—to hit. "Are you honestly telling me that anti-social, paper-pushing dwarf bastard didn't trust me to take the end of the freaking world seriously?"

"He didn't trust you at all."

A buzzing filled Sam's ears. He froze mid-step. "Why?"

Bob caught up with him, a little out of breath due to shorter legs. "He thought...Sam, you have to understand, it wasn't anything personal."

Heat rose up Sam's neck, leaving a prickling trail to his ears. "Why?"

"The terrorist asked for you by name, okay? Everyone thought you might be involved."

The edges of Sam's ears burned. "Everyone?"

"N-no, I didn't," Bob's voice dropped. "Beatrice refused to believe it, either."

The temperature of his ears dropped. He resumed his march. "Good old Bea."

"You have to believe me. I never believed, never."

He turned on his heel, scooped her up and hugged her tight to him. "You're the best, Tayanita, darling little bobcat."

She blinked up at him. "You remembered."

He set her down and winked. "Don't let it go to your head."

Sam approached his rig, scanning the many near naked Sun Cavaliers. A chuckle escaped him. "My kind of reception."

Bob laughed.

"What?" Sam asked.

She shook her head. "Inside joke."

Sam marched around the front of his rig toward the cab. He stopped mid-stride and turned back to look at its nose. A Decepticon symbol glared at him.

Sam scowled at the rig. "Really?"

Bob tilted her head side to side, searching for the problem.

"Phred, knife," Sam held out his hand. He snatched the blade from Phred and moved to pry it off, only to find it seamlessly part of the rig itself. Sam huffed. "Traitor."

"Sam?" Bob asked. "What's the problem?"

Sam mounted his rig and keyed the communicator. "Twenty-three to base. Get me that damned dwarf."

"Sam?" Beatrice said.

"Yes, I'm alive. Yes, I'm glad you're glad. Now, get me Alabastard."

"Don't do anything you'll be sorry for later," Beatrice warned.

"I'm sorry I didn't already beat the little jerk black and metallic."

"I'd like to see you try, Bridger," Alabaster said.

"The world is about to blow up and you didn't tell me?"

"If you'd done your job efficiently, you wouldn't have needed to know."

"Screw you, brother. Tell me everything, every detail."

"I hardly think--"

"Al, you've kept me out of the loop, and how has that worked out for you? You find the bomb yet?"

"The records here are atrocious."

Sam balled his fists. "Right, you can't do the job, so you blame the humans."

"It wasn't a Ryaloxian that made this mess."

"It was. And Audorian, Netaolian, Ferythers, all of you. All of you voted away the money to your special projects until we were left strangled. We limped along, but that's all right until you suddenly need something."

"To save *your* world, Bridger." Alabaster paused. "But you have a point."

"Tell me what you know about this bomb, about the job I'm supposed to do so I can get to it and lend my brainpower to the think tank."

Sarcasm dripped from Alabaster's reply. "Miracles are real."

"Bea? Can you send me the pickup and delivery list?"

"She hasn't the authority."

A holographic list materialized above Ren-2-3. Sam scanned it, his displeasure mounting with each item.

"This is nuts. It's got me running all over."

"The finest minds in the UPO have lent their expertise. I hardly expect you to see a pattern when it took them so long."

"What about the bomb and the bomber? What do you know?"

"I know you need to pick up the items list in order, Bridger. Leave the bomb to me."

"They think we shipped the bomb into Earth," Beatrice said.

"How else would it have gotten here?" Alabaster said.

Sam scowled. "Gosh, I don't know. You've got Laz shipping stuff in and out of the eleven worlds. Corlan sent an assassin squad after me with a passport strapped to their backs of all things. Then there are all the dwarf tourists."

"All dwarf visitors were delivered through official Ryalox transportation, Bridger."

Sam snorted. "And no one could have used such transports to get a bomb in?"

Bob laid a hand on his arm, startling him. He hadn't even noticed her climb aboard. "Sam, if we go down all those possible roads, we'll never find the bomb."

"Miss Zephyr, who is on report for unauthorized travel to Dorsun, is correct," Alabaster said.

Sam scanned the list once more. "What's with all the toys?"

"Maybe your terrorist has a lot of children."

Sam's thoughts swam. A pale, dirty blue face peeked at him from around a building's corner. Flashes of movement darted into and out of his peripheral vision without getting seen. An extra pillow weighed on his thoughts; a suspicious release order set atop of it with a basket of magical muffins.

"Could the terrorist be Vurian?" Sam asked.

"A few people have suggested the possibility."

Sam turned. His eyes bored into Bob's. "Didn't you once tell me about some kind of shapeshifter in Vuria, a blink?"

"Many universes have such things," Alabaster said.

"Shut up, Al. Bob?"

"Yes. A wink, why?"

Sam glanced around. "Because I've been seeing glimpses of it since I made that pickup on Vuria."

"*Botracl.* They're not intelligent enough to be behind this, and really, there's no proof the Vurians are involved?"

"Have you seen their world recently?" Sam snapped. "Anyway, it makes sense. The extra cargo you almost killed me over. The delivery note on the wagon seat when no one knew I was there, other odd occurrences - even the muffins after I'd complained about being hungry."

"Vurians are a peaceful people. We're dealing with hardened, power-hungry psychos," Alabaster said.

"Have they actually hurt anyone?" Sam asked.

"They killed Ambassador Hullis," Alabaster said.

"Another Vurian," Bob said. "And Sam, they threatened to blow up Earth."

"But they haven't," Sam shook his head. "No. I'm right about this. Sam Bridger knows people."

"Need I remind you about a certain elderly Tauron woman?" Alabaster said.

Sam dug through his memory. He remembered picking up the stranded old granny—even if doing so was against the rules. His rig ended up getting a few dings Ren hadn't deigned to fix but didn't remember her causing any trouble. "The sweet old cow was stranded. She just wanted to go to her grandson's wedding. Maybe it was against the rules, but someone had to help her. She wasn't some criminal. She gave me some wedding cake for Pete's sake. I'm certain these bombers are Vurian. I'd bet my mint condition number one Superman comic."

"Bridger, you've lost it."

An ear-to-ear grin spread across his face. He cranked the rig to life. "No. I've found it. Buckle up, Bob. I know where the bomb is."

"Sam, if you know where it is, tell us," Beatrice said. "You're not exactly close to a waygate."

"Don't remember the address, but Sam Bridger never forgets how to return somewhere once he's visited."

"Just give me the tracking number, Bridger. We'll find it in the records and send an assault squad."

"Not sure I ever turned it in." Sam rubbed his neck. "Been a hectic month."

"Of all the worthless, stupid...you're an idiot."

Sam chuckled and turned to his passport. "Ren, bud, I need wings, brother. We've got to save the world."

The passport beeped and chirped, the tones bright and positive.

"Knew I could count on you in a pinch." Sam ducked his head out the window. "Back up, this baby packs quite a punch."

Niri, Phred and Vyse charged the truck.

"Wait for us," Phred called.

Sam threw open his door. "Get aboard, we're in a hurry."

"What about my car?" Bob asked.

"We'll come back for it," Sam said.

Sam-2-0 put fists on his hips. "If the world needs saving, Sam Bridger 2.0 is the rig for the job."

Sam raised a brow at Bob.

She reddened. "Sam-2-0, delete sectored memory and return to the house."

The mecha kicked a boulder and pouted.

"Acknowledge command," Bob said.

He waved dismissively, "Yeah, yeah, I'll wait at home. Maybe do the laundry while you go off to save the world. Do you want dinner waiting? Forty-two course meal or something? It's not like I have anything *else* to do."

Bob sighed. "Acknowledge command."

"Command acknowledged," Sam-2-0 grumbled.

"Once in the garage, return to dormant mode. Acknowledge command."

Sam-2-0 moped. "You're ashamed of me, aren't you?"

"Pretty sure you're illegal, bud." Sam said. "Bob's precious secret little pirate friend."

"Friends? Like best friends? Forever?" Sam-2-0 asked.

"Acknowledge command," Bob growled.

Sam-2-0's attention shifted to Sam. He inclined his head, adding a wink.

"Command acknowledged."

"So, you have a hidden me to dress up, give oil changes, and whatnot?"

Bob turned back to find Sam's expression pensive. "It's not like that, Sam. Maybe my passport acts like you, but it wasn't intentional, okay?"

"How would that—"

Her face reddened, frustration hardening her words. "Do you *ever* intend to read the manual?"

Sam rubbed his neck. "Eventually...unless the world blows up. So, you make your little Sammie do laundry? Couldn't you let him get a job? A paper route, Mary Kay, something?"

Bob folded her arms. "World to save?"

Sam's toe knocked a rock from the rig. "I never saw myself as a garage wife."

The others looked at each other.

Sam brightened. "At least I can keep up with all my soaps."

The rig transformed and shot across the geonation's sky. He glanced at Bob, finding her glowering down at her clothes.

"What?" Sam asked.

"Nothing, just wishing for a change of clothes," she said.

"Don't you make me do enough housework? Besides, you look, like, totally awesome hot."

Bob smirked.

"I, too, wish for a bit more clothing," Niri said.

Sam glanced over his shoulder, casting his eyes up and down Niri. He opened his mouth.

"One word, Sam, and I'm slapping a fish across your face," Phred said.

A confused Bob sought Sam's eye. "What?"

"Long story."

"We've got time," Bob said.

Sam shook his head, but Niri launched into the story without an iota of hesitation.

They rocketed through Dorsun in record time, peoples above and beneath them staring as they passed. A moment before they hit the waygate, Sam cleared his throat. "Ren, bud, do the ladies a favor and alter their clothes however they'd like."

45: War of Wills

Vyse

Vyse struggled to take control of his mouth. In all of his time with Byron, the foci hadn't ever forced its will against Vyse's own until the arrival of the odd, flabby man in Vegas.

We were friends.

<We still are.>

This is how you treat a lifelong partner?

<Your lifetime. Mine stretches back many magus.>

Even so, isn't our friendship worth anything?

<This is about more than friendship.>

Byron maintained ever tighter control over Vyse. He prevented Vyse from acting out or warning the wayman about the disastrous fate completing their task would bring. His foci's thoughts occasionally flickered across Vyse's mind. They darkened the longer they travelled, portending Sam Bridger's doom more by the mile.

I thought this was about helping your people without hurting anyone. We were supposed to help Sam Bridger.

<Helping him now may doom my people.>

You said they were wasteful conquerors.

<I do not wish my peoples' destruction.>

Talk to the wayman, he'd help us.

<I cannot take the chance that you're wrong.>

Vyse eyed the Dorsun assassin next to him. He'd seen Phred's skill. If he could give himself away, Phred could stop him, especially after crossing into Eleventh World where magic was weak.

<I still have power enough to destroy everyone here if they assault us.>

Let me speak with them. I'm sure I can enlist their help.

<I fear I cannot trust you in this.>

What is happening to you? This isn't you. You've never hungered to kill before.

<Embracing necessity, that's all.>

Like with the star? That wasn't necessary. It was monstrous.

<Just because I'm siding with one of my people doesn't make me a monster.>

You're talking about the death or enslavement of every person in Eleventh World.

<That might not happen.>

It sounded to me like you thought it would.

<If it did, would it be so bad?>

Vyse didn't bother to answer. He worked to shield his thoughts so he could find a way to thwart Byron.

<The Masters built our governance. They provided for everyone within the framework of the original feudal-socialist system. They fed the peasants, put the magus in their place, and set order that benefitted all.>

You said they betrayed their own people for power and comfort. Now you're defending them?

<Their motivations don't negate their accomplishments. You said yourself that humans are barbarians. The Masters could bring humanity into line, end their wars, feed their people.>

Elmeddi wasn't a master.

<No, he's a high Linurian. Greater than those that became the Masters. He could-->

Kill all of humanity without a second thought.

<Elmeddi is High Linurian.>

Great, he's a more pompous, self-righteous, arrogant being than the Masters ever were. What would have become Netaol had he taken our world instead of the Masters?

Byron fell silent, shielding his thoughts. It made it easier for Vyse to shield his own, though he still felt Byron's iron grip on his body.

Byron, you know Sam Bridger is taking us to stop Elmeddi.

<Something I cannot allow.>

You must.

<I owe my people loyalty. I owe allegiance to-->

A stranger who ordered you around and told you to beat me like an animal?

<You don't understand.>

No. I don't.

46: Exploring Bob

Sam Bridger

Sam stopped his rig a few buildings short of the Versailles warehouse. A low fog clung to the dark streets beneath broken and failing streetlights.

"Neighborhood hasn't improved," Sam said.

"Making a delivery here didn't make you suspicious?" Bob asked.

Sam laughed. "Babe, this is hardly the seediest drop off point HQ's ever foisted on me."

"Once you identify the building for us, wayman, we should split up and encircle it, check for anything that stands out," Vyse said.

"A decent idea." Sam pointed. "It's that one next to the blinking streetlamp. Take a leisurely stroll around to see if anything looks wrong."

"As someone from a hot, dry world unlike any of this, I'd appreciate more specifics on what you'd consider as wrong," Niri said.

"Walk around the buildings that surround the warehouse," Phred said. "Look for people watching within, around or atop."

"Couldn't have said it any better, brother."

The five of them exited the truck. Sam glanced after Bob. He leaned back into his rig and pulled out his jacket.

"Bob."

She turned back to him.

He jogged up, offering his jacket. "Jeans and a button top blouse are a damn fine look, but you might need this."

She beamed at the jacket. "Thank you."

Sam returned a smile of his own. "Be careful."

"You too."

The Wink

The wink watched them spread out into the industrial park. From conversations, Sam Bridger's insights threatened Taleh's efforts. It felt compelled to stop them and protect her.

It shifted to an alley cat, slipping through the low mist relying on its superior sight to pierce the milky haze. It caught up with Phred first, changing shape to copy Sam Bridger.

Phred started. "Sam, I didn't know you knew such stealth."

"Princess Niri noticed men watching a little further out than we expected. I would appreciate it if you widened your search a few buildings, brother."

"I'll do so."

Phred snuck deeper into the complex, sliding in and out of sight. The wink changed back to a cat and resumed its search. It encountered Niri next. She took its instructions too.

The wink found Bob. One moment there was no one behind her, the next Sam stood on her heel. Bob jumped out of her skin, shoving a hand over her own mouth to stifle her scream. She punched Sam in the shoulder. "Damn you, you scared the life out of me."

"I am sorry, babe doll. Phred noticed people watching a few buildings further from the warehouse. Can you search a bit deeper into the complex, then come back to the rig?"

She smiled and extended a hand. "Come with me?"

"I must find Vyse and inform him as well."

Her expression fell. "I understand."

The wink smiled at her and walked back into the mist. It calculated a high possibility she would decide to follow, so it maintained form until it could be sure to slip free.

It checked over its shoulder to find Bob nowhere in sight. It turned back around to find Vyse nose to nose.

"Vyse, brother," the wink said. "I was looking for you."

"I was looking for you, wayman."

"Is there something you require of me?"

"I require two things. First, your forgiveness."

The wink calculated probable responses from Sam Bridger. "Of course, brother, what is the second thing?

"Die." Vyse thrust the head of his cane into Sam's chest. Pain and energy lanced into the wink. A hole spread out from the cane. The wink changed the surrounding tissue, creating layer after layer of varied substances until one halted the power.

To give it time, the wink fell backward, mimicking a human in agony. It wasn't that the magic hadn't hurt. It had, but survival was its first priority. As soon as the power hesitated at one of the materials, the wink thickened the barrier.

"You're tougher than I expected," Vyse raised the cane for another strike. "For the record, Vyse abhors this action. He is truly sorry."

The wink nodded Sam's head. It launched itself toward Vyse as it transformed into a vast fluid cloak of the resistive material. It wrapped around Vyse, covering head and shoulders while also fouling Vyse's arms.

The magus struggled. Lances of power beat at the wink. The magus changed the magic, carving chunks from the wink's form while it tightened its grip around Vyse's airways.

The crystal staff dissolved, rapidly forcing its way beneath the wink's surface. Before it could slide between the wink and Vyse's breathing channels, the wink changed to a more fluid form and flowed into both to block breathing.

Thwarted, the crystal cut a channel into Vyse's throat, creating a small breathing tube.

The wink flowed into Vyse's lungs, blocking its air receptors from receiving the entering air.

Vyse collapsed, yet the crystal struggled on against the wink. They tore at each other, both flowing through offensive and defensive forms as fast as thought.

Vyse's body convulsed once and ceased motion. The crystal froze as if stunned, solidifying for a moment. The wink squeezed it, cracking it through and through.

The wink released Vyse and its crystal, regaining Sam Bridger's form. It changed its mind, taking on Vyse's before striking off through the fog to find Sam Bridger.

Sam Bridger

Sam finished his circle. He was tempted to enter the warehouse, but he'd promised to meet back at the rig so they could all enter together. He turned toward his truck to find a shape in the fog.

"Hello?" Sam said.

Vyse edged into focus. "Wayman."

"Seen any of the others?"

"Princess Niri noticed something and ordered the others to help her check it out."

Sam chuckled. "Sounds like her high-and-mightiness."

"She felt you should check on the bomb without further delay in case your instincts proved incorrect. She said my assistance would prove sufficient."

"Guess so." Sam rubbed his neck. "I'm pretty sure this is the place."

"She's not a woman to trust men."

"She's improved."

Vyse shrugged.

Sam found the outer door unlocked. Fist-sized cockroaches remained, but either they'd usurped the ratosaurus, or it had moved on to better grazing. He stepped over a fire pit.

That wasn't here last time.

A silhouette of darker shadow filled the room's center. Sam felt around the doorframe but didn't find a light switch. He strode forward with cautious steps. His foot came down on something squishy, slipping a bit on the surface.

"Got a light, brother?"

Fluorescent lights flickered to life overhead with a characteristic hum. Sam looked down to find his foot surrounded by ripped fabric and writhing maggots.

Sam jerked away, kicking his foot repeatedly and praising his preference for thick, tall combat boots. "Ew, ew."

Sam turned to find Vyse's feet disturbingly near the maggots without any reaction from the magus. Sam bent down, examining the body on the ground. He recalled the truly ancient black Frenchman whose arms wrapped around a small chest probably liberated from the surrounding scavenged crates.

Medieval weapons littered the ground, spilled contents from an unknown crate.

Sam scanned the other crates. Whatever had been in them was gone now. He didn't think the terrorist had come for it, if only because the edges of the crates were bent and broken as if forced.

"Guess that's the bomb."

"Sure is, brother. Mistress didn't know where you had delivered it."

Sam's head shot up. His eyes widened, matched by a second set of his own eyes. "What the hell?"

"You delivered it to the wrong address."

"The blink."

"I cannot let you stop the mistress's plans," the wink said. "Our people need a new home."

"Hey, you've got my sympathy, even my help if you want it, but only if you're not threatening my planet."

"A pity," the wink said. "You might be sincere."

"I am, so what's the problem?"

"I cannot ignore the probability you are not. I must kill you," the wink raised his hands.

Sam brought up his fists.

Bob raced into the room, freezing on the doorstep with her mouth poised open.

"Bob, thank God," the wink said. "The wink is about to attack me."

"Leave Bob out of this."

Bob stepped into the room, narrowed eyes swinging back and forth between them.

The wink sighed. He put his back to Bob, keeping Sam in front of him. He swung high. Sam ducked and landed a blow into the wink's stomach. A tingle shot up Sam's arm. The wink stumbled back into Bob, the two falling to the ground in a tangle. A flailing leg kicked Sam's shin.

Sam stared down at two Bobs.

Which one was Bob first?

His hands caught his attention a moment later. He glanced down to find himself dressed in Bob's clothes, with Bob's breasts squeezed inward uncomfortably by what had to be a bra beneath blouse and jacket.

Niri and Phred raced into the room only to stop dead.

The wink, in Bob's shape, scrambled to her feet and bolted toward the new arrivals. "Help, I'm not sure what's going on, but--"

Bob leapt to her feet. "Don't let it touch you."

The wink stumbled, placing a hand on the leg of each newcomer to recover from the fall.

"Shit," Bob said.

The wink raised a hand to accept help up. It jerked both with considerable strength, sending them tumbling into the real Bob without releasing its hold. Sam and the others sprawled into a haphazard tangle of flailing limbs. In their tumbling, Sam lost track of which Bob he thought might be the wink. Around him, the others recovered only to freeze in shock at the sight of four identical spunky mechanics.

"Not sure if this is heaven or hell." Sam rubbed the back of his neck. "Damned confusing though."

"What just happened?" One of the Bob's asked. "And how?"

Sam pulled open the collar of his blouse, his expression a mixture of confusion and delight. He grabbed his breasts. "Okay, I get why you babes don't like 'em groped like that."

Bob's head shot up. "Sam Bridger, you take your hands off those this instant!"

Another Bob climbed to her feet. She shifted her weight back and forth. Her speech cadence and word choice pointed to her being Phred, but Sam couldn't be sure. "Your center of gravity seems a bit off, Bob. How do you compensate for being this top heavy?"

Sam rubbed his fingers beneath the uncomfortable bra. His surprise turned into a grin. "Oh, that's nice."

"You rotten—" The real Bob spluttered. "You rotten—Get your hands--"

The Bob Sam thought of as Phred rubbed gentle circles on his chest. "You're right, Sam. The sensation is quite pleasant."

Bob purpled. "Stop that right now, both of you."

"Are you familiar with this sensation, Mistress?"

"Mind your place, Phred!" The snappish tone and air of command suggested that Bob was Niri, except two of them had said the same simultaneously.

"That's a yes." Sam pinched a nipple. "Oh, like that too."

Bob whirled toward the other two Bobs.

One potential princess flexed Bob's body. "Not as tall, but good proportion and muscle tone."

A frustrated snarl escaped a red-faced Bob. "Damnit, Sam, stop, please."

Sam rotated his pelvis back and forth, with a baffled expression. "That doesn't feel right at all."

Phred mimicked the motion. "You're right."

Sam tucked his thumbs into his waistband to pull open the jeans.

"Samuel Oswald Bridger, if you open those pants even a half inch further, I'll see to it Buford can't restore your original equipment," Bob snarled.

Sam gaped at her. "I'm offended. This isn't about some cheap peep show. It's about education, understanding between the sexes. Surely you can't object--"

Bob's expression stopped him mid-sentence. He seized the waistband of his jeans and hiked them up.

"Thank you," Bob said.

Sam shifted his weight, lowering a hand reflexively to adjust his pants. A surprised expression turned into a mischievous grin. He rotated his hips once more "*Now* I understand the super tight jeans you girls wear."

Bob cradled her scarlet face. "Could you *please* stop fondling my body? Bomb to find? World to save? Ring any bells?"

"Bet you never thought you'd say *that* to me," Sam chuckled. "That first part. The latter seems kind of likely."

A Bob stumbled into Sam. Vertigo flooded his senses as he was jerked forward. He collided with another Bob and then another. When the vertigo faded, he sat in a pile of five visibly disoriented Bobs.

Sam frowned at the others. "Nobody move."

"Who's speaking?"

"I am," Sam said.

"Not helpful, you sound like me," the wink said.

"You all sound like me."

"Sam says stay where you are," Sam said. "Like Simon said, but better looking - actually right now *way* better looking.

Bob reddened.

The other four spoke in unison. "That's Sam." One added an extra word, "Bridger."

"Whoever said Sam Bridger is Niri," Sam said.

"No, Sam Bridger, I am me." The Bob Sam was pretty sure had to be the wink said, following with a groan. "We are never going to sort this out."

Phred pointed at the Bob next to him. "This is my Mistress."

"Niri, stand up please," Sam said.

"Princess Niri," Niri corrected as she stood.

"Yup, that's her," Sam said.

"What're we doing?"

"Figuring this out. Everyone line up. Before we go back to the battle of the clones, I'd like to make a point to the blink among us."

The four lined up in silence.

"If your people need help, I'm happy to help them. I'm sure the real Bob feels the same way."

"I do," two Bobs said.

"I bet if your people can survive on Dorsun, Niri and Phred would also be willing to lend a hand to a suffering people. We don't need to fight."

"I'll not harbor criminals, but my tribe will offer the innocent our compassion," Niri said.

"The way I figure it, a small group of you cooked up this scheme to get the help you needed, because let's be honest: the horses's asses at the UPO probably sat on their greedy laurels. You deserve help, and I'd like little Sammy back in working order. What do you say?"

Before one of the Bobs could reply, Niri kicked up a sword from those scattered on the ground. She snatched it from the air and whipped it across a Bob in two swift cuts. Blood flew everywhere.

Another Bob shrieked.

"Niri, what the hell," Sam gasped.

The cut Bob slid apart into four pieces.

"In deference to local vernacular, cutting through the bullshit," Niri said.

The pieces reformed into tiny Bobs, raising shaking fists. "You have any idea how much that hurts?"

Niri swept the blade once more, leaving eight tiny Bobs to glare up at her as they darted around her legs. They bolted out the door.

Bob glared at Niri. "You could have killed one of us."

"I didn't, and if I had, isn't one life worth all those in your world?"

Sam sighed. "She's got a point, but I really didn't want to have to walk into HQ like this."

"Grab the bomb. We should hurry," Phred said.

"Don't worry, I told Ren only to leave if I told it to."

"Shapeshifter," Bob said.

"Oh," Sam picked up the chest, surprised how heavy it seemed.

"Let's go, and keep your hands from yourself, cowgirls," Bob said.

Sam Bridger

Sam stared at the warehouse number, flicking the nine upward only to let the six fall once more. He shook Bob's head. "Wrong address."

Bob—the *real one*-placed a hand on his arm. "Look on the bright side. Things could've gone way worse if you'd delivered it where the terrorist could pick it up."

"I've never failed a delivery, Bob."

Her response was cut off by another Bob carrying the disemboweled body of Vyse. "I've located the magus, Sam Bridger."

"Thanks, Niri. What happened to him?" Sam asked.

"Suffocated," Phred-Bob said.

"And his—" Nausea washed over him, threatening to disgorge Bob's stomach. "Guts?"

"Ripped out from the inside," Niri-Bob said.

Sam lost the fight, rushing around the building corner to vomit. Bob laid a hand on his back. "Feeling better?"

"No."

"Let's get you back to HQ," Bob said. "Once you're out of my body...once you're...well, you'll feel more like yourself. One hundred percent the old Sam Bridger we all tolerate."

He smirked up at her.

She smiled.

"Thank you, Tayanita." He leaned in to kiss her cheek but froze. "I never fantasized about you and me having a girl-on-girl make out session. I need to add it to my bucket list, with lots of stars."

Bob covered her nose. "Ugh, making out with porcelain-worshipper me *isn't* going on mine. Come on. Let's save the world."

"Can we stop for breath mints on the way?" Sam asked.

She covered her nose once more. "Oh, yeah."

47: Cross Purposes

The Wink

The wink huddled its eight members behind a dumpster just outside the warehouse. The little Bobs pressed hard against each other, forcing the parts back into the whole with agonizing slowness.

One by one, it grew until a full-sized Bob panted behind the dumpster. It squared its shoulders and prepared to return to forestalling Sam Bridger.

Something the size of an alley cat flashed through the mist. The wink saw a flash of yellow as it leapt toward him. Claws dug into its torso, ripping the flesh it had just repaired.

The wink struggled to pull the small crystalline foci from its chest, but a magic inherent in the foci's nature overpowered the wink's limbs.

The wink slipped shapes.

The foci, functioning on instinct now that its bond was half built, slipped shape with it. The two slipped shape by shape, form by form, both in agony.

They collapsed, darkness taking both.

Bob

Sam got back into the rig.

"Where are the others?"

"Still shopping," Sam grinned. "Grocery stores are kind of a magical world for them."

"You can't leave them alone in there," Bob said.

Sam shrugged. "I gave Phred my expense card. He's shopped with me before."

She glared at him.

"Something wrong, baby doll?"

Heat built up in her gut. "Yes. You're a jackass."

Sam blinked.

"You hurt me."

Sam opened his mouth, but she placed a hand on his lips. "No, listen. Maybe you didn't mean it the first time. Maybe you really didn't realize your word choice made me think we were talking about feelings and not suspicions we weren't telling you things."

Her fingers muffled his words. "You weren't."

"But goddamnit Sam, I asked you to stop groping my body!"

Sam gestured and she lifted her fingers. "First, technically this is my body."

"Sam," Bob snarled. "What you did was worse than a casual grope—which is bad enough. *That* I could at least slap you for. This wasn't just nonconsensual, but there was nothing I could do to stop you. It was as if you were groping me while unconscious, except you made me watch!"

Sam reached for her hand, but she jerked it away. "Tayanita, I was just kidding around—well not about my desire to understand what it was like to be female, but we're friends, best friends, and friends kid around."

"No, not about something like this." Traitorous tears rolled down her cheeks. "What you did was like emotional rape. It's bad enough I have to deal with every other man treating me like a cheap object but you, you—"

"I didn't mean it like that, I swear." Both tone and his expression emphasized Sam's sincerity. "I'd never—"

"But you do it all the time, Sam. You objectify every woman you encounter."

Sam opened his mouth.

Before he could rebut, the doors opened. Niri-Bob and Phred-Bob climbed in with loaded arms. When Sam looked as if he intended to continue their conversation, she warned him off with a shake of her head.

"Sam?" Phred-Bob said.

Sam's tone was subdued. "Yes?"

"What's a Three's Company party?"

Bob snarled incoherently and punched the dashboard.

48: Hard Lessons

Sam Bridger

A parade of Bobs trudged up the icy stairs and into the HQ warehouse. Eyes followed them as they marched toward the mechanic bay, and Buford.

Gabriel Manx called out from a nearby loading door. "Hey, sugartits on parade! Shake it babies!"

Sam froze, sudden illness churning the coals in his gut. "Who said that?"

"Ignore them," Bob hissed.

Sam eyed her, seeing the same ramrod posture he'd witnessed when changing Phred back.

This is what she meant, isn't it?

"What do they mean by that greeting?" Niri-Bob asked.

"Ignore them, Princess. Let's just keep going," Bob urged.

Another voice ratcheted up the tension. "You ladies up for a Jane Fonda?"

"You know they are," Gabriel said.

A wolf whistle rang out across the warehouse.

Banked coals flamed to life in Sam's gut.

"I like not their tone," Niri-Bob reached for her sword.

Bob stopped her. "It's best just to ignore them."

Sam met her eyes. He didn't know what he saw there, but she paled. "No, Sam. Let it go."

"Wayman?" Niri-Bob asked.

"Think Corlan," Sam said.

The desert princess darkened. Blades slid from her hilts, and she stomped toward the offenders.

"Phred, help me," Bob pleaded. She grabbed Niri-Bob. "Please, Princess."

Phred-Bob stepped in front of his former mistress. "Niri, this is not your world. They will execute you if you harm these humans."

Sam circled around past them and strode toward Gabriel and the other smirking men. The unfamiliar swing of his hips at the higher speed made Sam stumble. He fell to his knees.

"Finally," Gabriel said. "A woman who knows her place."

Sam rose, folding his arms. He struggled to find a comfortable position with breasts in the way and instead planted his fists on his hips. "You want to apologize to the ladies."

"No, I don't," Gabriel said.

"It wasn't a question, Manx."

"What'll you do if I don't? Take more time fixing my rig?"

Tony, the warehouse worker who'd made the threesome crack eyeballed Sam. "Relax, babe. Take a Midol or something."

"Yeah," Gabriel said. "You bitches like the attention. Why else would you wear those tight pants?"

"Yum, yum," Tony chuckled.

"Sam, just leave it alone," Bob said.

Confusion clouded their expressions.

"Bridger?" Gabriel asked.

"What about it?" Sam asked.

They guffawed.

"Wow, talk about getting into Bob's pants," Tony said.

Sam balled a fist.

"Sam," Bob warned. "Let it go."

Sam punched Tony in the face. The blow landed without the strength he expected, but he swung again. Tony caught his second blow, spun Sam around and groped Sam's breasts. "Nice tits, Sam. Hey, does feeling you up make me a homo?"

"Nah," Gabriel squeezed Sam's breast. "Not bad Bridger. Come here, Sugartits, let's Pepsi Challenge these boobs."

Sam's rage doubled, but his struggles only increased their laughing, snide innuendos. Held effectively immobile, they grabbed Sam everywhere while Bob looked on white with shock.

Two more Bobs stepped up wielding swords.

"Let go or lose your hand," Phred-Bob said.

"Or your head," Niri-Bob said.

They released Sam, but he wasn't done. Not until he repaid them for what they'd done.

Bob dropped her voice. "Samual Oswald Bridger, if we really are friends, you'll calm down and proceed to Buford right this minute."

He looked into Bob's eyes. Jaw tight, he inclined his head. "Come one, girls. Let's go."

They exited to whistles and chorused laughter.

Sam exited Buford still steaming. One thing circled his head throughout the slow change process. It wasn't how much of an insensitive ass he'd been, though it crossed his mind.

Gabriel, Tony and the others had violated Bob. Even though it'd been Sam they'd attacked, he'd seen her face, remembered what she'd told him. Her rejoinder brought other scoldings from other women to mind, emphasizing just how big a jerk he'd been.

Bob had begged him to leave, to let it go. He'd left, going back with her to the safety of her domain.

But I'm not letting it go.

Phred-Bob grimaced "An uncomfortable process."

Sam nodded, unwilling to trust himself to talk.

"You all right?" Bob asked.

Sam nodded once more at the floor, unable to face her eye to eye.

"Princess Niri goes next." Phred-Bob guided her into Buford. "It is uncomfortable, Mistress, but all will be well."

Sam picked up one of Niri's swords from the counter.

"Sam?" Bob asked.

He shook his head. The sword's grip itched his tightening and loosening hand. He set it back down.

He paced the garage, jaw clenched.

"I know you're mad, Sam, but please don't do anything rash," Bob said. "We need your help dealing with this crisis. They're not worth getting yourself fired."

He stopped, eyes dropping to a familiar set of shiny tools. "These the wrenches I gave you?"

"Yes."

"The ones I sent after Gabriel made you feel bad?"

"It was around that time, yes."

Sam scooped up the largest. "Still looks new."

"Nobody ever gave me wrenches before," Bob said. "Usually, I make my own tools."

"So you don't really need these."

"Sam, don't." Her eyes flicked to Buford. She cursed.

Sam stormed out of the garage. Each footfall throbbed with the thundering boom of his heartbeat in his ears. Buford's lingering scent of burnt feathers covered pungent disinfectant. He stomped through the breakroom, eyes falling on the Pac-Man machine. His gut twisted.

His thoughts cast back to the missed anniversary, their miscarriage, the divorce and eventually to Morgan. She'd been hunted as a monster, but Sam couldn't get over the feeling he'd been the real monster. He'd been no different than Gabriel or Tony, not really.

He tightened his grip on the wrench.

I may be an idiot, but I sure as hell won't be the only idiot to learn my lesson today.

He charged toward the door. Beatrice came in through the doorway first. "Sam, did you find bomb?"

"Out of my way, Bea."

She narrowed her eyes. "What happened to you?"

Sam struggled to keep his voice even. "Please. Move."

Beatrice looked for an instant as if she might argue, but she stepped to one side.

Sam resumed his mission.

"Alabaster wanted me to send a message to him at the enclave the moment we learned something," Beatrice called from behind.

Sam's fury built behind his eyes. His neck burned like his shirt was aflame. He marched up to Gabriel and Tony.

They eyed him.

"Come back for more attention, homo?" Tony asked.

"Get all your pieces back, Bridger?" Gabriel asked.

"More important, did Bob get a piece of your--"

Sam lobbed the wrench. Their eyes followed the tool's arc through the air. Sam's fists slammed into Tony first then Gabriel. They tried to defend. Neither were bad fighters, but

Sam ignored their few connecting blows. He hammered fist after fist into them.

Workers crowded around the fight. A few tried to stop Sam, but the look in Sam's face made most step back. Those that intervened joined Gabriel and Tony on the floor.

He seethed above them, bloodied fists clenched tight enough the knuckles looked transparent. He spat words flecked with blood between heavy breaths. "You. Don't. Ever. Treat. Women. Like. That."

Beatrice drove through the onlookers. He reacted to her hand on his arm by cocking back his fist. She shied back but didn't let go. "Come on, Sam."

He let her lead him from the warehouse and into the hallway. "Dear God, Sam, what came over you? If Alabaster were here, he'd fire you in an instant."

Sam searched her eyes, seeing her for the first time since the red haze appeared. "Beatrice, for all of the things I said or should have said but didn't, I'm truly sorry. You're a wonderful woman, and you deserved better."

"Sam?" She checked his forehead for fever. "Are you ill?"

He stepped back, eyes dropping to her waistline. "Please forgive me, Beatrice."

She mouthed soundlessly, a hand going to her stomach. Tears brimmed her eyes. They locked gazes until she broke the silence. "You have no idea how long I've waited to hear you say that. This changes everything, but Sam, did you find the bomb?"

"Yes."

"Should you maybe deal with the galaxy-rending bomb first?"

Sam rubbed his neck. "Oh, right..., but after I apologize to Bob."

49: Only a Wayman

Sam Bridger

Sam kicked the doors open, lugging the huge chest into the UPO assembly chamber. Niri, Phred, and Bob formed the other three points of a compass around him.

He marched across the floor, setting the chest onto the nearest ambassador's desk - the Tauron Ambassador Onklus.

"What's the meaning of this?" Leahna asked. "By what right do you enter these chambers unannounced?"

"I granted him permission," Niri said.

"And who are you?" Gromoard demanded.

"Princess-Ambassador Niri Hivrus of Dorsun."

Onklus snorted. "Where's Corlan?"

"Dead. I claim his place by right of blood conquest."

"Excuse me," Sam said. "Universe shattering bomb here?"

Shocked gasps and murmurs ran through the chamber.

"What does this human mean?" Gromoard asked.

Alabaster raced into the chamber. "Blast it, Bridger, why did you bring that thing here?"

Sam smiled and gestured toward the chest. "I figured they'd want it. They're the responsible party in charge, right?"

"Am I to understand you brought a bomb into our midst?" Felisian asked.

An Anubian a half-dozen paces from Sam yipped and keyed an alarm. Lights and an alarm klaxon filled the hall.

Sam glanced around. "Are Klingons invading?"

The pixie ambassador Plix flitted around the room, eyes wide and mouth running full speed. "Be at ease, fellow delegates. It's obvious the industrious wayman, having located the terrorists bomb, disarmed it, and brought it to us as evidence in our continued investigation--"

"Whoa, slow down there, Tinkerbell," Sam said. "I didn't disarm anything."

"The bomb's live?" Alabaster said.

Sam folded his arms over his chest and added a gravelly baritone to his voice. "I'm a wayman, not an explosives expert."

Security guards summoned by the alarm swarmed the room. Several tackled Sam, while others drove the ambassadors to the edges of the room.

"Right," Sam said from beneath the pile. "Because that's far enough away from the universe-buster there."

A trio of gnomes in tiny versions of Feyrth mecha clomped into the room. Nangnome-robotic limbs shifted and transformed into varied tools and sensors.

Their leader addressed Felisian. "There's no trace of any known explosive fuels, but it's heavily shielded – Vurian in origin."

Sam spoke from his position pinned by twin Tauron guards and under gunpoint by a pair of Tuweinie. "Maybe it's a fusion bomb, fueled by peanut butter and banana sandwiches."

The gnome scanned the chest. "I'm not picking up any peanut residue."

"Damn," Sam said. "Could do with a sandwich."

"Shut up, Bridger."

"Leave Sam alone," Bob said.

"Now is hardly the time to become maternal," Alabaster said. "You should have thought of that before he brought a bomb to the enclave, threatening all of the ambassadors."

"He should have kept it in his world?" Phred asked.

"It would have been safer," Onklus said.

"For whom?" Bob asked. "On Earth it threatened billions. There aren't even ten thousand people here."

"Save your breath," Sam said. "It's quality over quantity with these folks."

"Then they should spend some time among your people," Phred said. "Seldom have I encountered better souls."

"Silence, slave," a Dorsun adjunct snapped.

Niri fixed the Dorsunian with her eyes. "Phred's a freeman, male, and he's right. Sam Bridger and Bob have evidenced the highest ideals of our people without thought to reward."

"I could still do with a sandwich," Sam said.

"We're going to open it," the gnome said.

"Is that safe?" Leahna asked.

"As opposed to letting it sit there and tick down to zero?"

"Shut. Up. Bridger."

"Geez, Al, just trying to help."

"Perhaps we should evacuate first," Gramoard said.

"Better we return the device to Earth first," Onklus said.

"Jackass," Sam muttered.

"I don't believe transporting explosives through a waygate would be prudent," a gnome said. "Better we open it now and see if it can be disarmed."

Several ambassadors cringed backward, though a few leaned in with interest. The gnome unlocked the chest and eased the lid open. Others leaned in when it didn't explode outright.

The gnome lifted out a small, blue, rubber doll.

Laughter exploded from Sam. It boomed off the high ceilings, filling the stunned silence.

"I don't understand," Bob said.

"Vurian squeaky toys," Sam guffawed. "Deadliest dolls in the eleven worlds."

"This isn't a laughing matter, Bridger."

"There's no sign of any danger from the toys," the gnome bomb technician said, squeezing it.

"Sam was right, right?" Bob said.

"It appears so," Phred said.

"This can't be the bomb," Leahna said. "It's a ruse to throw us off the trail and this buffoon is in on it."

"Just because I want bananas on my sandwich?"

"Buffoon, not baboon, Bridger," Alabaster raised a crumpled pink invoice. "This is the so-called bomb, ladies and gentlemen. The invoice number – never filed by Bridger – matches one that went missing around the time—"

"This idiot lost the bomb?" Onklus demanded.

"Hey, the number was all Wonka," Sam said.

Alabaster pinched the bridge of his nose. "I have a statement here indicating that this package was a matter of interest simultaneous to a communique by the terrorist with this body."

"Coincidence," Leahna said.

"The operator, one Marge Inpton, recorded the call due to..." Alabaster cleared his throat, "...excessive foreign language. Digital analysis--"

"What is your anal-ysis?" Sam asked.

"Grow up, Sam," Bob said.

Alabaster cleared his throat. "Digital analysis revealed faint voice traces of the esteemed council members in the background."

"Release the wayman," Felisian said.

"He brought a bomb here," Onklus said.

She shook her head. "He brought toys."

"Just call me Saint Nick," Sam said.

"Release him," Gramoard said. "Auditor Roxx, escort this buffoon from our presence."

"You people are still on about the bananas?" Sam asked. "Can't we all just get a song?"

Alabaster escorted Sam and Bob to the docking bays. Phred and Niri accompanied them.

"We owe you a great deal of thanks." Niri kissed Sam on the cheek. "Thanks also for rescuing me."

A petulant note rose up in Bob's expression. Niri turned to Bob before she could speak. "You've a good man. I suggest you chain him to your throne and keep him close."

Sam waggled his eyebrows. "Kinky."

Alabaster dragged Bridger away by the arm, keying the docking bay doors. "You will return to Crossways Transportation HQ under Miss Zephyr's supervision. You will stay there until I return. There'll be no side trips."

Sam adopted a hurt expression. "I wouldn't take any… right, sorry, I just can't finish that with a straight face."

Alabaster's sigh ruffled his mustache. "Just do what you're told for once."

The door opened and the five of them stepped inside. Everyone froze. Sam glanced back at the door frame, checking the bay number still read ninety-four. He turned back to the empty docking bay.

The cold of vacuum rushed into Sam's limbs, stealing his breath. When he regained his words, they were strangled to a higher than normal pitch. "Where, the hell, is my rig?"
Niri and Alabaster crossed the bay's empty floor.
Sam sought Bob's eyes. "I parked it here, didn't I?"
Bob nodded.
"This is the bay number," Phred said. "I checked it when we exited the vehicle."
Niri bent, retrieved something from the floor. She offered the stuffed animal to Sam.
"Did someone shrink it?" Sam asked.
"I don't know, wayman." Niri indicated the doll. "Could your change field have transformed the vehicle into this?"
Sam took the small brown furred doll. He ripped the horned head from it, snarling under his breath. "Laz. I'll kill him."

Sam slunk away while the UPO questioned his friends. He'd lost his rig. He'd lost Ren-2-3. It felt as if the loss left him with a gigantic hole. Without his rig, he wasn't a wayman.
He found the enclave's bar. It was quiet, clean, and empty save a robotic bartender and a pair of Tuweinie adjuncts - their bulbous heads pressed together in one corner.
Sam took a stool at the bar and slapped his wayman badge onto its immaculate surface. "Something strong, brother, and keep it coming."
"Please present vehicle ignition activator or access matrix."

Sam shrugged and dropped his keys onto the bar. The robot set a shot glass on the counter and added a bottle of violent neon green liquid next to it.

Sam threw back a shot. The burn, he expected. The sudden psychedelic lightshow, he hadn't. Sam turned the bottle around to scan the label. It fled, forcing him to keep turning the bottle to keep up.

"Holy fusion cuisine." Sam chuckled and shook his head - it didn't help.

"What're you drinking, Bridger?" Alabaster floated next to him on a flying carpet.

"Apparently, irradiated tequila spiced with Gogrian Dizzydust." Sam glanced at the robot, wondering briefly when it had installed a second head and third arm. "Glass for the dwarf please."

"Just an ale. You'd have to be an idiot to drink that."

A high-pitched titter escaped Sam's lips. "Came to cheer me up and fly me home then?"

The dwarf slapped a stack of paper onto the bar between them. "You're suspended."

Sam blinked at him.

"You didn't think we'd completed the audit yet, did you?"

Sam scanned the first page, staring hard and wishing the words would stop turning into ants at a hoedown. "Four weeks? I saved the world - universe."

The dwarf tapped lower on the page with a finger that kept severing itself, twirling like a ballerina then healing. "Yeah, I knocked off two days for that."

END

Crossways

Look for more great books like these at a book reailer near you and learn more at www.deliriousscribbles.com

Michael J Allen

BOOKS BY MICHAEL J ALLEN

Blood Phoenix:
1. ASHES OF RAGING WATER
2. RULED BY TAINTED BLOOD
3. VENGEFUL ARE THE DROWNED
4. RISE OF THE EXILED LADY
5. RAZING THE LAST BASTION

Scion (Original):
1. SCION OF CONQUERED EARTH
2. STOLEN LIVES
3. HIJACKED
4. UNCHAINED

Bittergate:
1. MURDER IN WIZARD'S WOOD
2. THE WIZARD'S BANE
3. FORGE OF WAR
4. SCYTHE OF ILLUSIONS

Guns of Underhill:
1. FEY WEST

Dumpstermancer:
1. DISCARDED
2. DUPLICITY

Delirious Scribbles:
(SHORT STORIES)

- WYRM'S WARNING
- SCRAPING BOTTOM
- CRIMINAL JUSTICE
- DREAMS OF TREASURE
- DESPERATE
- THE BOTTOM LINE

COMING SOON:

Binarai Online:
1. STORM REFUGE
2. ROGUE PLANET
3. POWER BREAK

Wayman Chronicles:
1. CROSSWAYS

Guns of Underhill:
2. METTLE KINGDOM

Dumpstermancer:
3. DECOY

Scion Rising (Remaster)

ACKNOWLEDGMENTS

We've come to the end of Sam Bridger's big adventure, and I appreciate you sharing it with me. Sam's special breed of insanity owes a lot to the crazy, campy movies I grew up watching in the 80's. This makes the big, lovable lug a flawed character typical of his time, but also gives him lots of room to grow.

I'd like to thank my protege Big D for his support on this one during trying times. My seeing eye daughter has also been invaluable, both for the seeing part as well as her exceptional editing, questioning, nagging and snarky comments. I'd like to thank Jacqueline Sweet for her cover art, which so succinctly draws o" the movie poster inspiration. I'd also like to acknowledge Hillbilly and Three Ravens Publishing for accepting this novel into their catalog. To paraphrase Deadpool, their crazy kind of $ts my crazy.

As for Sam, though I once thought it unlikely I'd be able to create another story with this kind of madness again, he's proven me wrong in the stories Stolen Night and Carpe Dentum, which both precede this novel. He's a stubborn sort, and I get the feeling he's unwilling to stop prancing around after only one novel.

Thanks again for reading. I'll "see" you in the next book.

ABOUT THE AUTHOR

Photo credit: Jim Cawthorne

Michael J. Allen is a star-lord, goofball, and USA Today bestselling author of character-driven, multi-layer, full-spectrum science fiction and fantasy novels - pretty much whatever madness sprouts from his head⋯ (Learn more at www.deliriousscribbles.

com)

DELIRIOUS SCRIBBLES READERS GROUP

Like free stories?

How about curated deals for Science Fiction and Fantasy books?

Get your first benefit—a FREE story sent right to you—by becoming a member of the Delirious Scribbles Readers Group.

Begin your journey, just scan this image with your phone camera!

LET'S CONNECT

I love chatting with my readers, and hope you'll join my reader groups. If you'd rather stay up to date without joining in on the fun, there are plenty of ways to follow along.
— MICHAEL J ALLEN

READER GROUPS:

Discord: https://discord.gg/WeM4bwq

Facebook: https://www.facebook.com/groups/dsreaders

MeWe: https://www.mewe.com/join/dsreaders

FOLLOW THE SCRIBBLER:

www.deliriousscribbles.com

amazon.com/-/e/B0096GEILG

bookbub.com/authors/michael-j-allen

facebook.com/deliriousscribbler

goodreads.com/deliriousscribbler

instagram.com/thedscribbler

twitter.com/Thedscribbler

www.ingramcontent.com/pod-product-compliance
Lightning Source LLC
Chambersburg PA
CBHW030658190726
48286CB00001B/74